CLIFF FARRELL divided his time between news-
paper work and writing fiction after he was lured out
West from his job as a newspaper office boy in Zanes-
ville, Ohio. He worked as an editor on several Cali-
fornia papers, including the Los Angeles *Examiner*.
More than six hundred of his stories appeared in such
magazines as *Liberty, Collier's,* and *The Saturday
Evening Post*. His more-than-twenty novels include
THE RENEGADE, TERROR IN EAGLE BASIN,
RETURN OF THE LONG RIDERS, RIDE THE
WILD TRAIL, COMANCH', CROSS-FIRE, and
others published in Signet paperback.

SIGNET Brand Westerns You'll Enjoy

Patchsaddle Drive

and

Shoot-out at Sioux Wells

By

CLIFF FARRELL

A SIGNET BOOK
NEW AMERICAN LIBRARY
TIMES MIRROR

PUBLISHER'S NOTE

This novel is a work of fiction. Names, characters, places, and incidents are either the product of the author's imagination or are used fictitiously, and any resemblance to actual persons, living or dead, events, or locales is entirely coincidental.

 SIGNET TRADEMARK REG. U.S. PAT. OFF. AND FOREIGN COUNTRIES
REGISTERED TRADEMARK—MARCA REGISTRADA
HECHO EN CHICAGO, U.S.A.

SIGNET, SIGNET CLASSICS, MENTOR, PLUME, MERIDIAN AND NAL BOOKS *are published by The New American Library, Inc., 1633 Broadway, New York, New York 10019*

FIRST PRINTING (Double Western Edition), JUNE, 1980

1 2 3 4 5 6 7 8 9

PRINTED IN THE UNITED STATES OF AMERICA

Patchsaddle
Drive

CHAPTER 1

Clay Burnet was trying to set down on canvas the dream of tranquillity that was always in his thoughts and which always seemed within reach and yet tantalizingly evaded him. He was peering, frowning, at the sketch, his homemade palette, his homemade brush poised, when, from the corner of an eye, he detected movement in the thickets along the creek.

It might have been a deer or a wild turkey. Clay could not be sure, for the distance was upward of two hundred yards. It could have been only imagination. He laid aside the palette and brush and picked up his rifle. It was a Henry that he had leaned against a pillar of the gallery near at hand.

"Micah!" he called.

"Comin'!" A black man stepped from the nearby kitchen door of the house. He was big and broad, in his middle thirties. He wore rundown, patched boots, a patched butternut shirt, and faded breeches inlaid with leather for saddle-work. He read Clay's expression, and, without asking questions, retreated into the house and quickly reappeared with his rifle in his hands. It was a muzzle-loading Sharps which had the initials CSA burned into the stock. Clay's Henry bore the same emblem, but the letters had been branded over the original mark of ownership, which was USA.

Clay waved the muzzle of his weapon in the direction of the creek. "There just below the ford. I thought I saw a rider. Not too sure of it."

"Injun?"

"Could be. No telling. All I got was a squeaky glimpse from half an eye."

He laid the rifle across his knees, picked up the palette and brush again, pretending to resume painting. He eased farther back of the easel, trying to make a smaller target of himself. Micah edged back into the shadow of the doorway. They waited.

The quiet landscape whose beauty Clay had been trying to capture on canvas remained silent in the early afternoon sun.

It was late March. The weather had turned mild; the air was laden with the bursting new fragrance of budding greenery and moist earth.

The first section of the new ranch house that Clay and Micah had raised stone by stone, beam by beam, lintel by lintel, stood nearly complete and livable. It was built in the hacienda style, low and rambling, with a roof of crooked red tile that they had packed by mule from the kilns in Mexico. A gallery flanked all the walls. Its clay floor would also be replaced by tile. The house now consisted only of a main room, a bedroom for Clay, and a kitchen. Later, according to his dreams, additions would be added. Rachel, the wife of Micah, had already planted morning glory, wisteria, and roses in the expectation they would climb the gallery poles and provide shade and coolness by the time the great heat of summer in South Texas arrived.

Nearby, the foundation and walls of the home Micah and Rachel would occupy had reached window level, with the empty frames of windows and doors rising skeletonlike against the sky. They lived now in a temporary structure beyond the main house. A saddleshop and blacksmith shop, also temporary, of chinked postoak poles stood down the slope near a holding corral that held four saddle horses. Half a dozen more horses were in sight in the bigger pasture along the creek. In the distance could be seen a few of the cattle that bore Clay's C-B brand. Southward, the land rolled onward to the wild country that led to wilder country in Mexico. A long day's ride in that direction lay the mysterious mountains of Coahuila which loomed above the horizon in pastel hues of mauve and burnt orange and pale violet. It was this that Clay Burnet had been laboring to imprison in paint on the oblong of canvas that had once been part of a chuck-wagon tarp. And failing, just as he had failed to capture contentment and peace in his heart.

Rachel's face appeared briefly over her husband's shoulder in the doorway. She was frightened. Little Lucinda peeked around her mother's skirt. Even at the age of six, Cindy was tuned to recognize the tensions and alarms of her elders, and to know the cause.

The Rangers had pretty well put a stop to the big raids. The Comanches rarely came down from the Llano Estacado in the numbers with which they had terrorized the Texas border during the war. Nor had the Apaches and the Kiowas been seen in more than a year in the San Dimas country.

Still, many of the young warriors had not given up. Small parties of Comanches from the north, Tonkaways from the refuge they had taken in Mexico, occasionally came through, hitting any settler's cabin they found off guard, but mainly bent only on stealing horses or butchering cattle.

"Tonk, maybe," Micah murmured. "I heerd talk when I was in Jackville a few days ago that some of 'em had crossed de rivah, accordin' to tracks thet was found."

They continued to wait, watching. Their hands suddenly tightened on the rifles. Then they lowered the weapons. Clay blew through his teeth in disbelief. Micah mumbled, "Oh, Lordy! It cain't be!"

A rider had emerged from the creek thickets. The horse evidently had been following the stream for safety's sake, for its belly dripped water. The arrival was a woman. She rode steadily up the slope toward the house, and pulled her mount to a stop at a few rods' distance.

She did not speak for a moment. She was a straight-backed woman well in her fifties, still handsome, with graying hair and fine gray eyes. She had a pistol in a saddle holster and a rifle in a scabbard. She rode sidesaddle in a riding habit. A straw sombrero was strapped to her head. Her mount was a broad-beamed, cat-quick cutting horse. A throw rope was coiled on the saddle.

"I came to talk," Rose Lansing said.

"About what?" Clay answered.

"About fools and feuds. About pride and conceit. About tombstones and weeping widows. About how it's time for the last of the Burnets and the last of the Lansings to act like human beings."

She continued to talk before Clay could frame his thoughts into words. "Don't say anything until you've heard me out. Oh, I know that I'm the first Lansing who ever set foot on your ranch, Clay Burnet. Just as—"

"Maybe not the first," Clay said.

"Lansings did not burn your ranch while you were at war," she said. "Indians did that. But no matter. That's in the past. I'm here, humbling my pride. No other Lansing has ever been in Burnet range to this day, just as you have never let your shadow touch anything claimed by the Lansings. I know about all the graves, and know who sleep in them, both Lansings and Burnets. I've wept for them, even for some of the Burnets, which you likely won't believe."

"You're right," Clay said. "I don't believe."

"And I don't give a hoot whether you believe or not. I said *some* of the Burnets. There were some that weren't worth a woman's tears."

"Even so, Burnet women wept for them," Clay said. "Now there's none left, even for weeping."

Rose Lansing made a hopeless gesture and touched her horse, starting to swing it to ride away. Then she halted. "No!" she said, throaty emotion in her voice. "No! I'm not going to go until I've been heard out. Even a Burnet should have sense enough to know I came in peace."

"Don't tell me you came alone?"

She waved that aside. "Listen to me, if you will, or stand on your foolish pride, if that pleases you, like all of the Burnets in the past."

She watched Clay's eyes search the brush of the creek. "There are no other Lansings there," she said. "I didn't come here to lure you into the open so that you could be shot. That's what's in your mind, isn't it?"

"Tonks are said to be in the country," Clay said. "They can shoot too and they'd like to get their hands on a woman. You know that."

"I'll make it as brief as possible," she said. "There's money to be made if men in this range will get off their tails and quit feeling sorry for themselves."

"I'm happy," Clay said.

Rose Lansing's eyes traveled over the surroundings. If she was aware of the evidence that this was only the beginning—the start of the restoration of the Burnet fortunes, she gave no sign. If she was thinking of the ashes that were all that had remained of the Burnet ranch house when Clay had returned from Appomattox a year in the past, her eyes remained stony. Clay believed the Lansings had destroyed his birthplace, thinking that none of the Burnets remained alive. They had been wrong. Clay had come back from the battlefields, where two of his brothers were in their graves.

Her gaze finally settled on the unfinished painting on the easel. She kneed her horse closer and took her time studying the canvas. She twisted around in the saddle to appraise the landscape that Clay had as his subject. She made no comment.

"Men can be happy, and still rot in their minds," she said. "Are you going to permit me to dismount? I've ridden quite a few miles today, and I'm not as young as I could wish."

Clay hesitated a moment, then moved to give her a hand down. She accepted it, and smiled bitterly as she watched him absently scuff his palms together afterward.

"Children in my family were taught to feel that there was contamination in touching a Burnet," she said. "I see that you were brought up to feel the same way about Lansings."

"You mentioned that you had something to say," Clay said.

"I believe you already know what's in my mind. Talk travels fast in the San Dimas. Some men have nothing else to do."

"I've heard something," Clay admitted.

"Jem Rance, I imagine. He'd ride forty miles to spread news, twice that far if it wasn't true."

"He only had to ride forty this time, I take it," Clay said.

"Well, it's true. I've asked the San Dimas ranchers to forget their petty jealousies and everybody pool together in shaping up a herd to drive north to find a market."

"Who's everybody?"

"Myself, Jem Rance, Ike Turner, Jess Randall, Ham Marsh, Pete Fosdick, and some others."

"Others like Parson Jones and Beaverslide Smith?" Clay asked. "Or Uncle Cal Pryer? I understand they're considering it."

"Like they've been considering getting off their rears ever since the war, but never quite getting around to it. They'd rather sleep on the bank of a creek, waiting for a catfish to bite, or wait in a blind to pick off a deer while they let their wives and kids live in shacks, wear rags, and go barefoot. They seem to think the world ended when Lee gave up the ghost at Appomattox. They talk big and think small. They just dream."

"Or maybe waste their time daubing paint on canvas," Clay said.

She did not yield. "There's a time to dream and a time to work. We all own cattle, plenty of them. All they're worth here in San Dimas is maybe four bits for their hides—if we can find a hide buyer. But there's a market for beef if we've got the gumption to take advantage of it."

"Just where would this market be?" Clay asked.

"There are places in Louisiana where cattle can be shipped by steamboat up the Mississippi to big cities," she said. "New Orleans, Shreveport. It's already been done."

"And the drovers came back broke, such as came back alive," Clay said. "I fought in that country. At Vicksburg and other places. Swamps, cypress jungles. And I've talked to men who made cattle drives to the Mississippi last year. They lost two thirds of their herds and the rest brought only hide money, for they were down to skin and bones."

"Then there's Missouri," Rose Lansing said grimly. "Railroads have built into Missouri, and into Kansas too, but I expect Missouri is the closest."

"That's been tried also," Clay said. "Half a dozen herds were shoved north last year. The most of them hit nothing but misery. Storms, stampedes, Indians. A lot of 'em were buried up there, and a lot of 'em came back afoot, busted."

"But some of them made money, good money. A man told me that cattle would bring fifteen, maybe twenty dollars a head at the railroad in Missouri. Do you know what that kind of money would mean to us here in the San Dimas?"

"Trouble," Clay said. "And grief. Plenty of both."

"It would buy silk dresses for every wife in the San Dimas."

"Black silk," Clay said. "Mourning dresses."

"And it might add twenty more years to their lives in place of working themselves into their graves, peeling hides, chopping cotton so as to put food in the mouths of their children."

"We fought people like the ones you'll find in this Missouri or Kansas," Clay said. "We won't be welcome. The hatreds of war don't die easy. That country's full of outlaws, guerrillas, cutthroats."

"Colonel Pierce says it can be done. Fact is, he's done it."

"Colonel Pierce? Who's he?"

"They call him 'Shanghai' Pierce. He passed through here a few weeks ago. He's a cattleman from the coast. He's making money and has great plans for grading up cattle, for bringing in humpbacks from India. He says they'll thrive on the coast, for they resist ticks, fever. He's a man who doesn't believe in waiting for catfish to bite."

Clay had heard of "Shanghai" Pierce. He was impressed but refrained from admitting it. He swept his arms to encompass the scene around. "Money can't buy this," he said. "Did you ever really look at what we have here? Did you ever really see the coming of spring, see the colors in the Del Burros across the line? There's more to this world than cattle and money."

Don't lecture me about beauty and peace," Rose Lansing said. "I was daubing away at trying to put all this on canvas when you were a wet-nosed brat, young man. I've had my dreams. I hunt for peace of mind too. But you can't live on dreams. Can't you see your future? Look around you. Look at men like Ham Marsh. Forty years old, and he looks sixty. All he does is move from place to place around the shack to let the sun warm him. He carries gossip instead of looking for something useful to do. Look at Pete Fosdick, at Nate Fuller, at *all* of them. I propose that we drive twenty-five hundred head of cattle to market. Think what that would do for these people—and for us."

Clay was staring at her. Her words, "I hunt for peace of mind too," kept echoing in his memory. Had that been an accidental figure of speech, or did she know about that day— that terrible day far from Texas at a place with the incongruous name of Hatcher's Run? The day Hatcher's Run had surged along as a red tide, the hue of soldier blood? Did she really know that the face of her son kept rising in his mind every day, almost every hour, tearing at his conscience, turning his dreams to nightmares, destroying his vista of the future? Did she know that he had ordered Phil Lansing to his death that awful day when the Yankees were driving relentlessly on the faltering men in gray?

"I'm happy here," he said. "I've got everything a man needs."

"Everything?"

Once more he suspected she was impaling him on the sharp point of her knowledge of that day. "You're still dreaming," he said. "Twenty-five hundred head of beef stock. It would take months to round up that many in the San Dimas."

"How many could you round up in two weeks' time?"

"I tell you I don't want any part of this!" he said.

"I happen to know that you don't sit here all the time smearing paint on that piece of canvas," she said. "You've been popping the brush for wild cattle ever since you got back from the war, branding young stuff, beefing mosshorns and barren cows for hides and tallow to earn a few dollars and cut down overgrazing. You've got a respectable start on a new herd. I would estimate that you could gather maybe two hundred head of good, strong fours and fives that could make it up the trail."

Clay was driven to boast a trifle. "More like three hundred if Micah and me put our minds to it. But that's a long way from twenty-five hundred."

"I can put around three hundred head into the pool from our Loop L," she said. "The other ranchers tell me they'll be able to get seven or eight hundred, maybe nine. They've all got some beef in their brands that are only growing horns and meanness."

"That still doesn't add up to twenty-five hundred."

"I've contracted with Pedro Sanchez across the river for a thousand head of prime cattle at four dollars a head. It's up to us to furnish the other fifteen hundred."

"That figures up to four thousand dollars for Pedro Sanchez," Clay said. "What are you going to use for money? This range is flat busted."

She ignored that. "He will deliver the cattle to our crew at the river on the fifteenth day of April. That's only three weeks away."

"Crew? What crew?"

"I've already named the most of them."

"You don't really mean—?"

"Why not? And who else? Ham Marsh, Beaverslide Smith, the Parson, Nate Fuller, Cal Pryer. They're men, aren't they?"

"You *are* dreaming," Clay said. "Parson Jones is past seventy if he's a day. Beaverslide is up in years too. Cal Pryer is maybe older than either of them. Ham Marsh is a tub of lard. He likely wouldn't last as far as the Brazos. He'd be afoot inside a week, for he's hell on horseflesh. Nate Fuller is too lazy to get out of his tracks. Some of them are moonshiners who drink their own rotgut. The lot of them haven't been too choosy about beefing cattle that wear other people's brands, including yours and mine. They steal horses, too, if the sign is right."

"It sounds like the makings of a good trail crew," she said.

"Lady, you don't know what you're talking about. The trail's rough, tough."

"Exactly. That's why we will need someone who knows how to handle a big outfit. You were an officer in the cavalry. They say Jeb Stuart considered you to be a top leader. You're to be trail boss."

"You must be out of your mind," Clay said. "And I'd be out of mine if I tried to handle a ragtag outfit like that."

"If these men are the weaklings you say they are, then they need a strong hand," she said. "The Burnets always posed as better than their betters. You're a Burnet."

"I'm telling you no," Clay said.

In the background Micah spoke softly. "Somethin' movin' ag'in in the shinnery."

Rose Lansing instantly moved close to the horse, using it as a shield, and dragged her rifle from the scabbard. She had lived through the days of the big Comanche and Kiowa raids. She had seen her husband die with a Tonkaway arrow through his lungs. The walls of the Loop L ranch house bore the scars of spears and fire arrows.

Clay moved to her side, also using the animal as a barrier. He crouched, scanning the creek brush from beneath the animal's belly. He saw movement in the thickets.

"Micah," he said. "Whatever is there is near that big bee

tree. You can notch on it from the front window. Take my Henry and put a few slugs through the nest. Maybe that'll smoke 'em into the open."

The bee tree was a hollow oak that had been taken over by a swarm. He heard Micah hurry through the house. Then came the shots. He saw dust rise from the punky wood of the oak where the bullets had struck.

There was a moment of silence. Then a rider came bursting from the thickets. Not an Indian. Again the arrival was feminine. A young woman. She crouched low in the saddle, urging the horse to greater speed. She headed the animal up the slope toward the house. She was being pursued by a comet tail of bees.

"She's bringin' 'em down on us!" Micah shouted. "De Lawd's goin' to punish de just an' de unjust. Everybody into de house! Slam de doors! Shet dem windows!"

The girl and the bees arrived. Rose Lansing tossed the reins over her horse, slapped it on the rump and sent it galloping away. She raced for the nearby kitchen door which Rachel held wide for her.

Clay, taken aback, waited until the victim of his inspiration leaped from her horse in a running dismount. "You damned rascals!" she screamed, and raced for the door. Bees buzzed like bullets. Clay felt the hot-iron thrust of their anger on his neck. He and the girl tore through the doorway together with such haste their legs tangled and they landed in a heap on the rag rug that Rachel had plaited for the kitchen floor.

She placed boot heels against Clay's chest and violently parted herself from him. "What in blazes are you trying to do?" she raged. "Break my neck?"

"Kick me once more, and I might consider it," Clay gasped.

She scrambled to her feet. It had been four or five years since Clay had seen Ann Lansing at close range, and even then no Burnet or Lansing would let on that the other existed. She had been fifteen or sixteen, a lofty-nosed, leggy, shrill-voiced impossible person who, in Clay's opinion, needed to be turned over a knee and tanned in the right place. As far as he was concerned, all the Lansings had acted as if they were heirs of the earth and planets, and Ann Lansing, the youngest of the clan, had been the snootiest of the lot.

She was in her early twenties now and still unmarried. Who'd want a wife who wore jeans under a divided calico skirt, rode astride, rolled her own smokes and could handle a throw rope from the deck of a hard-mouthed bronco? It was said she could handle strong language, and Clay knew for a

fact that she could stick in the saddle of a bucking horse
about as long as any cowhand.

She was glaring witheringly at him with those Lansing
eyes—gray-green, dominating. She swung a hand, knocking
away a bee that was trapped in one of the buns of golden-
bronze hair that she had plaited into two pigtails to fit under
the weathered sombrero she had been wearing. She had skin
tanned to the shade of fine chamois brown. She was slim and
straight, her chin and mouth well-tooled—and aggressive.

She apparently had escaped the major wrath of the insects
that still buzzed angrily around the walls of the beleaguered
house. Not so Clay. The bees had left fiery brands on his upper lip, a cheekbone, his forehead, and his hands. Rachel was
already coming with homemade lotions to aid both of them.

He returned glare for glare with Ann Lansing as Rachel
tended their hurts. "Only a Lansing," he said, addressing Micah, "would sneak up on a ranch like an Indian. Lucky we
haven't got a dead one or two on our hands."

Ann Lansing acted as though he was not present. She
spoke to her mother. "Mother!" she said severely. "What's
come over you to be found at a place like this? Haven't you
any pride?"

"You shouldn't have followed me, dear," Rose Lansing
said. "There *could* be Indians around."

"It wasn't Indians I was worried about. It was you. Are
you out of your mind, Mother?"

"It seems that you're not the only one who thinks so, dear.
I was asked the same question only a few minutes ago. As a
matter of fact, I feel that this is the most rational thought
I've had in a long time."

"Rational? You call it rational to come here and humble
yourself to this—this person? It's humiliating."

"I don't feel the least humiliated," Rose Lansing said. "I
came here to—"

"Some of our people will be turning over in their graves,"
Ann Lansing said. "What would Father say, if—"

"If some of them had forgotten their stiff-backed pride,
they might not be in their graves," Rose Lansing said crisply.
"I came here to discuss a business matter with Clay Burnet."

"It's this beef-herd scheme that's on your mind. What has
that to do with this—this person?"

"Burnet's the name," Clay said.

Ann Lansing continued to ignore him. "Bill Conners told
me you might do something like this, Mother, and I've been
watching you to prevent it. But you slipped away from me
this morning."

Rose Lansing smiled fondly. "I told Bill to hide your saddle," she said. "I knew you were watching me. I see that you had your old hull hid out somewhere."

"Never mind what saddle I'm riding! We're heading back home right now, Mother. Hurry, before I get to feeling any more crawly than I do. I'll have to scrub to get the smell of this place off me."

"Spoken like a true Lansing," Clay said. "I didn't want to mention it, but I'm beginning to feel a little itchy myself."

"It's time to let bygones be bygones," Rose Lansing said. "The San Dimas should be a good country where men could lift their heads and live decently instead of having to turn to thievery. They need a man with iron in his backbone who would shame them into getting out of their ruts—or bulldoze them into it."

"I'm not much for bulldozing humans around," Clay said.

"You were an officer in the Texas Brigade," she said. "That's why I came here. You are the man, the only one, for this."

"That was another time, another world," Clay said. "That was war."

"You can't convince me you'd prefer to stay here and hide from life," she said.

Clay stiffened. "All I ask is to live in peace. I saw enough of the other kind."

"Peace is a state of mind," Rose Lansing said. "You can't buy it with wishes. You can't win it by trying to paint it."

"Come, Mother," Ann Lansing said. "Leave him to his daubing. Let him live in peace, and in poverty."

"I want him to boss the herd up the trail," Rose Lansing said.

"What? Him? Boss it? Why, they'd never—"

"They all know Mr. Burnet's war record," her mother said. "They would respect him, at least."

"But—but, he's a Burnet. He's a coward! He just as much as admitted it."

Rose Lansing ignored her daughter. "You can't refuse," she said.

"I am refusing," Clay said. "I've talked to men who've been up the trail. They go without sleep, without grub, without all the soft things of life. They drown in rivers that no man ought to ask them to risk. Indians kill them, torture them. Outlaws waylay them. I've had my share of ordering men to their deaths. I want no part of it."

"Some things are worse than dying," Rose Lansing said. "Think of Jem Rance and his children who've never owned enough shoes to go around, and of his wife who looks like an old women when she's barely forty. Think of Parson Jones, trying to help grub out a living for half a dozen grandchildren, now that his three sons never came back from the war. And the rest of them. Ham Marsh, Beaverslide. Think of them when you're trying to paint this picture of beauty and peace."

She turned to Micah. "I think the bees are gone. If so, Micah, will you catch up our horses. We're leaving."

"Catch up the claybank for me, Micah," Clay said. "I'll be with you in a few minutes, ladies."

"With us? What do you mean?"

"I'll see you back to your place," Clay said. "I can't let females ride alone in this country—not even Lansings."

"That isn't necessary," Rose Lansing said.

"It certainly is not," her daughter sniffed.

"Rachel," Clay said. "Get my sidegun and shellbelt. See that there are a dozen shells in the loops, and fetch me a handful for the Henry. Where are my saddleboots?"

"I'd rather ride with a skunk," Ann Lansing said. "Stop acting like a tin hero. There are no Indians in the San Dimas, and you know it. Some people are always sending out scare stories. Those tracks somebody claims to have seen at the river likely were made by wild horses."

"I hope you're right," Clay said. "In that case I'm looking forward to being a tin hero. They're the kind that don't get killed. I've got no yearning to stop a slug, not to speak of an arrow or a spear. They all hurt. Then, again, you might be wrong. Even a skunk might be helpful if you ran into any copperskins between here and the Loop L."

Ann Lansing, finding she had no support from her mother, was forced to stand by, disdainful, but helpless while the preparations were made. When Micah brought up the horses, she helped her mother mount, a chore that was unnecessary, for Rose Lansing was supple and agile.

"Thet lady is might set in her ways," Micah murmured to Clay. "Brung up to hate the Burnets, an' keep the feud alive. Have you ever figured out what started thet feud, Claymore?"

Micah and Rachel were the only persons who ever addressed Clay by the full name that had been given him at birth. They had been free people from childhood, freed by Clay's father.

Clay shrugged. For the first time, it came to him that he really did not know the origin of that hatred between the clans.

CHAPTER 2

The Burnet-Lansing feud had its roots back in the hazy blue ridges of the Tennessee mountains before the Revolutionary War, when men wore coonskin caps and carried the long Kentucky rifles. That was more than a century in the past, and no man or woman seemed to know for certain what had started it. Clay's father had said he believed it had been something over a woman whose character had been assailed by the Lansings. The Lansings had it the other way and that it was one of their females who had been insulted. Clay had heard other stories, handed down from grandsires, that it had been something over the rights to a bear that had been felled by simultaneous shots from Burnet and Lansing rifles. Other stories had it that it began at a cabin-raising when young roosters from the Lansing and Burnet families had got into it, and it had ended in a shooting.

Whatever the forgotten cause, Burnets and Lansings had feuded and hated and dueled and slain in their native hills. It was the nature of the men of both families to be electrified by the saga of the Alamo in Texas's struggle for independence from Mexico. Unknown to each other, Burnet men and Lansing men had headed west to join in the Texan cause, with Davy Crockett as their martyred idol.

They had found Texas to their liking and had taken root there. Not until too late did the feuding families discover that once again they were neighbors. Perhaps it was because the hills of the San Dimas, the wilderness, the sense of independence and freedom in an untrampled land, was reminiscent of the Tennessee country, that they found themselves confronting each other in their adopted land.

Even though there were no longer ambushes along dark trails in laurel thickets, formal duels, and bitter hand-to-hand conflicts, the feud had been kept traditionally alive. Until now, no Lansing had crossed the deadline into Burnet range. No Burnet had set foot on land claimed by a Lansing. Rose Lansing was the first to break down the barrier. There were no Lansing men left to protest this defiance of family pride.

17

Of the Burnets only Clay remained. The men of both families had hurried to the battlefields with the same ardor that had brought the clans west to support Texas.

Clay remembered the kisses, the cheers, the kerchiefs that had been tied to his sleeves and those of his brothers by the women of Jackville, the thrill of it all, as they had ridden away to war that bright day in '61. Company A, San Dimas Volunteers, on their way to join the Texas Brigade. Four Burnets. Clay, his father and two brothers. And there had been three Lansings in the San Dimas contingent, two of Ann Lansing's brothers and an uncle. The demands of war and discipline had brought the feuding families into a common cause, but the old barrier existed. No Burnet had shared bivouac or campfire with a Lansing, no matter how harrowing had been the need for common comradeship. The feud had endured through the terrors of cannonfire and slaughtered humans.

Clay was the only one who had returned. During those nightmare years he had learned a bitter truth. They had all ridden off posing as crusaders, but the truth was that they had feared the finger of scorn. No Burnet, no Lansing had wanted to be branded as a coward.

The unyielding pride that had been the hallmark of the two clans was exemplified in the rigid posture of Ann Lansing. She urged her mount to a gallop as though she wanted to put as much distance as possible between herself and a Burnet. She was leading the way directly toward the creek brush from which she had come.

"Not so fast, dear!" her mother remonstrated, stirring her own horse into a lope in an attempt to keep pace.

Clay used spurs on his mount, lifting the surprised claybank into a full gallop. He swept past the mother and overtook the daughter. Before Ann Lansing realized his purpose he caught the bridle of her horse.

"Slowly, slowly," he said.

"Get your hands off my horse!" she snapped angrily. "What do you think you're doing?"

"It would be better if we crossed the pasture and forded the creek well beyond the brush there to the left," Clay said. He continued to keep control of her horse. She had a quirt on the saddle and she reached for it in a fury. Then she thought better of it.

"What do you mean?" she demanded. "That's a mile out of the way."

"But it will steer us clear of anyone who happened to have

trailed you and your mother and is hunkered down there in the shinnery."

"You're only trying to be dramatic," she said. "And you're only succeeding in acting like a fool. Like a Burnet."

"Maybe you don't think it's worth while to ride a mile out of the way to save your scalp, but I don't mind," Clay said.

Ann Lansing saw that she was again in the minority. Her mother had arrived and was obviously in agreement with Clay. "It's a waste of time," she said. She had been defeated this time, but there was no yielding in her otherwise.

Clay scanned the brush, which stood well to their right as they circled through open fields and crossed the stream. There was no sign of danger. If Ann Lansing found any vindication in this, she refrained from taking advantage of it. She continued to ride in silence at her mother's side.

Rose Lansing, evidently fearing that her daughter would refuse to follow if Clay took the lead, moved ahead and began picking out their route. She was accepting Clay's viewpoint that caution took precedence over pride, and was steering clear of broken ground and thickets that might offer cover to a foe. This added considerable distance to the ride. Even so, it was not always possible to stay clear of possible trouble, for these Rincón Hills were rugged and broken, clothed with scrub live oak or the inevitable tough, thorny growth of South Texas. The brush grew tall and heavy in the pockets of the draws that they were forced to cross, for seeps of moisture lingered there.

Clay's C-B spread was lost to sight in the tangle of hills back of them as they made their way eastward. The late sun was mild on the back of his neck. He rode with his rifle in his hands, for he had an uneasy sensation of danger. He had known that same harsh touch of fear in the past on battlefields. Here, there was nothing to explain it. The Rincóns dozed dreamily around him. Invisible fingers of breeze gently stirred the tufts of new grass and brought to life the brush in the swales.

A few cattle faded off into the land in the distance as they advanced. Some bore his brand, no doubt. Others might be neighbors' cattle, even belonging to the Lansings. Others could be mavericks. The country was full of cattle, some branded, but the majority at the disposal of any brush popper who wanted to take the trouble of roping them, building a fire to burn his mark into their hides, and cropping an ear. For the majority of the San Dimas settlers the game was not worth the trouble. There were often broken legs, arms, ribs and dead horses on the debit side of the ledger. And broken necks. Brush popping was a hazardous way of earning hide money. The only reward was a man's pride in himself. Clay and Micah had popped the brush. They had built up a respectable brand in the year they had worked together since the war.

Clay looked ahead and drew a breath of satisfaction. They were emerging from the Rincón Hills, which was regarded as Burnet range, and descending into an open flat. Safer country. Half a dozen miles away rose other low hills. These were the Lagunas—Lansing country.

As they advanced into the flat he relaxed still more, feeling that any danger, if there had been danger, was over. He was wrong. Rose Lansing uttered a wild scream of warning. Her daughter echoed it with fear. Clay saw the cause also—too late. He saw the bash of the arrow in the late sun an instant before it tore through the latigo leather on his saddle and buried itself in the calf of his leg.

He saw the Indian who had loosed the arrow. The warrior had been forced to stand erect in the small gully in which he had been waiting in ambush. He was a Tonkaway. A bullet struck him before he could fix another shaft to his bow. Rose Lansing had fired. The force of the slug knocked the Tonkaway down, but other Indians were there and arrows were coming. The horses were pitching wildly, and the shafts missed.

Clay felt the shock of his wound. He forced himself to ignore that, and came into action with his rifle. Rose Lansing's weapon was a single shot Springfield, but his Henry was a shock to the warriors. They leaped into view after he had fired once, expecting to race to hand-to-hand combat with quarry whose weapons were empty. They wanted the women alive. Clay downed their leader, who wore the single feather of a chief. He wounded another. There had been five in all in the charge, and the survivors raced back to cover again, dragging the wounded with them.

The horses carried Clay and the two women out of range. A few more arrows were loosed, but fell short. Then they were safe, letting the animals run at full gallop. They crossed a swale, tore through thin brush, and emerged once more into open flats.

Clay brought his claybank down to a walk. "Easy, easy!" he called to the women. "Your hair is safe this time. Lucky they seemed to be afoot."

Mother and daughter were pale, but maintaining taut composure. That was the Lansing code. Rose Lansing spoke.

"We'll go on to the ranch and send word to Dan King. They'll soon run those rascals down."

Dan King was Ranger captain, in charge of the San Dimas area, with headquarters in Jackville, which was the county seat.

Ann Lansing said nothing. She rode poker-faced, still refusing to acknowledge Clay's presence. He had been right about taking precaution against ambush, and she had been wrong. It was a dubious triumph over her, for his injury was taking toll, and he was in no mood to drive the harpoon deeper.

The stabbing pain suddenly nauseated him. He pulled his horse to a stop and slid from the saddle. The arrow was a hideous, snakelike length that clung to his flesh. Its head had driven entirely through the muscles of his calf and had emerged into the clear. He felt blood in his boot.

Until this moment the Lansings had not realized that he had been hit. They pulled up their horses. The mother uttered a small cry of dismay and swung from the saddle. She ran to his side. "Why didn't you tell us?" she cried. Clay feared she was going to faint.

He caught her by the shoulders, shaking her. "Get some sand in your craw, ma'am!" he said. "If there's one thing we can do without right now, it's a swooning woman. Get a bandage ready. That scarf around your daughter's neck will do. I'm going to pull this damned thing out of my leg now. I'll drip some, but I'm not going to die. It's only through the meat and not deep."

Ann Lansing had dismounted also. Her lips were the color of a tombstone, her cheeks hollow and ghastly. Like her mother, she was fighting off faintness.

"The neckerchief, the neckerchief!" Clay snapped. "Don't stand there gawking. If you expect me to beller, you're going to be disappointed. Give me that neckerchief, or do I have to take it off your gullet myself?"

Ann Lansing removed her neckerchief. It was of Mexican make, and of silk, yellow and blue, with a serpent design threaded through its center. Her fingers were quivering.

Her mother took the cloth. "I'll handle this," she said. She had fought off the faintness. She looked around, then took Clay by the arm and led him to a boulder on which he could sit. She knelt before him. "Knife?" she asked. "I've got to cut away your boot."

"On my horse," he said. "In the saddle pocket on this side."

Ann Lansing brought his skinning knife, and the mother

slit his trousers and the boot. Blood flower freely when she
removed the boot. She formed a tourniquet with the neckerchief and used the knife as a lever to increase tightness.

Clay broke off the head of the arrow and drew the shaft
from the wound. Pain became a searing flood, and the scene
swam crazily before his eyes. That eased, and he looked
sheepishly at Rose Lansing. "It did make me wince a little,"
he admitted. "Lucky it wasn't a war arrow. It was only a
small one. They must have been out for meat—rabbits or
prairie dogs—and happened to sight us."

Rose Lansing could not answer. She was sharing with him
the pain. So was her daughter. "What—what if—if it was
poisoned?" Ann Lansing mumbled.

"If so I'd know it by now," Clay said. "That stuff the
Tonks use works *muy pronto*, and for keeps, so they say.
That's one worry off my mind. Now, if you'll move that bandage down over that scratch I'd appreciate it. I got blood that
thickens in a hurry. I'll likely be as good as new by sunrise."

Dazed, Rose Lansing complied. Clay arose and moved
toward his horse. "Sorry I ruined your pretty scarf," he said
to Ann Lansing as he pulled himself into the saddle.

"Hold on!" Rose Lansing cried. "What in the world?
Where are you going?"

"Back home," Clay said. "You two will be all right from
here on. In another mile you'll be in sight of your place."

"You'll do nothing of the kind," she said. "You're going
with us to our house so that we can take proper care of that
wound."

"Rachel will look after it," Clay said. "She's doctored a lot
worse than this scratch."

Rose Lansing was angry. "I'm sure I can do anything
Rachel Stone can do. You're being a fool, and you know it.
It's ten miles to your place and those Tonks can still be hanging around in the Rincóns. Don't try to be so infernally
tough. That leg needs attention. It needs more than that
piece of silk. It needs a doctor. Do you want to lose your
leg? We can have Horace Peters out from Jackville hours
sooner than he could make it to your ranch."

Ann Lansing decided the issue. She swung aboard her
horse, moved in, plucked the reins of Clay's mount from his
hands, and said, "Come, Mother. Haven't you learned that
it's only a waste of time talking to mules or Burnets. They
have to be driven."

Clay tried to regain control of the situation—and of his
horse. He failed. He tried to glare Ann Lansing into submis-
sion, but discovered that there were two or three Ann Lan-

sing's gazing haughtily at him. They began to whirl crazily around him.

He heard Rose Lansing cry out, "Ann! Grab him! He's falling!"

He felt arms around him, steadying him in the saddle. His head cleared a trifle, and he found himself peering uncertainly into the eyes of Ann Lansing at very close range.

He tried to retreat to safer distance. "I don't want to be beholden to any damned, high-nosed Lansing," he found himself mumbling.

But she continued to hold him in the saddle. They rode in this position until they reached a trickle of water that bubbled along a small gully. Water was dashed into his face. That cleared his head somewhat. He suffered the humiliation of being helped to the ground by feminine hands.

"Ride to the ranch and fetch the men and the spring wagon, Ann," Rose Lansing said. "And send soneone to town to bring Horace Peters. We'll be all right here for a while."

CHAPTER 3

Clay came entirely back to reality. "I'm all right," he mumbled. "I sort of went wa-wa, I'm afraid. I was thinking I was in the field hospital at Petersburg, and . . ."

He quit talking, shocked. He realized he must still be a trifle wa-wa. He hadn't meant to mention the war, particularly to a Lansing and to Rose Lansing, above all. And Petersburg, above all. Petersburg had been the pivotal point in the major battle of which Hatcher's Run had been a small part. Clay still bore the scars of the shellburst that had sent him to the field hospital after Hatcher's Run.

Rose Lansing was gazing at him, and in her face was a pitiful hope that he would keep talking. He turned his head away, refusing to comply with that unspoken demand. She drew a sighing breath, then busied herself with the bandaging. "I'll have to use part of your shirt," she said, and Clay heard the knife ripping away at cloth.

Ann Lansing had been listening, and in her was the same demand that tore at her mother. When Clay did not speak she mounted and headed away toward the Laguna hills, in which the Lansing headquarters stood.

Rose Lansing said nothing more until she had finished applying a firm bandage. "Then you were at Petersburg?" she finally said, trying to make the question appear casual. "That is a place in Virginia where a terrible battle was fought in the last months of the war. My last letter from my son mentioned Petersburg. I—we never heard from him again. He is listed as missing in action, but—but we don't know how or where he fell."

Clay dreaded the next question. Rose Lansing knew Clay had been Phil Lansing's superior officer, knew that he must have been in the Hatcher's Run fight. She wanted to know how her son had died. Her lips formed the question, but the words did not come. She did not dare, for she seemed to fear the answer. Perhaps it was intuition, but she seemed to sense there was a dark shadow over Clay's knowledge.

She turned away. The situation that neither of them want-

24

ed to face was over for the moment at least. But Clay knew it would arise again, unless he was able to stay away from the Lansings. He tried to get to his feet with the intention of again mounting his horse. Rose Lansing pushed him back. "Wait for the wagon," she said. "You'll start the bleeding again. Do you want to die?"

"Quit treating me like a baby," he said. But he knew she was right. His attempt to move had offset the good effects of the fresh bandage. Rose Lansing had to cut more strips from his shirt to repair the damage.

He lay there expecting her to ask him again if he knew how Phil Lansing had died. He kept remembering how Phil Lansing's accusing, bitter eyes had kept looking out at him from his dreams, and from the darkness of the nights during all these months when peace of mind had evaded him. It was these visions that had robbed him of the tranquillity, the forgetfulness that he had sought here in the San Dimas—a thousand miles from Hatcher's Run.

Rose Lansing remained silent. She brought the horses closer at hand, tethering them to brush, then moved about on foot, rifle in hand, scanning the surroundings. Clay kept watch also, for there was always the chance the Tonkaways might have followed them, and could be creeping up on them.

Finally she spoke. "All right. The boys are in sight with the wagon."

The vehicle presently arrived. It was a long-reach, weathered old ranch wagon with a team of mules in harness, and driven by Dad Hoskins, an ancient cowhand who had been with the Lansings for many years. It was accompanied by Ann Lansing and the ranch foreman, Bill Conners. Conners was a bulky, muscular man, given to boasting of his strength and past exploits as a bare-knuckle boxer. He had served in the Rangers during the war, guarding against Comanche raids, and had been made foreman of the Loop L by Rose Lansing when the major conflict had ended.

The two men lifted Clay into the bed of the wagon on which blankets had been placed. "Easy, easy!" Clay remonstrated. "You're not bulldogging a maverick, you know."

"Too bad it wasn't your gullet that got stuck," Bill Conners said. "Then you wouldn't be able to beller like a branded calf—or like a Burnet."

Ann Lansing and Dad Hoskins laughed. Rose Lansing spoke. "That's enough of that. Now take it easy with that wagon, Dad. Walk the mules. If I see you trying any rough riding I'll drive the wagon myself. We don't want a dead man on our hands."

Even so, it was a rough ride to the Lansing ranch, but Clay refused to give Conners and Ann Lansing the satisfaction of complaining, even though Dad Hoskins failed to veer the mules away from some of the rough going. However, he was able to lift his head and peer with some interest when Lansing Manor finally came in sight.

Joseph Lansing had started it as a small adobe house to which additions had been added through the years—rock-walled wings, gabled frame structures, lean-tos—all connected by dogtrots or galleries until they formed a mansion that had somehow attained grandeur and dignity.

At a distance were quarters for servants and for the field hands who had once raised the crops that had fed the Lansings and their guests and the hay for their fine horses. Like the Burnets, the Lansings had never owned a slave. Free people themselves, the Lansings had believed in freedom for all. Also like the Burnets, they had gone to war because of loyalty to their adopted state.

Now Lansing Manor was a skeleton of its past glory. Decay had set in with the death of Joseph Lansing. Rose Lansing had fought a losing battle against Indians, against rustlers, against *bandidos* from across the river. The most damaging factor had been lack of market for cattle. The quarters for the field hands were now delapidated, with windows staring like toothless mouths, doors boarded shut. Only a small portion of the rambling bunkhouse was used.

The main house was forlorn. Apparently only the west wing was occupied. A few saddlemounts were held in the corral that had contained scores in the past. A lone, ancient foxhound came to challenge them, arising from the shade of the gallery. The Lansings had once maintained a fine pack of fox- and greyhounds for the pleasure of their guests at hunting parties.

Clay let his head fall back. He had the guilty sensation of having intruded into the chamber of the dying, of having committed sacrilege. A dreary emptiness gripped him. On him was the complete realization of the futility of it all, of the price of war, and of the toll of mistaken pride.

Rose Lansing was looking at him and must have been attuned to his thoughts. "Better that it had all been destroyed as your hacienda was destroyed," she said. "At least you have the advantage of starting anew again as your people did when they first came to the San Dimas. At least you don't have to live with ghosts that jibber at you from every doorway, from every window, every room."

"Mother!" Ann Lansing exclaimed. "Not now, please. And not in front of—of people!"

A venerable, bald-pated black man, with a fringe of white beard under his chin, came on rheumy legs to help, and was sent by Rose Lansing to fetch a stretcher. Ben Tibbs had been majordomo at the manor for years.

Clay, despite his protests that he could walk alone, was carried into the manor and down a long hall. He had a glimpse of wide, double doors of oak on which gilt paint was fading. These, he surmised, must open into the salon, as the Lansings had preferred to call the ballroom.

He was placed on cool sheets in a great wide canopied bed in a room whose windows were set in adobe walls a yard thick. A crèche in carved dark wood broke the blankness of one wall, and a great crucifix and chain, also carried from the same wood, was fixed to another. This, Clay realized, must have been the guest room in which famous personages had been entertained in the past.

Now Clay Burnet, the first of his clan ever to enter inside these thick walls, lay on fine linen in the remnants of his cotton shirt and worn saddle breeches, with the blood of his bandages staining the finery.

A vigorous, middle-aged black woman with fine features and a melodious voice took charge. Jenny Pleasant was the widowed daughter of Ben Tibbs. Between them, they kept the sinking pride of the Lansing clan alive.

"You git out of here, Anna Manana," Jenny Pleasant said, stabbing a forefinger in Ann Lansing's direction. "This ain't no place fer a young lady. I kin take care o' this hunk of person. I'll fix him up, even if he is one o' dem dratted Burnets."

"Anna Manana" meekly obeyed. "Is someone on the way to Jackville to fetch Horace?" Rose Lansing asked.

"Yep, I sent Luke," Jenny sniffed. "But, from de looks, it's a waste o' Mr. Peters' time. I kin do anythin' a doctah kin do. This heah man ain't hurt bad."

"That's what I'm trying to tell everybody," Clay said, attempting to get off the bed.

Jenny pushed him back. "You ain't *thet* perky," she said. "Now you jest lay there 'til I tell you that you kin git up. You hear me, Burnet man?"

Clay sank back. As a matter of fact he was glad to have an excuse to give in to the authority of the black woman. Jenny Pleasant removed the bandage from his leg and examined the wound. "You sure did git yoreself puncturated, didn't you?" she commented. "But you is lucky, like all you dratted Burnets. It missed de bone, else you might have had real trouble. But I got some salve dat will make you feel pretty frisky by tomorrow."

She applied medication and a fresh bandage. Then she brought a cooling lotion from the springhouse. It was a squeeze of berry juice, and it did wonders for his parched throat. The pain eased. Darkness came, and lamps were burning. He felt drowsy. He tried to fight that off, tried to get out of the bed.

It was Rose Lansing who held him back. He had not realized that she had been watching over him. "You must lie still," she said. "The doctor will soon be here."

"I don't need a doctor," he mumbled. "I need my horse—and a shirt. I can't ride home without a shirt at night. Mosquitos would eat me alive."

"And Tonkaways," she said. "You're staying here for the night at least."

"Micah will have fits if I don't show up at home."

"We've already sent word that you're here. He will come tomorrow to go back with you."

He realized that something had been put in the sweet drink. He surrendered to the drowsiness and slept. He was vaguely aware some time during the night that Horace Peters, the Range doctor from Jackville, was examining his wound.

He heard the crusty old doctor snort with disdain. "This fellow will be back on his feet in a hurry, Rosemary," Horace was saying. "He might be limping around for a while, but that's about all. You can't kill a Burnet that easy. You got me into a ten-mile trip for nothing, and furthermore, luck was running my way in the stud game at Hank's when I had to cash in. This will cost you about four fingers of whisky—good whisky—as a starter. None of that forty-rod heat lightning that Ham Marsh stills."

Clay drifted off again into sleep. He awakened to find the sun streaming through the windows. His leg was offering no pain. Whatever cure-all Jenny Pleasant had used, had been effective, evidently. Jenny came bustling in, bearing a tray that was loaded with a solid array of breakfast items.

"Good mornin', Burnet man," she said. "I declare, I was beginnin' to think you was goin' to be lazy all day. It's goin' onto ten o'clock. Don't you never git any sleep over at yore place? I fetched a considerable load of grub, figurin' that, as you didn't git any suppah last night, you'd be in the market for some fancy eatin'. Aftah you fill up I reckon you kin git dressed. Yore clothes are on that chair. We rounded up a shirt and boots that ought to fit you."

Clay dressed first, then ate. He ate heartily, even though he had imagined in the past that his throat would revolt against Lansing food.

He was sitting in a chair, finishing his coffee when Rose Lansing tapped on the opened door, then entered. "I see you are feeling better," she said. "Horace Peters is still here and says there's nothing he can do that Rachel Stone can't take care of without trouble. I'm afraid I won't get rid of him until that bottle of liquor I've been saving for medicinal purposes is all gone."

Clay was listening to voices. He arose and hopped to a window that overlooked the ranch yard. Half a dozen men, some saddleback, others in harness rigs, were arriving and being greeted as they alighted by other men who had arisen from chairs on the gallery, evidently having pulled in earlier. Stone jugs appeared and were passed around.

Clay knew them all—Jess Randall, Parson Ezra Jones, Ham Marsh, Beaverslide Smith, Uncle Pryer, among others. They were all San Dimas settlers. Some must have traveled a considerable distance to attend this gathering. Nate Fuller, for one, lived on Big Turkey Creek, some forty miles north.

"What's going on?" Clay demanded of Rose Lansing.

"Just a powwow among neighbors," she said.

"It's about this scheme of yours to put a herd on the trail, isn't it?"

"Why don't you go out there and ask them about it?"

"Not interested," Clay said.

"At least you could talk it over."

"You can't really be serious, ma'am," Clay said. "Look at 'em! Look, I say! Old men, beaten men. Patched saddles, patched shirts, patched britches. How long do you figure they'd last on the trail?"

She went to a window and called to the arrivals. "I'll be right out. I'm bringing a neighbor with me."

"I'm not going out there," Clay hissed angrily. "I told you I don't want to—"

"To have to tell them what you just told me? Afraid to tell Beaverslide and Nate Fuller to their faces that they're no longer worth a hoot, and that they drink a quart of rotgut whisky a day? Afraid to tell Pete Fosdick and Parson Jones they'd fade out before they got to the Brazos?"

"That's not fair. I said—"

Her daughter was standing in the doorway, listening. There was a twisted smile on her lips. "Go ahead," she said. "Go on

out there and tell them how much superior you are to them.
Tell them they're a bunch of failures."

"No," her mother said. "It's not that at all. What we're
actually saying is that these men haven't a chance to better
themselves. What Mr. Burnet will have to tell them is that
they might as well resign themselves to sinking deeper into
despair, that their future is in the past, and that if they want
to know what's ahead of them they only need to look back at
yesterday—or to this morning."

"Better that than to be in their graves far from home,"
Clay said. "I've got ghosts enough on my back, without that."

Again that had been a slip of the tongue. For again, Rose
Lansing was gazing at him, that wild question on her lips, the
question she was again afraid to ask.

Using a chair as a crutch, Clay hobbled to the doorway.
Ann Lansing stood for a moment as though deciding to block
his way, then thought better of it and moved aside.

"Wait!" Rose Lansing cried. "I'll help you!"

Clay kept going. Using the walls of the hallway for support, he hopped and stumbled through the outer door onto
the open gallery. The arrivals craned their necks, gazing in
amazement. The Burnet-Lansing feud was the great legend of
the San Dimas country. Every man, every woman and child
knew the story and treasured it as a perpetual source of
yarns and speculations that relieved a drab existence.

Clay saw his claybank horse in the holding corral, his saddle and headstall slung on a gear tree. He singled out Bill
Conners. "I'd like my horse, Conners," he said. "And I'll need
my sidearm and rifle."

Conners looked at Rose Lansing. She and her daughter
had followed Clay to the gallery. The elder woman made a
gesture of failure. Conners, with a shrug, nodded to Dad
Hoskins, who left the group, hurried to the corral and caught
up Clay's mount. Saddling it, he brought it to the gallery
step. It was all done in silence as the San Dimas ranchers
stared still not believing they were actually seeing a Burnet
on Lansing property.

Clay was handed his weapons. None offered help as he
dragged himself aboard the horse and arranged his injured
leg as comfortably as possible. Ann Lansing was the only one
who moved. She came to stand at his stirrup, holding a yellow ribbon in her hand. "This is for you," she said, tying the
ribbon to the bridle of Clay's mount.

Nobody spoke. The jugs of liquor that had been passing
from hand to hand were motionless. During the war it had

been the custom of Southern women to pin yellow ribbons on men they considered cowards.

Clay plucked the ribbon from its place and fixed it around his wrist. "Somebody might get the wrong idea that it was the horse and not me that you had in mind," he said.

He swung the claybank around and started to ride away. But Parson Ezra Jones stood in his path, forcing him to pull up. The Parson was a weather-blown oak of a man, craggy and knotty, with whitening hair, a hooked nose, and fierce eyes.

"Don't never mind what Miss Ann thinks, Clay," he said in his sonorous preaching voice. "We all know that you fought through the war, brave an' honorable. We are all hopin' you'll throw in with us. Rosemary Lansing has been proddin' an' pushin' us for weeks, so that we've begun to believe what she says. We're askin' you to forgit the past, forgit what you hold ag'in other folks. I know that me an' the others don't look like much to ride the trail with, but with the Lord's help, we'll git through somehow, for the sake of our women-folk an' our children. We're askin' you to gamble three, four months o' your time and a few head o' cattle that ain't worth anythin' to you down here in the thickets. The rest of us are a riskin' a leetle more than that. We're throwin' everything into the pot."

"What's everything?"

"Our Range rights. The roofs over our haids. Some of our holdin's don't amount to much, but it's all we got. An' the Loop L is all Rosemary's got."

"I don't savvy."

"You can't buy a thousand head of Spanish reds on promises," the Parson said. "Such of us are throwin' into the pool have borrowed on what little we own, an' put it in with what Rosemary raised by mortgagin' the Loop L. Them bankers in San'tone shore drive hard bargains. All they'd loan me was four hundred dollars, even though ah got a nice stretch of water frontage on Clear Crick. At one an' a half per cent interest a month. The rest o' the boys didn't do no better. Nor Rosemary either. Fifteen hundred dollars on the whole danged Loop L, lock stock an' barrel. Even in these days it's worth plenty more than that. We're all goin' for broke. Missouri or bust."

Clay glared accusingly at Rose Lansing. "So you talked them into this gamble," he said.

He kneed his horse into motion and rode past the silent group of San Dimas men, heading out of the ranch yard. After a moment he halted the animal. He sat fighting it out

with himself for a space. Slowly he swung his mount around
and returned. He slid from the saddle, sparing his bandaged
leg as best he could.

Beaverslide Smith was holding one of the jugs that contained the white lightning that had been passing around. Pete
Fosdick had just placed a second jug on the ground after im-
bibing. Clay drew his six-shooter and fired twice. The reports
kettled all the horses within hearing. Broken pottery tinkled.
The pungent fumes of spilled liquor drifted in the air. Pete
Fosdick and Beaverslide stared unbelievingly at the remnants
of the jugs.

"I can raise a little cash to sweeten the pot," Clay said.
"From now on there'll be a time for work and a time for
drinking. I'll be the one to decide when and where for each.
Right now we've got to round up about fifteen hundred head
of beef to add to that bunch of reds. I doubt if it can be
done. I figure I can get together up to three hundred head,
and Mrs. Lansing says she can do the same. What about you
boys?"

They stood in amazed silence for a space. Then the Parson
spoke, "I promise a hundred, maybe a few more."

A babble of voices arose as others estimated the numbers
they could gather that would be fit for the trail.

"Unless it's just moonshine talk we might wind up with
closer to three thousand head," Clay said. "As I understand
it, we're to take delivery of the reds in three weeks at the
river."

"But did you have to waste good likker thetaway?' Beaverslide said mournfully.

Clay looked at Rose Lansing. Her eyes were alight. She
seemed younger. But her daughter stood straight and stiff-
lipped, and still hostile.

Micah did the hard riding in the brush and coulees of the
Rincóns, bringing in cattle that measured up to Clay's stan-
dards. The majority were steers, along with a sprinkling of
strong, barren cows, all between the ages of four and six.
Rachel helped her husband, for she was a fine rider, and with
amazing endurance. She brought in her share of animals
from the hills.

Clay, fuming at his helplessness, could do little more than
the cooking, entertain little Cindy, and ride guard on the cattle that Micah and Rachel turned into the horse pasture
where the animals were content to partake of the rich grazing.

By the fourth day his leg had mended so that he was able

to trade places with Rachel, an arrangement that pleased everyone but Cindy, who preferred Clay's indulgence to her mother's discipline.

"Thet's about it," Micah said days later. "You shoah hit it about right, Claymore. I tally 'em at two hundred an' ninety odd. We've skimmed the cream an' a little more. Some o' them fours might not be what I'd pay money for."

"They'll all do," Clay said. "They'll fatten some, believe it or not, after we cross the Brazos, provided they have a smart trail boss who knows how to handle cattle. They tell me that grass will be stirrup high by the time we get there, and I've heard that the Nations beyond Red River is a paradise for cattle."

"These here Nations?" Micah asked uneasily. "Thet's a regular hornets' nest o' Injuns, so I understand."

"We might see a few," Clay said. "We'll give them a crippled steer or two and they'll let us alone."

"I shoah hope you ain't lyin' too much," Rachel spoke. "I don't want no truck with them no'thern redskins. They're meaner'n the ones we got down heah."

"Me neither," Cindy spoke. She was skipping a rope and playing hopscotch at the same time.

"Don't worry about Indians, Rachel," Clay said. "It's the gals in Missouri that Micah will have to fight off."

"I'll take care of that part o' the fightin'," Rachel said. "An' Cindy will help me. Any o' them black no'thern gals that makes eyes at my man will git them eyes damaged somewhat."

"Wait a minute!" Clay exclaimed. "You don't have any notion that you and Cindy are going along with the drive, do you, Rachel?"

"I am goin'," Rachel said. "An' I cain't leave Cindy here. I agreed it all with Missus Lansin' the other day when she rode over heah to see how things was goin'. I'm to help her with the cookin', an' such, an' drive the bedwagon. My brotha, who lives in Jackville, is goin' to come out here an' look after this place. He's married an' reliable."

"Did I hear you right? You don't mean to say that Rose Lansing is thinking of going along with the drive too?"

"Dat's kerrect," Rachel said complacently. "Us ladies ain't got any notions of bein' left behind to fret an' worry about what mischief you men folk air gittin yorselves into way up there. We figger we'll be needed."

"God help me!" Clay said.

"Miss Ann is goin' too," Rachel said. "I reckon that won't please you none either. She ain't got no more use fer you than a houn' dog fer a porkypine. I reckon she's goin' along to keep an eye on you."

Clay hurled his hat on the ground. "May the good Lord have mercy on me!" he frothed.

"I'm mighty happy to see that you're finally gittin' religion," Rachel said.

CHAPTER 4

Clay sat on his horse, looking at the river. The Rio Bravo, some called it. To the Mexicans it was the Rio del Norte, River of the North. Texans in this part of the world merely referred to it as the river. The Rio Grande's birthplace was in the high mountains of New Mexico, far away. Here, on the Mexico border, it bore the brown face of maturity and experience. It divided two nations. Armies had crossed and recrossed it. Outlaws from both sides used it to flee to sanctuary. Rustlers loved it. Cowboys feared it.

Clay was viewing a famous fording place that had been used since the days of the conquistadors. Here the river quieted, broadened to half a mile and offered fairly safe passage, especially in late summer. But this was spring. The river was rising. It had power. He could see the evidence of heavy current in the mid-stretches, a current that likely had gouged out deep holes that would offer the threat of savage undertows and strong eddies.

Around him were the men of the Patchsaddle drive. A dozen in all. A nondescript assembly. Jess Randall and Ike Turner still wore the infantry forage caps and ragged gray shirts in which they had returned after the surrender. Pete Fosdick had on a blue woolen shirt, faded by many washings, that looked suspiciously like one stolen from the Yankee garrison that had been stationed briefly at Jackville the previous summer. Among the others were patched cotton shirts, buckskin breeches, boots, and hats that had seen sad service.

In the background stood the chuck wagon and the canvas-hooded supply wagon. Rose Lansing in cotton dress, straw sombrero, and gauntlets sat on the seat of the chuck wagon, the reins of the four-mule team wrapped around the brake handle while she waited. Rachel and Cindy were on the seat of the supply wagon, in bright calico, and with bandanas around their heads.

Ann Lansing, mounted astride in breeches, leather chaps, flannel shirt, and brush jacket, sat with the men of the crew. During the work of assembling a thousand head of cattle, which were being held a day's ride north of the river, she had popped brush, hazed cattle, roped refractory animals, and had held up her end of the work in the thickets where even the horses wore bullhide breast-shields to protect them from the thorned cactus and mesquite.

At first, the presence of a trouser-wearing female had offended the old-timers, and also Clay. Now, even Clay had to admit grudgingly that it had been the only sensible thing to do. The other men now accepted her as though she was only another cowhand. Only young Lonnie Randall, the son of Jess Randall, seemed to remember that she was a comely young woman. Lonnie, sixteen years of age, was moon-eyed and love-smitten. A gangly, freckled, placid-natured youth, who was all elbows, knees, and Adam's apple, he managed to stay as close to her as possible whenever his duties as horse jingler with the *remuda* permitted. He was always eager to scramble hurriedly to anticipate her wants.

Clay gazed beyond the far shore of the river. Two riders were approaching the stream from the south. Both wore steeple-crowned sombreros. One was mounted on a saddle whose silver trim caught the glint of the sun. The other was evidently a leathery *vaquero*.

Clay lifted an arm and raised his voice to the utmost. "*Buenos días, Señor Pedro!* We are ready!"

On the flats beyond the river he could see the brown scatter of cattle that were being held on grazing by more *vaqueros*.

The Mexican ranchero answered with a beckoning arm, but what words he uttered were carried away by the wind.

Clay looked at his crew. "All right," he said. "He's got the cattle. Let's cross."

His glance traveled from face to face. He saw them appraising the river. They knew the Rio Grande, knew it very well. He waited for the fear to show, for some to shrink. None did.

It was Beaverslide Smith who spoke. "Come on, you brand-pickers. Shake a laig. The quicker we git them Mex cows acrost to God's country the better. Thet river's raisin', an' raisin' fast."

Next to the elderly Parson Jones, Beaverslide was the one Clay had picked to cave in the earliest. But it was the old bald-headed cowman who now led the Patchsaddle crew into the river. He led with a whoop and slap of his hat on the rump of his horse. The others, yelling also, joined him. Spray flew, horses kicked up sheets of water that drenched all riders. But the day was turning hot. It didn't matter.

Clay and Ann Lansing rode to the chuck wagon to which Lonnie Randall had brought up a packhorse and Rose Lansing's mare, equipped with her sidesaddle. Clay and the girl pulled two heavily laden canvas bags from the wagon and lashed them on the packhorse. Rose Lansing mounted, and the three of them rode into the river, leading the pack animal. Rose Lansing, still refusing to follow her daughter's example of riding astride, adamantly ignored the inconvenience of soaked skirts as the water splashed high.

Ann Lansing had a double-barreled, sawed shotgun across the saddle and a six-shooter in a holster at her waist. Her mother also carried a pistol and had a rifle in the saddle-boot. Pedro Sanchez had a reputation for having built up his holding of cattle from the American side. His rancho was said to be a haven for outlaws.

Sanchez was waiting to meet them as they rode ashore. He lived up to his reputation, as far as appearances went, at least. He was a big, pock-marked, cold-eyed man, wearing expensive *charro* garb, with barbered sideburns and a waxed mustache.

Two more *vaqueros* had left the herd and came riding up to augment the bodyguard. They joined in the *"Buenos días!"* greeting that Sanchez uttered, taking their cue from their *patrón.*

Sanchez was mounted on a fine bay horse, astride a heavy silver-mounted saddle with a dinnerplate horn and ornate *tapaderas.* He and his men had cartridge bandoliers over their shoulders, with carbines and machetes slung on the saddles. Sanchez had a gold-hilted dagger in the red sash that circled his waist.

"Buenos días, señor," Rose Lansing said as her horse splashed to dry land. "I see you have the cattle ready."

"Si, señora," Sanchez said, beaming. "One thousand head of prime animals. I am giving them away for nothing at the price of only five dollars a head. In addition, I have thrown in a few extra. I am a generous man. They are road-branded, as you requested, and ready to be driven to market."

The man was really an American who had adopted a Mexican name and mannerisms. At least one of the three *vaqueros* was an American also.

"Did you say five dollars?" Rose Lansing said. "You are mistaken. We agreed on a price of four dollars a head."

Sanchez moaned and clapped a hand to his forehead. "Four dollars?" he cried. "You are joking, *señora*. I—"

"Four dollars," Rose Lansing said. "Take it or leave it.

There are other rancheros who would be glad to do business with us at that price."

"Do you have the money, *señora?*"

"You'll get it, and in gold—after we've tallied out your cattle. We pay only for sound animals that you deliver."

Sanchez was not offended. He smiled almost admiringly. He gave an order in Spanish to one of his men who went riding away to the herd.

Clay moved in. "We'll tally before they're shoved into the river," he said to Sanchez. "Parson, you and Senor Sanchez will tally on the left. I'll count on the right, along with any man the *señor* wants to name. We pay on average count if there's any small difference. If there's a big difference we'll tally again."

That was agreeable to Sanchez. He looked at the river. Then he looked dubiously at Clay's crew. "The river is growing mean," he said. "You may have trouble. My cattle are wild."

Clay nodded. "Tell your men that I'll pay a dollar each for any that want to help shove the drive across. And tobacco."

Sanchez's bodyguards beamed and immediately volunteered. American tobacco was worth far more than the dollar as far as they were concerned. They rode away to carry the news to the *vaqueros* with the cattle.

"You're bein' a leetle free with our money, ain't you, Clay?" Beaverslide complained. "There's a whole passel of them Mex riders. Maybe a dozen or more. That'll add up to as high as fifteen dollars gone for nothin', not to mention a big hole in our tobacco stock. We kin handle this alone."

"These cattle aren't trail-broke," Clay said. "By the time we hit the rivers up north they'll be toughened to it. Better to risk a few dollars now than to regret it later. With a double crew we ought to make it without losing a head—or a man. We can stock up on tobacco later."

What he actually meant was that his crew needed to be toughened to the trail also before attempting a river crossing of this caliber. But if they knew that also, they wouldn't admit it. Ham Marsh gave a snort of scorn. Pete Fosdick squirted a stream of tobacco juice and uttered a grunt of contempt.

Bill Conners saw his chance to challenge Clay's judgment. "If you're afeared, I'll shove them cows acrost with just our own boys, Burnet," he said. "We don't need any help from them Mex."

Conners had been sullen and antagonistic, resenting being subordinated to Clay's authority. He had been palpably seeking a showdown ever since he had learned he was to be only a member of the crew instead of trail boss.

"We'll do this my way," Clay said.

Conners uttered a snort of disdain, intending to make an issue of it, but Rose Lansing spoke. "That ends the talk, Bill." Conners was forced to drop the matter.

Pedro Sanchez discovered that Ann Lansing was more than just a member of the crew. *"Hola!"* he exclaimed and swept off his bangled sombrero. "A *señorita*. This *is* a surprise."

His eyes took in her masculine attire. He moved his horse closer. Ann Lansing lifted the shotgun and pretended to take a bead on some target just beyond the man. "I'll bet a peso I can knock the top off that clump of pear," she said. "And still have a barrel left for other forms of pests."

Sanchez halted his horse. He grinned weakly. "She's what you would call a chip off the old block," he said to Rose Lansing.

It was late afternoon when the tally was completed. Rose Lansing counted out the payment in gold coins from the two canvas bags on the packhorse. Sanchez and his *vaqueros* stood by, gazing fascinated at the double eagles that she stacked in tallies of five hundred dollars each on a spread blanket.

"We'll settle for one thousand even," she said. Actually the tally had been fifteen cattle short of the agreed number, and Sanchez knew it, but he also knew that, with the river rising fast, neither Clay nor Rose Lansing would ask for a recount.

Sundown was at hand when the combined crew prepared to push the cattle into the river. The animals were wild and agile, and difficult to control. The Rio Grande had grown more ugly, more dangerous. Evidently there had been heavy storms upstream, and Clay feared that the crest of the rise had not yet arrived.

He saw some of the *vaqueros* crossing themselves as they prepared to earn the dollar and tobacco. He tried to assign his older men, such as the Parson and Beaverslide to the drag of the herd, where they would be in less danger if trouble came.

They huffily refused. "I was handlin' cows afore you was born," Beaverslide snorted. "These here air our own critters, paid fer with Rose Lansing's money, which we aim to see that she gits back. I ain't trustin' them *pelados* to try very hard at this job if'n we git into a tight squeeze."

Clay was at right point and Micah took the opposite point as the herd, strung out in a ragged column, headed down the long sloping sandbank toward the water. Clay had already picked out the leader, a rangy, rawboned, belligerent steer, the biggest in the herd. This animal had a magnificent spread of horns, and was distinguished by a band of pure white from neck to tail down its back, its hide otherwise being a rich red—a lineback, in cow parlance, but the *vaqueros* had named the animal Blanco because of the white stripe.

The cattle had been held off water all day and were thirsty and eager to cool off in the river. The Blanco steer led the way into the water, with the stronger animals at his heels. They attempted to tarry to drink, but Clay and Micah, with the help of *vaqueros*, kept them moving deeper into the current.

Blanco, a dozen yards ahead of the others, finally reached swimming depth. Clay lifted a shout. "It's going to be swimming water most of the way. Be careful. Don't let them turn back or they'll mill."

Quirts began to pop, lashing water in the faces of steers that tried to swing out of line, forcing them to stay on course. The *vaqueros*, with their long Mexican quirts, were in their element at this art. The reports of the whips were like pistol shots.

The river's direction was north to south at this point, and that put the setting sun at their backs, which was a factor in favor of success. Clay knew that cattle could be kept swimming as long as they could see their destination. The Texas shore was nearly half a mile away. The distance was broken by small islands and spits of sandbars that still stood above water, and which would offer brief respites for the cattle, but the far shore was distinct in the clear air, and the cattle could see it.

Clay's horse was swimming strongly. It was a big-bellied bay from his string of seven animals that he knew was a good water horse. He unbuckled his gunbelt and draped it around his neck, and did the same with his boots, a shift in weight that nearly capsized the horse. The animal righted itself and continued to push powerfully ahead.

Blanco reached shallow water that led to a dry sandbar and Clay's horse, along the vanguard of the herd, found bottom also, and waded ahead. Blanco willingly crossed the dry bar and moved into the river again. Clay found wading water for his horse until they were in midstream. Then the river deepened again, and the current ran stronger.

Looking back, Clay could see the herd, a long, black rope, winding across the sandbar and into the river, bending here, curving there, stretching out back of him.

A blocky, mustached, tough-jawed rider from Sanchez's crew was riding in the first swing position a dozen rods back of Clay, using his quirt and talking to the cattle, casual talk that soothed the animals. The man was speaking in Spanish, but it was broken Spanish. He was, like Sanchez, an American—an outlaw, no doubt.

Clay found the current increasing. It began to carry Blanco and the leaders downstream. He peered and saw that there was a wide expanse of water in that direction. It was an eddy where the current swung in a circle, capturing driftwood. If the cattle were carried into that swirl, they were almost certain to become confused and that would bring on that terror of river crossings—a mill.

Other riders saw the danger also. The *Americano* near Clay lifted a shout. "Keep 'em headed upstream, cowboys! They kin make it, if you squeeze 'em! Don't let 'em drift down!"

Clay, forcing his mount ahead, was already managing to turn Blanco into fighting crosswise against the current in a more direct line toward shore which was now only a hundred yards away. The *Americano* was also working furiously to achieve the same purpose with the swing of the herd.

The lineback steer seemed to sense the danger, and cooperated. The head of the long line of animals swung sluggishly back toward the shore.

Clay heard a shout of alarm. The *Americano* was in trouble. His horse apparently had caught a hoof in a stirrup and was floundering. Then the animal capsized and went under. Its rider could not swim. Claw saw the sick fear of death in the man's hard face as he tried to struggle clear. He succeeded in escaping from the struggling horse, but he then went under.

Clay left the saddle and headed for the spot where the man had vanished. Some of the steers swung out of line and began drifting downstream. Riders on the flank urged their swimming horses faster ahead to close the gap and prevent others from following.

Clay was caught among the animals that had left the column. The cattle were splashing water and snorting and bawling in a panic. He fought his way among them to where he judged the man had gone down. He was forced to dive among thrashing hoofs. A hoof grazed an arm, another struck his leg where the arrow wound was still tender.

Forcing his eyes to stay open, he sighted a shape in the murky water. It was the *Americano*. He grabbed the man and fought his way to the surface. He was starved for air, and weakening, but he managed to lift the head of the man clear of the water. The *Americano* wheezed and coughed, but he was alive, and oxygen revived him enough to respond to Clay's gasped order not to struggle.

The current carried them, along with the loose cattle, into the big eddy. Clay treaded water desperately in order to support his burden. He was at the end of his strength when the eddy carried them near shore. Micah was there. He had left his horse and stood waist-deep whirling his lariat. His cast settled expertly around Clay.

Clay found himself being pulled ashore along with his burden. Reaching shallow water he looked up at Micah, trying to grin. "Good throw," he gasped. "I was running out of ambition."

He struggled to his knees and peered. The bulk of the herd was under control and beginning to stream ashore well above the eddy. The animals that had drifted into the pool were still struggling. *Vaqueros* and Patchsaddle men came riding to help, and began roping animals that came within reach. But many were going down, giving up the struggle.

Ann Lansing was among the arrivals. She swung down from her horse, looking at Clay, then at the man he had saved from the river. "What were you trying to prove?" she demanded, her voice shrill. "You should be dead. You know that. Look at you! You're bleeding!"

The blows from hoofs that had seemed so inconsequential under water had ripped a gash in Clay's left shoulder. The arrow wound had been reopened.

Rose Lansing rode up and dismounted. "Another bandaging job," she said tersely. "Help me, Ann."

She too gazed accusingly at Clay. "You shouldn't have tried it, you know," she said. "It was a big risk. Why?"

Clay was asking himself whether Ann Lansing might not have answered that question already. Had he really been trying to prove something, prove that he had a right to the tranquillity that he had been seeking so vainly since that day at Hatcher's Run—that morning when the cannon roar was an affliction no human nerves or human ears should be forced to hear—that morning when he had ordered Phil Lansing to his death?

Vaqueros and Americans were reviving the man he had saved in the river. Rough jests were uttered as they pumped water from his lungs. They thumped and belabored him until he was breathing normally.

Finally the man sat up, propping himself weakly on his

arms, watching Rose and Ann Lansing bandage Clay's injuries. *"Gracias,"* he said to Clay.

"Da nada," Clay said, grinning, using the polite Spanish phrase. "It was nothing."

"It was a lot to me," the man said, abandoning any pretense that he was Mexican. "I'd be food for the gars by this time. I'll make it up to you some day."

"There's nothing to be made up," Clay said. "Forget it."

"Could you use another hand on the drive?" the man asked. "I'd work for nothing."

"We could use a good hand," Clay said. "And you'll be paid, if you really want to go up the trail. What's your name?"

The man showed a trace of a sardonic grin. He thought it over for moment. *"Sabe,"* he said. "That's the last name."

"First name's *Quién*, I take it," Clay said. "Who knows."

"It's as good as any," the man said.

"If you ride with us, you take care of your own miseries," Clay said. "We've got worries enough without loading mistakes in the past onto the chuck wagon. Is that clear?"

"I *sabe*," the man said.

"If so, I'll cut you a saddle string when we get squared away," Clay said. "We pay off at the end of the drive. We expect every rider to hold up his end of the work."

The man moved away to care for his saddle, which the *vaqueros* had retrieved from the drowned horse in the river. Ann Lansing spoke indignantly. "What do you mean by giving that man a job? He's an outlaw. It's written all over him. And that name *Quién Sabe*. He's probably wanted by every sheriff on this side of the river."

"He's tough," Clay said. "Made of leather and catgut by the looks. We'll be needing more of that kind before we're through with this affair."

"I won't stand for—"

Her mother spoke gently. "Mr. Burnet is foreman. He will do the hiring as he sees fit."

"And the firing," Clay said.

And so *Quién Sabe*, or Q, as the others began calling him, joined the Patchsaddle crew. Clay judged that he was about forty, and the history of a violent life was written on his scarred face and a nose that had been broken many times. But, outlaw or not, in him was that vital thing which for a better name was called character.

Rose Lansing paid off the *vaqueros* in silver dollars from the common fund and gave pouches of tobacco to each man from the stores in the supply wagon. "The cost will be apportioned among us at trail's end," she told the San Dimas men as they watched the whooping *vaqueros* head back across the river.

CHAPTER 5

Clay rode in the supply wagon with Rachel and Cindy for a few days until he was able to take saddle again. The Mexican cattle were trailed slowly, carefully northward to the Lansing ranch, where the cattle of the various brands from the San Dimas pool were being held by men who were not making the drive north.

The united herd was given three days to settle down, and two more days of casual driving to permit the animals to become accustomed to the presence of riders and to discipline. The morning came when Clay awakened before daybreak and began beating on the dishpan that Rose Lansing had hung on a nail on the chuck wagon.

"Rise and shine!" he yelled. "School's over. So's the fun. Today we head 'em north for keeps. Roll your spurs, men. Today you become trail drivers."

Beaverslide Smith rolled out of his bed and came groaning to his feet on aching, complaining bones. He uttered a quavering Confederate yell to prove that his spirit was willing, even if the flesh was weak. The others exhibited equal enthusiasm, some real, some feigned. Clay could see that doubts were already beginning to arise among some of the Patchsaddle crew.

He discovered that one man was still in his blankets. He had stirred, then had turned over, resolutely burying his head in the blanket. He was Bill Conners, the malcontent.

In his career as a prizefighter in the past, Conners had survived savage, bare-knuckle endurance contests that lasted until one or the other opponent admitted defeat or could no longer stand on his feet. He bore the scars of those days, bore them boastfully. He had held down riding jobs at the Lansing ranch between bouts, and had gravitated into the foreman's job at the end of the war mainly by default, since there were few men around to choose from.

It was evident he longed to prove his boxing ability, with Clay as his target. Clay had assigned him to the last night shift, which was regarded as one of the most responsible, for

45

herds on bedground were more prone to restlessness and to stampeding in the predawn hours when the animal world was on the prowl, particularly natural enemies such as wolves and cougars.

Conners had not finished out his shift, and had come in alone to turn in, leaving the responsibility to the other two riders. These were Pete Fosdick and Jess Randall. Their blankets were still vacant, showing that they had remained with the herd, a task that would continue until the entire crew rode out to throw the cattle on the trail.

Desertion of a herd green to the trail was akin to a mortal sin in the code of cattlemen. In this case it was a calculated challenge to Clay's authority. Around them the other men were pretending not to be aware of what was happening. They were making a great show of yanking on their boots, of going to the nearby creek, and of dousing water on their faces.

But they knew! Ann Lansing knew also. She had appeared from the small tent attached to the supply wagon, which served as sleeping quarters for herself and her mother. Her face held the residue of restful slumber and forgotten dreams. She was plaiting her hair into the customary two pigtails, which she would form into buns that would fit beneath the sombrero she wore on the trail.

She gazed at Clay, and there was something like pity in her eyes. She had known that this was inevitable, and that now the moment had come. Clay had known it also. By reason of his rank, he slept beneath the chuck wagon where he was sheltered from weather, while the men of the crew took their chances under tarps if rain came. It was the foreman's privilege. He had left his belt and holstered six-shooter hanging on a wagon strut until time to mount. He walked to it now, lifted the belt, strapped it on and nudged the holster into a comfortable position.

He heard men draw sighing breaths and look for cover as they began edging away. They all knew Conners had a pistol concealed under his blankets, and that he had only been feigning sleep, and was ready for this showdown.

It was Ann Lansing who came out of the trance that held the camp. She rushed at Clay and tried to snatch the Colt from his holster. He backed away, defeating that purpose.

"No!" she cried shrilly. "There's no need for anyone being killed! Haven't you seen enough of that?"

There it was again—the question. The question her mother had wanted to ask so many times. How had Phil Lansing died?

Clay turned and walked to where Conners still lay in his blankets. "Get up, Conners," he said. "Quit playing possum. I know you're awake."

Conners came out of his blankets. He was fully dressed, even to his boots. He got to his feet, but the six-shooter he had taken to bed with him still lay there, and he moved out of reach of it. "What do you want, Burnet?" he asked. It was evident that, of all things, he did not want a gunfight now that Clay was armed and ready.

"Rig your horse and pull out," Clay said. "Don't linger for breakfast. We don't feed bunch quitters."

"You can't fire me," Conners said. Fury was a storm in him. The ache to mash Clay with his fists was shaking him, crimsoning his heavy jowls, knotting his fists.

"It's got to be that way," Clay said. "You pushed this. You know I can't let you get away with this."

"Take that gun off you," Conners said. "Then we'll see how big you talk. I'll show you who's the best man in this drive. I'm the one that's entitled to ride as foreman, an' you to stand night guard."

Clay unbuckled his gunbelt and hung the weapon on the chuck wagon. He returned to face Conners.

"No, Bill!" Rose Lansing cried. "Stop it! He's no match for you, and you know it. He's injured, and he's still limping."

Conners paid no heed. The hunger to right the wrongs he believed had been done was too keen. He came moving in on Clay with the poise of a skilled boxer. He was big, with the litheness of a horseman.

Even so, Clay was able to weather the first storm and do some damage. He blocked the first heavy punches that Conners threw, and drove a right to the throat that drove the man back, fish-mouthed. But Conners came in again, punching. Clay found his injured leg giving way under him. He could hear Rose Lansing screaming for Conners to stop.

His leg buckled, and Conners caught him with solid punches. He felt nausea. He managed to duck a knockout blow that came at his jaw and staggered forward, driving his head into Conners' stomach. Both went down. The breath gushed from the bigger man, and his flailing arms lost power.

Clay realized that Rose Lansing was trying to pull them apart. "Help me, you idiots!" she gasped. "They'll kill each other."

Men moved in and ended the fight. Clay sat up, too spent to move. Conners finally got to his feet.

"Rig your horse, Bill," Rose Lansing said. "Get out of camp as fast as you can."

"That's a harsh way to treat a man who's been foreman of your ranch," Conners said.

He bundled his bedroll, shoved his effects into the canvas bag that served as his war sack, and saddled and mounted his personal horse.

"You'll regret this," he said to Rose Lansing. "An' so will you, Burnet." Then he rode out of camp.

The man they called Q moved to Clay's side. "I better trail him aways to make sure he keeps headin' south," he murmured.

"No need," Clay said. "It's over."

"That I doubt," Q said. "That feller has a black grudge workin' inside him. Things like that fester 'til they become pure poison. I know the kind. He could turn into a killer."

Clay shrugged it away. He signaled for Lonnie Randall to bring up the *remuda*. The crew moved out, ropes dangling, to cut their first mounts from their strings for the start of the day's drive.

"Your hawss, boss," Lonnie said importantly, roping and leading up Clay's first mount. "You sure took care o' that big shorthorn. Good riddance. You should have put a bullet in him."

"How old are you, Lonnie?" Clay asked. "It's a question I've been wanting to put since we left the San Dimas, but I've been too busy to get around to it."

"I'm goin' on eighteen," Lonnie said. He drew from a shirt pocket a tobacco sack and started to roll a brown paper smoke. The result was not what he had planned. It more resembled a crumpled leaf.

Ann Lansing walked in, plucked the quirlie from his hand, and confiscated the sack of tobacco. "He's not quite sixteen," she told Clay, "and ought to be in school."

"Aw shucks, Ann," Lonnie moaned. "I saw all the school I want. *Years* of it. You was my teacher when I was a yearlin'. Now I'm the best damned horse jingler—"

"From now on," Ann said, "I'll be your teacher again. You'll do a little studying while you're loafing along with the *remuda*. It happens that I brought some books along just for you and Cindy."

"I'd just like to see you try to—" Lonnie began.

Clay reached out, caught him by the belt, and hop-scotched him stiff-legged to stand directly in front of Ann Lansing. "Say 'yes ma'am,'" he said. "Say you'll be mighty glad to have her waste her time trying to drive some book learning into that knothead of yours. Say it."

Lonnie was lifted almost bodily from the ground so that he

was ignominiously spider-legged. "Yes ma'am!" he managed to gurgle. "If the big augur says so, I'll do my best, no matter how it hurts."

Clay released him. Lonnie's father was standing by, grinning. "I couldn't prevail on him to stay home," Jess Randall explained. "He said he'd follow us up the trail, an' he'd have done it too. He's knotheaded, like you said. Takes after his mother for strong will. So I figgered it better to let him ride along. He'll earn his keep."

"See that you earn your own," Clay said. "You were on late nighthawk along with Pete Fosdick and Bill Conners this morning. You let a string of loafers drift loose. What were you doing, sleeping in the saddle, like Conners was in his bed?"

"Cattle? No loafers got by me!" Randall declared.

Clay pointed. In the brightening light of day a scattered band of some score of cattle were visible, meandering south over the back trail of the drive. They were a mile or more away, but in no hurry.

"Fetch 'em in," Clay said. "You and Fosdick. You lost 'em, you bring 'em in. Any that are missing when we tally next time will be charged up to you two when we settle up at the finish."

He walked away amid silence. When he spoke again, ordering them to saddle and throw the herd on the trail they moved with alacrity. Fosdick and Jess Randall brought in the loose cattle by riding extra miles and enduring the badgering of comrades who were, in fact, secretly thanking their lucky stars that they had not been caught in the same situation.

"You're being a little hard on them, aren't you?" Rose Lansing asked Clay.

"That's nothing to how I'll rawhide them if it happens again," Clay answered.

Ann Lansing spoke. "Maybe you're only trying to act important. Maybe being named trail boss has gone to your head. It happens that Bill Conners doesn't own any of these cattle, but the most of the others have a stake in this drive. It's their stock to lose if they make a mistake."

"And their lives," Clay said. "I don't want any more of that on—"

He broke off, mounted and rode away. Once more he had almost said too much. Once more it was all back before him—that grisly day on the battlefield.

He rode hipshot on the ambling horse. The fight with Bill Conners was two weeks in the past and fading from memory.

He looked only at the peace of the moment, knowing that it would not last. The cattle were tractable, the weather mild. Grass was rich and greening. He had talked to men who had traveled north. He had hand-drawn maps in his pockets and had memorized verbal descriptions of what lay ahead. There would be sufficient water for the next two or three days. Then would come the first real test.

They were crossing the mighty Edwards Plateau, and a sixty-mile dry stretch lay ahead, with the gamble that the creek they hoped to reach might be dry also. It was a risk drovers from South Texas always faced. The majority won. Some lost.

Slowly the interlude of peace of mind drained away. He rode listlessly, completely alone even amid the droning, ceaseless presence of life around him, of the rattle of hundreds of hoofs in motion, of the intermittent call of a swing man turning a stubborn animal back into line, of the ever-present bawling of bovine protest. It was a massive host that moved with him, and its fate was all in his hands. All the decisions would be his, as it had been that day at Hatcher's Run.

The chuck wagon rolled along abreast of the leaders of the drive, with Rose Lansing handling the reins of the mules. Rachel followed on the supply wagon with Cindy beside her on the seat.

Cindy held aloft a papermade whirligig that her mother had formed and had pinned to a long, slender branch. The toy began revolving dizzily in the warm morning breeze. Clay could see the bright delight in Cindy's face as she watched the success of the improvised plaything. He was long to remember that joy, that young, innocent moment of happiness.

Then the herd stampeded. One moment the cattle had been complacently peaceful. The next instant they had become a frightful juggernaut, mindless, deadly. They had run a few times in the past several days, but these had only been half-hearted efforts that had died of lack of interest. This was the real thing.

Clay touched his horse with steel, hoping to turn Blanco and the leaders. He carried with him as he rode little Cindy's sudden change of expression. Her joy had shifted to fright and self-accusation. She believed the whirligig had spooked the herd.

One of the San Dimas men, Tom Gary, was riding into the teeth of the avalanche, firing his six-shooter across the faces of the leaders in an attempt to turn them. Then his horse pitched head over heels.

Clay saw Gary's body being flung free. Then he vanished beneath a flood of horns, hoofs, and dust.

The panic faded after the cattle had run for nearly five miles. The scattered animals, as though obeying a single impulse, slowed to a trot, then to a walk. They halted and began grazing.

Clay rode back to the place where Tom Gary had gone down. Other Patchsaddle men were already there. Ann Lansing was approaching, her face ashen. Clay waved her back.

"Go to Rachel and 'specially to Cindy," he said. "They will need someone with them. Tell Cindy the run was started by a coyote, or a rattlesnake. Make her believe it. *Make her believe it!* She might have to live with this the rest of her life. With ghosts."

They buried Tom Gary on higher ground in a coffin of green planks that the crew sawed from cottonwoods. Parson Jones intoned the invocation. Rose and Ann Lansing sang a hymn. Rachel, holding Cindy's hand, joined in.

". . . yet shall he live," the Parson said. "Amen!"

They repeated a final prayer together. Clay and four other men fired a soldier's volley over the grave, for Tom Gary had worn the gray. Gary had been a quiet, reserved man with whom Clay had little more than a casual acquaintance. He was leaving a widow and two children back in the San Dimas, and it came to Clay that the location of this grave in this lonely land would be forgotten soon.

He turned away from the grave. He had turned away from so many graves, heard the crash of so many volleys for the departed soldiers. It was over. Over for all, he thought, except small Cindy. The child had stood forlorn during the services. In spite of all attempts to solace her, she believed the toy she had so innocently held to the warm breeze in her moment of happiness had caused Tom Gary's death.

Clay took the child's hand, walked to where he had left his horse and lifted her astride across the animal's neck. He mounted and rode to where there were no cattle, no humans. Only the peace of the great plain.

He felt the taut agony in the child as she leaned against him. He felt the deep quiver of grief, of despair in her. "Once upon a time," he said, "I was a soldier. I was in a battle. It was a place called Hatcher's Run. Back in that country a creek was called a 'run.' It was a long, long way from here. It would take a month to ride to Hatcher's Run. We were losing the battle. The other side had more guns, more men. They were men just like me."

"Why was you fightin' them?" Cindy asked.

Clay was at a loss for an answer. It was a question he had asked himself many times. He had asked it during the fury of a dozen battles. He had asked it at Hatcher's Run, but he had never found an answer that was really an answer.

"I guess you'd call it pride," he finally said. "I guess neither side wanted to admit they were wrong, or that the other might be the best fighter. Something happened that day that still makes me very sad when I remember it. Sometimes it even makes me want to cry."

"Cry?" Cindy echoed incredulously. "But you are a man— a big man. You are the trail boss. Big men don't cry."

"Sometimes a man wishes he could," Clay said. "I was an officer, a captain. That's a sort of a trail boss. My outfit was surrounded by Yanks. We were protecting a battery of cannon that were very valuable to our side. There was only one way to save the guns. We had to create a diversion. That means making the other side think you're going one way when you really are taking off in the other direction. That also meant sending some of our own men to do this. There wasn't much chance any of them would come back alive. I couldn't go myself. I had two hundred men in my crew and it was up to me to see that as many of them as possible got out of that fix they were in, along with the cannon. I had to pick the men who would likely be killed. It happened that the man who was the only one who could lead a thing like that was not my friend. His family and mine had not been friends for years."

"Like the Lansings an' the Burnets?" Cindy asked.

Clay tried to look at her, but decided that her small, young face was innocent of any accusing knowledge.

"Yes," he said, his voice becoming hoarse and shaky, now that the memories were back in full flood. "This soldier was young and very popular with the men in the ranks, maybe much better liked than I was. That's one of the penalties for being the trail boss. I had to order him to lead the diversion. He knew it was an order for him to die. Everybody knew it. I saw it in his eyes, and in theirs, that they believed I was doing it because we were not friends. He never came back from where I sent him, nor did the eleven other men I ordered to their deaths. But they succeeded in saving me and the other two hundred, and the cannon. They drew the enemy away from one point long enough for us to fight our way out of the trap and get back to our main lines."

Cindy looked up at him, and tears were glistening on her small face. She was sobbing. She said nothing, but he knew that, young as she was, she understood his torture just as he understood her own travail. And she knew why he had talked to her, talked as though she was a grown-up who needed consolation, just as he needed consolation.

"I'm sure they're in heaven," she wept. "Jest like I pray that Mister Gary is in heaven."

"Never blame yourself, Cindy," Clay said. "Many things might have brought on the stampede. Many things that we don't know about."

Ann Lansing rode up and lifted Cindy onto her own horse. She studied Clay briefly, then moved away, asking no questions. Clay followed her. In the distance men were filling the grave and rolling up boulders to protect it. Rose Lansing and Rachel returned to the wagons, and with the help of men who swamped for them, were preparing to hook up the teams and move to the next night's camp.

The roundup of scattered cattle began. The bulk of the herd had clung together, but several hundred animals had seized the chance to again head south for home. They were overtaken and brought back by weary men on tired horses. By sundown the herd was mainly intact again. Half a dozen animals had been killed, their carcasses already torn by coyotes and buzzards. Clay judged that perhaps a dozen more were missing and would become prey to the wolves, or would join the mavericks that wandered in the wild draws and thickets.

He rode slowly around the bedground. The cattle were at peace once more. Downwind, the breeze brought the stale, wild smell of the Longhorns, their body heat, the knowledge that here was a mindless force as elemental and impersonal as the wind, the stars, the sun, a force that had already taken one life and could take more.

Clay picked out a prime young steer and cut it from the herd. "Beef it," he told Dad Hoskins, who acted as cook's helper, swamper, and butcher, as well as assistant horse wrangler. "Let it cure until ready. Until further orders everybody eats good steaks. All they want. And at breakfast too."

Ann Lansing looked questioningly at him. The custom was that inferior stock, the lame and crippled, serve as fare on the drive. Strong cattle with tallow on their bones graded up a herd, and the more of them the better the price would be for the entire herd if the bidding grounds were ever reached.

"Men last longer on dry drives if they're on good fodder at the start," he said. "So do cattle."

The dry drive was ahead. Clay had sent Micah north three days earlier to scout the way, and the big black man had returned, saddle-worn, thirsty with dry canteens, and on a spent horse, in time to attend Tom Gary's burial.

"Tuk me more'n a day to reach watah enough to fill a herd," he had told Clay. "Only a seep in between. Rain water caught in rock tanks, but dryin' up, an' hardly more'n enough at that to take care o' the saddle stock."

"How much time for a cow to walk to this running water?" Clay had asked.

"Three days, maybe," Micah said. "Less if'n you keep 'em walkin' nights."

CHAPTER 6

They let the cattle graze for two days on the feed that grew around the marshy stream on which they were camped. They filled all canteens, pans, and kettles in the wagons. Clay awakened the men two hours before daybreak, and they threw the herd on the trail under the light of a waning moon.

The quirts began cracking. "Hi-yuh! Hi-yuh! No yuh don't, yuh jug-headed critter. Back in line. Hi-yuh! Git movin'. Hi-yuh!"

The drive strung out once again. Blanco marched in the lead. The strong young steers made a pretense at breaking line, but it was only a show, and they stepped out in the big steer's wake. The other cattle followed, the meek, the humble.

The wagons surged ahead, made a breakfast camp where riders ate hurriedly and swigged coffee in relays. Clay was the last to partake. Ann Lansing was cooling coffee also, taking respite from her place with the drive.

"Are you all right, Cindy?" she asked the child.

Cindy was grave-eyed, older in aspect. She remembered Tom Gary. "Yes, Miss Ann," she replied.

"There's a settlement called Fort Worth that will be within reach in a few days," Ann said. "I'm riding in when we get there to buy supplies and maybe a new dress for you. Would you like to go with me? It won't be far out of our way."

"I'd like that, Miss Ann."

Clay was aware that Ann Lansing was studying both himself and the child. Again he was sure she wanted to ask a question. Then she decided not to try to pry into whatever secrets he and Cindy had exchanged.

He returned to the herd. He pushed the pace. By midafternoon he estimated that the cattle had walked twenty miles. He kept them moving. Twilight came, and darkness settled. He was gambling now against the chance of a stampede. In the bovine scheme of things, darkness multiplied the long rosary of imaginary terrors that even daylight held.

The animals began to bawl and grow sullen. Flank men

were riding continuously to maintain discipline and hold the line. Drag men were wearing out horses each hour. Lonnie Randall and Dad Hoskins grew bone-weary as they kept meeting the demand to replace jaded horses with fresher mounts from the *remuda*.

The moon came up, and Clay finally gave the order to throw the herd off. The cattle grazed on scant forage and milled restlessly in futile search of water. The night air had turned cool, but dry. There was none of the dew Clay had hoped for on the grass that might have eased the situation.

He let them bed for five hours. Every man in the crew slept with his boots on, night horses tethered within reach. Clay slept not at all, maintaining a constant circle around the bedground to reinforce the shifts of men who stood watch.

He looked at his watch. The half moon was bright in the sky at three o'clock, the air keen and bracing. The slow draw of breeze brought the fresh tangy spice of sage and grass as he reluctantly gave the word.

"Hi-yuh!"

Sleep-drugged men, mumbling thickly and hopelessly staggered out of their blankets, clawed bedrolls into a semblance of order, carried them to the wagon where Rachel and Dad Hoskins were backing the mules to the swingles. Ham Marsh, whose girth was now beginning to dwindle, moved like a man in a daze, but he was moving. Clay particularly watched Uncle Cal Pryer. He was a patriarchal, gentle-speaking man who had never mentioned his age, but Clay was sure he was older than Beaverslide and the Parson. He was thin and long-geared, and his straggly gray beard fluttered in the wind. Clay could hear Uncle Cal's teeth chattering, could see him shaking with the cold. He watched the old man try twice before he could pull himself into the saddle after he had quaffed coffee and refused any other choice of breakfast. He wanted Uncle Cal to give up, turn back for home. He had suggested that as diplomatically as he could a day or so previously.

Uncle Cal had stiffened with hurt pride. "Maybe I ain't quite as spry as you, Burnet," he had said, "but I can still fork a bronc and spill a loop along with any of you younger whippersnappers. An' I'll drink all of you under the table when we hit this here Missouri."

Ann Lansing came from the wagon, carrying an extra cup of coffee for Uncle Cal. He refused to accept it. "Don't need it, Annie girl," he said, bracing himself crisply erect in the saddle. "Give it to old Pete Fosdick over there. He looks like he's goin' to shiver hisself right out'n his skin."

She gave Clay a hopeless look and turned away. Micah, who was riding swing as the herd was thrown on the trail in the pale morning light, began to sing softly in his deep voice:

> As I was walkin' down de street,
>   Down de street, down de street,
> A handsome gal I chanced to meet, chanced to meet,
>   Oh, she was fair to view.

Ann Lansing's clear contralto joined in from somewhere down the line, and the voices of more riders took up the refrain.

> Buffalo gals, can't you come out tonight,
>   Can't you come out tonight,
> And dance by the light of the moon?

The nervous bawling of the cattle faded. The singing soothed them, and they struck out in the wake of Blanco and the lead steers.

Dawn came, pink, then bright golden. Clay had been hoping, praying, for clouds, for rain. His supplication was not fulfilled. The chill of dawn faded. The day was turning hot. He sent word down the line to let the cattle graze as they moved, but to never let them stop.

"How far?" he asked Micah at noon.

They were moving across a rolling plain that had no horizons, no offer of mercy to men or cattle. It was a brassy gridiron on which they seemed to make no progress. Weaker cattle were lagging, and Clay assigned more riders to the drag. Wolves and buzzards were following the herd.

Canteens were about exhausted. At midafternoon Rose Lansing and Rachel managed a tepid drink, flavored with brown sugar and lemon extract with the last water in the cooking supply. It was at least liquid and offered some nourishment. There was nothing for the cattle and horses. The tanks of rain water that Micah had found on his scouting trip had vanished.

They pushed on past the drying mud of the tanks with the sun beating down savagely as the afternoon advanced. Clay touched his listless horse with his knees suddenly, lifting it into a shuffling trot. He reached the side of Uncle Cal Pryer in time to catch him before he toppled from the saddle.

Micah came riding to help. Between them they carried Uncle Cal to the wagon where Rachel and Rose Lansing were waiting with cloths they had dampened in water that Rachel had held out for just such an emergency.

It was too late. Uncle Cal looked up at Clay and tried to grin. "No regrets," he said. "Don't blame yourself, you young whippersnapper. This is the way fer a cowboy to go, ridin' with his pals, with spurs on his boots, an' the cattle headin' north. Buy thet drink for the boys for me when you hit Missoury, Clay."

Then he was gone. Rachel and Rose Lansing covered their faces and sobbed. After a time Clay stood up. The cattle were still moving stolidly ahead. Their dismal lowing was a dirge. The outriders were peering toward the wagon, not knowing exactly what had happened, fearing to learn.

Clay waved them ahead. The drive must go on. "Uncle Cal would be the first to say that," he said hoarsely to anyone who would listen. "He'd say to keep 'em moving."

Dad Hoskins had left the *remuda* to come in to the wagons. He had seen Uncle Cal die. He and Cal Pryer had been lifelong friends. As young men they had fought under Sam Houston in the Texas war for independence from Mexico. They had been at San Jacinto the day Santa Anna's army had been wiped out.

Dad Hoskins glared at Rose Lansing. His beard was as gray and windblown as had been that of Uncle Cal. His hands were gnarled by saddle work and rheumatism. Time was bending his shoulders.

"I blame you, Rosemary," he said hoarsely, and tears were on his seamed cheeks. "First Tom Gary, an' now Cal Pryer. You was the one that kept naggin' an' tauntin' us. Cal told you that he was too old, when you prodded him. You laughed an' told him it'd be better to die livin' like a man than to keep on rottin' in poverty in a shack. Look at him! Look at what you done! You'll have this on your soul, Rosemary, as long—"

"No," Clay broke in. "Mrs. Lansing was right. Uncle Cal died happy—a proud man. He was here, among his own kind. He had been *alive* these days on the trail. He wanted to do this. He'd have died in shame if he stayed behind. He was a cattleman. He died among his own kind. Don't blame her. Don't blame anyone. She gave him the right to die proud of himself. You don't know what you're doing, trying to brand her guilty of killing a human being. *You don't know!*"

He walked to his horse and mounted. "Put Uncle Cal in the bedwagon," he said huskily. "We'll bury him when we camp."

He rode back to the herd. He carried with him the memory of Rose Lansing standing over Uncle Cal Pryer's body, her hands clasped, complete agony and grief in her face. His words had failed to console her. She blamed herself.

He rode like a demon the rest of the day, changing horses often, keeping Lonnie Randall busy furnishing him with fresh mounts. He drove the cattle. He drove men. He spent the greater part of the time with the drag where the weaker animals were falling farther and farther behind. Normally there would be only a score or so of cattle in the drag, needing only the presence of one rider to haze them along. Now there were more than a hundred animals straggling along in the wake of the main herd, with three riders working to keep them moving.

The westering sun had no mercy. Clay shot a cow that had gone down and could not rise. Better that than to leave the animal to be torn apart alive by the gray shadows that were following the herd in force now, and by the black wedges floating in the sky.

It was a duty he repeated again and again before sundown. "Keep 'em moving," he told the men from a throat cracked and parched. "How far, Micah?"

"Five miles," the black man said. "Maybe farther. I cain't exactly locate myself. Every danged gully an' clump o' brush looks like what I seen an hour ago."

They drove on in twilight, in darkness, for hours. The glow of the old, fading moon was beginning to show in the east when the cattle caught the scent of water. The terrible moaning that had been a hymn of agony changed to a wild roar.

There was no holding them. "Ride clear!" Clay shouted. "Let 'em run!"

At least it was only cattle that died in the terrible race for water, and no men. A few more animals drowned in the crush as the herd piled into the bed of the creek, churning it into a froth of mud.

Clay rode upstream on his jaded horse until he found a pool of unsullied water. It glinted like a great diamond in the first strike of moonlight. He fell limply from his horse, crawled to the brink, and slumped forward on his face in the resurrecting coolness of the stream.

After a time he realized that someone had followed his example. Ann Lansing lay nearby, drinking prayerfully. She loosened her hair and let it float free in the water. Using her hands for cups, she drenched herself and kept making that grateful little sound of thanks.

Satiated at last, she flirted water from her hair and let it hang down her back while she sat up and looked at him. "I'm sorry," she said.

"Sorry? For what?"

"For, for many things. That yellow ribbon, for one."

"I've still got it," Clay said. "Waiting for a candidate. But there's been none."

"I'm afraid there soon will be," she said. "Some of the men are talking of quitting."

"Let them," Clay said.

"Mother is desolate," she said. "She blames herself for Uncle Cal, and for Tom Gary. She wants to turn back, if we can."

"There's no turning back now."

She was silent for a moment. "I want to thank you," she finally said. "For telling them it wasn't her fault. Otherwise I don't know what she'd have done. She's taking Uncle Cal's death very hard."

"He died happy," Clay said, "She must understand that."

She was silent a moment. "You were in command of the company in which Phil was a sergeant during the last campaign of the war, weren't you?" she asked abruptly.

Clay had to force himself to answer. "Yes."

"Were you in the last battle?" she asked slowly.

"I was there."

She hesitated a long time before speaking again. "Do you want to tell me about it?" she finally asked.

Clay had faced this moment many times in his thoughts, searching for an answer and finding none. It had haunted him all those months before he found that he had fallen helplessly in love with Ann Lansing. Now the spike in his heart was driven deeper.

"No," he said harshly. "What good would it do? Men are forced into situations in war that can't ever be understood by others, and never can be forgiven."

He walked to his horse which had drunk its fill, mounted, and rode back to the herd alone, leaving Ann Lansing there—and also alone.

They dug their second grave the next morning and laid Uncle Cal to rest. On that same day they lost more men from the crew. Pete Fosdick and Dave Wilson decided that the trail was no place for them. After standing beside the grave, they came to Clay and said they'd had enough and were heading back to the San Dimas.

"An' the rest o' you better do the same," Pete Fosdick told the remainder of the crew, who were listening. "We've already buried pore Tom Gary an' Uncle Cal an' this drive ain't even half way. There'll be more graves to fill if'n you keep goin'. Rosemary Lansing sweet-talked us into this. Bein' a woman, she don't have to ride stampedes or stay in the saddle eighteen hours a day. She don't have to be rawhided by a foreman who's managed to git two of us dead already."

Ann Lansing walked up to Fosdick, who was a thin-necked, hook-nosed man. "That's not true, and you know it, Pete," she said. She turned to the others. "If any or all of you are thinking the same, either about my mother or about Clay Burnet, now's the time to say so and cut your string to head for home."

There was silence for a space. Then two more men moved to join Fosdick and Dave Wilson. One was Ike Turner, the other Dad Hoskins.

Parson Ezra Jones spoke harshly. "Go on home, you yaller-bellied leppies! None o' you was worth a pint o' sour beans anyway. Tell yore kids an' womenfolk to pin the ribbons on you. You know the color."

"What about our cattle?" Fosdick demanded. "I got forty head in the bunch. Dad's got none, but Ike an' Dave's got enough. More'n a hundred, all told."

"Take 'em back with you," Clay said.

"You know we cain't do that," Fosdick said. "No cow could walk back acrost thet dry stretch after what you put us through."

Rose Lansing spoke. "You'll be paid for them at whatever price we get when the herd is sold. After all expenses are paid we will share in proportion to the number of cattle each of us had in the herd. We signed a paper, remember, on which all brands owned by you and the rest of us are designated."

"I don't reckon we'll ever see a cent for our cattle, but we ought to git somethin' considerin' that we've already risked our necks bringin' 'em this far," Fosdick said. "We figure we ought to be paid off right now. We know you got some money in the fund, Rosemary."

"Get out of camp as fast as you can and be damned to you!" Ann Lansing exploded. "Before I take a quirt to you."

"Daughter!" her mother spoke reprovingly. "Don't forget you're a lady."

Ann Lansing looked down at herself, at her dusty chaps, her hands, her general appearance. She looked at her mother and at Rachel. Rachel had given up after the first week, and had stored away her petticoats and skirts and had re-tailored masculine jeans to fit her good figure. She had managed to give the jeans a jaunty Mexican style, with a slashed bell bot-

tom effect, and had added to the picture with a colorful calico waist and gingham sash. But Rose Lansing had held out.
She still wore ground-length, voluminous skirts, and her waist
was obviously reinforced by stays and whalebone. Both she
and Rachel had on the floursack aprons that were the badges
of their servitude when meals were being prepared.

Ann's eyes traveled over the crew, taking in their patched
garb, their dog-eared, rundown boots, their general appearance of having been thrown together in a ragbag. She looked
at Clay. He had fared little better. His injuries had all healed
but he had paid a greater penalty, at least to his garb, than
the others during the hard journey.

She began to laugh. "I beg your pardon, gentlemen," she
said. "I'll try to be a lady from now on, no matter what I
look like."

She laughed harder, wildly at first, then with full-throated,
vast, and healthy amusement. Rachel joined in. Micah's deep
bass chuckle started and increased to rolling thunder. Clay
began to laugh.

Beaverslide uttered a yelp. He and the Parson clasped
hands and began a wild, heel-kicking buck and wing.

"Missouri, here we come!" Beaverslide howled. "We're the
Patchsaddle boys, an' we ain't quittin' until we git there."

Other men joined in. The camp became a madhouse of
cavorting humans, some of whom might have passed as
scarecrows.

Rotund Ham Marsh took Rose Lansing's hands and started
to whirl her. Startled, stiff, for an instant, she suddenly began
to laugh and let herself be swung wildly, the hem of her skirt
flying. This, she realized, was more than a dance. It was a
memorial to their comrades who had died.

Clay found Ann Lansing standing before him, her green
eyes alight. "Missouri, here we come!" she cried.

He caught her hands and they joined the rigadoon.
Lonnie Randall struck up a tune with his harmonica and Jess
Randall joined in with a fiddle. On the bedground, the cattle,
which needed no guarding after the rigors of the dry drive,
gazed with bovine surprise, horns glinting in the sun.

The four men who were leaving all this withdrew to a
safer distance. "They're loco," Pete Fosdick assured his companions. "They've gone clean off their rockers. We're lucky to
be shed of 'em."

CHAPTER 7

"I might be able to round up a few hands," Q said to Clay the next day.

Clay eyed him. "Where?"

"I'd need a little time," Q said. "I might be gone as long as a week. I might find 'em, I might not. But it's worth a try. You can't drive ahead with six men, an' most of 'em old an' creaky. You've got to lay over here for a spell anyway to let the cattle git back in shape."

Since that day at the Rio Grande, when Clay had saved the life of the squatty, flat-nosed, taciturn man, Q had done his work phlegmatically, without complaint. He had proved to be an average trail hand, obviously experienced in handling cattle, but also obviously not interested in that occupation as a way of life. The other members of the crew avoided him. It wasn't that they were afraid of him. Young or old, creaky or not, the Patchsaddle riders were beginning to be afraid of nothing. They were firming into a hard-core unit that had an unspoken objective. They meant to put this herd through to the finish, or die in the attempt. And there was no doubt in the minds of any that more of them would likely die before they saw the end of this trail.

They steered clear of Q mainly because they didn't want to intrude. He always slept with his rifle, his six-shooter, his hiding knife within quick reach of his bed. He was the only one who never talked of his past, or his future. In fact he did not talk at all, except on matters in connection with the welfare of the cattle. It was taken for granted that he was an outlaw. Because of his hard-case appearance, the others could not believe that Q was paying out a debt. Only Clay was certain of that. Q was with the drive because of an unshakable belief that he must repay Clay for saving his life.

"Care to tell me where you figure to find these men?" Clay asked.

"Hackberry, maybe," Q said. "It's a piece west o' here. Not too far, but it might take a little time to look up the boys I have in mind."

63

Clay had heard of Hackberry, and its reputation. It was headquarters for buffalo hunters and Indian traders, and a haven for outlaws.

"You seem to be acquainted in these parts," Clay said.

"I've been around," Q said, shrugging.

Rose Lansing was listening. She was wearing her apron, and there was flour on her hands. She had been mixing sourdough-biscuit batter in the top of a sack of flour. The Dutch oven stood heating on the wood coals. Clay did not dare look in her direction, for he could picture her expression of disapproval.

"If you find these boys," he told Q, "let them know that all we can pay is twenty-five a month and grub, with maybe a little sweetening of the pot if we get through to end of steel without losing many head. Make sure they understand one other thing. We don't help fight off posses or reward hunters."

Q displayed one of his rare, twisted grins. "I'll tell 'em."

"Got any money?" Clay asked. When Q shrugged, he turned to Rose Lansing. "Give him a ten-dollar piece out of the fund," he said. "He's got to eat and buy fodder for his horse."

She held her nose high, but disappeared around the wagon and presently returned with a gold piece which she gave to Clay, who turned it over to Q. It came from the dwindling expense fund that remained from the mortgage money she had received.

She did not speak until after Q had saddled a fresh horse and had ridden away. "So now we're going to hire more outlaws," she said grimly.

"Our job," Clay said, "is to get these cattle to market."

She walked away, stiff-backed, to join Rachel at the cooking duties. Her sense of guilt was bearing heavier on her each day.

Clay watched Q vanish into the country westward. There was no doubt in his mind that this was dangerous ground for Q and that he was unquestionably taking a risk in showing himself in Hackberry, where he evidently was known, and where there might be Rangers or other law officers. This was one of Q's ways of paying off the obligation he believed he owed Clay.

He and the remainder of the Patchsaddle crew settled down to wait. The dry drive had taken forty or fifty pounds off every animal, Clay estimated, but after a few days on water and forage he could see the wrinkles vanishing from their hides.

The men too had thinned, but the efforts of Rose Lansing and Rachel at the cook fires took care of that. Clay did not realize that he might have lost more than the others until he became aware that Rose Lansing and Rachel were favoring him with extra tidbits, and standing by aggressively to see that he ate them.

"I declare!" Rachel said in despair. "I never did see a human what was harder for to take on tallow. This here man is an insult to our cookin', Missus Lansing. Look at that Micah man of mine. He's fattenin' up like a shoat in a harvest field, but this one only gits narrower. He *worries* it off."

Four days passed. Five. The cattle were recovered now, and ready to be thrown on the trail again. But no word came back from Q.

"You'll never see that man again," Rose Lansing said, almost hopefully. "I couldn't blame him. I must say anybody would be a fool to come back to this ragtag outfit."

"He'll come back if he can," Clay said.

She sighed. "Yes," she said. "You're right. He's a strange one. He believes in paying off a debt."

Clay continued to hold the herd, concealing his burning impatience. For one thing, he could not move the herd ahead with this skeleton crew. But he had faith in Q. He believed the man would return if he was alive and free. But he might be dead, or in some sheriff's jail.

Riders appeared late in the afternoon of the sixth day. None among them was Q. As they came closer Clay made out a badge on the vest of the burly-chested, red-bearded man who rode in the lead.

"A posse, or I never seed one," Micah said.

Micah was correct. The posse rode up, and all the members dismounted without awaiting the customary invitation to alight. There were six of them, all saddle-weary, dusty, hungry, and palpably in no mood for idle talk. All were exceedingly heavily armed.

The big man glared belligerently around. His lips were cracked; his large nose was peeling from windburn. Alkali dust had whitened his stiff stubble of beard.

"What in hell do you call this outfit?" he demanded.

Ann Lansing answered that before Clay could speak. "And who in the hell is asking?"

That rocked the officer back on his heels. He peered closer, then took a second look and a third. He gazed at Rachel, then at Cindy, then at Rose Lansing. He blinked owlishly. He fumbled for the brim of his hat and removed it.

"I'm sorry, ma'am," he mumbled. "Didn't know there was

ladies present. I'm Deputy Sheriff Sim Kimball from Hackberry. And you might be Missus—Missus—?"

"The name is Miss Lansing," Ann said crisply. "We would ask you to dismount, but it seems you've already done so."

Sim Kimball had lost the initiative. He tried to regain it. He glared officiously around. He studied Beaverslide Smith, who, at the moment, was trying to mend the heel of one of his worn short boots, using the shoe last that was carried in the supply wagon. Beaverslide's yellowish bald head glinted in the sun. His puckered old eyes were gazing at the visitors with disdain. "They never did teach 'em manners up here in no'th Texas," he observed scathingly.

Kimball's attention turned to Parson Jones, who was washing his socks in the creek. His gaze swung to Ham Marsh and his tubby stomach, who was endeavoring to repair his old saddle, which had suffered some new disaster. Then to Lonnie Randall, who was wearing a pair of his father's oversize breeches and shirt.

Kimball looked at his possemen to make sure they were seeing the same sights. They were staring, bug-eyed. Kimball wagged his head as though still not believing it.

"We been ridin' three days, an' maybe four," he said. "I ain't quite sure of it. I ain't sure of nothin' anymore. It makes a man a little testy. Who's roddin' this here outfit?"

"I am," Clay said. "This is a mixed herd out of San Dimas down below the Nueces. We're bound for market in Missouri."

"Missouri? You mean you figure you can really?—I mean how soon do you aim to git there?"

"We'll make it," Clay said. "What's on your mind, Deputy?"

Kimball produced a much-creased paper from his pocket, carefully unfolded it, for it was about to fall apart. It proved to be a poster of the kind put out for wanted men, to be posted in railway stations and law offices. The subject of this particular dodger, according to the black-type headline, was wanted for bank robbery. A picture was printed, along with a detailed description. The name of the wanted man was listed as Kirby Kane. The picture was smudged and had been taken years earlier, but there was no doubt as to Kirby Kane's identity. He and Q were one and the same.

"Ever seen this feller before?" Kimball asked.

Ann Lansing had moved to peer over Clay's shoulder. He knew she was about to speak, and believed she was going to deny any such knowledge, but he got there first.

"Maybe," he said.

He heard her draw an angry sigh. She had expected him to lie.

Sim Kimball was enlivened. "Where? When?"

"Three, four weeks ago," Clay said. "Down on the Rio Grande. We were taking delivery of that big jag of reds you see in the herd. A fellow who looked like this one was working with the *vaqueros* under a rancher named Pedro Sanchez."

Kimball's burst of hope faded. He sagged back into apathy. "In Mexico?" he moaned. "Weeks ago? What good will that do me now? He was up here in Hackberry only a few days ago, an' shore raised hell, shoved a chunk under it, an' left it tilted."

"My goodness!" Ann Lansing cried. "What did he do?"

"What didn't he do? He's wanted for kidnappin', mayhem, unlawful entry, torture, an' half a dozen other items that they'll git around to after they ketch him, not to mention stickin' up a bank."

It was Clay's turn to be a trifle staggered. "How could he do all that way up here when I saw him in Mexico?" he asked.

"Mexico ain't so fur away he couldn't git here ahead of a bunch of cow critters in four weeks' time," Kimball said. "Not satisfied with havin' nigh ruined pore old Jonathan Pickens by robbin' his bank a year or so ago, he rides into Hackberry a few nights ago, busts into Jonathan's house, marches him out, an' rides away with him. We find Jonathan the next day, tarred an' feathered, an' tied to a tree with the sign of the double cross dabbed on his chest."

"This fellow on this law dodger did all this?" Clay asked incredulously. "This Kirby Kane?"

"He had help. Jonathan allowed there must have been four or five more in on it. But he was blindfolded, an' all he heard was voices an' footsteps and the horses when they rode away."

Clay was nonplussed. It sounded fantastic. Rose Lansing spoke. "I can round up a bait of food for you men. I know you're in a hurry, so I'll have to serve it cold. Leftover corn-bread and meat from the pot. I'll open some tomatoes and peaches. It will be filling at least. It's a long ride to Mexico."

"Mexico?" Kimball echoed, wincing.

"This man you're looking for came from there," Rose said. "Where else would he be heading for after committing all those awful crimes? How much of a start did he have on you men?"

One of Kimball's posse spoke. "Damned if I'm headin' for

Mexico, Sim, beggin' your pardon, ma'am, for the slip of the tongue. I've had enough. This feller didn't actually hurt that old skinflint anyway. Just tarred an' feathered him up a leetle. There's a lot o' folks around here who figure that Jonathan was overdue for it."

Other men in the posse voiced firm support of that viewpoint, both as having no desire to proceed to Mexico and as to the nature of Jonathan Pickens' character. Sim Kimball was plainly glad to be ruled by majority opinion. "We accept your offer, ma'am," he said gallantly, and became affable, now that he saw a graceful way to escape from a futile pursuit.

Clay faded into the background while Rachel and Rose, with Ann's help, fed the possemen. Finally Ann joined him. "You got out of that gracefully and without telling an actual fib," she said. "I always knew the Burnets were accomplished at slippery doings. What in the world was on Q's mind, do you suppose? Did he go loco?"

"I doubt that," Clay said.

"We'll never see him again, of course," she said.

"We'll see him."

"Why are you so sure?"

"Because of that notion he carries that he owes it to me to see this drive through and watch over me. He'll show up."

"But if he doesn't what will we do?"

"Hit the trail. What else?"

"With this crew? That's impossible!"

"I never thought it was possible that I'd be standing here talking to a Lansing, and driving Lansing cattle to market," Clay said. "But here we are. Anything's possible after that. We'll hang around a while longer. I still think we'll hear from him."

He was right. But it was not until after dark more than twenty-four hours later, and the confidence he outwardly exhibited was beginning to wear thin, when Q returned. He was sitting apart from the wagon, a tin cup of coffee in his hand, when he heard a low, cautious whistle from the background. He arose and located the whistler. It was Q, or Kirby Kane, as he was named on the law dodger.

"Have they gone?" Q whispered. The posse?"

"Long ago," Clay said. "Yesterday afternoon. They were heading back to Hackberry and glad of it. They'd had enough. We sort of pushed them into believing you were on your way to Mexico, and that they didn't have a chance of catching you. Fact is, I got the idea that some of them weren't too much interested in catching up with you anyway."

Q chuckled. "Jonathan Pickens ain't exactly the most popular citizen in Hackberry."

He uttered a low whistle. There was movement in the darkness. Several men, leading saddled horses, presently came out of the shadows.

"Here are some fellers who are lookin' for ridin' jobs," Q said. "Some of 'em has worked as trail hands, an' you'll find 'em worth their pay. One or two might need a leetle proddin', bein' as they was born lazy, but they'll stick with us if things get touchy."

Clay eyed Q's companions. Rose Lansing and her daughter, attracted by the sound of voices, left the campfire and came walking to join him. They also peered in silence.

Rose Lansing finally spoke. "Heaven help us!"

Q had brought five men with him. The glow of the wagon fire faintly reached them. Two were wearing knee-length black coats in the plantation style, along with ruffled shirts and stocks, all frayed and threadbare. Clay tabbed them as tinhorn gamblers at best. One was rail-thin and over six feet, the other short-coupled, with a wide mouth. Two others wore brush jackets, foxed breeches, and cowboots, garb that was also far from new. The fifth had on a blanket jacket, checked shirt, striped pantaloons that were stuffed into knee-high Conestoga boots, and a round pancake felt hat. A bull-whacker's garb. Still, he did not exactly stack up in Clay's eyes as a man who followed that arduous and dangerous profession regularly.

They were of different sizes, different faces, different dress, but all had one trait in common. They were young, hard-bitten, reckless, with a go-to-hell set to their mouths and their postures.

"This one here goes by the name of Zeno," Q said. "We call him Z for short." He was indicating the bullwhacker.

"And I take it that these others are known as A, B, C and D?" Rose Lansing spoke caustically.

"Now how did you guess it?" Q responded.

Rose Lansing clapped a hand to her forehead in despair. "If you think for one minute we intend to—"

"The pay's twenty-five a month and found," Clay said. "Is that satisfactory to you men?"

"Provided the grub is what Kir—I mean Q here—says it is," one of the cowboys said. "He tells me you git real home cookin' with this outfit. Female cookin'."

"Best fodder any trail crew ever had," Clay said. "But, if

you throw in with us, you're to stick all the way. Our destination is a railroad somewhere in the state of Missouri. That means crossing the Indian country."

"Do you think I'm going to stand for traveling with these men?" Rose Lansing moaned. "Why—why, they're nothing but a pack of out—"

Her daughter spoke hastily. "Mother, you're taking the wrong view. They look like righteous, upstanding men to me."

"How can you say that?" her mother groaned. "We know they just tarred and feathered some poor man there in this Hackberry place, and are wanted by the law for that and heaven knows what else."

"We didn't really tar that old buzzard," the tall tinhorn said. "All we did was smear some axle grease on him an' dust him with cockleburs."

"We couldn't find no tar," the smaller tinhorn explained. "So we had to use whatever was handy."

Q spoke to Clay. "You can call me Kirby. I reckon the law man told you that was my name."

"We'll continue to call you Q," Clay said. "As far as we're concerned you've never had any other name."

"Thanks," Q said. "But, so that we don't get the alphabet mixed up, maybe we better call some of these others by name. The tall one, dressed like an undertaker, is Bass. The short-coupled one is Ace. Them two there are Cass an' Des. You've already met Zeno. Clear enough?"

"Clear as a hole in a patch of quicksand," Clay said. "We'll get them straightened out in time. I take it that Ace and Bass aren't really undertakers. My guess is that they're better at burying dead hands in the discard than burying the real thing."

Q grinned. "You could be right. Don't get into any poker games with 'em. Nor with Zeno either. He ain't exactly as stupid as he looks."

"How about you two?" Clay asked the pair who called themselves Cass and Des. "What's your speciality?"

"Punchin' cattle," Cass said with an injured expression. "What else."

"I wouldn't want to guess," Clay said. "I'll cut saddle strings to all of you in the morning, The herd's rested and snorting to hit the trail. We'll string out at daybreak."

"We got clothes in our war sacks that will do better than what we got on," Ace said. "We better camp out in the brush tonight. No use crowdin' in on you folks right away."

Clay understood that Ace and his friends did not want to

take a chance that Sim Kimball and the posse might decide to make a return visit.

Rachel, who had been listening, spoke. "See to it dat you stay dar. I'm goin' to sleep mighty light, an' I'll have a butcher knife under my pillow, I tell you. I don't cotton to havin' bank robbers an' such wanderin' around my bed."

"Be quiet!" Micah rumbled angrily. "Dese men come here to help us."

"To cut our throats, most likely," Rose Lansing said.

"Don't listen to her," Ann Lansing said. "I want you to know we appreciate your coming here to help us."

"An' we ain't bank robbers either," Ace, the short-coupled tinhorn said, injured, "Kir—I mean Q here—got double-crossed by that old miser, Jonathan Pickens. He's charged with a whizzer that ol' Jonathan pulled for his own profit."

"Do tell us more," Rose Lansing said with tart skepticism.

"You wouldn't believe us anyway, ma'am." Q spoke mildly. "You've got your mind set ag'in us. Anyway, we're sort o' weary. We been dodgin' that posse for days."

Clay walked with the six men as they retreated from reach of the firelight. Q had given him a glance that indicated he had more to say, but wanted to say it away from the ears of others.

Reaching the brush, and inspecting what they carried on their horses, he discovered that the newcomers lacked bedding of any kind, and intended to make the best of it for the night, as they evidently had been doing during their flight. He realized they probably had little or nothing to eat recently.

He returned to camp to speak with Rachel and Rose Lansing. They responded with speed, if not with enthusiasm, by pitching in to prepare a second meal. Clay rounded up tarps and what spare blankets he could find, and carried them into the brush where Q and his men were waiting, smoking pipes and cigarettes.

When the food was brought on tin plates by the women, the six men fell to with appetites that aroused comment from Rachel. "I declare, if they're gonna stow away provisions like that, we'll git to Missoury with nothin' but hides an' bones. They'll eat de whole herd."

"Don't worry, gal," Zeno said with a wide, friendly grin. "As a rule we don't eat our own beef. We got a tooth for slow elk."

"Dat's one thing I kin believe," Rachel said. "An' dis slow elk wears brands, I take it. Other folks' brands."

After the women had returned to the wagons, Clay looked around at the shadowy figures. "Do you want to tell me anything?" he asked. "You know our side of it. We're driving cattle to market. That's enough to keep us busy. We don't hanker to take on any side lines."

"Such as robbin' banks?" Ace asked tersely.

"That's right," Clay said. "That's what I want made clear."

Q spoke. "This is the way it is, whether you will believe it nor not. About a year ago Jonathan Pickens run a high blaze on me. I was hangin' out in Hackberry, doin' this an' that, mainly buffalo huntin', pickin' up jobs with cow outfits, an' with freight outfits. Even drove stagecoach for a while. The country is full of fellers like me who'd fought in the war, an' was jest driftin' around, tryin' to keep body an' soul together, like me an' my brothers an' cousins here."

"Brothers? Cousins?"

"These two shorthorns that look like tinhorns are my brothers," Q said. "Ace is older than me, an' Bass younger. Cass an' Des are first cousins. Their paw and my paw were brothers. We're a sort of clannish family. Root stock in Georgia. We cling together. When a feller does dirt to one of us he sorta takes on all of us in a bundle."

"What about this one?" Clay asked, indicating Zeno.

"No relation," Q said, grinning. "Just a friend what sorta speaks our language. An' a bluebelly at that. He fought ag'in us. Now we're pals."

"You're referring to this Jonathan Pickens as the one who did you dirt, I take it?" Clay observed.

"Us six had scraped together enough to start a little brand of our own a few miles out of Hackberry," Q said. "We figure that the buffalo will soon be thinned out an' that cattle might be worth somethin' if you could hang and rattle long enough. Jonathan Pickens owned the bank in Hackberry. It wasn't much of a bank, o' course, but Jonathan had a way of talkin' big, walkin' big, an' impressin' folks. Wore a stovepipe hat, quoted the Bible, an' was a real buttermouth. He also liked to play poker, a habit no banker ought to indulge in. He was a bad poker player, but he believed he was a cyclone on the plains when it come to playin' cards. He got to owin' quite a few folks. It was money he didn't own, of course, but nobody knew just how poor off the bank really was. I finished two hundred dollars ahead of him in a stud game one evenin'. He said he didn't have the money on him, but asked me to go over to the bank where he'd git it from his private safe."

"My brother was a danged fool," Bass said. "He might have known Jonathan had somethin' up his sleeve."

"I'd had a few drinks an' was happy," Q said, sighing. "It

was near midnight. I went to the bank with him, waited while he fumbled around in his office. He gave me the money, an' I rode on back to the ranch, callin' it a night.

"I was woke up about midmornin'. It was Bass here, tellin' me to hit the trail. Seems like they'd found Jonathan Pickens hog-tied an' gagged in the bank, the big safe busted wide open with a sledgehammer, an' all the bank's money gone. Jonathan allowed that I was the one who'd done it an' had scooted away. It seems that I was supposed to have got away with more'n ten thousand dollars, which busted the bank an' cost the depositors everything they'd put into the place. O' course, it was what Jonathan had stole from the safe that night, cached it, then come back, tied hisself up an' waited until he was found the next mornin' so he could accuse me."

Q paused a moment, then said dryly, "I was mighty sure they'd believe Jonathan rather than me or my brothers. We wasn't exactly what you'd call leading citizens. Maybe we had sold a few cattle that we didn't have sales receipts for, an' maybe some of us had run in a cold deck at times in poker games. But we never really hurt nobody. Even fellers like us have to eat when our bellies pinch our backbones. So I lit out for Mexico on a fresh horse that Bass had ready for me."

"And the rest of you have been hanging around Hackberry ever since?" Clay asked. "Why?"

"Wal," Ace explained. "In the first place we didn't take kindly to bein' swindled. Our little cowspread was took over when they liquidated what assets the bank had after Jonathan hid the cash. We'd borrowed from the bank to buy the water rights. At ten per cent. Jonathan bought himself a good ranch, which included our place, pretendin' he'd borrowed the money from a brother back east. So we figured he owed us a living, an' stayed on."

"Living?"

"Jonathan's beef tasted better than anything else we could think of," Ace said modestly. "An' didn't cost anything. Jonathan knew we was slow-elkin' him, an' tried every way he could think of to ketch us. I reckon he might have succeeded in time. But we sort of enjoyed seein' him stomp and froth. We knew we had about run out our string when Kirby showed up an' told us about a man he admired who needed a little help on the trail. We had a few drinks, an' as a partin' gesture, rode over to Jonathan's ranch an' greased him up some. He's likely got it all swabbed off by this time."

"You're all hired," Clay said. "We'll be across the Red and out of Texas in less than a week with luck. Until then you'll have to keep your eyes peeled for law men."

"There's another little matter," Q said. "I bumped into a man you know in Hackberry. It was Bill Conners, the feller you fired down the trail."

"In Hackberry?" Clay responded. "You must be mistaken. Conners is back in the San Dimas, a long way south by this time."

"No mistake," Q said. "It was Conners. He's sort of gone maverick. He hangs out with a tough bunch whose speciality is stampeding herds in order to rustle strays. They also stick up a stagecoach or so now and then. An' Conners is figurin' on doin' a little more stampeding of a certain cattle drive ag'in which he packs a grudge."

Clay came to taut attention. "Say that again."

"It wasn't the whirligig that pore little darkie girl had made, an' for which she blames herself because that cowboy got killed that day. It was Conners who spooked the herd. He sneaked up a gully on the flank where there wasn't anybody in sight, waved a blanket in the faces of some animals that was grazin', an' that did it. It just happened, by bad luck, that little Cindy had started her whirligig on the far side of the bedgrounds at the same time."

"How do you know this?"

"Conners showed up in Hackberry nigh onto two weeks ago. Cass an' Zeno got into some poker games with him. No big stakes, o' course, but just to pass the time. Conners wasn't much of a poker player, an' he couldn't carry his likker either. He'd heard that Cass an' Zeno had reps as hard noses, an' he wanted to build himself up. He got to talkin' about how tough he was. He did some whisky talk one night about how he'd stampeded a herd which was bossed by a feller he didn't like. Said he'd been headin' north waitin' a chance to repeat the trick until that herd was wiped out or so spoiled nobody could drive it. He was waitin' in Hackberry 'til this herd come on up the trail."

Clay didn't speak for a long time. "This will be mighty good news to Cindy," he finally said. "She's been heartbroken. Maybe she'll start smiling again. She's been breaking my own heart with those sad eyes."

"Mine too," Q said. "How are you goin' to make her believe it? She'll figure that you're making it up."

"You'll see," Clay said. "How far away is this Hackberry?"

"Four, five hours ride."

"Where would a man be likely to run across Bill Conners there?"

Q stared closer at Clay in the darkness. "Now wait a—"

"Where?"

"You know that I can't go in with you," Q said slowly. "Nor any of us. Sim Kimball would throw us in jail an' lose the key."

"Where?" Clay repeated.

"If he's still there he'll likely spend part of the evenin' at a saloon hangout called Hunter's Rest," Cass spoke.

"Did Conners see you, Q?" Clay asked.

"No," Q said. "It was Cass an' Zeno what had anything to do with him. I spotted him a few times, but kept out of his way, once I'd made sure it was really him."

CHAPTER 8

Pale smoke from the juniper firewood laid a fragrant haze in the morning air as the crew ate breakfast, mingling with the aroma of frying meat, of cornbread, of coffee. The herd grazed quietly in the distance on a rolling prairie. The breaks of the Double Mountain Fork stood purple and peaceful to the northeast. The sun had not yet pushed its golden eye over the rim of the land.

"A mornin' like this makes a man forget thar's sich things as saddleburs, night guard, an' buffalo gnats," Parson Jones said, finishing off a slab of cornbread, sweetened with sirup. "There's days when the Lord is more'n good to us."

Tiny Cindy Stone was standing, with widening brown eyes, watching Clay. He sat by the supply wagon with a stiff square of paper in his hands. It was a sheet from a calendar advertising a railroad, the same material with which Cindy's mother had fashioned the whirligig the day of the stampede in which Tom Gary had died.

Clay was shaping another whirligig. He completed the toy. Pinning its center with a sliver of cottonwood that he had whittled, he fixed it to a small stick.

"No!" Cindy suddenly sobbed. "No!"

Ann Lansing turned from the iron cook pot where she had been helping her mother and Rachel and became aware of what was going on. A spatula still in her hand, she came walking to stand beside the terrified Cindy. She did not speak as Clay got to his feet and held the toy aloft so that it caught the morning breeze.

"Don't!" Cindy screamed. "Please!"

The whirligig began to spin nicely. Clay moved to Cindy, took her hand. She hung back in terror, but he said, "Cattle aren't afraid of these things, darling. We were wrong that day. It was something else that started the stampede. A bad man who was hiding on the other side of the bedground scared the cattle into running."

He and Cindy moved toward the cattle as he held the spinning whirligig aloft. He could feel Cindy's small fingers

76

gripping tighter and tighter. He was taut inside. Cattle were unpredictable. Bill Conners could have been boasting.

But the cattle were paying no heed. A few raised their heads from grazing, staring with bovine indifference, then returned to foraging.

Clay laughed. "See!" he exclaimed. "It's not scaring them now, and it didn't scare them that day." He swung Cindy up on his shoulder, placed the toy in her hand and walked back to the wagon. "Tomorrow," he said, "I'll make you a paper arrow that will sail on the wind."

Cindy began to smile. It was only a feeble, tremulous smile at first, but it slowly blossomed. Cindy's young mind was free again, her heart lighter.

He walked to where Lonnie Randall had driven the *remuda* into the rope corral. He cut out the mount he wanted, roped it, saddled it, and thrust a rifle in the sling. He buckled on his six-shooter and mounted the horse.

"I'll be gone a day or two maybe," he said. "I'll pick up the herd along the way. Jess, you rod the drive until I get back."

Jess Randall, the man he was placing in charge, stood dumbfounded. "But—" he began to stammer.

"I've got a little business to attend to," Clay said. "Personal business."

Rose Lansing and her daughter became aware that he was leaving and came hurrying, questions on their lips. He did not look at them, but rode away. Jess Randall had proved to be a levelheaded, capable man. The weather was mild, and according to Clay's information conditions were ideal for driving cattle for the next seventy or eighty miles to Red River.

He headed west. Hackberry lay in that direction. He took his time, throwing off at noon for a leisurely nap in the shade of brush along a small stream. He again let the horse set its own pace. The sun was casting long shadows back of him when he sighted the haze of smoke that marked the location of the settlement. He dallied again, resting alongside a sizable stream above the town until twilight settled.

Mounting, he rode into Hackberry. It was an unplanned scatter of nondescript structures, some built of sod or stone, others of adobe or logs. It stood at a stagecoach crosstrail and was the last jumping-off place for the Indian and buffalo country. It served as a supply point for the Army, and for cattlemen, and had attracted a population of perhaps two thousand persons, Clay estimated.

The principal street meandered aimlessly. The mud of spring had dissolved into gritty dust under a summer sun that blew in blinding curtains from the churning wheels of passing freight wagons. Bull-team, mule, and horse freightyards fringed the settlement, and the air was foul with the stench of buffalo hides that were stacked in great ricks, awaiting transport north. Livestock grazed by the hundreds in corrals and feedyards around the town.

More than half of the establishments were gambling houses or saloons. Some were shacks of sheetiron and mud, with plank bars set on sawhorses and candles for light. These catered to the besotted, the penniless, the vicious.

Higher up on the scale were emporiums which had mirrored backbars and gambling layouts that included roulette tables and birdcage games. At least two of these sported small stages with velvet curtains where entertainment would be offered during the evening.

The name painted across the false front of the largest of these places was the one Clay was seeking.

Hunter's Rest,
Mort Quinn, Prop.

Clay rode slowly past Hunter's Rest, glancing over the top of the slatted swing doors. He gained a partial view of the interior. There were only four or five patrons at the bar at this early hour. One poker table was in operation with four men holding cards. He saw no sign of the person he was hunting.

He found an eating place, tied up his horse at the front where he could keep an eye on it through the window, and entered.

Soldiers, buffalo hunters, bullwhackers, men of uncertain callings occupied the tables. Eyes turned briefly toward him as he stood his rifle in a wall rack along with other such weapons, and selected a space on a bench at a table. They took in the holster gun, measured his height, his garb, his boots, which classified him as a trail man. They lost interest in him, and returned to the business of eating as much food as possible in the time allotted.

A tin plate was slapped in front of him, along with a mug for coffee. "Gimme a dollar, mister, an' eat yore fill," the waiter snarled. "Then make room fer others."

The food was served in huge platters and bowls, which sprouted big iron forks and spoons. It was solid, and filling—and heavy with grease. Clay helped himself but only pretended to be hungry. He sized up all who were leaving the place, trying to determine if they might have recognized him and were on their way to carry the news to someone. He found no such evidence.

He finished eating, and strolled into the full darkness of the town. He led his horse to a livery, paid another dollar for stall and board. The animal would be reasonably safe from theft in the livery. He cased the town which was now growing livelier as the evening advanced. Women stood in doors beckoning. Barkers appeared in front of dance halls, bellowing the advantages of the establishments where there were percentage girls, entertainment, and crooked gambling tables, no doubt.

He passed a building which was now a saddlery and leather shop, but on whose walls, beneath a coat of white-wash, could still be made out a printed sign which identified it as the past location of the Hackberry Safety Bank, Jonathan Pickens, Prop. Farther on, a new bank, with new names in gilt paint, had taken the place of the bankrupt establishment.

Clay finally returned to Hunter's Rest. It was a sizable place as such things went. It had originally been built in the slat-length style, but business had been so rushing that an addition had been added in a wing at the side to accommodate the gambling layouts.

He moved to the bar, taking a position where the light from the lamps did not reach him directly. He ordered a beer, which came in a mug, mainly foam and not too cold.

Bill Conners was not in the place, which was growing increasingly busy. All the tables were in operation, and the bar was lined with men drinking, smoking, and yarning. A piano player began tinkling out a tune near the curtained stage.

Clay had ordered his second beer when Bill Conners came through the swing doors into the place. He was accompanied by two men. Conners had changed in the weeks since he had parted from the Patchsaddle crew. As range boss at the Lansing ranch, he had been somewhat of a dandy, dressing with a flash and a flair, a frequent visitor to the Jackville barbers and clothing stores.

Evidently he was now drinking hard. His white shirt was soiled, his features had thickened, and his eyes were bloodshot. A fold of flesh overlapped his belt. He packed a brace of six-shooters, whose handles jutted big and clumsily from his sides. In the past he had never posed as a gunman, preferring to depend on his reputation as a pugilist to awe lesser men.

He moved to the bar, shouldering aside patrons who happened to be in his way. "The red stuff, Al!" he called to the bartender, who was busy with a group of customers. "*Pronto!* I'm thirsty. Where's Gloria?"

"She'll be around," the barkeeper responded. "She's never this early. You know that. She don't sing till nine o'clock."

Clay sized up Conners' companions. One was a puffy, alcohol-soaked man who had the earmarks of a thug who would cut a throat for a dollar. The other was young, cotton-haired, with thick lips, coarse features, and the vacuous smile of a child. Both he and the puffy one packed six-shooters in holsters. Clay decided they were the kind who had knives, sheathed in handy hideouts, which they preferred to use. Of the two, he rated the cotton-haired one as the more dangerous. This one was brainless, heedless, with no conscience, no future, no past.

Clay moved into the nearest circle of lamplight. Bill Conners sloshed whisky into a glass, raised the glass, then stood in that attitude, peering.

"It's really me, Bill," Clay said. "Imagine finding me here. And you also. You really should have gone back to the San Dimas."

Conners carefully placed the untasted glass back on the bar. "What's on your mind, Burnet?" he asked.

"One or two things," Clay said. "One concerns Tom Gary. His best friends wouldn't have known him after that stampede went over him that morning down the trail. But we all knew him anyway, and gave him Christian burial."

"I don't know what you're talking about," Conners said.

Conners' two companions were standing open-mouthed, taken by surprise. Clay spoke to them. "Stay out of this. It's between me and this leppie here. He stampeded my herd a while back. One of my crew was ground to mincemeat under the hoofs. I happen to know that he has bragged that he aims to stampede me again and again."

Around them, men began backing hastily away, looking for cover. The alarm spread to the gambling tables. Play stopped, faces were staring, startled.

"Don't try to draw," Clay said. "I don't want to have to kill you. I figure you're going to live with Tom Gary's ghost the rest of your life, and that's what you deserve. You knew Tom Gary, you were even a friend of his. I came here to beat you with fists, and to let you know that if you ever come near a drive of mine again I'll do it over and over again until you'll look worse than poor Tom Gary did when we found him that day."

He added, "Take off all that iron that's hanging on you. It won't be of any help to you now. You're no gunman, anyway, only a false front."

A pudgy man with a paste diamond in his necktie appeared back of the bar with a double-barreled buckshot gun in his hands. "Take it outside, boys," he said. "I own this place, and I don't want it wrecked."

"More light in here," Clay said. "And this won't take long."

He moved in, yanked the guns from Conners' holsters, and slid them out of reach down the bar. He handed his own pistol over to the saloon man.

Conners was thirty pounds heavier. He had not wanted a gunfight with Clay, but he was now eager, for this was in his element. He thirsted to maim and maul the man to satisfy the hatred that had darkened his life. He charged in greedily. Clay moved inside the arc of Conners' blows and they lost power, expending themselves harmlessly on his shoulders. He drove punches to Conners' stomach, and heard the rush of agony from lungs. He took a smash to the jaw that had stunning force. He weathered that and again delivered punishment to the body.

Conners reeled back. He braced himself against the bar and caught Clay to the forehead with a sledging right, then a left to the chin that sent Clay staggering back against a table. Conners rushed in to finish the fight. Clay caught the chair that had been vacated by a poker player and sent it spinning against Conners' shins. Conners was tripped to a hand and knee in the sawdust but lunged to his feet.

Clay met him with punches to the face. Conners' blows suddenly lacked steam. Clay drove a right to the jaw, and then another right. And Conners went down, horrible disbelief in his eyes.

A kicking, fist-mauling, cursing weight landed on Clay's back. It was Conners' young, cotton-haired companion. He was squealing profane, insane promises that he would kill Clay. He was pummeling with both fists, but his own berserk fury was defeating his purpose, and he did little damage.

Clay plunged forward and bucked his new opponent head over heels in a somersault. The cotton-haired one struck a poker table with solid impact. The table was strongly built and withstood the weight. But the cotton-haired was left motionless, the wind knocked out of him.

A gun roared. Clay turned. Conners' second companion, the puffy-eyed one, was standing with a shocked expression on his hard features. A six-shooter was dribbling from the limp fingers of his right hand. It landed in the sawdust. His right arm, which had managed the gun, drooped sickeningly.

A bullet had broken his arm midway between elbow and wrist. Blood was appearing.

Powder smoke came spinning past Clay from the bore of a pistol in the hands of a newcomer who had stepped through the swing doors. The arrival was Ann Lansing. She was pale, and palpably horrified by what she had done, but she still held the six-shooter ready to fire again if necessary, her lips set in a tight, determined line.

The place became bedlam, with men diving to cover. That gradually stilled as no more shooting erupted. Heads began to cautiously appear.

"Come on!" Ann Lansing said to Clay, her voice thin, high-pitched. "Let's get out of here!"

Clay lifted his six-shooter from the hands of the stunned saloon owner and walked to join her. Together they backed through the swing doors—and into the arms of a big man wearing a deputy's badge—Sim Kimball.

"Stand right there!" Kimball thundered. "Turn aroun', while I peel them guns off'n you. Stand quiet, till I say you can move."

Clay looked wryly at Ann Lansing. "Better uncock that gun," he said. "It might go off. You don't want to add shooting a peace officer to your crimes, do you?"

Kimball took their six-shooters and laid them carefully on the ground. He ran his hands over Clay to make sure he had no hideout. He started to do the same with Ann Lansing. There was a sharp report and the deputy staggered back, holding a hand to his face that had been thoroughly slapped.

"Keep your paws off me!" she snapped.

"M'God!" Kimball moaned, continuing to nurse his jaw. "If'n it ain't the pants-wearin' female! An' this other one is thet long-legged boss of that ragged-bottom trail outfit I come across out there. What in blazes are you two doin' startin' a ruckus here in my town?"

Bill Conners, blood crusting his damaged face, came out of the saloon, helping the puffy-eyed man, who was gripping his broken arm and stumbling, dazed by the shock of the injury.

"We got to git a doctor!" Conners snarled. "Gotch, here, has got a bone busted by a slug, an' is bleedin' bad. Them two there done it. Thet gal shot Gotch. Tried to murder him."

"I shot at his arm," Ann Lansing said. "He was the one who was trying to murder someone. He was going to shoot Clay Burnet in the back."

"Arrest 'em!" Conners demanded.

"Don't neither of you try nothin'," Kimball warned Clay and the girl. "I'll have to take you two into custody till I find out what happened."

A few minutes later Clay and the girl found themselves in the dingy office of a stone-built structure that served as the Hackberry jail. Sim Kimball, with two assistants standing by to watch the prisoners, was laboriously filling out entries in a soiled ledger, and muttering aloud.

"One male, one female, charged with disorderly conduct, attempt to commit murder, resistin' arrest, an—" he mumbled.

"Who resisted?" Ann demanded indignantly.

"—an' assault on a law officer in the performance of his duty," Kimball rumbled ahead.

"My only regret is that I didn't swing harder," she said. "What right did you have to lay hands on me?"

"For all I know you might still have a sneak gun or a pigsticker cached on you," Kimball said. "You wouldn't let me find out."

"If I had a pigsticker I'd use it," she said.

She glared at Clay. "You are the biggest, conceited fool this side of the River Styx," she said. "Which river you will likely cross before you are much older unless you quit trying to demonstrate how brave you are. You're still trying to prove something, but you're only succeeding in being childish and insufferably heroic. You know you should never have come here alone."

"As long as we're calling names I could think up a few for you," Clay said. "Nobody with an ounce of brains would have followed me here, let alone a rattleheaded girl."

"Somebody had to follow you," she said. "I knew you were going to get yourself into hot water."

"How soon do we get out of this sweatbox?" Clay asked Kimball.

The deputy ran a finger over a calendar that hung on the wall. "Three weeks," he said. "Maybe four."

"Three weeks? Maybe four?" Clay and the girl echoed the words in unison.

"Circuit court just closed its session here a few days ago, an' won't be back for a while," Kimball explained. "Then you'll likely be bound over to the grand jury an' taken to the county seat to await trial if you're indicted."

"Good heavens!" Ann Lansing said. "Such a bother. If you think for one minute that I'm going to sit in your filthy jail for weeks, waiting to go through all that rigmarole you're mistaken. Can't we put up bail?"

"That'll have to be set by the judge," Kimball said. "An' from the looks of you two I doubt if you could raise bail, no matter how low it was set. As for sittin' in my jail, which ain't filthy, I want you to know, we don't keep females here. After all, you're a lady even if you don't dress like one. You'll be held at my house. I'm a married man, an' we've got a room all ready fer female prisoners. Last one we had there was a lady who'd kilt her husband with an ax. She's in Huntsville now, life sentence. Should have hung her. My wife's deputized, an' I warn you she kin handle half a dozen yore size, if'n you git any ideas about escapin'."

He looked at Clay. "You'll be held here in this calaboose, an' I don't want no complaints. My jail is the best the county kin afford."

He turned to one of the jailers. "Go fetch Sadie. Tell her we got a prisoner fer her to look after."

After the man had left, Kimball gave Clay and Ann Lansing a wink. "County pays a dollar an' a half a day fer board an' keep when a prisoner is held in special quarters. I don't care if'n the circuit judge never shows up."

Clay and Ann sat on a bench waiting while Kimball again busied himself at his desk. "You weren't fool enough to have come here alone, were you?" Clay murmured.

"No," she whispered. "I've got a little more sense than one person I could name."

"Who came with you?"

She was reluctant to answer. Finally she said, "My mother."

"Your *mother*? My God! Of all people! Where is she?"

"She waited outside of town while I rode in to scout the situation. Then I got involved. I heard you fighting with Bill Conners in that saloon and looked in in time to see that man trying to shoot you in the back."

"Well at least your mother must know that we're in jail. I hope she has savvy enough to clear out and get back to the wagons before she gets involved too."

The jailer returned, accompanied by Kimball's wife. She was a very broad-beamed, bosomy, muscular woman with an untidy mop of red hair. She wore a brown skirt over many petticoats, a man's saddle jacket on which was pinned a deputy's badge, and had a pistol in a holster strapped around her ample waist.

"Come on, gal," she said, and grasped Ann firmly by the arm. "George tells me you shot up Hunter's Rest tonight an' likely killed a man. It's you smarty, pretty-faces that are always the worst underneath. I'm Deputy Sadie Kimball. You an' me air goin' to git along—if you know what's good for you."

Ann looked back wildly as she was led away. Then the outer door closed behind her. Kimball pushed Clay toward the open door of a cell at the rear. A moment later the door banged shut and a key turned in the lock. Clay was a prisoner in the Hackberry jail. Moths and mosquitos flew freely in and out of the small barred window from which the glass had been removed for ventilation. He heard the dribbling of a rat or lizard in the heavy beams of the roof overhead. He sat down on the bunk which had a thin mattress, evidently stuffed with cornshucks. He was to discover that this was also his chair and table. There was nothing else in the tiny cell.

"There's water, buckets, soap, and mops in the washroom at the back," the turnkey said. He was a wizened, bowlegged man with a sad handlebar mustache. "We'll tell you when we want to let you out to wash up yourself an' yore cell."

Clay tried to imagine what Rose Lansing might be doing. No doubt she would carry the news back to the trail camp. But when then? He had no answer for that. What could a skeleton crew manned with oldsters like the Parson and Beaverslide do? As for Q and his five companions, they did not even dare show their faces in Hackberry, else they would find themselves in the same predicament as Clay and Ann Lansing. Jailed.

He turned in presently. The turnkey furnished him with a ragged cotton quilt, which was not needed, for the cell was stifling in spite of the open window. He lay wondering about Ann Lansing, about the herd, and about what would happen to it now that he no longer could carry the responsibility.

He slept fitfully. At daybreak he left the bunk and stood with his face pressed to the bars of the window—an opening too small for a man to wriggle through, even if the bars were removed. Hackberry was still asleep at this hour. It awakened slowly, the sun came up. He ate the coarse flapjacks, moistened with molasses, that the jailer brought, along with a cup of water that was tepidly warm.

He returned to his vigil at the window. Hours of it. He had a slanting view into the main street, and his entertainment was the parade of passing freighters, pedestrians, riders, and pack trains. Noon meal was a bowl of stew, prepared by Sim Kimball's wife. Brought from the Kimball home, it was cold by the time it reached him.

The afternoon dragged by, the heat in the cell became a torture. Sundown came and darkness fell, bringing a measure of coolness. He paced his cage, listening to the sounds of conviviality that drifted from the music halls and saloons.

Surely the next day would bring at least some word from Rose Lansing. But the next day passed as monotonously as had the first twenty-four hours. Something must have happened to Rose Lansing.

When twilight came, he furiously rattled the door of his cell until Kimball, who had been cooling himself in a chair on the sidewalk, was forced to take heed. "What's eatin' you?" the deputy demanded.

"I want to see Miss Lansing," Clay snarled.

"What fer?"

"What for? What the hell! So we can find a lawyer who can get her, at least, out of here."

" 'Tain' no use. Ain't no lawyer in town now thet court is over. Wouldn't be no use anyway, bein' as both o' you are flat busted. She didn't have a cent on her, Sadie says, an' all you had was little more'n seven dollars. Ain't no lawyer what would be interested in that kind o' money."

Clay gave up the discussion. Another day passed. He again demanded that he be allowed to speak to Ann Lansing. Kimball again refused. "I don't want you two gittin' your haids together to hatch up some deviltry," he said.

A fourth day passed. A fifth day. Clay had the sensation of living in a nightmare. He began to fight the desire to yell and tear at the cell door and the stone walls. He began conjuring all sort of grim theories. They had been deserted. Or, *he* had been deserted. Rose Lansing probably had managed to gain her daughter's release and was on the way north with the drive, leaving him to face the music alone. The feud had been revived.

"You got a visitor," Kimball growled on the afternoon of the sixth day.

The visitor was Ann. She was accompanied by Kimball's buxom wife who stood, arms folded, listening to what was to be said.

Ann came to the cell door. She was thin, drawn, seemed much smaller. "I forced them to bring me here," she said. "I wanted to make sure you were all right."

Clay said weakly, "My God, the things I've been thinking about you. You and your mother. I thought you had—"

"Deserted you? I've been imagining the same thing. Awful things. I believed Sadie Kimball was lying to me, and that you had been turned loose or had escaped. After all, I'm the one who shot that man."

"What's happened?" Clay asked. "Where are they? Why

doesn't someone come? Why don't they at least send word?"

"I don't know," she said, fighting back tears. "I just don't know. Clay Burnet, you—you look terrible. Just terrible."

He started to say the same about her, then refrained. Sadie Kimball took her arm, pulled her away. "If'n thet's all you two got to say to each other, then we're all wastin' our time," she said, disappointed. "I figured you two might be sweet on each other."

"Now, whatever made you imagine a thing like that?" Ann said, and wiped away more tears.

"Come on, then," Sadie snapped. "I got a bakin' to do before suppertime."

Clay was again left alone to sweat out the mystery of the apparent desertion of Rose Lansing and the Patchsaddle crew. He knew in his heart it could not be desertion. So he began to picture new wild visions. Something had happened to all of them. Outlaw attack. Rustlers. Indians. They might have been wiped out, the herd stolen.

These demons marched with him. It was sundown again, and he was lying listlessly on the pallet. He suddenly lifted his head, listening. Then he leaped to the window.

"Come to salvation and enlist in the army of the Lord," a deep voice was booming in the street. "Revive your faith in the sacred word of the Testaments, and humble yourself in the knowledge that there will be a Judgment Day."

A hooded wagon creaked into view in the street. On the seat, booming the message in bell-like tones, was Parson Ezra Jones. He held the reins of a team of mules in one hand and brandished the Bible in the other. Stork-thin and cadaverous, he wore a rusty frock coat, a battered top hat, a celluloid collar, and a black string tie. Clay recognized the garments as having once been worn by the tall tinhorn who called himself Bass. The canvas tilt of the wagon bore messages, dabbed on in axle grease. "Come To The Lord. Piety Is The Path To Heaven. Blessed Are The Humble."

The vehicle, which was the Patchsaddle supply wagon, proceeded out of sight down the street, with the Parson's voice continuing to roll out the appeal. Along the way, faces were turning, following the progress of the wagon. The majority were grinning tolerantly.

Clay waited. He could follow the location of the Parson by the distant droning of his voice. It became very faint, then began to strengthen. Soon the wagon reappeared. This time the Parson swung the team off the street into a vacant lot alongside the jail.

Sim Kimball, who was smoking a cigar, with his feet on

the desk, was annoyed. "I ought to run that old fanatic out o' town," he said. "We git one of 'em every month or so. He'll take up collections 'til he figures he's milked all the fools dry, spend it on red-eye, then move on to find another town what will stand for his racket."

It was evident that Kimball had not recognized the Parson as having been one of the crew at the trail camp he had visited with the posse. However, he did not follow up his threat to ostracize the pseudo evangelist, evidently because that would require effort on a warm day.

The Parson ended his declamation, and began unhitching his mules and making preparations for what was evidently to be both an overnight camp and a preaching session. Clay left the window and returned to the bunk. The Parson had not once glanced in his direction, but he knew that he had not been deserted after all, and that action was impending.

He ate the coarse meal that was brought from Sadie Kimball's kitchen, lukewarm, as usual. Darkness settled, and torchlight flared alongside the jail. Parson Jones began preaching, using the wagon seat as a pulpit. A few listeners gathered and more began to drift in. It was a way of passing time. There were catcalls and groans of derision. This brought protests from some of the gathering.

The sermon ended with the collection. Clay heard a few coins clank into a metal object. Then the impromptu revival was over. "Thet old faker will be as drunk as a skunk inside an hour," Sim Kimball predicted. "I shouldn't ever have let him light in this town."

The torch was extinguished. Silence came, as far as the Parson was concerned, although Hackberry was settling down to its nightly round of drinking and gambling. Nine o'clock came, and Sim Kimball locked his desk and headed home, leaving the jail in charge of the turnkey.

Ten o'clock. Midnight. Hackberry was mainly asleep, except for four or five of the gambling traps and music halls. The turnkey was asleep on a cot in the office.

Clay became aware of faint activity outside his window. He heard the snuffling of mules and the creak of harness being adjusted.

A man spoke softly from outside. "Clay, where are you?"

That was Q's voice. Clay moved to the barred window. "Here," he said. "This one." He dangled a hand to mark his location.

Metal clinked. A length of chain was passed through the bars into his hands. It was one of the chains used to lock the wheels of the wagons on steep descents.

"We're goin' to jerk them bars out of their sockets," Q whispered. "Pass the end back to me so I can hook up."

"I doubt if that'll be enough for me to squeeze through," Clay breathed. "This cussed window is child-size."

"I figure part of the wall will go when we give it a yank," Q said. "Stand back. That whole danged jail might come down around your ears. It's only a crackerbox."

Clay stood back. He could hear ropes being attached to the chain. Riders were out there with lariats. The wagon was being backed into position to join in the effort.

"All set," Q said.

"Praise the Lord, an' down go the walls of Jericho!" Parson Jones cried. "Hike!"

His whip cracked. The mules leaped into motion. Clay heard riders grunt as they leaned against saddles to help take up the strain.

Q had judged the strength of the structure correctly. The bars were not only snatched from their seatings, but with them went a section of the stone wall.

Clay leaped through the opening, taking a shower of dust and broken mortar, making it into the clear just as a portion of the roof sagged down, blocking the opening.

The turnkey awakened and began yelling. "This way," Q said. "Don't mind that feller. He cain't git out. We slipped some wedges into the outer door, so he'll be some time gittin' it open."

Clay ran with Q. Riders loomed up. One was Zeno, another Beaverslide Smith. They were cutting away the ropes that had been attached to the wagon, and which had helped breach the walls of Jericho.

The whip cracked again and the wagon took off, swinging through the dark back areas of the town, with Parson Jones handling the reins. Clay was guided at a run to where saddle-horses waited.

"Hold on!" he panted. "Ann Lansing! She's being held at—"

"Here I am," Ann spoke. She was mounted on one of the waiting horses. Clay and Q leaped aboard saddled animals, and they rode away in the wake of the wagon. In addition to Beaverslide and Zeno, he recognized Ham Marsh and Cass as members of the party.

"They got me out first," Ann explained. "It was even easier than wrecking the jail. I was locked in a room, but it was easy to open. Cass, here, seems to have had experience at picking locks. Sadie and Sim Kimball are sound sleepers, especially after they found a bottle of whisky in the kitchen that they didn't know they owned."

There was no sign of immediate pursuit. Clay was sure that would come later when Sim Kimball would have time to organize a posse.

"Take it easy," Q said. "We've got a hundred miles ahead of us, an' we ain't goin' to make it right quick."

"A hundred miles? Where's the herd?"

"The other side of the Red," Q explained. "We forded 'em a couple days ago, then come back to git you two."

"So that's why you let us hang and rattle?" Ann exclaimed wrathfully. "You got the cattle safely out of reach of Texas law before worrying about us. I could have died of anxiety."

"Yore maw figured you'd last it out," Q said complacently. "An' Burnet too. She said you was both young an' tough. Once we got the drive across the Red, we could thumb our noses at Texas badge toters like Sim Kimball. Otherwise he might have clapped a lien on the cattle to hold 'em as security for fines or such."

"Just as I said," Ann Lansing moaned. "My mother thinks more of those blasted cattle than she does of me. She'll never know what I went through with that big ox of a woman, Sadie Kimball. Do you know what Sadie actually asked me?"

"I'm waitin' to hear," Q said.

"She asked me how many other people I had shot during my wicked career."

"And how many is it?" Clay asked.

She glared at him in the starlight. "I might state here and now," she said, "that the next blasted time you try to act like a big hero, I'll not interfere."

"Amen," Clay said.

"I'll just let you be carried out on a slab!" she cried shrilly. Then, amazingly, she burst into tears.

They overtook the wagon. "Welcome, my children," Ezra Jones said. "We have shattered the walls of Jericho. Now we will wait for the waters of the Red River to part for us."

"I won't count on that," Q said. "I'll just figure on swimmin' it—provided we git there ahead of Sim Kimball. He'll be right red-eared, an' in a mood to do some shootin', after drinkin' that rotgut we left for him, which had the label of good likker, an' after what we done to his jail."

The lights of Hackberry faded back of them. There was still no sign of pursuit, and they slowed the horses. At daybreak they came to where relay horses had been left in a patch of timber, guarded by Des. Food was available. They changed saddles, ate and headed north again, leading the horses they had been riding.

At noon, with seventy miles behind them, they found a second relay of Patchsaddle animals in charge of young Lonnie Randall. Mounted on these fresh mounts and driving with them their augmented *remuda*, they rode on through the afternoon.

At twilight they pushed through scrub pecan, willows, and sycamores into view of Red River. The stream was low, and there was little swimming water to contend with as they crossed, herding their horses, and floating the wagon ahead of them.

The chuck wagon was camped in the fringe of the river brush. The herd was bedded peacefully on open flats of grama and buffalo grass, with Micah and Nate Fuller drowsily singing the cattle to sleep.

Rose Lansing came hurrying to meet them. She took Ann in her arms and wept. "You look thin, darling," she sobbed. "They didn't treat you right, did they? Rachel, fix up a plate for my little girl. And for Clay Burnet too. He's nothing but skin and bones. They've been starving them."

Ann kissed her mother and clung to her. "It's nice to be home," she said, weeping. "Home—and wanted."

Riders appeared in the purple dusk across the river. Clay made out the bulky form of Sim Kimball. The deputy sat there with his posse for a time, shouting threats. Then, defeated, he turned back from the river, and he and his men vanished into the brush.

CHAPTER 9

Clay twisted in the saddle and looked back. The herd was strung out for nearly half a mile, straggling raggedly along. Riders slumped hipshot on shambling horses that bobbed aimlessly along. Bluestem grass was almost stirrup-high here, but it only added to the suffocating heat of the summer afternoon.

A man had to turn his face away to parry the lung-parching aridity of the gusts of wind. Dust devils were springing into life from the yellow face of a parched stream bed off to the right. Clay watched the dusters, for one had built itself into a high, whirling column in sand hills the previous day, and had come dancing down on the herd, causing a run that could have been dangerous at another time, but which had faded away out of the sheer inability of the cattle to keep going in the heat.

This was the Indian Nations. The blue lacework that were the Witchita Mountains had faded to the southwest days ago. Since then the drive had been traveling through a vacant world, with no horizons to reach, no goals for a man's future.

No Indian really claimed this land, but all nations hunted buffalo, deer, wild turkey, and other game that was as plentiful as the hair on a warrior's scalp. This was the game paradise of the Pawnee, the Cherokee, the Southern Cheyenne, the Crow, the Comanche, half a dozen other tribes. Even now, in the heat of midday, Clay glimpsed a band of deer to the north, and the wind brought the unmistakable odor of a great buffalo herd somewhere nearby.

But the great danger now was Indian. Here the tribesmen killed the buffalo that came, they believed, in an endless river from caverns somewhere far to the south in the Llano Estacado, which white men called the Staked Plains. Here they feasted, made medicine, danced to their gods, fought rival tribes, counted coups, stole women and children, and lived as free and undisciplined as the wind. They wanted no white man to despoil their paradise.

Every man in the Patchsaddle crew was aware of the possibility of attack. Each morning when they were topping off their first day horses Clay made a point of reminding them to be always on watch. Each night he added an extra man to the shifts on the bedground—an added burden on men who were already in the saddle two thirds of the time.

He wheeled his horse and rode down the flank of the drive. His horse responded listlessly. The riding stock was as dispirited as the men, beaten down by the long days, the monotony, the dust that was always in their nostrils, the heat that never offered mercy, the hot nights that brought the mosquitos, the buffalo gnats, the deerflies.

One rider had strayed wide of his position on the second left swing, mainly to avoid the dust which was being driven his way by the wind in a cloud the color of a shroud. He was Parson Jones.

"Close in, Parson, close in!" Clay shouted. "They're beginning to scatter all over hell's acres. If they ever spook they'll explode in all directions and we'll have half The Nations to search. Keep 'em in line."

The Parson obeyed angrily. "That's all I hear," he snarled. "Saddle up! Git movin'. Tighten up them cattle! Eat dust. Eat more dust. If'n I wasn't a God-fearin' man I'd say fer you to go to hell an' take these dem-blasted horns an' hoofs with you."

Clay rode on. The angular, hawk-nosed Parson was in a mood for a real clash. So were all the other members of the crew. Micah, usually the most placid, who accepted hardships as part of life, came charging belligerently up as Clay neared the drag.

"That there feller what calls hisself Cass ain't gittin' along with me none at all," Micah raged. "He's fixed it so I'm always taggin' along with bunch-quitters, an' ridin' my bottom down to the bone. Look at me. I was black dis mawnin'. I'm yella now. Sweat an' dust. I could scrape me off an' build me a 'dobe house. You tell dat Cass man dat—"

"I'll tell him," Clay said hastily. Cass, as a matter of fact, was as dust-caked and in as much of a fighting mood as Micah, from the looks. "Simmer down, you two. There's a lake ahead. Nice cool water. Everybody will have a swim and forget the dust and sweat for a while."

"Lake?" Micah exclaimed. "Ah don't recollect anybody sayin' anything about a lake in dis part o' dis forsaken country."

"Look for yourself," Clay said. "Can't you see the shine of water dead ahead. We'll be there in less than an hour by the looks."

Micah and Cass rose in the stirrups. Then they both climbed onto the saddle standing erect. Their ponies were too jaded to object.

"Glory be!" Cass breathed. "There sure is water ahead. Blue an' cool-lookin'. Water!"

They slid back into the saddles. They were enlivened, suddenly eager. "Watah ahead, boys!" Micah yelled to swing men ahead. "Swimmin' watah! Bathin' watah! Whoopee! We'll be there before sundown."

Cass, whooping, slapped Micah on the back. They both were laughing like idiots. Their bickerings and frustrations were forgotten. They ignored the dust that crusted them and their horses, forgot their hatred of the unpredictable bovines they had been herding for so long. Once more the country looked beautiful to them. They even forgave it for the blistering heat.

The word passed from rider to rider. Wild yells of joy arose. The tempo changed. Even the horses and the dull-eyed cattle seemed to respond to the lightening spirits of the riders and began stepping ahead faster.

Ann Lansing came riding up to join Clay, her eyes alight. "It's a miracle," she said. "I'm going to ride right into that water, clothes and all."

"Go to the wagons," Clay said. "And stay back. You and all the ladies."

"What do you mean?"

"You'll see."

He circled the herd, speaking to the men. "Better start shedding your duds, boys. No use ruining boots and such. You'll have plenty of time later to do a washing. I'll send the ladies and the wagons off out of sight."

Soon the Patchsaddle drive was traveling ahead through westering sunlight, accompanied by a dozen men clad only in their hats. Clay faded to the rear, then dropped out of sight and joined the women at the wagons.

Rose Lansing, tooling the chuck-wagon team, was standing erect, gazing ahead. The herd was a mile or more to the west. She suddenly glared at Clay. "They'll kill you," she said. "They'll hang you up by your heels—and you deserve it."

Her daughter, who had placed her horse alongside the wagon to profit by its shade, had been peering eagerly ahead also. Suddenly she uttered a gasp. For an instant she went limp in the saddle. Then she snatched up the quirt that hung around the horn and rode toward Clay, swinging the lash aloft.

Her mother snatched the bullwhip from the socket on the

dash of the wagon, and sent its length sailing in time to intercept the braided length of the quirt in midair, foiling the girl's blow at Clay.

"No, Ann!" Rose Lansing said. "Wait! It might work. Something had to be done. They were ready to go at each other, tooth and nail. They had to be made to think of something else. Maybe to laugh at themselves. At least to laugh."

"Dar ain't any watah there," Rachel spoke from the seat of the supply wagon. "Mistah Claymore Burnet, you bettah be ready to run fer yore life when dem naked men find out you've made fools of 'em. I can't help laughin'. I'd shore like to see their faces when dey find out dat lake ain't nothin' but a stretch o' dry sand that looks blue, like a mirror under de sky."

Then Rachel began laughing. She laughed harder, rocking back and forth on the seat. Little Cindy joined in. Rose Lansing began chuckling, then burst into uncontrollable laughter. Ann was drawn into the rising hilarity. She draped the whip on the horn, covered her face with her hands, shaking with laughter. It spread to Clay.

In the distance he could see that the point men were becoming aware of the hoax. The nearest was Q. He was standing in the stirrups, craning his neck, staring in disbelief. Clay could visualize the incredulity in Q's tough face, the dawning realization that he had been duped.

Q was also aware that the best way to treat a humbug was to make the best of it. He turned, waving energetically, urging the others forward. They left their places with the jaded cattle and prodded their horses into a gallop.

Clay watched the small, white figures on horseback as they pulled up, far away, staring at the stretch of hot sand that lay across their paths in the sun. They sat, stunned on their mounts, for a space. Clay waited—waited. Then he heard their whooping, their jeering, their laughter, laughter that swelled to Homeric proportions. He watched them begin slapping at each other with their hats and gigging their surprised horses into sunfishing and humpbacking. Once more laughter had returned to ease the tension in the Patchsaddle crew.

Rose Lansing spoke to Clay. "It has worked, but I still pity you when they catch you."

"There's a creek with real water in it about two miles farther on," Clay said. "That is, if my map is correct. We'll hit it by sundown. There's a trading post and army fort a couple of miles east if the map is still right. We'll lay the drive over for a day or two so that the boys can really cool off. They can ride into the post in shifts to whoop it up a little."

"What's the name of this place?" Rose Lansing asked suspiciously.

"I believe it's called Comanche Ford," Clay said reluctantly.

"So that's it," she said, her lips pursed. "I'm quite sure you have heard of it. And so has everybody else. It's worse than this Hackberry. It's so wicked no decent person is safe there. Outlaws, cutthroats, gamblers and—and—"

"And painted women," her daughter said.

Young Lonnie Randall had been listening. "Man, oh, man!" he breathed. "Comanche Ford! I can hardly wait till I git there. I'll shore give that place a spin."

"Well, you're one young one who'll never see it if I can prevent it," Rose Lansing said. "I could never face your poor mother when we get home if I let you go into that den of iniquity."

Lonnie dashed his hat on the ground. "I never did have no luck!" he raged.

Clay waited until the crew had calmed and dressed. He cautiously returned to the herd. They had resumed their places as before. They were suspiciously silent, making no mention of the big event of the day. He kept close watch on them, trying to have eyes in the back of his head.

Sundown came and the brushline of a creek loomed ahead as the drive snailed its way over a long swell in the land— their real destination for the night. The vengeance Clay had been fearing did not come until after the cattle had watered and settled down on the bedground.

Then it struck. Jem Rance engaged his attention at the wagons, with an inquiry about some detail in connection with the first night trick with the herd. The loop of a lariat descended over his shoulders and tightened. He leaped aside— and stepped into another loop which heeled him as a calf would be heeled on its way to the branding fire. The cousins Cass and Des were handling the ropes.

The crew surrounded him, whooping and grinning. They had cut a bony, high-backed steer from the herd and had left it tied up in the brush nearby. Clay was carried there and placed astride the steer—facing the wrong way.

"Ride 'em, cowboy!" they whooped, and sent the steer lumbering and pitching into the stream with Clay aboard, fully clothed.

They stood howling and jeering as he was thrown by the outraged steer. They were happy. They mudded him when he came to the surface and tried to scramble his way to dry land. They finally permitted him to come ashore. He floundered to a sandbar and sat down, gasping. He pried off his boots, poured water from them. They joined him, joshing him, telling him that they'd skin him alive if he ever pulled a "batter," their term for a joke, on them again.

At the wagons Rose Lansing and Rachel had a special meal ready, topped off with hot dried apple pie, generously sprinkled with brown sugar and nutmeg.

Clay changed to dry garments and sat in the background, content. The antagonisms, the petty irritations, the endless discomforts and hardships—and the danger—were forgotten. At least for the moment. Men who had been at the point of blows hours before were now swapping tall stories and telling it big and long. Once more they were a crew, working together.

The men turned in, one by one. Rose Lansing and Rachel and Cindy retired. Only Ann remained. The cookfire embers cast warm, flickering shards of light. On the distant bedground they could hear Parson Jones and Micah singing softly, reassuringly to the cattle in their deep, melodious voices.

Ann sat with arms folded around her knees, staring dreamingly into the fire. She finally spoke. "It's over."

Clay stirred from his own reverie. "You mean the crew? For a while, anyway. But they're only human. We've got a long, tough way to go. They'll likely get stretched out again. That's why I want to give them a blowout in Comanche Ford. The trail gets to a man, and he's got to get away from it for a spell. A man needs to cut loose or explode. I'll have to think of something else when things get edgy again."

"I wasn't thinking of the crew," she said. "I was thinking of us."

He looked at her, and she nodded. "The Lansings and the Burnets," she said. "It's over. The feud. That's what I meant."

Clay did not speak. Her voice was low, level as she resumed. "I was a fool. Stubborn, spoiled. I was the one who tried to keep it alive—the hatred of the Burnets. I have been taught from childhood to believe you were evil. I know now how wrong I was."

"How wrong we all were," Clay said.

She arose, moved nearer, and sat close beside him. "I had to say these things," she said. "I *had* to know how you feel. You see, my punishment for my conceit in the past is that I'm now falling in love with you."

Clay looked at her, feeling the blood drain from his face. He was thinking of Hatcher's Run. "You must never say a thing like that again!" he said hoarsely.

She sat for a space, all her surrender in her eyes—and all the hurt. "There's something else, isn't there?" she finally said, her lips quivering. "There's something between us. It's something about my brother. About Phil."

He wanted to take her in his arms and tell her how wonderful she was, how much he desired her, tell her that she was the tranquillity he had always sought.

"I'm sorry," he said.

She continued to sit like a statue for a time. "There's torment in you," she said. "I want to help you, but you won't let me. It was the war. Something in the war. I can't fight ghosts."

She arose and left him, entering the tent. Clay continued to sit there. The entire camp was silent. He was still sitting there long after the embers of the fire had faded into gray ashes. Parson Jones and Micah continued to sing their sad songs in the night.

Presently the Parson rode in, awakened Ace and Zeno to stand the midnight watch, turning over to them the heavy silver watch that belonged to Ham Marsh and which was the official timepiece for the crew. They pulled on pants, shirts, and boots, buckled on guns and spurs, and rode away to the herd, still yawning and heavy-eyed. The Parson and Micah, their cocktail shift ended, turned in. They knew Clay was sitting awake in the background alone with his thoughts, but they did not intrude.

However, after a time, the Parson spoke from his bed. "Do you want to talk, my son?"

"Does it show on me that plain?" Clay asked.

"Not for all eyes, perhaps, but I've been privileged to carry on the Lord's work, so that it is possible I see farther than the others. You carry a great burden, Clay. Greater than the responsibility of these cattle and all us humans. You desire a woman, but you cannot claim her. Would it help if you told me why?"

"A man can't talk himself out of the deepest pit of hell, Parson," Clay said. "I had to send twelve men to their deaths. One was an enemy of mine. I could have gone myself, but I had an obligation to two hundred other men. That's the whole of it."

"I see," the Parson said wearily. He lay silent for a long time, but evidently could find no more words to say. Finally he wrapped the blanket around him again, and Clay was left alone once more.

When morning came, Clay picked by lottery the half of the crew that would be first to visit Comanche Ford. He talked Rose Lansing into advancing each man ten dollars from the reserve fund. Over the objections of the men, he insisted that they leave their guns at the wagons. "I can't afford to lose any more riders on this trip, now that you've learned to be drovers," he said. "No guns."

The group returned at midnight, singing, staggering, and hilarious. And broke. Cass sported a fancy red garter as a sleeve supporter. Ham Marsh flaunted a lacy feminine pair of pantaloons, which he hastily concealed when Rose Lansing appeared from the tent. Expecting the worst, she had remained awake. She was swathed in a heavy dressing gown, and felt that she had been vindicated in her fears. "Look at them!" she said to Clay. "They call themselves men. Why, they're worse than children. Even Ezra Jones is drunk. And he's a *preacher!*"

"Right now he's a trail driver," Clay said. "And a good one."

"He's a disgrace to his preachings," she said. "I'm going to give him a piece of my mind when he sobers up."

Clay, helped by the sober men in camp, headed the celebrants to their blankets. Clay counted noses. "Where's Nate Fuller?" he asked.

"Nate got rambunctious, an' tried to run Comanche Ford up a tree," Q explained. "He got throwed in the calaboose. The marshal allowed that five dollars fine an' three dollars costs was needed, but by that time none of us had more'n a total of two simoleans among us."

"Imagine!" Rose Lansing said acidly. "Nate Fuller, of all people. A married man, with children. How will I ever be able to face Aimee Fuller when I get home—if I ever dare go home after all this?"

"I'll bail him out when I ride in tomorrow with the other half of the crew," Clay said. "The boys will need the same financing these drunks had, and I'll need a little extra to get Nate out of the *cárcel*."

"You mean we've got to go through all this again!" she moaned. She threw up her hands in defeat and fled to her tent.

Q, who was not so noisy as his companions, spoke to Clay alone. "I run into a feller in Comanche Ford who knows you," he said. "Leastways, when he found out that this outfit hails from down San Dimas way, he asked if any of us happened to know a man named Clay Burnet."

"Who was he?"

"I don't recall him mentionin' his name," Q said. "But he seemed mighty interested when he found out that Clay Burnet was boss of this drive. I got the impression that he might have soldiered with you." He paused, then added, "I also got the feelin' that he wasn't exactly a buddy o' yours. He looked like he'd seen more of the war than he needed. Gaunt, thin, like a steer that had wintered mighty poor. Eyes burnin' out from deep in the sockets. Gave me the creeps, like I was seein' a ghost."

Clay felt a cold, bristling sensation at the back of his neck. "What did he look like?" he asked.

"He wasn't big," Q said. "I'd say about five, eight. Hair had been black, but was sort of a mouse gray now, though he couldn't be any older'n you. Does that mean anything?"

"No." The clammy sensation faded a trifle. Phil Lansing had been tall, fair-haired. At any rate Phil Lansing must be in his grave back there at Hatcher's Run. "I knew a lot of soldiers," he added. "Maybe I'll run into him tomorrow."

"You still going in with the boys?"

Clay knew he was being warned. "Why not?"

"Be sure and pack a gun," Q said. "I already told you I don't think this jigger is friendly."

The next morning Clay hid his gun and holstered belt in his saddle jacket, which he rolled and laced on the horse as he prepared to ride with the second group to Comanche Ford. He continued to ban weapon carrying on the part of his companions. "I don't want anybody brought back on a plank, or heading for Texas with a posse after him," he told them. He did not mention that he was breaking his own rule because of Q's warning.

The settlement was a step or two down from even the crudeness of Hackberry. It straggled among thin timber along a small stream, whose banks had been flattened by the freight and Army wagons which used the military trail through this area. Its nucleus was an Army fort, built of logs, and a stage station of rock. Both had walls thick enough to stand off arrows and bullets. Passing by the fort, whose gates were open, Clay noted that the garrison was thin. The sentry on duty informed him that the major part of the command was in the field hunting raiding Indians. A gaggle of some score of shabby buildings fronted on the crooked street.

"It'll look purtier after we've cut the dust from our gullets with a slug or two of refreshments," Beaverslide said.

"Nothin' will improve the looks of such females as I've seen," Zeno said glumly, peering at the harrigans who beckoned from doors and windows.

Clay visited the jail, paid the fine and costs that freed Nate Fuller, got his horse out of the livery, and sent him on his way back to the wagon camp.

He took young Lonnie Randall in tow. Lonnie had prevailed on Rose Lansing to permit the visit. He allowed Lonnie a small glass of beer, which went to Lonnie's head, causing him to stride grandly through the town, viewing the dubious sights, and even ogling a woman or two. Lonnie finally noted that Clay had his holstered six-shooter on his side.

"How come you sweet-talked us cowboys into leavin' our artillery at the wagons?" Lonnie demanded. "Come to think of it, you ain't drinkin'. Not even a beer."

"That's a lot of thinking," Clay said. "How about some grub, then a little game of pool? There's a parlor down the street."

"Pool?" Lonnie said disgustedly. "Grub? Man, I'm a shaggy wolf from the fork o' the crick, never been curried below the knees. I aim to stand on my laigs an' howl. I don't want no grub. I don't want to waste my time playin' pool. I got other notions."

Clay steered him, almost forcibly, into a beanery that promised to be a speck cleaner than its competitors. They ate the usual buffalo steak and fried spuds, canned tomatoes and coffee that Lonnie allowed was heavy enough to float a railroad spike.

Afterward, they made their way to the billiard parlor. Lonnie, resigned to his fate as Clay's companion, broke the wedge of balls on a pool table with a vicious drive of the cue. "Wait'll we git to this Missouri town," he said. "Then I'll cut loose an' take the whole danged place apart."

"Missouri is a state, not a town," Clay said. He drove a ball into a pocket. He paused, watching two of the Patchsaddle crew pass by on the sidewalk. Zeno and Bass. They were walking high in their boots, eyes alight and eager for action.

Clay sighed. "Chances are I'll have some more of 'em to bail out of jail by dark," he predicted.

A red-nosed, unkempt man owned the place. Clay and Lonnie were the only patrons at this afternoon hour. Now a newcomer entered. He was only a silhouette against the sun as he moved through the door. Clay was standing, cue grounded, watching Lonnie prepare to attempt a bank shot.

"Hello, Captain." Clay turned, peering.

The arrival laughed harshly. "No, I'm not a ghost, cap. But I've come back to haunt you."

"Owens," Clay said slowly. "Joe Owens."

"Correct, cap. Corporal Joseph P. Owens, listed as missing in action at Hatcher's Run, near Petersburg, Virginia, an' presumed dead. You recollect the place, I reckon."

"I remember," Clay said.

"You ought to. You sent twelve of us out to take on an army of Yankees so you could save your own skin and—"

"So I could save two hundred other men, along with six pieces of artillery, and pull back to close a break in General Lee's line, which we did," Clay said.

Joe Owens moved away from the flare of the doorway. He was no longer a black shadow. He had been a young, happy-go-lucky soldier, moon-faced, lighthearted. He was now skin and bones, his hair colorless, his thin wrists dangling from the sleeves of a ragged shirt that was too small. As Q had said, his eyes burned out from deep in their sockets. He wore the weight of premature age.

"Unlucky for you, cap," Owens said, "only ten of us died over that ridge. I thought I was the only one still alive till I run into Phil Lansing a couple of weeks ago right here in Comanche Ford. Sergeant Phil Lansing. I reckon you remember him also, don't you, cap?"

"I remember him," Clay said levelly.

"I sorta washed ashore here in this place a few months ago, takin' jobs skinnin' for buffalo hunters, swampin' out saloons, doin' any odd jobs that nobody else would do," Owens went on. "I was hit by a Minié ball, an' was picked up still alive by the bluebellies. I wound up in a Yank prison hospital an' camp until the war ended. Sergeant Lansing, it turned out, had been hit too, but came through alive. They kept him a lot longer, for he was hurt real bad, an' then he wouldn't agree to sign parole, for he thought the Yanks was foolin' him about the war bein' over. So they jest kept him in a Yank prison until he saw the light. Do you know what it was like to be a prisoner of war?"

"I'd like to help you, Corporal," Clay said.

"Help me? Do you think I want help from a man who was responsible for what I went through? I ought to put a bullet in you as you stand there."

The pudgy proprietor came to life in the barrel chair in which he was sitting. He produced a pistol and its maw was directed at Joe Owens. "I don't want no killin' in my place, fella," he said. "If'n you got to settle this, take it outside."

"Keep your hair on," Owens said. "I ain't goin' to rub out

this yella-belly. I'd consider it a pleasure, but I want him to sweat a little while he waits for it to happen. And I promised Phil Lansing I wouldn't rob him of the fun."

He leered at Clay. "Sergeant Lansing said that all that keeps him alive is that he wants to put a slug in your guts. He was on his way back to the San Dimas country when I run into him here at the Ford. He aimed to look you up when he got there. He must have missed your outfit somewhere down the trail, but he's had time to git home by this time an' learn that you're headin' north. My hunch is that he's well on his way back to find you."

Owens let that sink in for a space. "It could be that the sarge is close around already, cap. From now on, every hour, every minute, you can expect another ghost to show up from the battlefield in Virginia. His name will be Phil Lansing, and he has a bullet in his gun with your name on it. He aims to put you in your grave like you tried to put him in his. He knows he's supposed to be dead, an' he let it ride that way. He didn't want you to be warned, so you could light out. He wanted it to be a surprise. Maybe I made a mistake in tellin' you this. Maybe you'll run for it, but I just couldn't deny myself the satisfaction of seein' your face when I told you that, from now on, you can think of every minute as likely to be your last."

Owens walked out of the place, his thin figure blotting out the glare of the sun for an instant. His scuffing footsteps faded on the sunbaked clay sidewalk.

Lonnie Randall had stood pop-eyed, mouth gaping, still poised for the bank shot, frozen in that position. He looked at Clay and finally managed to speak. "Good gosh! What are you goin' to do, Clay?"

"It's your shot," Clay said. "Side pocket, you say. I say a quarter to your nickel that you miss."

Lonnie missed. By a wide margin. Clay moved to the table. His was also a bank shot. A difficult try. He stroked the cue ball evenly. It clicked against the target ball which rebounded from a cushion, crossed the table, and dropped into a pocket.

Lonnie glanced nervously toward the door. "I reckon I don't want to play any longer," he said.

Clay racked his cue and paid the proprietor, who had put away his pistol. "Did you hear anything said in here?" he asked the man.

"Not me," the owner said hastily. "I've learned to live all these years by stayin' out of other folks' affairs."

"I'll be coming back this way after we deliver the herd,"

Clay said. "If I was in the mood I could build a fire under you as long as a Mex lariat."

He and Lonnie walked out of the place. "Holy gee whiz!" Lonnie breathed. "Phil Lansing's still alive. Wait 'til I tell Missus Rose an' Miss Ann that their—"

He broke off, peering at Clay. He gazed for seconds. In that brief space he matured considerably, grew grave, and bore a burden. "Maybe I better not," he finally said. "Maybe I better forget I ever saw Joe Owens."

Clay's silence was his answer. They walked along the hot sidewalk, past the doors of saloons and music houses. "What are you going to do, Clay?" Lonnie finally asked.

"Drive the herd on through to Missouri."

"But—but—"

"Nothing's changed. Why should it be?"

"But—but what about Miss Ann? She likes you a lot. I've seen the way she looks at you."

"You must be imagining things, Lonnie."

"If her brother killed you, or you had to kill him, why it would just break her heart. It would—"

The enormity of it was too much for Lonnie. He went silent, staring into an adult world that he had never imagined—a tangled world made up of terrifying conflicts.

CHAPTER 10

Clay and Lonnie herded the happy members of the crew back to the wagons at midnight and wrangled them to bed. The great spree was over.

"Thank the merciful Heaven that none of them were killed," Rose Lansing said. She and Ann and Rachel had remained awake, with hot, black coffee ready. "I hope we don't have to go through anything like this again." She glared accusingly at Clay.

"Not unless they get ranicky again," Clay said. "Maybe we can make it to Missouri before that happens. Then my guess is that we'll see some real fireworks."

"May the good Lord spare me from seeing it," she said.

Clay mounted and rode to the bedground to visit the men on the middle shift to see how the herd was faring. A half moon swam in a clear sky. The only sounds that came from the cattle on this peaceful night were contented sounds.

No sound, except the hard, heavy slam of a rifleshot. Before the report could reach Clay's ears he heard the crackling of displaced air. A bullet had passed within inches of him.

It struck his horse in the back of the head. The animal was killed in its tracks. It pitched forward in a somersault. Clay wore only a right spur, and it caught in the stirrup. He could only try to throw himself aside and hope the horse would not fall on him, or that he would not sustain a broken leg.

His foot came free in time and he managed to roll clear of the animal's weight as it lurched in its death throes. He got shakily to his knees. The breath had been driven from him. He crouched there, wheezing heavily, trying to get at his six-shooter. His holster had been twisted around by his fall. Still half stunned, he had the sensation of moving sluggishly in a nightmare. He expected another bullet. He believed the shot had come from the shadows a considerable distance to his right.

He heard the faint pound of hoofs receding. At the same moment the herd took off in a stampede, the animals alarmed by the shot.

He realized he was right in the path of the stampede—on foot. He remembered Tom Gary in that instant. He started to run, trying to estimate the direction of the stampede and to hope that he was taking the shortest way out of its path. But that could only be guesswork.

A rider loomed up, screaming his name. The arrival was Ann Lansing. Her hair was a dark, rippling cascade in the moonlight, and she was bare-armed, wearing only a skirt and a camisole, evidently having been in the act of turning in for the night. She had appropriated one of the night horses that were always kept at the wagons, saddled, for use of the men who would go on the late bedground tricks.

"Here!" Clay shouted.

She came riding toward him, leaning and offering an arm, which he seized and swung up behind her. She veered the horse and rode clear of the oncoming stampede.

"What happened?" she shouted above the uproar. "I heard a shot. What happened to your horse?"

"Killed," Clay said. "It was rustlers, I reckon, stampeding us so that they could get away with some beef."

It was an answer that didn't answer anything. Stampeding trail drives so that theft of scattered cattle would be easier, was a common practice. But that did not explain the single shot and the fact that this shot had killed Clay's horse. She seemed to sense that she would get no further answer, and did not pursue the matter.

There was nothing more that Clay could tell her. How could he say that he believed it had been her brother who had tried to murder him?

She took him to the wagons where he roped out a new horse from the *remuda* and rigged it with a worn saddle that was carried as a spare. He took off in pursuit of the crew that had cleared out of camp to ride down the stampede.

As a stampede it didn't amount to much. The cattle were paunchful of water and grass, and in no mood to run far. The crew already had them milling. The riders who had just returned from Comanche Ford were nursing aching heads and vowing that if they ever touched another drop of red-eye they hoped someone would take a blacksnake whip to them.

They had all heard the rifleshot and knew that Clay's horse had been killed. They had questions on their tongues, questions that only he and Lonnie Randall could answer. But the questions were not asked. It was taken for granted that if Clay had anything to say he would say it.

They found Clay's dead horse. What damage had been done to the rigging could be repaired. When daybreak came, men of the crew scouted the country. But the stampede had gone over the brushy area from which the shots had been fired. Sifting any particular trail from the maze of hoof and horse tracks was impossible, particularly with only moonlight to help.

"Get what sleep you can," Clay told the crew. "We're throwing them on the trail at daybreak. We've lost enough time here."

He saw worry darkening Ann Lansing's eyes. She knew something was wrong—something that concerned the visit to Comanche Ford. But she asked no questions.

Clay did not turn in, remaining with the three men he had named off to stay with the herd. None of them mentioned the shot that had been fired. The fact they kept so carefully away from that subject showed that they did not believe that rustlers had been responsible. They knew that shot had been aimed at someone. Aimed to kill. And Clay had been the target.

The night faded. Rachel clanged the triangle at the wagon as a signal that sleep was ended and that a new day was starting for the Patchsaddle crew. The swift breakfast was served, the herd thrown on the trail. The cattle were tractable in spite of the night's stampede. They reeled off nearly twenty miles before dusk.

Clay followed the foreman's routine, riding two miles to one for the members of the crew, answering questions, making decisions as to route and procedure. The herd was a machine, half a mile long, mindless and stolid, but packed always with explosive energy that might erupt from the slightest cause.

A stampede from a neighboring herd that was paralleling their route three miles to the east came thundering across the prairie in late afternoon, with riders spurring desperately to swing the leaders north. Clay and his men braced, expecting their Patchsaddle cattle to join in the run. But the Patchsaddles moved placidly along, letting the running cattle race past only a few hundred yards ahead of Blanco and other leaders. Clay sent some of the men to help the harassed crew of the spoiled drive. They came back at dark, tired and vowing they'd never seen such blundering handling of cattle.

Two days later they forded the Canadian River, which was high and swift. The herd, veterans of the trail now, arched across the current in a column beautiful to behold and especially beautiful to a herd boss. Clay had led the way. He sat on his dripping horse on the far bank, watching the long string of cattle snake across the stream. Blanco came ashore followed by his pals, the calico steer, the big twisthorn cow, the playful black one known as Clown, and Moose, so named because of the width of his horns.

The animals in the herd were becoming individuals. Even more so were the men. There was Beaverslide, for instance. Clay had tabbed the old-timer at the start as a complainer and a troublemaker. On the contrary, Beaverslide had never mentioned hardship, never objected to drag duty or to standing double-guard on stormy nights when the herd was on the roam.

And there were Parson Ezra Jones and Nate Fuller. They had no future when they had started the drive, but now they were proud men in their patches and colorless, washed-out denims, linseys, and butternuts. They had brought a herd up through hundreds of miles of Texas into the perilous Nations. They had seen country they had never expected to see. Now they wanted to see more.

One by one, group by group, they came stringing ashore, the cattle, the men. The wagon was rafted across on floats of dead cottonwood trunks that Q and the men roped from sandbars and lashed together. Rachel and Rose Lansing rode the wagons, watching over their precious mules which swam strongly.

Rachel, especially, was now an experienced wagoneer, who feared no stream, no distance. Clay remembered a day now more than a week in the past when the mules, which hated snakes above all other dangers, had taken off in a runaway when they found themselves amid a colony of hissing, buzzing rattlers. The wagon had capsized in the midst of this horror, but Rachel had freed the tugs, releasing the mules, then had climbed higher on the frame of the vehicle, with Cindy in her arms until help arrived.

"Shucks, I ain' skeered o' snakes," she had told Bass. "I been livin' wid 'em all my life. Have you ever seen a real Texas rattler, Mister Bass? Dey grow ten feet long down whar I come from. Dey use 'em fer bullwhips down thar. Sorry I spilled de wagon, but it don't look like it's gumbled up too bad."

The oldsters like the Parson and Beaverslide clung together in camp, for they found that their yarnings of a past that was fresh to them and ancient to the younger ones, drew only polite, forced interest outside their own age circle. And Q, with his alphabet friends, formed their own group. There were the three women and Cindy. Then there was Clay, and there was Micah, islands who stood alone. But when it came to moving the herd they were a unit, pulling together, bound by a common pride in their accomplishment.

Micah's horse came splashing ashore, and the big black man unslung his boots which he had tied around his neck. He cocked an eye at Clay, and said, "You are ridin' kinda light, ain't you?"

He was referring to Clay's lack of weapons. Since the attempt on his life, he had not carried even the customary six-shooter which was looked on as a necessary part of a trail man's equipment while with the cattle. It was stored in the supply wagon.

This was the first time the omission had been mentioned, but Clay knew that everyone in the crew was well aware of it and was puzzling over it, particularly Micah and Q. One or the other of these two had been finding a way to being close to him the greater part of the time since the shooting and the stampede. Both always carried rifles on their saddles in addition to their side guns.

"I don't understand you, Claymore," Micah continued. "Are you *tryin'* to git yoreself bushwhacked? You had no business ridin' up thar as pilot, after what happened the other night. You made a good target o' yoreself the way you pushed ahead o' the cattle jest now."

"That's over with," Clay said. "I've decided it must have been some Indian who thought he saw a chance to pick off a *Tejano*."

Q had joined them and was rolling a brown paper cigaret. "How about that fella that was askin' about you in Comanche Ford?" he observed. "I got the idea he might have had somethin' in his craw ag'in you. Maybe he's the one who notched on you."

"I reckon there are plenty of folks who don't like me," Clay said.

They studied him, baffled. Ann Lansing had ridden up in time to hear what Q had said. She sat silent also, the same worry in her face.

"Anyway, you ought to at least pack a gun," Q said. "I got a feelin' you're goin' to need it. That wasn't any Indian who took that shot at you. Indians don't rack around alone at night—not these days."

Clay broke up that inquiry by riding away. They were forcing him into shaky grounds. It was evident they had quizzed Lonnie Randall, and even though Lonnie hadn't talked, they were aware he was holding something back as to what had taken place in Comanche Ford.

Clay waved his hat. "Keep 'em moving," he shouted.

"Don't let 'em overfeed or water, or they'll be no good the rest of the day."

The routine of the drive took over. Men, including Q and Micah, began hazing cattle away from the river. Soon, with Blanco and his pals striding ahead, the Patchsaddle herd was bound northward once more. Now it would be the Arkansas River that lay across their path—the last big hurdle on the way to their Golconda, which was named Missouri.

Clay was glad to escape from searching eyes, especially from the gaze of Ann Lansing. Micah and Q might be right in suspecting that Joe Owens was the one who had fired from the darkness, but always in Clay's mind was a man whom Owens had named as having sworn to kill him. Phil Lansing. That was why he had stored his six-shooter and rifle in the supply wagon. He could not shoot it out with the last of the Lansing line. If he killed Phil Lansing he could never again face Rose Lansing. Above all, he could never face Ann.

He rode pilot again, well ahead of the drive, to the despair of Micah and Q, who rode at the points and could only watch over him from a distance. He nearly paid for his life for disregarding their advice before the day was over.

The sun and the shadows were long-legged hobgoblins that marched stride for stride with a mounted man. A great buffalo herd had gone through this prairie recently, leaving a juggernaut scar of cropped forage, littered with droppings and the wolf-torn carcasses of weaker ones that had been cut from the fringe of the herd.

The sun went down, purple dusk came, and broken ground appeared to the east where a network of gullies and ravines was backed by miles of timberland and brush.

A rifle flashed from one of the coulees. The bullet was a savage thrust that knocked Clay askew in the saddle. The second shot missed. If there was a third, he did not see the flash, for he was letting himself plunge from the saddle to the ground. His horse, a thin-necked, tough sorrel that was the youngest and wildest in his string, took this opportunity to go to pieces and went bucking away, trying to rid itself of the saddle.

He lay flat in tall grass that protected him. He explored his thigh with his hand. He found no blood, no flesh injury. The slug had torn through the folds of the worn bullhide chaps he was wearing, and the only damage was the ragged slit in the leather.

Micah arrived, his horse at full gallop. He had his rifle in his hands. He yanked his mount to a stop, his face a picture of concern. "You hit bad, Claymore?" he asked.

"Not hit at all," Clay said. "It only tore through my leggin's and jerked me around in the saddle."

Micah started to dismount, then thought better of it. He peered, vengeance in his eyes, and was about to head for the dark gullies, but Clay halted him. "Don't do anything foolish. It might be an ambush. Indians. And whoever did it can be well on his way by this time. It'll be dark soon."

Q and others arrived, Ann Lansing among them. Ignoring Clay's warnings to stay back, the men rode toward the breaks in the prairie. Q was already forming a hangnoose in his lariat.

But in the approaching darkness the network of draws and barrancas defied easy search. All they could report when they returned was that the bushwhacker evidently had investigated the terrain before choosing the spot to shoot from, and had made sure he knew a safe path of escape into the tangled timber beyond.

There was little talk around the wagon fires that night. Clay sat in shadow near the supply wagon, and Micah saw to it that he was shielded by tarps, hung to block points from which a shot might be fired from darkness at a distance.

"Quit babying me," Clay said.

"Now, will you pack a gun, stupid man?" Micah growled.

Clay did not answer. Micah withdrew like a disgruntled crab, complaining in grunts to Q, who shared his disapproval of Clay's obstinacy. And there was another. Clay was again aware that Ann Lansing was studying him moodily. There was an increasing dread in her face.

He tried to avoid her, but she managed to maneuver him apart from the others where they could speak alone. "Do you want to tell me anything?" she asked. "Or would you prefer to tell my mother?"

"I don't know what you mean," Clay said.

"Whoever keeps trying to kill you will try again," she said. "That's for certain after tonight. Do you still intend to let him do this? Do you still intend to go unarmed, deliberately giving him every chance to murder you?"

Clay did not answer. She waited a moment. When he remained silent, she said, "It's tied in with something that happened back at Comanche Ford, isn't it? Lonnie Randall knows. I can see it in his face. He wishes he didn't know. He's scared, worried. I could probably force it out of him if I tried, but that would not be fair, for he's little more than a boy. I'd prefer that you tell me."

"There's nothing to tell."

"It has something to do with my brother," she said. "Something about Phil. What is it?"

"Stay out of this," Clay said. His voice was hoarse, shaking. "There's nothing for any of us in this but—but—"

He couldn't finish it. She finished it for him. ". . . but death for you—and heartbreak for me. You know how I feel about you. And I'm sure I know how you feel about me."

Clay gazed at her, agonized. "You've got to forget all that, stop saying things like that."

"Phil is alive, isn't he?" she said. "You believe he is the one who is trying to kill you!"

She saw that he could not deny it. She covered her face with her hands. "Oh, God!" she sobbed. "My own brother! He's trying to murder you! Why? The feud? Is it that awful feud?"

She tried to clasp her arms around him. Clay held her away. "No," he said. "That's impossible. We must not."

She believed that the gulf that had always separated the Burnets and the Lansings had opened again. She stood looking into grisly, appalling possibilities.

"You'd let him kill you, rather than try to defend yourself and kill him," she said brokenly. "Because of me, because you love me. I know you do. I know you will never tell me that in words, but it's true. Don't you understand that if you are dead I'll have this to live with all my life? I won't let this awful thing happen. I'll find Phil. I'll stop him, make him see how wrong he is."

Her mother came through the darkness and took her daughter in her arms. "What is it, darling?" she asked gently. "What has happened?"

Ann could not answer. She could not share her burden with her mother, knowing the grief and terror it would bring. She could only weep in Rose Lansing's arms as they walked away together.

CHAPTER 11

When Clay rode ahead of the herd, piloting the way, as the drive was thrown on the trail in the morning, he found that he had a companion. Ann Lansing was at his side, riding stirrup to stirrup with him.

She did not speak. Her face, with its delicate, high cheekbones, was a thin wedge, framed by the chin strap that held her hat on her plaited hair. Her eyes seemed larger, and there were dark shadows under them, evidence of a sleepless night.

She had been in the habit of carrying a pistol in a saddle holster, but the holster was now empty. So was the rifle sling. Clay was again unarmed.

He looked back. Q was riding right point, with the taciturn big, bronzed man who called himself Zeno at left point in place of Micah who had dropped back to first swing. Zeno packed a six-shooter, but in place of the big, bullhide holster he had used in the past while in the saddle, the gun was now in a tied-down, halfbreed affair—a gunman's equipment.

Clay knew that the weapon had always been within quick reach of the big man, day or night. He had never asked questions of Q as to the past of his companions, but on occasions he had seen Zeno brush up on marksmanship when the firing was too remote from the cattle to cause alarm. He had learned that Zeno was swift on the draw and deadly of aim, and that he continually honed these skills, as though he knew that someday he would need them against someone. There was dark tragedy beneath the casual, easygoing manner of the big man. In his past lurked depths that Clay hoped would never be plumbed.

Micah was riding fully armed, even to a belt knife. These men, Clay understood, were his bodyguards, self-appointed. As for Ann Lansing, she had gone even further. She was stationing herself where she believed her presence would not only serve to deter a bullet from her brother, but where she might even be able to offer her own body as a shield. Knowing the Lansings, he knew she would do such a thing. He also knew that nothing he might say could change her decision.

A lump came in his throat as he considered the devotion of this girl and the three men. He remembered little Cindy saying that strong men could not weep. Micah and Q might feel that they had great obligation to him, but Zeno owed him nothing but the loyalty that had evolved during the days of hardship and monotony on the trail. Clay felt that Zeno, too, must have his ghosts which might rise from the past at any time to put a bullet in his back.

One of those ghosts was near at hand now for Zeno. It was mid-afternoon when Clay rose in the stirrups, squinting ahead. Dust was rising in the distance.

"What can it be?" Ann asked, peering.

Strange objects were taking form, miraged to fantastic proportions by the reflections of the sun. Gaily painted vehicles became visible, with streamers whipping from their gilded turrets. Some were drawn by ponies bearing purple and golden cockades. One had a camel and bullock in harness. Another was drawn by mules, painted with stripes to represent zebras.

"Gypsies!" Q shouted.

"Comancheros!" Micah pronounced.

"Mexican circus!" Ann exclaimed.

"Looks to me like a little bit of all three," Clay said.

The exotic caravan evidently had been aware that it would meet the trail drive and had decked itself out for the occasion. It had been bound down the trail for the Indian country, and for Mexico, no doubt. Now that it had sighted the oncoming Texas trail men and their cattle, the wagons swung into a circle, halted, and prepared to camp.

As the distance lessened Clay heard music—cymbals, drums, bells. Women in Oriental and Spanish costumes appeared, cavorting and beckoning. They had bells around their ankles. Men joined them, turning handsprings and some juggling gilded spheres.

"Go fetch my guns," Clay said. "Rifle and sidegun."

Ann, surprised, hesitated. Clay rose in the stirrups and signaled Rose Lansing and Rachel to halt the wagons and camp. He waved his hat, ordering the crew to throw the cattle off the trail.

"Surely you're not afraid of that scabby bunch, are you?" Ann asked. "Look at them now that we can see. Paint peeling from the wagons, those poor animals skin and bones, men who look like cutthroats. And those women! Such hussies, and some of them half naked."

"They're bad enough," Clay said. "They're not exactly harmless, even by themselves. Some look like genuine gypsies, and my guess is some were *Comancheros* in the days when there was money in trading guns to the tribes. It looks like they all flocked together to make whatever living they could off the country. But they've got help. Big help."

He pointed. Another haze of dust was rising in the wake of the gypsy caravan. "Indians!" Ann exclaimed tremulously.

"Fetch the fieldglass as well as the guns," Clay said. He waited until she had made a fast round trip to the wagons, which were being camped by the women drivers, and adjusted the glasses.

"Some are Indians," he said slowly. "But not all."

"What else could they be?" she asked.

"Nothing good. Some call them border runners, or Bully Boys, or Jayhawkers. What they actually are is an outfit of cutthroats who prefer to call themselves unconstructed rebels. Guerrillas, in other words. During the war they joined up with renegade Indians to kill and rob both Secesh and Unionists. And they stayed in business after the war ended. I was warned to look out for them. They're bad business. There's likely a single name for every man in that outfit. Murderer."

"How many are there?"

"I can't tell exactly. I'd say at least thirty, maybe more. That's not counting the ones with the circus. Now circle the herd and tell the men to come into the wagons."

"The cattle?"

"Will have to take their chances," Clay said. "We may be in for a fight, we may not."

She rode away, spurring her horse, fright in her eyes. Clay rode to the wagons. Scanning the terrain he selected a position clear of all but scrub brush, with a scatter of small boulders which would serve as barricades against attackers. A wide, shallow wash, dry except for a tiny trickle of water in its center, broke through the flat a short distance beyond the site he had selected.

He spotted the wagons so that they would serve as barriers for riflemen. Rose Lansing and Rachel handled this task, backing the mule teams expertly into the positions that satisfied him.

The crew came in, sober-eyed and tense. At Clay's order, Rose Lansing dealt out rifles and spare ammunition from the supply wagon.

"It could be Major Blood, along with Stone Buffalo's bunch," Q said. "There was talk at Hackberry that they was ridin' together an' had jumped some wagon trains an' a trail outfit or two. Ever hear of 'em?"

"Who hasn't?" Clay said.

The renegade who was known as Major Blood had made a black reputation as a guerrilla during the war, having been the leader of a band of cutthroats that had preyed on settlers whose men were with the armies. Blood's speciality, in addition to murder and looting, had been the kidnaping of white children whom he sold to the Indians, then profited by acting as go-between in ransoming the captives back to grieving parents. Blood was said to have once been a freebooter on the Caribbean, and Clay had been told that the man glorified in dressing like a pirate and that he used the Jolly Roger as his emblem.

Stone Buffalo was a Comanche chief who had taken his sacred oath to kill all white invaders of the buffalo country and was followed by Indians of half a dozen tribes who joined in that cause.

Clay noticed that Q was intently watching Zeno. "Take it easy, Matt," Q said. "There's still a chance it isn't Blood's outfit."

Zeno, whose real front name evidently was Matt, was standing gazing fixedly toward the oncoming body of guerrillas. He did not turn, as he still sat on his horse peering. The guerrillas halted near where the gypsy circus had pulled up, preparing to camp. The music and tinkle of bells went on, along with the distant, tantalizing laughter of women.

"Fix barricades," Clay said. "For the women. Wagon boxes, boulders, whatever is handy."

He continued to watch Zeno, chilled by something in the man's face. And Q was watching also. "Don't do anything crazy, Matt!" Q spoke urgently.

Zeno finally spoke. "It *is* Blood. I see him now. He's the big man wearin' the red sash an' the flair boots, like a pirate. Like the woman-killer he is. Like the child stealer!"

Zeno stirred his horse. Clay had never seen such cold rage in the face of a human, such consuming desire to kill. Zeno meant to ride into the guerrilla camp alone, but Q seized the bit chains of the horse, halting the animal. "Take it easy, Matt," he said.

"I've waited three years for this," Zeno said. "I've thought of nothing else."

Clay interceded. "Whatever it is, Zeno, we can't let you go alone into that nest of killers, and we can't go with you. We're outnumbered, and we'd be wiped out. The odds are up to five to one against us."

Zeno drew a long breath. Some of the frenzy faded out of him. "Four years ago I enlisted in the Union Army," he said. "I had a wife and a daughter. My daughter was seven years old. I was a farmer on the Missouri border. That man over there hit my farm with his renegades one night. They murdered my wife and her parents and sold my daughter to the Kiowas. A company of border militia raided the Kiowa camp later on and found my daughter—dead. She'd been killed by the squaws when the soldiers hit the camp. All I want is to get this man who calls himself Major Blood in front of me, an' tell him I'm goin' to kill him. Then I'll start shootin'. I'll put bullets in his arms. Then I'll break his legs. Then I'll put a slug in his heart. I've practiced. I've made a gunman of myself, just waitin' this chance."

The Parson moved closer, and was listening. "Do not take the Lord's work in your own hands, my son," he said. "Vengeance is mine, saith the Saviour."

Zeno looked at him without seeing him. The Parson shook his head, knowing that his appeal was useless.

Rose Lansing spoke. "Look!"

Two riders had left the guerrillas and were approaching the wagons. One was a leather-clad, mahogany-skinned man, mounted on a black horse, who bore in his right hand a white pennant fixed to the shaft of a spear. He bore a ingratiating, white-toothed smile. Accompanying him, on a cockaded, spotted pony, was a young woman wearing a male Spanish costume of brocaded vest, pleated shirt and belled, laced velvet breeches over high-heeled boots. She was wickedly comely, but obviously hardened to her way of life. Like her companion, she was of Mexican-Indian blood. She returned the gaze of Ann and Rose Lansing with mocking challenge.

Clay swung into the saddle and rode to meet them, halting them at a distance, for he was sure one of their purposes was to assess their numbers and the strength of their position. He found Ann had joined him. "Go back," he said.

"No," she said, and he did not press the point.

"*Buenas tardes!*" the man cried. "We greet you, *señor*. You are from Texas, no? And with the cattle to sell in the north. We are very, very happy to meet. We invite you to our camp where you will feast and drink, and be entertained."

"*Gracias,*" Clay said. "I regret to say we are in a hurry to get to market. My men need rest tonight. We regret our inability to accept your invitation."

The girl spoke. "I will tell your fortune, *Tejano*. I will tell you whether you are in for much trouble."

"And does your fortune say that those who cause us trouble may not live long enough to regret it?" Clay asked.

The girl's lips tightened. "Do you not know who is our leader? He will consider your manner an insult."

"We know your leader," Clay said. "He is the woman-killer who calls himself Major Blood."

"Woman-killer?" It was the girl's companion who spoke. His pretense at friendliness had gone. "He will not be happy when he learns what you have called him."

Zeno moved into the foreground. "Then let him come out alone," he said. "I will call him a woman-killer to his face. I am not a woman. Tell him to come out armed. I will let him go for his gun first—before I move. Then I will break his arms with bullets, break his legs, then kill him."

The leathery man peered closer at Zeno. "Who is it who speaks so bravely and who will likely turn tail like a rabbit and run when Major Blood comes to meet this braggart?" he asked Clay.

"His name is Zeno," Clay said. "That's all you need to know."

The pair began to back their mounts away. They were frightened by the cold rage in Zeno. "We won't shoot you in the back," Clay said. "We leave that sort of thing to you people."

The two remained wary until they were at a safer distance. Then they wheeled their mounts and rode at full speed to where the guerrillas had camped a distance apart from the gypsy caravan.

"I can't say you went out of your way to handle that diplomatically," Ann said to Clay. "You might as well have given them a few slaps in the face. Wouldn't it have been better to have?—"

"Acted like we were afraid of them? That's why they sent those *mestizos* here—to find out if we were loaded for bear. They were supposed to size us up, find out how tough we might be."

"But they invited us to—"

"To walk into their spiderweb and be murdered," Clay said. "That gypsy circus is only a trap to bait people like us into easy reach of Blood and Stone Buffalo and their cut-throats. That would be the easiest way for them to get our cattle."

"They're after the cattle?"

"What else? They must know that trail outfits aren't loaded down with cash, especially this one."

"How—how are they going to try to take the herd from us?" she asked, frightened.

"Depends," Clay said.

"On what?"

"On Zeno, and this Major Blood. If Zeno is too fast for Blood, that might settle it, and Blood's outfit might go away. If it goes the other way, we're likely in for it."

She was staring at him with growing horror. "You don't mean you're going to let Zeno fight that terrible man?"

When Clay did not answer she turned to look wildly at the others who were listening. The men of the Patchsaddle crew stood in brooding silence. Zeno, who stood apart, was staring off into the distance. Rachel had Cindy at her side, an arm around the child. Cindy was weeping softly. Even she understood.

Rose Lansing moved to Zeno, took his face between her hands and kissed him on the lips. "I will pray for you, my friend," she said. "We will all pray for you."

Ann whirled on Clay. "No!" she cried. "No! You can't let this go on! Why, this man, this Major Blood, is said to have murdered twenty men in gunfights. Zeno wouldn't have a chance. You've got to put a stop to—"

Her voice faded off. Born and raised on the frontier, she knew the code. Major Blood had been challenged to come out and duel an opponent with his followers looking on. The guerrilla leader had his choice. He could meet the issue or back down. Refusal to meet the challenge would mean loss of face with his men, and perhaps worse. It was the law of the pack that he headed that its leader be all-powerful, or be pulled down.

Her mother came and tried to draw Ann away. She moved free and grasped Clay by the arm. "Don't let Zeno go through with this," she pleaded. "He—he might die. Let him stay here with us. You must stop it. It's your responsibility."

Clay stood, remembering another day when something like this was his burden. A day when powder smoke lay like a curse over the battlefield, pierced by the sheet lightning of cannon fire.

He looked at Zeno. The big man was inspecting his six-shooter, making sure of its action and the charges. It was a long-barreled, single-action Colt, the kind Union officers had carried during the later stages of the war, replacing the heavier cap-and-ball weapons. There was now only a stony purpose in Zeno, a purpose that was not to be thwarted.

Clay moved to him and extended a hand. Neither man spoke. Q and others also shook hands with Zeno. Then Zeno swung into the saddle and rode into the open. He halted his horse when he was midway to the guerrilla camp and sat there in the saddle, motionless, waiting.

There was turmoil in the guerrilla camp. Clay could hear the far, faint sound of excited voices. Faces kept turning in the direction of the Patchsaddle camp. This suddenly quieted.

A rider emerged from among the tawdry wagons of the caravan. He was a broad, paunchy man on a powerful sorrel horse. He wore the jackboots, doublet, and pantaloons of a pirate. A great black beard masked his jowls. He wore a tri-cornered hat that bore the skull and crossbones in white. He now threw this back to his followers, and came riding forward, bareheaded. His hair was black, thick, and curly. A six-shooter was thrust in his red sash, along with a dagger. A curved sword was in a scabbard at his knee. This was Major Blood.

He was confident, arrogant. He shouted something, an insult, Clay imagined, in Zeno's direction, but the words were lost in the distance. Blood came advancing slowly on the horse, and finally halted some hundred feet from where Zeno waited. The guerrilla leader dismounted. He beckoned Zeno to approach, daring him, taunting him. Major Blood was playing out his role. He knew he must bluster and swagger, knew he must win.

Zeno swung from the saddle, slapped his horse so that it moved out of the way of possible bullets. He stood facing Major Blood. Clay heard Ann and Rose Lansing and Rachel begin to pray. That was the only sound in the Texas camp.

Blood, the killer, was the picture of death itself in the garb he affected, which was so out of place here so far from salt water. Zeno, in dog-eared boots and shirt and breeches that had faded to neutral hue, seemed pallid and inadequate in contrast to the colorful bandit. But Clay's gaze was riveted on the one feature of Zeno's appearance that counted—the holstered six-shooter on his right thigh.

Zeno moved toward Major Blood. They were now within easy shooting range. It came then like gunfights always do—like the wicked flicker of lightning and the crash of thunder. Major Blood's nerve was the first to break. He shouted something and drew. He was very fast. Split-second work. His gun erupted flame, but the trigger was pulled by the finger of a man already doomed.

Zeno had fired first. Clay watched Blood whirl around, his weapon falling from his fingers to the ground. He stood stricken, broken not so much by the impact of the slug, but by the knowledge that he was a dead man.

Zeno fired again, then again. Blood's arms were broken by the slugs. Zeno was keeping his promise that the man would pay. Blood reeled as though in an attempt to run. Zeno fired again, and Blood went down, rolling like a stricken chicken, a leg shattered by the slug.

Zeno moved toward his man. In the silence that followed the gun thunder his voice was distinct. "Remember that little girl you stole the day you scum murdered my wife and parents on a farm near Joplin?"

He raised the gun to fire again. But Ann had left Clay's side and was running toward him. "No!" she screamed. "No! He's dying. Don't do anything more that might be on your conscience the rest of your life. No, Zeno."

Zeno did not fire the shot. Ann reached his side and stood with him. He remained for seconds looking at Blood, who lay writhing in the grass. Ann took the six-shooter from his grasp and swung him around. Then he came walking with her back to the wagons.

Blood's people came scurrying and carried their fallen leader back to the camp. Clay looked at Zeno. Ann still stood, an arm around the dark-haired man. The black, taciturn shadow that had marked Zeno's nature seemed to have lifted. He had not put the finishing shot in the man he had sworn to kill, and Clay felt that Zeno was finding solace in that forbearance now.

Rose Lansing spoke to Clay. "It's over. Thank God. We can throw the herd on the trail and be miles away from this awful place before dark."

"I'm afraid it isn't over," Clay said.

The tawdry gypsy circus was moving onward, stringing in a ragged line over the rolling prairie. But the circus was merely moving out of range, taking its women with it. The main body of guerrillas remained in position. Now they began to mount and move toward the wagons.

They moved in two segments, the white guerrillas being led by the leathery man who had first acted as emissary and who evidently now had taken over in Blood's place. All were armed, with rifles slung in their arms. The Indian contingent, feathers and paint showing, were being directed by a chief who wore only a breechclout and a single eagle feather and had a large shield of buffalo hide poised.

"Stone Buffalo," Q said. "Look! He wants to palaver. I'll side you."

Stone Buffalo had moved ahead of his warriors. They halted and so did the guerrillas as Stone Buffalo advanced, making the sign that he wanted to talk.

Clay, with Q at his side, rode to meet him. Stone Buffalo peered toward the wagons, and it was evident he also was trying to determine the strength of the Texans. His gaze came back to Clay. Stone Buffalo was scarred by time and battle. He was a "Naini" Comanche, a term for that segment of his people who were "alive" and inflexibly committed to oppose any invader of their hunting grounds. The shield was in his left hand; his right hand gripped the handle of a pistol that was thrust in the belt of his breechclout.

Clay looked at the hand on the gun. "You ask palaver, Stone Buffalo, but you are ready to kill."

The chief spoke English fluently. "You are the ones who have killed. My friend Blood is dead. And you are on the sacred hunting grounds of the red man. Because of you and people like you the buffalo are growing hard to find. We eat birds and rabbit. That is not good for warriors. Because there are no buffalo, we need _vaca_ to fill our bellies."

"There are buffalo around," Clay said. "Many more buffalo than cows. Why do you not try to find them?"

Stone Buffalo pointed toward the herd. "We take _vaca_," he said.

Clay raised two fingers. "Two cows," he said. "I will give you two cows to feed your warriors who can't find the buffalo that are so easy for others to hunt."

Stone Buffalo spat contemptuously on the ground. He raised both hands, with all ten fingers extended. He closed them, opened them twice, three times.

"This number we will take," he said. "If we need, we will take more."

Stone Buffalo was saying that he would take forty head of cattle, and that he would take the entire herd if he so desired. To emphasize his demand he looked back, made a gesture, and both the Indians and the guerrillas moved in closer.

"We have many mouths to feed," he said. "Many guns to shoot. You are not so many."

Clay spread all the fingers of one hand. "Five cows," he said. "That is all. We are not so many as your people, but we have guns that shoot all day, and men who never miss. You saw what happened to your Major Blood. It will happen to very, very many of your warriors, and even to you, Stone Buffalo. Five cattle."

Stone Buffalo's dark eyes flickered a little. Clay felt that there was little doubt in the chief's mind that any attempt to rush their position would be costly. He also believed the chief was not in a mood for a fight. A young, tall, wild-eyed warrior left the ranks of the Indians and came riding up to join the chief and began angrily berating him, urging him to fight. But Stone Buffalo continued to waver, evidently deciding to bargain for more cattle. He began lifting his spread fingers again, evidently to reduce his demand, but he never finished the haggling.

A bullet twitched at Clay's hatbrim. It had been meant for him. It missed and struck the young warrior alongside Stone Buffalo, smashing into his shoulder. He would have toppled from the pad saddle, but a moccasined foot caught in the plaited leather sling that served as a stirrup. He managed to hang to his tough muscled buffalo pony until it stopped rearing.

Stone Buffalo uttered a cry of fury. "You have tried to kill my son!" he screeched. He drew his six-shooter and fired at Clay. But all the horses were rearing, and the shot missed.

Q had drawn and would have shot the Comanche chief, but Clay shouted, "No! Wait! It's a mistake!"

Clay had drawn his own pistol. He could have killed Stone Buffalo, whose pony was still unmanageable, but held his fire. So did Q. The Comanche chief, his face contorted with rage, gained control of his horse, caught the headstall of his son's pony, and rode out of range. The young Comanche was clinging to the neck of his mount.

Clay and Q looked at each other in dismay, then rode back to the wagons, where their people were milling about, guns in their hands.

"We're in fer it now," Q said.

Clay hit the ground in a running dismount. "Who fired that shot?" he demanded.

"Nobody from here," Ann Lansing said. "It came from somewhere beyond the wagons. From the riverbed." Then she cried, "Look!"

Two riders had appeared from the dry wash. One had a rifle in his hands and was covering the man who rode ahead of him.

Rose Lansing uttered a heartrending cry. "Philip! Philip! My son! My dear son!"

She stood an instant, staring at what she believed was the ghost of her son. She began to sway, and Clay caught her as she fainted.

CHAPTER 12

Ann and Rachel took Rose Lansing's limp body from Clay's arms. Rachel looked at the oncoming riders with terror. "De Lord help us all!" she mumbled. "De graves are givin' up dar daid."

The two women placed Rose Lansing on a blanket near the wagon. Ann arose, leaving the care of her mother to Rachel, and came back to Clay's side.

"Phil!" she called. "Phil, you *are* alive."

Phil Lansing did not answer. He kept his rifle covering the rider ahead of him. He was a thin and emaciated shadow of the dashing, handsome Phil Lansing who had ridden off to war at the age of twenty with the kerchiefs of more than one feminine admirer on his sleeves.

The man Phil Lansing was bringing in was Bill Conners. Even in the weeks since Clay and Conners had fought with fists in Hackberry, the former Loop L foreman had gone farther down the scale. He was grimy, had not shaved in many days, and looked as though he always slept in his clothes. His face beneath its matt of whiskers was bloated; his eyes were hooded and cloudy.

Phil Lansing brought both horses to a stop at a short distance. His sister started to run toward him, but he waved her back. "I'm alive, Ann," he said. "I'm not a ghost. I didn't come back from the grave. I came back from far worse than that."

He looked at Clay. "You know why I'm here, Burnet," he said.

Clay nodded. "Joe Owens told me. I ran into him at Comanche Ford. But I'd like to hear it from your own lips."

"You're hearing it," Phil Lansing said. "I came here to kill you."

"You seem to have lost your touch," Clay said. "You had a reputation as the best sharpshooter in the Texas Brigade. But you've missed me three times."

Lansing slid from his horse. He motioned to Bill Conners

to alight also. Conners obeyed listlessly. In him was the fixed despair of a man who had lost the desire to live.

"You ought to know better than that, Burnet," Phil Lansing said. "You should know that when I came after you it would be face to face and not from a bushwhack. It was Conners here who did the missing. At least he missed a few minutes ago and winged that young Comanche. He told me he had a score to settle with you, but that you've been lucky. Your luck has now run out."

"No," Clay said. "I'm happy that you finally showed up. I've been waiting for it. I want it ended."

"I've been on your trail for a long time," Lansing said. "I've been all the way to the San Dimas where I found out that I must have passed you somewhere in Texas. So I headed back north. I came in sight of the herd in time to see that you got yourselves into a tight fix with that bunch of crossbreeds out there. I took to the arroyo, sighted Conners skulking along. He'd left his horse tied up. I saw him take that potshot, then stopped him as he was trying to get back to his horse to get away. I didn't know what it was all about until he told me. I figured I better bring him in."

"I apologize," Clay said. "Fact is, I never could really bring myself to believe you were notching on my back. But I never thought Conners had the sand to even try that."

"Conners might be satisfied with trying to assassinate you," Phil Lansing said. "But I want you to be looking at me when I throw down on you. I've traveled a long way for that pleasure. Now is the time. You've got a gun on you. Draw!"

Phil Lansing snatched out the six-shooter he was carrying in a holster. He meant to kill. But Clay made no move toward his own weapon.

Ann uttered a scream, and shoved Clay aside, placing herself between him and her brother's vengeance. Phil Lansing could not hold back the shot he intended. The six-shooter roared.

Clay was staggered by her strength, but he steadied himself and clung to her, horrified, believing she had taken the bullet. She continued to grasp him desperately and shield him.

Her brother's shot had missed, partly because he had been shaken by his sister's intervention and partly because she had managed to veer herself and Clay out of line.

Phil Lansing swung the pistol around again, seeking a clear shot at Clay. "No, no!" his sister screamed. "No, Phil! You can't! It's a mistake. It must be a mistake. I am in love with Clay Burnet."

Rose Lansing had revived. She came hurrying shakily into

the line of fire and threw her arms around her son. "It *is* you!" she moaned. "My son! My darling son! You *are* alive!"

He tried to wrest free, the fury for vengeance still upon him, but his mother clung. She pushed his pistol down. "Why are you trying to kill Clay Burnet?" she sobbed. "Have you lost your mind?"

"I *am* going to kill him," her son gritted.

With galvanized strength his mother wrested the gun from his hands. "I won't let you do this terrible thing!" she panted. "Oh, my son! My son! You look like a ghost. Where have you been all this time? You were listed as dead. But I never really gave up. Somehow I knew it wasn't so."

"I was wounded in a fight near the end of the war," Phil Lansing said. "I was picked up for dead by Yankee soldiers, but they found that I was alive. I had been hit in a dozen places. I've got a leg that will never be worth much."

For the first time Clay realized that Phil Lansing was favoring a crippled leg.

"I didn't know who I was for months," Lansing continued. "I was in a Yank hospital for weeks. After I was able to move around on crutches I was taken to a penitentiary at Columbus, Ohio, where they were still holding Confederate prisoners that were classified as too dangerous to turn loose. It seems that I was one of the worst of the lot. I didn't remember it, but I had tried to kill some of the hospital people, and had tried to escape several times."

"Why didn't you let us know, my darling son?"

"I had my reasons. It was only a couple of months ago that I really came out of the fog. That was the first time I clearly knew who I was and remembered what had happened."

He looked at Clay. "I remembered it all, Burnet. I remembered everything that happened at Hatcher's Run. I realized that I had been given up for dead by that time. I let it ride that way. The Yankees were glad to get rid of a person like me. I signed the parole and was turned loose. I made it to Kansas by stealing rides on trains and wagons. I got a job swamping for a bull team that was freighting into Texas. That was the direction I wanted to go. I was on my way back to the San Dimas when I ran into another ghost at Comanche Ford a few weeks ago. Joe Owens. He had been a corporal in our outfit. He was the only other one who came out of it alive that day. So you talked to him at the Ford, Burnet?"

Clay nodded. "He told me you were alive and that you'd

likely be coming back up the trail to kill me. I've been expecting you."

"I don't understand," his mother said frantically.

"Burnet ordered me and eleven more men to their deaths so that he could save his own skin," her son said icily.

Ann spoke. She was still standing in front of Clay, thwarting his efforts to force her to stand aside. "This is no time for bringing up the old feud, Phil. That's ended. Because of Conners we're now all in deep trouble."

"Is all this true?" Rose Lansing asked hollowly of Clay. "About ordering my son to his death?"

"I gave the order," Clay said.

"But—but—" She couldn't finish it.

Clay looked at Bill Conners. "I didn't give you credit enough, Bill. It probably takes a certain type of nerve, I imagine, to hate a man enough to trail him for weeks and try three times to kill him. But you didn't have quite enough nerve to hold a steady bead."

He looked at Phil Lansing. "Now what?"

"Nothing's changed," Lansing said. "I'm still here for only one purpose."

Clay nodded. "That's your choice. However, I'm afraid you'll have to wait your turn. There are other people who think they have first claim on my scalp—and on yours. We seem to be in this together."

He pointed. Stone Buffalo's warriors were milling around, brandishing weapons. The chief's sonorous voice could be faintly heard, inciting them. The guerrillas had moved in and were listening.

"It'll be a pony charge by the Indians," Clay said. "With Blood's renegades helping. All you men who were in the war know how to act. All take cover. You women, get back of the barricades under the wagons and stay there. Horses can't overrun wagons. Lonnie, you stay under the wagons too."

"Sorry, sir," Lonnie Randall said. "That's only for the women. I'll stay with my father."

"Of course," Clay said. "Of course. And you'll be needed on the fighting line."

He spoke to Phil Lansing. "You will stay near the women and Cindy. If worst comes to worst you know what to do."

He added curtly, "That's an order."

Eveyone knew what the order meant. The women and the child were to be killed by Phil Lansing, rather than let them be taken captive. Years of Army discipline prevailed on Phil Lansing. His right hand automatically started to rise to the brim of his ragged hat. Realizing that he had been about to salute the man he was sworn to kill, he stopped the gesture in time.

"I'd prefer that someone else—" he began hoarsely.

His mother spoke. "No, Phil. You are our loved one. Do as Clay Burnet says."

Lansing turned and limped away with the women to make sure they were made as safe as possible. Around Clay the men were grimly preparing to stand attack. Selecting cover, they were looking to their weapons. Clay moved among them, placing them so that their positions protected each other from flanking attack. Clay turned the horses loose and sent them trotting away to freedom to avoid danger from stampeding.

He sent Bass and Ace worming their way to positions to right and left well beyond their main line of defense. "Cavalry is at its worst when it's being outflanked," he said. "Don't kill ponies. Get the riders. Wild ponies only upset mounted men trying to charge. Dead ponies only serve as breastworks for such as are on foot."

"You tellin' me, Captain!" Q said, squinting over the sights of his rifle as he estimated range and windage. "I fought ag'in Phil Sheridan's Yank cavalry at Spotsylvania. You don't stop fightin' men by killin' horses. Them damned bluebellies fought afoot as hard as they did on hawsback. Ain't that right, Zeno?"

"Correct, grayback, except it was me that had to try to stand off Jeb Stuart an' that pack of crazy men what called themselves the best ca'vlrymen in the world," Zeno said.

"I keep forgittin' you was a bluebelly," Q said. "You almost act like a human bein' at times."

Parson Jones and Beaverslide had taken positions back of rock outcrops near each other. "Keep yore danged hat on, Beaverslide," the Parson said. "Leastways till the sun goes down. It shines so it'll bring the whole passel of 'em down on us two an' we'll have to handle it alone."

"I figure the best way is for you to rear up, start one of your hell-fire sermons an' talk 'em to death," Beaverslide said.

Ann Lansing and her mother, rifles in hands, crouched back of the barricades that had been set up against the wagons. With them was Rachel, who had armed herself with a huge muzzle-loading, single-shot blunderbuss. Clay did not know it had been in the wagons. She had Cindy at her side and was talking calmly to the child, assuring her that everything would be all right. Micah was hunkered in a firing position near them. So was Phil Lansing.

Bill Conners had squirmed to cover nearby. Phil Lansing spoke harshly to Clay. "What will we do with him?"

"Give him back his rifle," Clay said. "If he can't hit the back of a man who's standing still he likely won't be worth a hoot against warriors coming at him, but we'll at least give him a chance."

Lansing frowned. "He might not miss a fourth time."

"Meaning that he might cheat you out of your fun?" Clay asked.

Phil Lansing did not answer. Clay studied the mass of riders across the flat. The speech-making had ended. A battle line began to form. Indians moved to the left, and their guerrilla allies formed the right wing. Stone Buffalo could be seen toward the center. Evidently he had taken command in place of the fallen Major Blood.

Q spoke from his position. "No squaws, no camping stuff with the Injuns. That means this must be only a scouting or hunting party, riding ahead of the main bunch. There must be a lot more of 'em somewhere around."

"Let's hope the others don't get here until too late," Clay said. "We might be able to hold off this bunch until dark and get a chance to wriggle away."

Nobody spoke. They knew that what Clay was saying was that it was now a case of saving their own lives, even if it meant abandoning the cattle they had driven so many hundreds of miles.

"Here they come!" Jem Rance shouted.

"Don't open up until I give the word," Clay warned.

The Indian-guerrilla charge was wild, primitive, and not too well organized. Red men screeched shrilly to intimidate their opponents. They brandished buffalo spears and hatchets in a promise of horrible death. Scalping knives were gripped in teeth; bronzed faces and dark eyes were ablaze with the threat of torture and agony.

The renegade whites were even more fearsome in aspect as they came charging to battle. They were yelling too, screeching obscene threats. Their bearded faces were aflame with the lust of expected conquest. They had seen the women. They expected easy slaughter, easy victory.

Around Clay rose a savage, shrill response to the challenge. The Rebel Yell, the battlecry of men in gray which had been the death knell of so many in the great war.

Clay joined in the Rebel Yell. Once again the conflicting emotions of battle were upon him, emotions he had hoped he would never have to endure again. He was torn by fear of death, and at the same time by the vengeful urge to shatter

these humans who were seeking to kill him. One part of him
kept urging him to turn and run, but the dominant part of
him demanded that he stand fast and deal out what destruction he could to these foes who were challenging his fiber. He
was torn between the urge to cower, and the eagerness to
come to grips with these arrogant strangers.

He heard feminine voices around him joining in the Rebel
Yell. Zeno, who had worn the blue, aided in that challenge.
The battle fervor had gripped them all. The oncoming riders
heard. Clay fancied that they had wavered for a moment. It
was not the first time that sound had driven fear to attackers.
Then they kept coming, but he was aware they were suddenly
knowing doubt, and that this doubt might be greater than
their thirst for captives and scalps. They were wondering now
if they had not found a lion instead of a rabbit.

They were now so near that Clay could make out the la-
ther on the ponies, the shine of grease on bronzed bodies.

"Fire!" he shouted.

He began shooting. He was battlewise, hardened by the
terrors he had seen at Antietam, in the swamps around
Vicksburg, in the blinding thickets of the Wilderness where
friend fired upon friend by mistake. Around him other guns
were crashing. The shooting was steady, restrained. Parson
Jones, to Clay's right, was kneeling, taking time to follow his
target carefully before pulling the trigger, then settling back
to ram a new charge into his muzzle-loading Sharps. But, to
his left, Lonnie Randall was emptying a Henry as fast as he
could work the action.

"Slowly, son," Clay shouted. "Slowly. Pick your man and
hold down on him."

He saw Beaverslide suddenly reel back and crumple into
limpness. A sickness came upon him. He had seen so many
go like that.

Jem Rance was hard hit. He staggered back, fell, then
gamely got to his knees, picked up his rifle and began firing
again.

Bill Conners was shooting frenziedly, the fear of death
graying his face. Saddles of the attackers were being emptied
and loose animals were running wildly, impeding the guerrillas and the red men. A heavy Comanche spear passed by
Clay's head and thudded into the wooden side of the chuck
wagon, splintering a plank.

The guerrillas broke, and their retreat spread to the Indians. What had really broken the charge was the gunfire from
the flanks where Clay had stationed Q's brothers. That and
the blood-chilling Rebel Yell which was being carried high

into the sky by the voices of women—women who were using rifles also.

The attackers fled out of range. Loose ponies wandered aimlessly among scattered bodies on the battlefield. Clay could hear the herd stampeding away in the distance.

The frenzy of battle faded. He became aware that he was still alive, still breathing. He was gasping for air, as though he had been in a long, heart-bursting race. This was a terrible sensation that had been all too familiar with him in the past on many battlefields. He sank down on hands and knees, gulping, unable to find the strength to arise for a time. Battle at close quarters had always drained him thus.

Women were weeping. Rose Lansing knelt beside the body of Beaverslide, wringing her hands. Ann and Rachel wept over another still form. This was the bluebelly, Zeno. A spear had been driven through the big man. Q stood looking down at Zeno, the same futile grief in his homely face that was driving Rose Lansing and the others. The alphabet quartet, Ace, Bass, Cass, and Des, joined him and had no words to say.

Micah moved in, lifted Zeno's body in his strong arms and carried him to a spread tarp, then brought Beaverslide to lie beside him. "Dey are both in de happy land now," he said. "Zeno's wid his family. Mr. Beaverslide kin tell how he fought a man's fight, an' he won't be tellin' a lie."

Parson Jones, gripping with his right hand an ugly bullet wound in his left forearm, stood over the body of Beaverslide, his comrade of many years, raised a rigid clenched fist, and said in a bitter voice, "Why? Why, O Lord? He believed in You. He lived by the Golden Rule. And now he is dead, and I, who have doubted You many times, am alive. Why?"

Micah was leading the women in prayer. Parson Jones bowed his head, sank to his knees, and prayed also.

Lonnie Randall was wounded. A slug from one of the fearful, bell-mouthed *escopetes*, handed down through the tribes from the early Spanish days, had torn a gouge in the flesh of his left shoulder. Ann Lansing, with the help of Lonnie's father, doctored the injury from the medicine chest and bound it. She kissed Lonnie, and that did more for him than the medication.

Jem Rance and Ace had wounds, the first a bullet in the calf of his leg, and Ace with a shoulder slash from a Comanche knife in the hands of the only warrior who had managed to penetrate the wagon defense line. There the Indian had been shot dead. His body still lay near the wagon barricades.

Rose Lansing and Rachel had fired simultaneously at this tragic red man who had tried to leap at them over the barricades. Neither would ever know which had fired the death shot, but neither would forget that moment as long as she lived. The Comanche had been very young, very handsome, very brave.

Clay assessed their losses, estimated their strength. They had won the first round, but at heavy cost. They had dealt fearful punishment. The bodies of five Comanches and three guerrillas lay on the field, and many more of the foe had been carried away wounded, and some dead, no doubt.

The guerrillas and the Indians had withdrawn farther into the prairie to where the gypsy circus had made its new camp. Silence came. The hot afternoon breeze drove away the acrid tang of powdersmoke, the smell of blood and death.

Clay helped carry Beaverslide and Zeno into the nearby wash where graves were dug. He stood while the Parson read the sad and achingly lonely words. "Ashes to ashes, dust to dust." They caved a cutbank over the tarp-wrapped bodies, marked the spot for future reference, and went back to care for the wounded and to fight for the living.

In the distance Clay listened to the lamentation of warriors, mourning the dead. Buzzards soared over the battlefield, but the Texas men cursed them and drove them away with thrown rocks. Comanches and guerrillas came under white flags, and the defenders lay silent and let them carry away the bodies.

The hot afternoon waned, dusk moved in, and the mauve shadows deepened. The attack had not been resumed, but it was evident that the foe was not in the mood to withdraw.

"They're waiting for the main bunch to come up," Q said.

His prediction was soon confirmed. A new commotion arose in the twilight. Clay climbed onto a wagon, peering. The reinforcements that Q had foreseen, were arriving in the camp of the allies. He could see many ponies, many riders, many travois approaching. Soon he could hear the wailing of squaws joining in the ceremonies for the dead.

"Ain't there an Army fort somewhere in these parts?" Jess Randall asked.

"None in more than a hundred miles, according to the map," Clay said reluctantly.

"A hundred miles? We'd all be dead before we could get to them an' back—if we could git out at all."

Phil Lansing spoke. "I passed a big company of freighters yesterday down the trail. They came from San'tone and are heading for Leavenworth, loaded with leather and such truck.

They had a troop of Union cavalry with them as an escort, but they didn't look like they needed it. There must have been fifty wagons in the outfit, manned by tough whackers and swampers, most of whom likely had been soldiers not long ago."

"Where?" Clay exclaimed. "When?"

"Two days ago," Lansing said. "That was about fifty miles south, I reckon, but they were heading north. Likely they might be only fifteen, twenty miles away by this time, camping on a stream I crossed this morning."

Hope soared. Then it faded. "They might as well be on the moon," the Parson said. "Nobody's goin' to git out of this fix. Them devils out there are likely expectin' somethin' like that. They're already spreadin' all around us. They're in the wash, both above an' below us, an' acrost from us."

There was silence. The slow darkness was settling. The knowledge was in the minds of every man that if help was to arrive in time the messenger must be soon on his way.

From the darkness came a burst of sound, the thudding footsteps of a running man, the faint pad of moccasined feet, the crash of disturbed brush. A scream came. It was the despairing sound from a frenzied human. A struggle was taking place down the dry wash. More strangled outcries came, then faded.

Clay peered around. "Where's Conners?"

Bill Conners was no longer among them. He had seized a chance to attempt to creep away. Faint sounds came for a time. Then, nearer at hand, a man began moaning in torture in the darkness. The moaning increased. Horrible screaming came.

Ann Lansing covered her ears, sank to her knees. Her mother tried to comfort her. From the darkness, savage, taunting voices arose, laughing, jeering, mocking, promising in Spanish, broken English, and dialect the same fate for all of them.

Presently silence came again. It was over—for Bill Conners, at least. But not for the Patchsaddle crew. The taunting and the promises of torture and death for them were resumed by the warriors and guerrillas in the darkness. They tried not to listen, but that was impossible. They had no doubts about the vigilance of the foes who surrounded them. The voices came from all points. Nor were there any doubts as to the torture that awaited any, like Conners, who were taken alive.

Clay broke the bitter silence around him. "Someone has to get through to that wagon train and fetch help."

Again the silence. No face was turned toward him. None wanted to look at him, to be placed in the position of forcing the decision on him. But the decision had to be made.

Once again he was thinking of that day at a stream whose waters had been turned to crimson when the loneliness of command had been a spike in his heart, a spike that had never been removed. That was the day he had sent Phil Lansing and eleven other men to what seemed like sure death. Now he was living it over again.

He looked at Phil Lansing. "Two of us must try it," he said. "Two strings to the bow. We'd have a better chance of success. Remember Hatcher's Run, Sergeant? Remember how two hundred men lived and ten died to save them? Remember how it was done? I made the decision that day. Now it's your turn. These are your flesh and blood, your neighbors, your friends. There's only two who should go. You name them."

CHAPTER 13

Phil Lansing stared at him for long seconds, a bitter trapped hopelessness in his eyes. "You can't do this to me, Burnet," he almost whispered.

"You have no choice and you know it," Clay said. "I'll be one to try it. I'm unhurt, strong. There's only one other person among us who is uninjured, young, strong enough to have a chance of making it through. You can't go. Your leg. This has to be done by persons who can move fast and have endurance. The rest of you will have to make a diversion so as to draw them away long enough for us to slip through. It will be a diversion like you and Joe Owens and ten other men made that day at Hatcher's Run to save me and two hundred other soldiers."

Phil Lansing did not speak for a space. His face was gray, without trace of life or blood. "It worked that day," he said with an effort. "It just might work again. Damn you to hell, Burnet. I wish now I'd never come out of it alive that day."

"The rest of you will start shooting and act like you're stampeding down the wash in an attempt to break out," Clay said. "That might draw them all there while we make a try for it in the opposite direction. We might head for their camp, for that could be the one direction they're likely to leave open, figuring nobody will try it."

There was a silence. "Who's to go with you?" the Parson finally asked reluctantly. "I ought to be the one. I'm strong, an' unhurt, an' I'm mighty spry."

Every able man in the group spoke up, volunteering. But Clay did not speak. He was looking at Phil Lansing, waiting.

"You've got no right to put this on me, Burnet," Lansing said, his voice mirroring the torture inside him. "I'll kill you for this, if for nothing else, if we both live."

He looked at his sister. "You're the one, Ann," he said huskily. "The others, like Micah, are too big, too clumsy, or they're old or wounded, or crippled like—like me. You're young, strong, quick."

135

"Of course," she said calmly above a chorus of protest from the men. "I knew that from the first."

"God forgive me," her brother said.

Rose Lansing kissed her daughter. "You will come back to us, darling. I know that. I feel it. Our prayers will go with you."

Her brother spoke hoarsely. "Ann, if they catch you . . ." He could not bring himself to finish it.

"I know what to do," she said with that same calmness.

Clay sat on the ground and began pulling off his boots. "You do the same," he told Ann. "We'll make less noise in socks. Hang your boots around your neck. We'll black our faces from the cook pots."

He gave his rifle to Phil Lansing, along with what spare ammunition he had for the long gun and his six-shooter. "I'll keep my sidegun," he said. "Extra shells won't do us any good if luck runs against us and they might be more needed here. You're in charge now."

He drew Ann into his arms and kissed her. "At least we'll be together, no matter what happens," he said.

"Yes," she said, weeping a little. "Oh, yes, my darling."

Clay released her and spoke to the others. "Mrs. Lansing and Rachel and Cindy should stay with the wagons. The rest of you begin yelling and shooting. Make a big commotion, as though you're on your way down the draw. Then drop flat in case they open fire, and slowly work your way back to the wagons. But keep yelling all the time to hold them."

He waited for suggestions. None came. "Now," he said. "The sooner we start, the better."

The attempt at a diversion began. The men ran to the rim of the wash and dropped into it. They began yelling and crashing through brush, creating what uproar they could. Grasping Ann's hand, Clay left the barricades and they scuttled on hands and knees into the open. Starlight seemed agonizingly bright in the sky. He heard Ann breathing hard and knew that she entertained terrible fear.

The glow from the distant campfires of the attackers lifted a faint crimson curtain, outlining the crest of a low swell ahead. Shadows were moving fast there. Indians and guerrillas, some on foot, some mounted. They were all speeding like mannequins, in a mad puppet show across their route, heading toward the uproar in the stream bed.

They flattened out and did not move until the puppets had cavorted past. Then they began squirming frantically ahead. The Patchsaddle men were performing their task nobly. The pandemonium behind them was increasing. Guns began to explode.

Clay led the way, seeking to avoid what obstacles he could on the rough terrain. He paused abruptly, again pressing Ann flat to the ground. Someone ran past them scarcely a rod away. Clay judged that he was a guerrilla because of his heavy, booted tread. The man vanished in the direction of the uproar.

They moved again. They crested the low rise and the encampment was in sight within rifleshot ahead. Cookfires burned there and they could make out the squaws moving about, staring, talking, and gesticulating.

They circled far away from this danger. They chanced getting on their feet, but ran crouching to avoid being skylined. The snuffle and stir of horses ahead warned them in time that they were moving toward the big herd of ponies on graze beyond the camp of their foes, and they were forced to veer far wide of this peril also.

"If we could only steal horses . . ." Ann said in an excited whisper.

"Too dangerous," Clay said. "They'll be guarded."

They put more distance between them and the crimson glow. "All right," Clay said. "I think we're out of the frying pan, at least. Faster!"

They straightened and began running. They ran until they could run no more, then fell flat, their lungs laboring. Clay's agony eased, and he listened. All sounds had died back of them. The diversion attempt had died of attrition. By this time the guerrillas and Stone Buffalo would know that it had been a trick, and that someone likely had managed to steal out of the trap. There would be pursuit.

"Not even a Comanche can find our trail in the dark," Ann said hopefully.

Clay said nothing. Presently they heard the dogs—a far, heart-freezing sound, a shrill, coyotelike screeching.

"Dear God!" Ann sobbed. "Help us now!" They began running again.

They suddenly found themselves among cattle. They had blundered upon a remnant of their own scattered Patchsaddle drive. A horned animal loomed in their path. Clay was caught by a wild inspiration.

"Up!" he panted. "Ride 'em, cowgirl."

He lifted Ann off her feet. Before she realized his intention she found herself astride a Longhorn. In the next moment Clay joined her aboard the startled creature. Luck was with them, for their mount was a cow, one of the smaller animals in their herd. Even so it was a Longhorn with its share of strength and wildness.

Ann clung to the spread of horns and Clay clung to her. The cow was too dumbfounded to move for an instant. Then it took off with a wild snort of terror. Its flight set off a stampede among other cattle nearby in the darkness.

The cow ran blindly for a short distance, then began to rid itself of its burden. It sunfished, swapped ends, and the girl and Clay went sailing. They crashed into a clump of brush that cushioned their fall and lay there in a tangle of arms and legs. The stampede thundered away into the blackness of the night.

Clay scrambled to his feet. "Are you hurt?" he asked.

"No," she gasped. Then she began to laugh hysterically. "Ride 'em, cowgirl. I tried my best."

He drew her to her feet. They could still hear the ululation of dogs in the distance. Clay was sure that any chance the dogs might have had of trailing them was ended now, wiped out by the stampede of cattle.

They headed southward again. Phil Lansing had estimated that the wagon train encampment would be on a stream where the Patchsaddle herd had bedded on its last camp, some fifteen miles away at the speed a cattle drive normally travels. Their route was easy to follow, even in darkness, marked by the cropping of grass and the droppings of cattle.

They had donned their boots earlier during a breather, but cowboots were not intended for this sort of use. Clay knew that his feet were blistering, and he was sure Ann was suffering the same misery. Neither mentioned it.

Clay estimated the time was nearing midnight, according to the position of the Dipper, when he caught the acrid tang of herded livestock. They followed this downwind until they were challenged by a sentry. Beyond, lay the scattered night fires of an enormous camp, ringed by the towering hoods of freight wagons.

The sentry was a lank young soldier who told them to advance and be identified, and who shouted for the sergeant of the guard. To his consternation, the trooper found himself being kissed by one of the ragged, breathless arrivals.

"Hurry, soldier!" Clay said. "We're from a trail crew that's in bad trouble ahead. I want to talk to your commander."

The commander was a lieutenant, a West Pointer, who was groggy with sleep, and confused. "You say you were an officer in the rebe—I mean the Confederate forces?" he mumbled, trying to pull on his jacket and stuff his shirt into hastily doned trousers as he realized he was in the presence of a member of the opposite sex.

"That war's over," Clay said. "We're in another one, and you'll soon see action, Lieutenant."

Soon he was in the saddle heading north. Back of them rode the lieutenant's detachment of thirty troopers. Reinforcing them were that many more men from the freight caravan, tough mule skinners, hardened swampers and game hunters, all of whom knew how to use guns. The majority had served in one army or the other during the war.

Ann rode with them. She had scorned the lieutenant's objections and laughed at his doubts as to whether she could stand the hardships of the return trip. "After what I've been through I could ride all the way to Missouri and back," she said.

Clay watched the first small radiance of dawn in the sky. "Faster, Lieutenant!" he said. "Faster, for God's sake! It's coming! Daybreak! We'll be too late!"

Full dawn came. The miles that had seened endless to him on foot in the darkness were visible miles now, and even more endless. The horses and mules on which the motley aggregation was mounted were beginning to tire under the hard pace.

Clay stood up in the stirrups and said hoarsely, "Hear it?"

The lieutenant could hear nothing, but a civilian scout in buckskins who had been riding ahead, along with three Pawnees, returned, with his horse at a gallop to report. "Fight goin' on ahead, Lieutenant. Guns talkin'."

The Lieutenant ordered his followers ahead faster. Clay, forcing his horse into the lead, was first to come in sight of the fight.

A pony charge by the reinforced Indians was forming and it was evident that the wagon camp was sure to be overrun. Stone Buffalo's warriors were unaware that help had arrived. They were moving in a long double line toward the barricaded camp, warriors hanging on the far sides of the ponies, preparing to ride down the defenders.

Stone Buffalo gave the signal and the ponies broke into a gallop. The charge became thunder and color and ferocity. Clay's appearance was the first intimation that Stone Buffalo had of danger. Other warriors turned too, staring, and now the head of the oncoming column of cavalry and wagon men could be seen.

The bulk of the pony charge continued for a moment. Clay, riding to the wagons, was caught in the melee of ponies and warriors, some of whom were wheeling to face the new threat, and others still intent on their original targets.

Around him guns were exploding, and Indians were screeching amid terrible confusion. Clay found himself falling. His horse had been killed by a bullet. Stone Buffalo loomed above him, a spear aloft to skewer him. A bullet struck the chief. The spear thrust wavered and weakened. It missed Clay, the heavy metal head burying itself in the earth at his side.

It was Phil Lansing who had fired the shot. Clay looked at him, and he knew that it was over. The feud, the hatreds, the misunderstandings. Over forever. He got to his feet and they stood side by side to meet further challenge.

But the battle was also over. With Stone Buffalo fallen, the odds evened, the guerrillas had already deserted their allies, and the Indians were forced to flee. Warriors were riding back to their camp where they were being joined by the squaws in a flight that was successful, for the horses and mules of the arrivals were in no condition for pursuit after the night's ride.

The lieutenant called off the chase. He returned and dismounted. He stared at Rose Lansing and at Rachel and Cindy. "What did you say you called this outfit?" he asked Clay.

"The Patchsaddle drive," Clay said. "Seven weeks out of the San Dimas country, with a mixed herd of twenty-five hundred head of beef. Leastwise we had that many when we set out. I don't know how many we'll tally now, if any at all."

The officer continued to gaze around disbelievingly. The Parson was binding the wounds of Q, who had fought hand to hand with a Comanche, whom he had disarmed and then had permitted to ride away. The brothers Ace and Bass were standing over the body of Des, who had been struck down by an arrow. Cindy was with them, and all were weeping. Strong men do not weep?

"And where are these cattle now?" the lieutenant asked.

"Around somewhere, what's left of 'em," Clay said. "We could use a little help rounding them up. We're on our way to find end of steel in the state of Missouri. We're not sure how far away it is."

"Only another hundred miles or so," the officer said, still acting as though he was dreaming. "It happens we're on our way there also. We'll ride along with you. Rounding up cattle isn't exactly in our line, but we'll give it a try."

The shipping point was a settlement called Springfield in Missouri. The railroad had reached Springfield, and engineers and surveyors were there, preparing to help extend the line on into Kansas and The Nations. The town had changed from a collection of log houses into a hell-on-wheels, with all the attractions, including women.

"Painted hussies!" Rose Lansing sniffed. She sat in a rocking chair in the upper parlor of the best rooming house the town afforded. She wore a new dress. It was of economical cotton, for she had resisted her daughter's urging to buy silk.

On the bed lay gunnysacks containing some thirty-eight thousand dollars in gold coin. Buyers had been waiting at Springfield with cash, for beef was at a premium in eastern packing houses, and the Patchsaddle drive had been one of the first to arrive. The herd had tallied out at nineteen hundred and ten head of the original twenty-five hundred and had brought twenty dollars a head. The San Dimas men would return home with more cash in their wallets than they had ever seen in their lives.

Clay and Phil Lansing were in the room, rifles and side-guns handy. Lonnie Randall, recovered from his wound, was there also, sitting in a corner, gloomily listening to the sounds of revelry that drifted from the street. The Patchsaddle crew was celebrating.

Rose Lansing had been prevailed on to advance fifty dollars to each man from the Patchsaddle stake so that the members could shake the saddle kinks out of their "laigs," as the Parson put it. The shaking was well started. Night had fallen, and the drinks were flowing freely. For all except Lonnie. Rose Lansing had firmly refused to let him join the hurrah. "You just stay put where I can keep an eye on you, young man," she had said.

Ann was in the room also, along with Rachel and Cindy. They wore new, comely garb which they had bought on a shopping spree at Springfield's newly stocked stores.

Rose Lansing arose and brought into view a sizable object, covered by a piece of wagon sheet. She stood in front of Clay and removed the cover. It was the homemade easel on which he had been working the day it had all started back in the San Dimas. She placed on the easel the half-finished landscape he had been attempting.

"Now you can go ahead with it in peace," she said.

Clay kissed her. "Would you object to having a Burnet as a son-in-law?" he asked.

"It's about time," she said. "Fact is, that is one of the

things I had in mind right from the start when I rode over to your place that day."

Ann sprang to her feet. "Well, if that isn't the damnedest proposal I ever heard of. Only a coward would go to a girl's mother and—"

She got no further, being crushed in Clay's arms. "Just because you're a tough trail hand doesn't give you the right to do any cussing," he told her. "Mind me now."

Shoot-out
at Sioux Wells

Chapter 1

Brandy Ben Keech, owner and trail boss of the K-Bar-K herd, slid from his horse, removed his hat and hurled it on the ground. The hat was hand-made of brushed beaver and had cost him thirty dollars in San Antonio. It had suffered considerably from wear and weather, and now Brandy Ben leaped high in the air, and landed on it with spurred boots, completing its destruction.

"Drat the danged, double-dratted, pig-headed, triple-cussed sons of Satan!" he screeched. "Dang all cow cattle to condemnation! Drat! Drat! Drat!"

Some months previously Brandy Ben had taken a solemn vow to his wife and to their community preacher at the little cow-town church in the Brazos country that he would forgo the use of strong language and would never again take the Lord's name in vain. Therefore, he was somewhat handicapped in attempting to express his feelings.

Along with the K-Bar-K crew, he had trailed the herd nearly a thousand miles up the country from deep in Texas, enduring his share of the customary miseries that go with handling three thousand head of wild Longhorns. He and his riders had survived dry drives and the crossing of such items as the Red River and the Arkansas. They'd had their stampedes on nights of storm and lightning. They had lost two men, one from natural causes— a broken leg when a horse fell, and the other still lingering in the Dodge City jail after an attempt to run Marshal Wyatt Earp and the town up a tree.

Now they were in the short-grass country of the plains, and they could not force the cattle to cross a measly railroad track that had cropped up unexpectedly, blocking their route. The track stretched across the swells as far as the eye could carry into the plains.

The cattle had never before seen a railroad track, and it was the nature of the Longhorn to be wary of objects that were not within its past experience. Brandy Ben had been lucky when the herd had approached the Santa Fe Railway right-of-way near Dodge two weeks in the past. A cloudburst had washed out a long section of track, through which the Longhorns had passed peaceably.

When a Longhorn made up its mind to be obstinate, it was obstinate indeed. In this case, its strength was three-thousand-fold. Brandy Ben and the crew had been trying for three hours to induce the mass of perversity to cross that narrow stretch of imaginary danger. They had coaxed, wheedled, threatened and prodded. The only result was a growing spirit of rebellion among the cattle. The animals were on the knife-edge of stampeding.

Brandy Ben's son rode up and dismounted beside his enraged father. "Easy, easy!" he said. "Quit dancing around like a drunk yahoo. You'll start the herd running. We don't want that to happen, and 'specially not here. We'd lose a lot of them if they headed into that stuff to the south."

Brandy Ben's jowls swelled and became crimson under his stubble of wiry, graying beard. He wasn't in the habit of taking advice from anyone, least of all his son. It graveled him that he had to look up into his son's face. Zack Keech was an inch past six feet, and Brandy Bill fell five inches short of that height, much to his secret chagrin.

"What in Tophet do you say we do, if you're so danged smart?" he demanded. "Maybe you figure we ought to stay here 'til we decide they won't be et up by that railroad track? An' where did that blasted thing come from anyway? Nobody told me there was a railroad across this stretch of country."

Zack looked around. His father did not make many mistakes in rodding a trail herd, but he had made one this time. He had failed to have the route scouted ahead, taking it for granted that the going would be easy across open plains for the next hundred miles or more. But the herd was milling uneasily in a cul-de-sac, with the railroad track blocking the way north, and a maze of coulees and alkali marshes stretching to the east and south. The only path was the area over which the cattle had traveled into this unexpected blockade, and it would take time and patience to induce them to return over grass they had so recently trampled.

Bib Olsen joined them. "I've heard that Shanghai Pierce had a herd that wouldn't cross the U.P. tracks up Julesburg way a year or two back," he said. "Shanghai an' his crew built a sod an' dirt path across the tracks, an'—"

"Yeah!" Brandy Ben raged. "An' it took them days of hard work. They sent into town for shovels an' such. All we've got is the wagon shovel an' a pick with a busted handle. Maybe I haven't told you, Bib Olsen, that I've got a contract to deliver these jugheads to the Crow agency on the Missouri River by the middle of September, with a penalty of one hundred dollars a day for every day I'm late. It's well into August already, with us a week behind schedule. Maybe you don't know that."

"You've told me this before," Bib Olsen said. "More than once. I admit we shore cain't bury them tracks under dirt with only our bare hands."

Zack spoke. "Our best chance is to easy them out of this place and trail them west until we can scout for a trestle or a bridge big enough so that we can try to push the herd underneath the tracks instead of over. If we mill around here much longer, a train might come along. That might scare the liver out of them, and they'd run."

"Train already comin'," Bib Olsen said.

Zack and his father whirled, staring in the direction Bib was pointing. A smudge of black smoke had appeared over the swells to the east. A train *was* coming.

Zack hit the saddle. "I'll stop it until we can move the herd out of range," he shouted. He headed the horse east along the railroad track, pushing the animal to a full gallop.

He had one factor in his favor. The approaching train was mounting one of the long swells in the plain, and the upgrade was telling on the wood-burning locomotive. It proved to be a combination train consisting of two passenger cars, a mail and baggage car and half a dozen box and flat cars. The thud of the exhaust from the coalscuttle stack was growing more and more labored. Zack, as he rode into closer view, could see the heads of the engineer and the firemen poking from the windows, peering down at the slowing driving wheels.

The train was moving at a pace which Zack's horse could easily keep abreast of as he arrived alongside. The engineer was a young, redheaded man with a lantern jaw and hayrack shoulders, who sported a flaring red mustache.

"Stop it!" Zack yelled above the roar from the straining machinery. "We've got a trail herd sulled alongside the tracks ahead. You might stampede 'em, and we'd lose a lot of them most likely."

"What?"

Zack repeated his statement. The expression on the lantern-jawed engineer changed to disbelief, then to outraged scorn. "You don't think for a minute I'm goin' to stop a Rocky Mountain Express train just because some dumb Texas cowpoke has got some cattle grazing where they shouldn't be?" he screeched. "If I stopped this train on this grade, I'd have to back down five miles or more an' start over ag'in."

"We've got three thousand Longhorns on the prod," Zack yelled. "They're caught between the railroad tracks and the breaks. They might—"

The rawboned engineer was thumbing a nose at him. Zack snatched out his six-shooter. The engineer ducked out of sight, yelling profanity. Zack holstered the gun. He had been bluffing, having no intention of putting a bullet in the man.

The train, having topped the crest of the grade, was beginning to pick up momentum. Zack's horse began to lose ground. Passengers lined the opened windows of the two cars. Taunts and jeers were shouted at him as the cars moved ahead.

He tried to board the last car of the train, but his horse refused to move that close to the mechanical thing. The engineer was looking back from his window and making more insulting gestures.

"I'll look you up, my friend!" Zack panted. He knew the engineer could not hear the words but he was sure his intentions were plain, for the man clenched a fist and lifted it in a challenge.

The race had brought Zack back within sight of the herd. He could see his father and the crew riding frantically, trying to move the cattle as far from the track as possible, seeking to soothe them in preparation for the passing of the mechanical terror.

They might have succeeded in preventing a stampede, but the redhead at the throttle, leaning from the cab window so that he would not miss the spectacle, turned loose the whistle of the locomotive.

That did it. Zack uttered a moan. He kept moaning in pity as he watched. The blasting whistle had been the last straw. The cattle ran, scattering blindly away from the railroad track and the bellowing monster. Some headed back over the path by which they had entered the area. But one wing of the herd was stampeding blindly toward the coulees and alkali marshes.

Cold sweat in his clenched fists, Zack watched men ride clear of the cloud of dust that was kicked up by hundreds of hoofs. Will Nix, Bib Olsen, Johnny Summers, Juan Hernandez, Len Duvall. Others. All but one. All but one.

Then that one emerged from the dust and confusion and wearily dismounted. Zack drew a long breath, staring at his father, knowing the agony in Brandy Ben's heart. "Blast him," he mumbled weakly. "Why did he cut it so thin? He couldn't stop them. Nobody could."

He rode to his father's side. "You ought to have known better than to try to turn them," he raged. "Do you want to be buried in this forsaken country?"

Brandy Ben did not answer that. He sat watching helplessly as disaster piled upon disaster. "The poor critters!" he kept saying. "The poor, poor cattle!"

Zack discovered that tears were mingling with the dust on his father's unshaven cheeks. He sat humble. He had never before seen his father weep. He had never believed that tough, gruff Brandy Ben Keech was capable of tears.

He found himself forced to brush guiltily at his own eyes. Side by side, tall son, and weeping, graying father watched the cattle die. The coulees caught many of the stampeding Longhorns, piling them in heaps. Others were mired in the marshes, some moaning in terror as they sank until the sounds were smothered. Finally it was over.

"Two hundred head, give or take a half dozen or so," Zack told his father. "We came out of it better than I expected. We'll get an exact tally tomorrow, if they settle down."

It was sundown and they had succeeded in moving the

survivors of the stampede out of the trap and to safer
distance from the right-of-way of the railroad.

"What did you say was the name of this railroad?"
his father asked.

"Rocky Mountain Express, according to what the engineer said when I asked him to stop his train," Zack said.

"Never heard of it," Brandy Ben said.

"What's your plan?" Zack asked.

"If we can get these judheads movin' north again, I'll
try to buy up enough beef at Ogallala or from ranches
along the trail to fill out the herd. I still aim to make
delivery date."

The cost of two hundred head to replace the lost cattle
would come to at least six thousand dollars, and likely
more, for prices would go up once the sellers realized
that old Brandy Ben Keech had got his tail in a crack. It
wasn't that he couldn't afford it. He owned a big outfit
in Texas and had a reputation for reaping fat profits on
trail herds he had been driving north for several years.

"First we've got to get these cattle across the track,"
Zack said. "I'll scout west of here and try to find a trestle
or a bridge. Bib, you ride east in the morning."

They found a feasible path the next day where the
Rocky Mountain Express bridged a wide riverbed which
was mainly dry at this season. After waiting for two more
days they chanced driving the cattle under the track,
making sure there were no railroad trains due along that
area at that time.

A talkative section hand who came by with three other
workmen on a handcar furnished the trail men with that
information and much more. As Brandy Ben had surmised, the Rocky Mountain Express, despite its fancy
name, was considerably less than a major operation. It
was independently owned and operated on some two hundred miles of track. Its traffic consisted of intermittent

freight runs and a single combination train east and west daily.

"But if'n the Tollivers kin hang on long enough they'll be settin' purty," the man said. "The country's startin' to build up, with sodbusters an' cattlemen movin' in. An' if the Tollivers kin last it out, they'll tap them gold camps in the Rockies. Then their troubles will be over."

"Who are the Tollivers?" Zack asked.

"Cowboy, you sure must have lived fur out in the tules. You mean to say you never heerd of the Tollivers? Why, they've been railroad people since way back. J. K. Tolliver is president an' head of the board of the Rocky an' runs the railroad along with whatever other Tollivers air left. If it wasn't for them highbinders, they might make a million."

"Highbinders? What does that mean?"

The section hand suddenly became less talkative. He looked around as though to make sure his fellow workers had not been listening. He changed the subject abruptly.

"There's plenty of hustle in Sioux Wells," he said. "Town's growin' fast. Lots of action. They brung in Wild Bill Hickok a couple o' months ago to keep law an' order. I seen Wild Bill operate in Abilene a few years back. He's a tough man, but even he will need luck in Sioux Wells."

"Where is this Sioux Wells?" Zack asked.

"About thirty miles away. It's headquarters for the Rocky in these parts, but the main office is in Kansas City. As I was sayin', I saw Wild Bill tame some tough ones back in Abilene. He's somethin', he is."

Zack wasn't interested in Wild Bill Hickok, although he had heard of the man and his reputation. He did have interest in another person. "There's a Rocky Mountain Express engineer with red hair and a red mustache," he said. "About my size and age, I take it, with big teeth and a long nose. Do you happen to know that kind of a man?"

The section hand grinned. "That'd be Stan Durkin," he said. "I heerd about how he stampeded yore cattle. He was tellin' about it the other day in the Good Time, which is a first-class honky-tonk in the Wells. You wouldn't be wantin' to look him up an' try to take it out of his hide, now would you, Texas man?"

"Why would you think anything like that?" Zack asked.

"Forget it," the man said. "I'd hate to see a good-lookin' feller like you have his face mussed up permanent. Stan Durkin ain't never been licked in barroom or in the ring. He picks up some extra money fightin' all comers on Saturday nights at the Grizzly Bear Club, an' practices through the week on anybody who comes along, such as cowboys an' sheepherders. Take my advice an' steer clear of him."

"That's real considerate of you," Zack said. "I'll keep your words in mind."

After the cattle were safely north of the Rocky Mountain Express track Zack had Pinkie Lee, the Chinese cook, iron the wrinkles out of his going-to-town clothes and got out the polish to tone up his Sunday boots.

"Where you goin'?" his father demanded, discovering this activity.

"Make out your bill," Zack said.

"Bill?"

"A claim rather. A claim against the Rocky Mountain Express for six thousand dollars in loss of cattle. And a further statement that if this delay costs you penalty money on the delivery contract we'll bring a second claim against the railroad."

"Son," Brandy Ben said solicitously. "You're twenty-five years old, but you don't seem to know the facts of life. Railroads are owned by rich people what have high-priced lawyers to advise them. They pay the taxes that pay the salaries of judges an' lawmen. We got no more chance of gettin' a dollar out of a railroad up in this country than I have of yankin' up a piece o' sagebrush an' findin' a gold mine. Forget it. Next year we'll educate the cattle to railroads before headin' 'em north."

"I'll make out the claim myself," Zack said.

Brandy Ben sighed. "Do you think I don't know what's really gravelin' you? You're goin' in there to look up that railroad engineer what turned loose the whistle to spook the herd."

"Whatever gave you that notion?"

"I talked to that railroad hand too, son. I hear that this Stan Durkin is about the toughest knot in the timber. I don't reckon you'd stand for me goin' along with you?"

Zack gave his father a frosty look. "Or maybe Willie Nix," his father said hastily, naming the giant of the crew who had a reputation for brawling in cattle towns.

Zack did not answer. He saddled a horse and swung his war sack aboard. The section hand had said there was a sidetrack two or three miles west where the train to Sioux Wells could be flagged to pick up passengers.

Bib Olsen rode with him and kept relating stories about fools who had taken on more than they could handle, and had been crushed. "Just because you knocked out a few cowpokes in boxing matches at roundup camps don't mean you can stand up to every bucko that comes along," he said. "Remember that young professional pug what knocked you kicking in the second round at San'tone when you got too big fer your britches? If this railroader has got savvy enough to keep away from that right hand of yours, you're finished."

"Who said I aim to pick a fight?" Zack replied.

"I do," Bib sighed. "I only wish I could see it."

They found the siding, turned the faded red flag down, and settled down to wait. The train, two hours behind the schedule the section hand had mentioned, finally came creeping across the plain and ground to a stop. Stan Durkin was not at the throttle. The man handling that task was a plump, middle-aged individual.

Zack tossed his belongings aboard and followed them, leaving Bib to return his horse to the remuda. He stepped inside a coach and took a seat as the train jolted into motion again. A burly conductor came barging into the car, rattling a brass key chain that could be used as a bludgeon.

"Whar to, fella?" the man asked, instantly hostile as he saw that he was dealing with a cowboy, and a Texan at that.

"Sioux Wells," Zack said.

"One way?" the conductor asked, peering with a leer out at the empty plain.

"That'll do," Zack said, "though I doubt that I'll settle there."

"That'll be a dollar," the conductor said. "You a drover?"

"Nope," Zack said, paying the fare. "I'm a swatter."

"Swatter?"

"Fly swatter. A fly squats, I swat."

"Texans," the beefy man sniffed, and went away mumbling.

The majority of the seats in the car were occupied. Two painted ladies with false bangs hanging from beneath straw bonnets, sat midway in the car, one with high-buttoned shoe extended into the aisle. They were being ogled by two tough-nosed, swarthy passengers whom Zack tagged as cheap roughs whose specialty was likely to be back-alley muggings of unwary strangers. Both wore double-breasted shirts, striped breeches and boots of surprisingly good quality, and packed six-shooters in holsters, all of which seemed new and expensive.

Among the other passengers were the usual drummers

and business men and a homesteader with a wife and baby. An elderly woman and a young companion occupied a seat ahead of Zack. The elderly woman was small and gray-haired, with gold-rimmed spectacles and a tiny bonnet perched on the side of her head. She had knitting in her lap and her hands were busy.

Zack's attention turned to the small lady's companion and he sat up straighter. Even from the back, this one was a stunner. Thick, glossy hair, very dark. A nice, slender neck. Good, proud line of chin and cheek. She had animation, interest in the passing of even the drab sweep of buffalo grass. She turned once so that she glanced at Zack, and he felt that he was instantly appraised and found wanting. She had eyes to match her hair and manner. Snapfinger black eyes.

He hadn't seen a pretty girl in some time. Nor even a woman of any age or shape since the drive had laid over near Dodge for a few days, and that was far down the trail. He enjoyed just looking at the back of this one's lovely head.

Someone stirred from the heat apathy that claimed the passengers and exclaimed, "Antelope!"

A band of pronghorns had appeared out of the loneliness of the land and was bounding along with their stiff-legged, grasshopper gait, keeping pace with the train in what was an antelope's idea of a frolic.

One of the two roughs picked up a rifle that had been lying on the floor beneath his feet and moved to an unoccupied seat, lifting the window.

He raised the gun and fired twice. "Whoopee!" he screeched. "Got him! Busted his laig!"

The antelope were scattering and vanishing into the plain. All but one. This animal was hobbling on a bullet-broken front leg. The man emptied his rifle at the other fleeing animals. Zack could see the bullets kicking up puffs

of dust around the target, but all shots evidently had
missed.

The man, laughing shrilly, sank back in his seat. "I sure
winged that ol' goat," he boasted. "Two hundred yards if
it was an inch."

The train suddenly began to slow, the whistle sounding
hoarsely ahead. Zack realized that the small, grandmoth-
erly person had risen from her seat and had jerked the
bell cord which was the signal to the engineer to bring
the train to an emergency stop. The wheels ground to a
halt.

"You just go out there and finish off that poor suffering beast," Grandma said to the tough with the rifle.

He looked at her, tobacco-stained teeth gaping, his
hard face the picture of amazement. "What's that?" he
mumbled.

"You heard me," Granny said. "Put some shells in
that gun, pile off this car and finish what you never
should have started in the first place."

The man glared disbelievingly, then began to laugh
scornfully. "Go back to knitting your doilies, old lady,"
he said. "Do yuh think fer one minute thet I'd go out
there in that hot sun and waste not only a ca'tridge but my
time on a stnkin' goat? The world's full of pronghorns."

Granny lifted a folded parasol that had been leaning
at her side and brought it down with a smart whacking
sound on the tough's head. It came so unexpectedly that
he had not even attempted to dodge. The blow drove his
hat down around his ears. He reeled back in the seat,
somewhat dazed.

The he recovered. He reared to his feet in a seething
fury. "If you wasn't an old woman," he roared, "I'd . . ."

His voice thinned and faded off into nothing. He was
looking into the maw of a derringer. It was in the hand of
the beauty with the snapfinger dark eyes. It was a double-
barreled weapon that Zack estimated was .50 caliber. At

short range a slug of that size would tear a fearful hole in flesh. Two slugs would tear two holes.

The tough was aware of these possibilities. He cringed back. "What'n hell!" he croaked.

"Get off and finish that animal as my grandmother told you to do," the young lady said. She was the calmest person in the car, with the probable exception of her grandmother. Granny was inspecting her parasol. Satisfied that it had suffered no permanent damage, she laid it aside and said in a very positive voice, "Now git! An' don't waste any more time. This train's hours late already, and I'm growin' weary. Git out there an' do as any decent person ought to do."

The tough glared around. His stare was avoided by the eyes of other passengers who had ben jolted out of their heat torpor, and who obviously wanted no part of this. The man's glance finally rested on Zack—and remained there.

"Better do what the lady says," Zack said. "You're wasting our time."

Zack sat with his six-shooter muzzle resting on the back of the seat in front of him. The hammer was tilted back, but he was not pointing the pistol at anything in particular.

The tough turned to his companion, but found no sign of help there. "I cain't fight women!" he snarled. He gave Zack a glare and said, "I'll remember you, mister."

Reloading his rifle, he stumbled down the aisle and dropped off the train. From the window, Zack watched him head on foot through the hot grass to where the wounded antelope had halted at a distance, head drooping. Two shots sounded.

The peppery Granny peered from a window and said, "The poor, poor beast. At least its agony is over."

The heavy-jowled conductor came bursting into the

car. "Who pulled that bell cord?" he raged, his stomach vibrating.

"I did," Granny said calmly.

"You?" the conductor exploded unbelievingly. "Old lady, don't you know that—?"

"My name is Mrs. Julia Smith," Granny said. "And don't you know enough to take off your hat in the presence of ladies. Where was you brought up? In a pig sty?"

The conductor had to try several times before he could speak intelligibly. "Don't you know it's ag'in the law to stop a train carryin' the United States mail without permission of the conductor in charge—namely me?" he thundered.

"Fiddle-faddle," Julia Smith said. She picked up her knitting and seemed to lose interest in the conductor. Her granddaughter had returned the wicked derringer to whatever hiding place from which it had emerged. Zack suspected that it had come from a garter holster.

The tough returned, panting, hot and vengeful. He glared at Julia Smith and the handsome girl as he resumed his seat. He engaged in mumbled angry recrimination with his friend who was apparently denying all responsibility for his companion's humiliation. He gave Zack a scowl, but Zack only returned that with a beaming smile.

The conductor angrily yanked the bell rope twice. "You ain't heard the last of this, lady," he told Granny.

"Go polish your brass buttons," Granny said.

The train lurched ahead, couplings clashing.

Chapter 2

Zack holstered his six-shooter and relaxed in his seat. Julia Smith turned and thoroughly inspected him through the spectacles perched on her nose. Finally she lifted a hand, crooked an imperious finger, beckoning him to approach her. Irritated at her arrogant manner, he ignored her for a moment. Then he realized that this might be a chance to become acquainted with the granddaughter.

"What's your name?" Julia Smith asked.

"Keech," Zack said stiffly. "Anything else, ma'am?"

"A cowboy," she said. "I'd say south Texas by your accent. I don't like Texans and them from the south are the worst. They're pig-headed, rude."

"Texans don't cotton to other rude, mule-headed folks," Zack said. *"Adios!"*

"Keep your hair on," Julia Smith said. "In addition to your other shortcomings you're impudent also. And maybe stupid. I doubt if you knew what you might be letting yourself in for by horning in with me and my granddaughter against those two over there."

"I'll worry about that for at least five minutes," Zack said. He seized his chance and turned to the girl with the snapfinger dark eyes. "I didn't catch your name, miss."

Her smile was frigid. "How sad." She turned her back on him. Granny Smith gave him a leer, and he retreated to his seat, defeated.

The train built up to its top speed, which wasn't much. The roadbed seemed new and rough. The August afternoon heat increased. The majority of the passengers sank back into their torpor and were tossed around in their seats. The buck-toothed, swarthy tough remained awake. He kept darting menacing glances at Zack and at Granny and her granddaughter, both of whom remained pointedly indifferent.

Granny turned in her seat and spoke to Zack so that everyone in the car could hear. "Stay out of dark alleys in Sioux Wells, Texas man," she said. "Stay sober. There are rats around, but if anythin' happens to you, I'll see to it that someone is strung up for it."

Zack grinned. "Thanks, ma'am. I'll remember."

That ended the glares and unvoiced threats. Silence came, except for the creaking and groaning of the train. Their route descended from the dry, higher plains and advanced into better, greener country, veined by creeks which fed a winding, small river. Homesteaders had taken over much of the land, and fields were lush with crops or pasture for cattle. The number of passengers in the two coaches indicated that the Rocky Mountain Express was doing a comfortable business.

The conductor returned on his rounds, carefully avoiding looking at Julia Smith. Zack accosted him.

"When was this railroad built?" he asked.

"Three, four years ago," the man said.

"Looks like it's doing pretty good."

"It might look that way, but it ain't," the man growled.

"How's that? This country seems to be filling in."

"The country's doin' fine. What's needed is half a dozen good hangin's."

"Hangings? Why?"

Like the section hand a few days earlier, the conductor grew cautious. He looked around, then ended the conversation and hurried away.

Zack settled back, frowning. Evidently the Rocky Mountain Express's outward appearance of prosperity was tarnished. If so, he began to suspect that this would go against his chances of collecting his claim.

However, there was this J. K. Tolliver whom the section hand had named as head of the railroad. Zack had been brought up to believe that all railroad presidents were rich beyond imagination. He had never met a railroad president, nor any rich easterner, as a matter of fact. What few tenderfeet he had encountered were weirdly garbed tourists who were as likely as not to mount a horse from the Indian side, and get kicked over the corral bars. It was very probable that J. K. Tolliver was wealthy enough to pay an honest claim against his railroad, no matter what the situation of the railroad itself. It occurred to Zack that he might have to travel east and take it up with J. K. Tolliver in person. That gave him cold chills. Not because of J. K. Tolliver. He had heard of people coming to no good end in those crowded eastern cities.

"Sioux Wells!" the conductor bellowed, returning to the car. "Sioux Wells, next stop!"

Passengers, including Zack, aroused and began groping for their luggage. Grandma Julia Smith stored her knitting in a handbag. Her gorgeous granddaughter, who had fallen asleep, was arranging her hair and pinning on a small straw bonnet trimmed with daisies.

When the train ground to a stop, Zack shouldered his belongings and alighted on a plank platform which flanked a two-story depot whose upper floors evidently contained the offices of the railroad. He looked at Sioux Wells beyond the station. Sioux Wells looked back at him. The settlement was a one-street, one-sided stringtown that stretched along the railroad yards for a considerable distance. The tracks narrowed to a pin point in the distance, and were swallowed by the glare of the sun. At Zack's back were sidetracks, cattle corrals and chutes and idle rolling stock. He could make out the faint dots that were the soddies and shacks of settlers here and there in the distance.

East of the depot were freight sheds. Great ricks of buffalo bones were stacked along the tracks awaiting shipment to eastern grinding plants. A stack of buffalo hides, dry as wood, made its odorous presence known. The great herds were about done for in this region and their bones now served as a source of income for the settlers.

A buffalo hunter, a rare specimen now, was just in, and his two swampers were unloading fresh hides at the buyer's yard across from the railroad station. The hunter had a jug of whiskey in his hand, which he passed up to the swampers. From appearances the jug had been going the rounds very liberally, for the hunter pulled his Sharp's buffalo rifle from the wagon, loaded it and peered around for a target.

He found one and fired. Zack heard feminine screams of outrage from somewhere down the street. A stream of water was spurting from a wooden water tank that was mounted on the roof of a two-story building whose sign proclaimed it as the Good Time Music Hall. Heads appeared from the upper windows, using language that ladies do not utter.

The hunter lowered his rifle and hid it back of him, grinning into his month's growth of ragged beard, acting for all the world the picture of innocence. But the haze of powder smoke that hovered overhead betrayed him. A pistol appeared in front of one of the feminine heads at a window. The hunter ducked in time and the slug from the pistol only whacked into the load of buffalo hides. The pistol kept roaring, but the hunter and the swampers had disappeared back of the wagon.

"Hey, Gussie!" the hunter yelled. "Quit smokin' us up, afore you hurt somebody. Cain't you take a joke?"

A tall, long-haired man wearing an immaculate white shirt, string tie and an expensive Panama hat, appeared from a gambling house. A marshal's badge was pinned to a suspender. "Quit it, Gussie!" he shouted. "It's Ed Hake again. I'll see to it he pays for any damages. He's been on the buffalo range for weeks an' is just havin' a little fun."

The speaker was equipped with a brace of pistols in holsters that had ben made with an eye to permitting a quick draw.

"By glory, it *is* Wild Bill!" one of the train arrivals nearby said. "I heard he was marshal here, but didn't believe it."

Order was restored instantly in Sioux Wells. The heads withdrew from the windows after another barrage of language at soprano pitch.

"Be in court in the mornin' to pay fine and damages, Ed," the marshal said to the buffalo hunter, and then headed back to his interrupted game in the gambling house.

A man appeared on the roof of the music hall, set up a ladder, and plugged the bullet hole in the water tank, ending the spurt of liquid. Evidently this was not the first time the tank had been a target. Zack could make out other plugs in its sides. He heard a windmill pump begin operating to refill the tank. Apparently the Good Time had very up-to-date facilities. Zack had heard that some establishments up north had running water in the rooms. It came out of faucets through pipes. He had to see this with his own eyes.

Grandma Julia Smith and her granddaughter assembled their baggage, not lacking assistance from male bystanders, and boarded a waiting hack that carried them away toward a hotel, which like the Good Time, was a frame, weatherboarded structure with a water tank on its roof too.

Zack walked across the street toward the Good Time. He was thirsty and was thinking of a cold, foaming mug of beer. He stepped through the swing doors and headed for the bar, which was unexpectedly elegant with a glossy, varnished surface and polished brass rails. The big, mirrored backbar sported pyramids of glassware.

There were several patrons at the bar, glasses before them, smoke curling from their cigars and pipes. They wore denim jackets, striped caps and pants to match, and heavy brogans. Railroad men.

One was the big lantern-jawed, redheaded engineer who had been at the throttle when the K-Bar-K herd had been stampeded. Stan Durkin. He had a mug of beer in his hand and was holding the floor, relating some tale which his listeners were not interrupting. Zack gained the impression that Stan Durkin was in the habit of dominating the conversation.

Zack placed his belongings on a chair at a poker table that was covered and not in use at this hour. He unbuckled his gun belt and hung it over the back of the chair. It was evident that Stan Durkin was unarmed. In any event Zack felt that this matter required something more satisfying than gunplay.

Stan Durkin was unaware of Zack's arrival. He was reaching the climax of his narrative, and his listeners were waiting with fixed attention. Durkin was a big man, taller than Zack by maybe an inch and many pounds heavier. His long arms were knobbed by big hands. His nose had been broken more than once and there were a few white scars along the jawline and a permanent one in crimson above his right cheekbone. He had seen considerable fistic action, as the section hand had mentioned.

Zack tapped him briskly on the shoulder, halting the tale at its important point. Durkin, with an impatient snort, tried to continue without turning to look at his annoyer. Zack tapped him again on the shoulder—harder. Much harder. So hard it jolted Durkin into realization that trouble was hunting him.

He whirled, rage boiling in his eyes. "What the hell do *you* want?" he roared.

"Remember me?" Zack asked.

Durkin peered. Rcollection began to dawn.

"Yeah," Zack said. "You didn't kill any humans the other day. Otherwise I'd be even meaner than I aim to be. But you cost us around two hundred head of cattle. I'm here to collect for the loss from the railroad and to take the interest out of your ugly hide."

Stan Durkin believed that offense was the best defense. "Why, you fool!" he snarled. "I'll beat you to a pulp, cowpoke."

He began moving in on Zack, swaying on the balls of his feet. But a man moved between them, shoving them away from each other. The intruder was Wild Bill Hickok.

"No fightin' in here, gentlemen," the marshal said, and Zack was surprised by the softness of his voice. "All you'd do is wreck glassware an' tables. Take it outside if you've got to settle whatever is in your craws. There's plenty of room in the street. And there'll be no foul fightin'. No gougin', kneein' or jumpin' on a man when he's down. I'll decide when one or the other has had enough."

"I couldn't be happier," Stan Durkin said. "I'll wipe up Railroad Street with him."

Durkin led the way outside, followed by Zack, Wild Bill and every person in the place, including the bartenders. The marshal picked a likely spot in the dusty street and said, "All right. Go to it."

Nearby stood the hotel. It sported a veranda at the front equipped with chairs and a porch swing. Granny Smith's granddaughter came from the lobby and stood on the porch. With her was a good-looking man in a neat business suit and starched collar.

"Better go inside, ma'am," Wild Bill said, lifting his

Panama. "There's goin' to be some roughin' around here. Not a sight for ladies."

The girl with the snapfinger eyes spoke. "I've got ten dollars that says the railroad man wins."

There was silence. Zack spoke. "I'll take the bet, ma'am. Cash."

"It'll be easy money, miss," Stan Durkin said, bowing grandly in the direction of the girl. "This won't take long."

He and Zack faced each other in the dusty street, circling for a space, measuring each other. Durkin came in, feinting, dancing, displaying fistic experience. Zack stood, his fists only half-raised, as though he was timid. That encouraged Durkin into the belief that he had an unskilled victim.

Durkin charged. He was confident. He presented a shoulder, crossed with a left, and expected his opponent to be in position for a knockout with the right. Zack had fallen for some such maneuver himself one evening in the past in a makeshift ring in San Antonio when he had the temerity to get into the ring with a young professional pugilist who was picking up spending money by barnstorming through the hinterlands.

Durkin swung the right just as Zack had swung at the professional pug that night. Durkin missed, just as Zack had missed. However, a fist did connect. But it was Zack's right and not Durkin's. It landed on Durkin's jaw, and it had back of it all of Zack's strength.

Durkin stood a moment, swaying, a glassy look in his eyes. Zack refrained from swinging again, for he had seen that same vacancy in the expressions of other men on whose jaws he had connected solidly.

Then Durkin pitched on his face. He did not move.

Dead, unbelieving silence descended on Railroad Street. The faces of the girls who crowded the upper windows of the Good Time remained fixed there. Julia Smith's granddaughter and her companion stared from the veranda of the hotel. No one spoke. All eyes were on the recumbent body of Stan Durkin.

Wild Bill broke the silence. "I reckon there's no point in countin' him out." He bent over Durkin. "He might have a busted or dislocated jaw," he said. "Some of you boys better pack him to a doctor. Fetch a stretcher. There's one at the depot."

One of the railroad men spoke resentfully to Zack. "You must have got in a lucky lick, mister. Ain't nobody could knock out Stan Durkin like that with one punch unless there was somethin' crooked about it. You likely had somethin' wrapped up in yore fist. Let's take a look."

"Sure," Zack said. He moved close and let the man see that his right hand was empty. Then he clenched the fist and knocked the man as cold as Stan Durkin with one blow.

Howls of fury arose. The bystanders surged in. "We'll fix him! He cain't come into this town an—"

They surged back. They found themselves facing, not Zack, but Hickok. He hadn't drawn his guns—as yet.

"I'll take care of this," he said. "He's guilty of assault an' battery, but this feller here asked fer it. He questioned this man's integrity an' got what was comin' to him if you ask me. But he'll have to pay a fine. Five an' costs will likely cover it when he faces the justice. Meanwhile, I'm releasin' him on his own recognizance, an' I don't want no mob talk from nobody. You hear me?"

They heard him. He addressed Zack. "Keep out of any more trouble while you stay in Sioux Wells, which stay I hope will be short. What's your name?"

"Name's Keech," Zack said. "I've got business here, an' I don't aim to leave until it's settled."

Hickok looked him over from head to foot. He had sad eyes, expressionless eyes on the gray-green side. Zack had heard that this man had killed at least a dozen persons.

"You're a sassy rooster," Hickok said in his mild voice. "Be at the justice court at nine o'clock tomorrow mornin' to pay your fine."

A stretcher was brought and Stan Durkin was carried away. He was already reviving, and Zack was sure he had suffered no more damage than a jaw that would be swollen for a few days.

Zack got his war sack and gun belt from the Good Time and headed for the hotel, whose name was Traveler's Rest, according to the sign on the veranda.

To his dismay he found half a dozen wide-eyed, barefoot urchins tagging along at his heels. They were nudging each other and whispering that this was the man who had licked Stan Durkin.

Zack was embarrassed. "Go home, lads," he pleaded. "Don't they teach manners to young ones in this town?"

The youngsters dropped a dozen paces back, but that was all. They gathered around the steps of Traveler's Rest as Zack mounted to the veranda. The dark-haired girl and her male companion were still on the veranda. So was Wild Bill Hickok.

Hickok turned and discovered he was blocking Zack's path. He said, "Here's the winner, ma'am. He cost you ten dollars, I reckon, but I suppose you want to congratulate him."

"I certainly do," the girl said. "First the ten dollars. He seems to have earned it."

Her companion tried to move in, reaching for his wallet. She pushed him back. "It's my pleasure," she said, and produced a gold piece from her reticule and handed it to Zack.

Then she brought the heel of her slipper down very forcefully on the toe of Zack's boot. The slipper was high-heeled.

"And congratulations," she said. "Come, Frank."

She swept past, drawing her companion with her, and vanished into the lobby. He was a well-proportioned man in his thirties, Zack judged. He gave Zack an amused smile as he passed by. Zack watched them mount to the second floor.

Not until then would he permit himself to give any sign of pain. "O—oo-f-f!" he groaned. He dropped the war sack and grabbed at his foot, dancing around until the pain subsided.

"Why'd she do that?" he asked Hickok. "She's a right hard loser."

"There's only one thing you can take for granted about a female," Hickok said. "They'll always be cantankerous an' flighty when you figure you got 'em estimated as all sugar an' spice. Especially the lookers."

Hickok strolled away in the direction of the gambling house from which he had originally emerged.

Chapter 3

Zack entered the lobby, still favoring his foot. The wrinkled, turkey-necked man back of the counter eyed him without warmth and said, "I suppose you want a room. That'll be five dollars a night."

"Your sign says rooms are a dollar to a dollar and a half a night," Zack said. "I'll take the best. I need a shave an' a bath. That's another two-bits, according to the sign."

The hotel man wanted to refuse. Several railroad men had mounted to the veranda and were peering into the lobby with scowls. But he looked at Zack's face and did not have the sand.

"I'm anxious to see this water running out of a pipe that I've heard about," Zack said as he picked up the change from the gold piece he had won from the girl. He looked at the key and the tag attached which indicated that his room was Number 209.

He mounted the stairs and found the room which was midway down the hall. A sign at the rear and an arrow pointed to the bathing facilities.

The room was average, with a limp rag rug on oiled pine flooring, a bed, commode and a rack for hanging clothes. Zack lost no time getting out his shaving material and heading down the hall.

A wizened flunky came stumping from downstairs and handed him soap and a towel. "Don't waste water, mister," he warned. "I'm here to see that if you do you'll pay another quarter."

Zack shaved, amazed at the convenience of a wall basin into which sun-heated water was piped. The bathing equipment was equally novel. A pipe jutted from the ceiling. When he turned on a faucet, water sprayed from a perforated gadget. He had never before taken a bath standing up. He stood beneath the spray so long that the flunky came to the door and informed him he would have to come up with another two-bit piece.

Zack finally emerged, toweled himself and got into fresh clothes that he had brought from his war bag. "What do you do in winter to make folks comfortable under that thing?" he asked the attendant.

"Winter? We close up this here thing. Anybody in need of a bath in winter kin wallow in a tub. Feller, it gits down to forty below in these parts at times."

Zack, refreshed, headed down the hall toward his room. Deep twilight was at hand, but the one lamp in the hall had not yet been lighted. A man emerged from a room toward the front of the hall and came brushing past him. He was Wild Bill Hickok. Zack, surprised, said, "Howdy, Marshal!"

Wild Bill replied briefly and moved past. He left by way of a rear door which led to an outer stairway at the back of the building. Zack had the impression that the marshal had not particularly wanted to be recognized. Evidently he had come to the Traveler's Rest instead of the gambling house, and must have entered by the rear stairway while Zack had been in the shower.

Zack heard faint voices and laughter from the room from which Hickok had emerged. Feminine voices. A man's voice. The girl with the wonderful dark eyes, of course, and the man who had met her at the hotel. He made out the more positive voice of the grandmother. Hickok apparently had been a visitor in the quarters of Julia Smith and her kin.

Zack's toes on his right foot still smarted. There was

a small bruise to charge up to the granddaughter. He shrugged, and unlocked the door of his room. He had left his wallet, his watch and other pocket possessions in the bureau drawer and had hung his gun belt on a wall peg. The key to his door was a cheap skeleton affair, a duplicate of which could be bought in any hardware store.

A shadow warned him in time and he was fading away, ducking as the first of his assailants came at him. The man was swinging a club. It grazed Zack's shoulder, doing little damage. Driving a fist from a crouch he felt it bury in the man's stomach. He felt great satisfaction as he heard the gushing moan of agony. He rolled aside, certain that this one, at least, would be out of it for a few minutes.

The second man was braced to move in. He also had a club—a wagon spoke—in his hands. He was the bucktoothed one who had come out second best with Granny Smith in the matter of the wounded antelope. The one who was slumped on the floor, gasping agonizingly for breath, had been Bucktooth's seat-mate on the train.

Bucktooth lost his ambition. The door was open. He wheeled and tore through it, abandoning his partner. Zack lunged, trying to tackle him but missed and sprawled on the floor. He came to his feet, but was tangled in the rag rug. He skidded and fell again. By the time he got into the hall his quarry had vanished through the rear door. Zack could hear him taking the downsteps in long leaps.

Zack raced in pursuit. Dusk was deepening into darkness. He did not risk a broken leg leaping down the stairs as his quarry had done. He could hear receding footsteps. The man was vanishing among a maze of barns and corrals, heading toward the railroad yards evidently. Zack ran in that direction for a time, then realized it was useless.

He came hurrying back to the hotel, mounted the steps and ran down the hall. The door of his room was still open. Granny Smith, her granddaughter and the dark-haired man, along with several other hotel guests, were peering into his room. They parted to let Zack through. The open window told the story. Bucktooth's partner had recovered enough to drop from the window, which was a comparatively short descent, and had fled.

"What'n blazes happened?" Granny Smith asked waspishly. "It sounded like a buffalo stampede."

"I had visitors," Zack said. "They were friends of yours, by the way. They seemed to have a grudge to settle with me, and all the time you were the one who made them eat crow."

"You're talking about the bully boys who was on the train," Granny said. "I warned you to look out for 'em, now didn't I?"

Hickok had heard the commotion at the hotel and had returned. "What did they look like?" he asked.

Granny Smith supplied the descriptions quickly and accurately. Trashy, mean-looking as wet skunks. One's got teeth like a gopher, an' his pal's pitted with pockmarks. Both need a bath and a shave—an' a rope around their necks. Both about thirty, cotton shirts, denim pants, cowboots. Armed, dangerous."

"You've got a mind for detail," Hickok said. "If they're still in town, which I doubt, I'll run 'em in."

He eyed Zack. "You're right busy, my friend. You hit town only a couple of hours ago, and you've been in two ruckuses already. What did you say your name is?"

"Keech," Zack said. "Zachary Taylor Keech."

"You wouldn't be related to an old Texas hellion named Ben Keech, who's better known as Brandy Ben, now would you?"

"He's my dad," Zack said. "You acquainted with him?"

Hickok smiled. "I've bumped into Brandy Ben a time or two. First time at Abilene, if I recollect. Later on, he come through Baxter Springs with a drive when I was stayin' over there a few days. Would you take it kindly if I asked you just why you're in Sioux Wells?"

"Same reason why I had the ruckus with that Durkin fellow," Zack said. "I came here to press a claim for six thousand dollars against the Rocky Mountain Express Railway. Durkin stampeded our herd some days ago, and we lost around two hundred head."

He became aware that a strained silence had come. Everyone was looking, rather embarrassed, at the natty, dark-mustached, dark-haired man who stood with one hand laid possessively on the arm of the handsome girl.

He looked at Zack and laughed. "It happens that I'm Frank Niles, superintendent of the Rocky," he said. "I'm the man who will have to handle your claim." He laughed again, tolerantly. "Six thousand dollars, you say. For cattle that our engineer was supposed to have stampeded. Well, that *is* quite a claim. This is hardly the place for us to discuss it. Come to the office tomorrow, Mr. Keech, and we'll see what can be done."

Zack understood that Frank Niles was already of a mind not to pay that amount of money, and, in fact, no money at all. The group broke up. Granny and Frank Niles and the girl returned to the suite at the front. Zack entered his room and took stock. His wallet, watch and pistol were still in place. His assailants had not had the time to rob him.

He left the room, locking the door, and descended to the street, heading for an eating place which was some distance away. He found Hickok waiting for him.

The marshal fell in step with him, and they strolled along. "About that claim against the railroad," Hickok said. "You must know that you've got as much chance as an icicle on a hot stove."

"Would it help if I got a lawyer?" Zack asked.

"Ain't a lawyer in five hundred miles that would

touch you," Hickok said. "And in Sioux Wells, least of all. This is a railroad town. The bread and butter of most everybody here comes from sidin' in with the railroad—or stealin' from it."

"Stealing?"

"That's another story," Hickok said.

"It's a fair claim," Zack said. "If Durkin hadn't touched off the whistle, the boys likely would have been able to have held the run down to where it wouldn't have amounted to much."

"You're buttin' a stone wall," Hickok said. "All I can do is wish you luck. For one thing, the Rocky couldn't come up with six thousand dollars right now, even if you got a judgment handed down from the Almighty."

"How's that? Why, six thousand dollars ought to be pocket change for a railroad."

"Not with the Rocky," the marshal said. "If things keep goin' as they have been, the Rocky will be bankrupt or in receiver's hands before long."

"Everybody says railroads make piles of money," Zack said.

"That'll be news to most of 'em, and to the Rocky above all. The Rocky had enough trouble with Indians in summer an' blizzards in winter buildin' into this country without bein' plagued by these highbinders just when they might have seen their way clear."

"I've heard this mentioned before," Zack said. "Just what is a highbinder?"

"Thieves is a better word for them," Hickok said. "They started out a couple of years ago as petty robbers, stealin' a packin' crate from a boxcar here an' there. Then they got bolder an' began stealin' by the carload."

"Carload? How did they get away with that?"

"They got bolder an' bolder. They ditched a freight train east of here less than a year ago, an' got away with enough freight to load a dozen wagons. The engine crew was killed in the wreck, an' they murdered the conductor and a brakeman. They didn't want any witnesses who knew them. They seem to know when there's valuable freight aboard, an' that's when they strike."

"What kind of valuable freight?"

"They got a carload of sewing machines, cookstoves an' kitchenware in one haul. Worth plenty in the mining camps that are boomin' in the Rockies. Miners are hittin' it rich, an' their wives want the best that money can buy. Another time they got away with a carload of lighter stuff—women's dresses, shoes, things they wear underneath, hats, bustles an'—"

"Bustles?"

"Don't tell me you don't know what a bustle is?"

"Of course I do," Zack snorted. "Do you think we live in caves down in Texas? They're contraptions that ladies wear to make 'em look—well, make 'em look more important. But what kind of robbers would bother with stealing things like that?"

"That shows your ignorance," Hickok said. "These particular objects came from New York, an' was wholesaled at three dollars apiece. There was a thousand of them, along with crates of slippers, dresses an' all the other truck that females need to keep 'em happy. About seven thousand dollars' worth, in all. Then they got into another car which had ten crates of Remington magazine rifles, late models. Twelve rifles to a crate at fifty dollars a gun, wholesale. They got a dozen kegs of Galena lead an' five kegs of DuPont powder. All that run into money. Close to ten thousand dollars, all of which the Rocky was liable for."

"What in blazes do they do with all that stuff?"

"Some of it is being sold right here in Sioux Wells," Hickok said. "Some in Denver, some in Hays City. Likely the bulk of it goes back to Kansas City where there's a bigger market. It's shipped back over the Santa Fe and the Union Pacific, or maybe even the Rocky, labeled as pickled buffalo tongue or some such. It just vanishes onto store shelves where it's sold cheap an' fast, but at a big profit, for it don't cost much. It's a leetle difficult, for instance, to identify a stolen bustle when a lady is wearin' it."

"How often do things like that happen?"

"Too danged often. An' it's growin' worse. They are gettin' bolder. They got away with forty thousand dollars in gold dust just about six weeks ago."

"Forty thousand?"

"It had been brought by wagon out of the minin' camps to a little station forty miles west of here that is the end of steel for the Rocky. It was to be shipped to the mint in Philadelphia. The highbinders ditched the train, killed another railroad man, an' got away with the dust. Nobody but a few was supposed to know it was aboard."

"You're trying to make it sound like I'm picking on a poor, ragged-bottom railroad that's on its way to the poorhouse," Zack snorted.

"Well, it's something like that," Hickok admitted.

"How about this J. K. Tolliver, who's said to be the big augur back of this outfit?" Zack sniffed. "Likely he's rolling in gold notes or such somewhere back east, living off the honey and fruit of the land. He's the one I aim to gun for. I reckon he's in the clear like most of these sharpers who let other folks take the losses."

Hickok gave him a slanting look. "The Tollivers own about all there is of the stock in the Rocky," he said. "It's a family affair. This here railroad ain't in the same class with the U.P. or the Santa Fe. It was dreamed up by a Tolliver an' built by the Tollivers who've put all their money into it."

Zack eyed the marshal. "Why are you telling me this sad story about the Tollivers, Mr. Hickok?" he demanded. "I don't like to pick on a man when he's in trouble, but this railroad still owes my father six thousand dollars. I aim to collect."

"Of course, of course," Hickok said. "I ain't usually in the habit of sounding off to a stranger. Maybe I sort of cottoned to you from the way you took care of Stan Durkin. I liked the way you leveled him with one punch, with all his friends around. It reminded me of a friend of mine who is a law man in Dodge City the last I heard of him. Name of Earp. Wyatt Earp. I saw him hit a man who had it comin' an' lay him low with one punch, just as you did. Have you ever considered goin' into the ring? Prize fightin' for money?"

"I tried it once," Zack said. "I was knocked kicking. I'm a cowman from here on in. That's my trade."

"How are you with a gun?"

"Gun?"

"Ever shoot a man? Ever have to draw in earnest?"

"That's sort of a leading question, isn't it, marshal?"

"It's not idle curiosity," Hickok said. "You've got the earmarks of a man who'd make a good law officer. You've shown that you can use your fists. You might have to use something faster than fists if you decided to take over this badge I'm wearin'."

Zack was out of his depth. "Wait a minute! Who said anything about—?"

"I'm here only temporarily," Hickok said. "I took over this law job as a favor to J. K. Tolliver, who is an old friend."

"You know J. K. Tolliver? In person?"

"Yes. J. K. Tolliver hoped I'd be able to break up this gang of highbinders. It was a tougher job than I had expected."

Zack eyed the marshal. "If you couldn't swing it, you could hardly expect a greenhorn like me to do it, now could you?"

"The trouble is," Hickok explained, "they knew just why I came here an' took the job. They know every move I make. If I could drop out of sight, I might be able to ramble around and maybe get some information on these thieves. But somebody's got to wear the badge."

He paused for a space, then added, "The fact is that I'll be dead if I hang around here much longer. I've been lucky this far."

"You mean they've tried to—"

A gun blasted a spurt of flame from between buildings down the street. Hickok's hat was knocked slanting over his ear. The gun exploded again, but by that time both Hickok and Zack were diving flat on the sidewalk.

Hickok was firing as he fell, a chilling demonstration of his reputation for gun speed. Both of his six-shooters were thundering, raking the blackness from which the attack had come. Zack's gun was in his own hand, but he held his fire, awaiting the outcome of Hickok's volley.

The guns went silent. The echoes quit bouncing from the town's walls and nearby windows ceased shuddering in their frames. Zack could now hear the sickening, agonized breathing of a dying man.

Hickok ran, crouching, down the sidewalk and halted at the corner of a building, listening to sounds from the darkness. "You there," he called. "Come out!"

The burbling sound continued. Hickok reloaded his guns, then advanced cautiously into the darkness. He returned dragging a limp body with him. In the lamplight from the windows of a nearby gambling house Zack looked down at a hard-faced man, a stranger. The tough was breathing his last. Life faded from him in a convulsive quiver of fingers and legs.

"Name of Glover," Hickok said. "He's been a barfly around here. One of the highbinders, of course. Paid to get me. If I'd stopped that slug he might have tried to knock you over."

"Why me?"

"He runs in the same herd with the two who laid for you in your room."

"You mean those two are highbinders too?"

"The one with the big teeth calls himself the Ogallala Kid. His pal goes by the name of Matt Pecos. Likely he's never been within five hundred miles of the Pecos River. Their specialty is wrecking trains and robbing boxcars."

"You know that for sure?"

"I know it, and I know half a dozen more like them and Glover who hang out here in Sioux Wells are in on it too. But knowing it in your mind and catchin' them red-handed so it can be proved in court are a long piece apart. What the Tollivers are after are the brains back of these fellers. These are small fry, who only take orders. Someone who plans the jobs has a lot of gray matter between his ears. That's the one—or ones—the Tollivers want."

A crowd gathered. The majority were railroad men. They stood gazing down at the twisted body of the dead man. Someone in the rear spoke, "Another notch on Hickok's gun."

The majority of the gathering shifted uneasily. No other voice was raised to back up the unseen speaker.

Hickok ignored the matter. "Send for Doc Appleton," he said. "Tell him it's a coroner's job this time."

The medical man arrived and asked the routine questions, for he also served as coroner. When he was finished, Hickok motioned Zack, and they moved away from the crowd.

"I withdraw my request," Hickok said.

"For what?"

"For askin' a man to make a target of himself in my place. I'll stick to the job here 'til it's finished, one way or another. What I was really wantin' was a chance to look around to see if I could find out what's happened to a friend of mine."

"Friend?"

"Name of Mel Sanders. Around here he was known as Jimmy Broom. I talked him into comin' to Sioux Wells not too long ago to see if he could get some information on these highbinders. He used to be a deputy under me back in Abilene. An' a good one. He acted the part of a bum, sweepin' out saloons, an' hangin' around honky-tonks. He dropped out of sight four days ago."

"The highbinders? They got onto him?"

Hickok shrugged wearily. "If so, God help him. And God help them if they've done away with him."

He changed the subject abruptly. "See to it that you show up in court tomorrow," he said. "At nine o'clock, sober. You've got to answer charges of disturbin' the peace."

Chapter 4

"Five dollars an' costs, which makes a total of seven dollars," the justice of the peace said, slapping a palm down on the table which served as his bench.

The courtroom was part of the marshal's office and the jail. Zack fished in his pocket, found a ten dollar gold piece, which brought a frown from the court.

"Five an' costs an' three dollars for contempt of court," the justice thundered. He was a bald-headed buzzard of a man.

"Contempt of court?" Zack questioned incredulously.

"For not appearin' in this court with the proper change," the justice said.

Zack was crimson with rage. But he happened to look at Wild Bill Hickok who was hiding a grin back of a hand. The marshal wagged his head, warning him to be silent and accept the verdict.

Zack retreated to the spectator's benches, scowling. The judge called the next defendant who happened to be the buffalo hunter, Ed Hake, who had punctured the hole in the water tank on the roof of the Good Time. Hake pleaded guilty.

"Ten dollars an' costs," the justice thundered. "I ought to give you thirty days, Ed, but it happens our jail is full right now, lucky for you. An' another ten dollars to Gussie Bluebell for damages to her dress from water which came down through the ceiling, an event for which you were responsible."

"Here's your ten bucks an' two fer costs," Hake said

amiably. "I'll deliver the ten dollars to Gussie in person an' glad to do it. Me an' Gussie air old friends."

"Oh, no you don't!" his honor snarled. "I'll see to it myself that Gussie gets paid. Put that other ten dollars here on the judicial bench alongside the fine an' costs."

Zack and Hickok retreated from the courtroom into the marshal's small office. "Some day a real lawyer is goin' to wrap that old devil up in graft charges until he'll never be able to talk his way out," Hickok chuckled. "But it's only penny-ante stuff."

He lowered his voice. "We're out for bigger game. Are you still of a mind to insist that the Rocky owes your dad six thousand dollars?"

"I sure am," Zack said. "I'm more than insisting. I want that money."

"I happen to know that J. K. Tolliver has offered five thousand dollars to anyone who figures out a way to put an end to these highbinders," Hickok said. "I reckon the ante could be tilted to six thousand."

Zack crocked a cynical eye at the marshal. "Now I've heard everything. The railroad owes me six thousand dollars. It's a legitimate claim. But you've got the gall to ask me to risk a bullet in the back by gumshoeing around, acting like a detective or something. Just to earn what's honestly coming to me."

"That's right," Hickok said mildly. "But it happens that I'm not the one who's asking you to take on the job."

"Who, then?"

"J. K. Tolliver."

Zack stared disbelievingly. "Now, wait a minute. How could a big gun like that know anything about me?"

"That's beside the point," Hickok said. "But it's true. Frank Niles can vouch for it."

"Niles? The white-collar man I saw with the pretty girl at the hotel?"

"As superintendent of the railroad he's in close touch

with J. K. Tolliver, naturally," Hickok said. "Niles knows all about this."

Zack pretended to clap a hand to his forehead in bewilderment. "Let's go over this again. I came to Sioux Wells only yesterday as a Texas trail driver to press a claim for damages against this railroad. I gathered from the way Niles acted yesterday that he had decided I was wasting my time. Now I'm being asked to risk being killed just to pull the railroad's chestnuts out of the fire."

"Six thousand dollars," Hickok said. "It's the only way you'll ever get the money. You can't squeeze water out of a stone, nor money out of a railroad near bankruptcy."

He added, "My advice is for you to forget the six thousand and clear out of Sioux Wells."

"You'd make a good trout fisherman," Zack growled. "You know how to whip a fly just above the water. You know I won't clear out."

"I generally catch a few when I go fishing," Hickok admitted.

"This time it's a sucker you're after, not a trout," Zack said.

"Get moving," Hickok said.

"Where to?"

"Down to the railway station to have a talk with Frank Niles. His office is upstairs above the waitin' room."

"What would we talk about?"

"Your claim, for one thing."

"Something tells me that won't be all, nor even the most important part of it. I take it he's expecting me."

"Yes. It would be best for you to walk right down the street and ask the man in the ticket office how to get to Niles' office. Ask it so that anybody around can hear it."

"Sort of advertise that I'm calling on Niles to demand my money. Is that it?"

"It's pretty well known already why you came to Sioux

Wells," Hickok said. "You've established yourself as not among the Rocky Mountain Express's fondest admirers. First you level their star fistfighter with one punch. You have made it known that you're here to collect that money, even if you have to take it out of somebody's hide. It would only look like common sense for you to take on Niles this morning at his office to lay down the law to him."

Zack eyed the marshal in silence for a time. "I've got the feeling I'm being led around like a bull with a ring in his nose," he said. "As a matter of fact, I had in mind a visit with this Niles gentleman as first order of business. Now, I find it's all been arranged."

"Then I'm wasting my time talking to you," Hickok said jovially, slapping him on the back. "Here's luck. By the way, don't take Frank too lightly. He wears a stiff collar and dresses like a dude, but he might not be as easy to level as Stan Durkin. I happen to know he can take care of himself in a roughhouse. He was some sort of a boxing champion when he went to college back east, so I understand."

"It's J. K. Tolliver I'm after," Zack said. "I've got no bone to pick with Niles."

"Sure, sure," Hickok said. "By the way, how's the foot that Miss Smith stomped on?"

Zack took the bait. "So her name is Smith too," he said.

Hickok laughed. "Frank Niles wants to change it to Niles," he said.

Zack realized he had been trapped. "So what?" he snarled. He left the marshal's office and headed down Railroad Street, mumbling to himself. Why would he give a hoot if Frank Niles was sweet on the girl with the snapfinger eyes?

He began to understand that he was becoming sort of a marked man in Sioux Wells. Railroad men off shift were having a morning beer in some of the less pretentious saloons. Many of them were moving to doors and windows to watch as he passed by. Their interest was not actively hostile, but neither was it friendly.

Zack could hardly blame them. To them he represented another peril to their livelihoods. He was another burden on the already financially burdened Rocky. They had heard how Stan Durkin had stampeded the K-Bar-K herd. Although local courts might rule in favor of the Rocky the chances were that if the claim was carried higher, it probably would be allowed, along with the assessment of heavy legal costs. That might be the straw that would break the Rocky's back.

The morning westbound combination train would soon be due, and a gaggle of passengers were on the platform and sitting on the hard benches in the stuffy waiting room, along with the customary quota of idlers who were there to see a train come in.

Zack strode to the ticket booth, making sure everyone heard not only what he said, but the thud of his high-heeled boots.

"I want to see a fellow named Niles who seems to be the ramrod around here," he said. "Where does he hang out?"

The ticket agent, who was a thin man in an eyeshade and sleeveguards on the arms of his white shirt, almost swallowed his Adam's apple and acted as though he wanted to duck out of sight. He was forced to face it out, and pointed weakly toward a stairway that led to the second story. "Up there," he croaked. He fluttered around for a moment as though having the notion to leave the cage and race upstairs to warn his boss. But he decided against it, for Zack was already on his way to the stairs.

Zack mounted the steps and found himself in a hall that served several offices. Telegraph sounders clattered, and operators were busy at the keys. One room gave forth the inky odor of ledgers. Clerks were mounted on high stools laboring with pens on bills of lading.

The farthest door was closed, and its frosted glass panel bore the information that this was the office of Frank M. Niles, Division Superintendent.

Zack opened the door and entered. Frank Niles had a female secretary in the ante room. She was forty and plump, with china-blue eyes. Her eyes started to rove over Zack. Then she realized who he was, and she uttered a startled gasp.

"I came to see the boss," Zack said. The door to the inner office stood open and he could see Niles sitting at a big, varnished desk. He walked past the secretary into the inner sanctum.

Niles did not arise. "Well, well," he said crisply. "Do you always barge into business offices without being asked?"

Before Zack could answer, Niles arose, moved to the door and spoke to the secretary. "Jenny, I missed breakfast this morning. Would you mind going down to the Delmonico? Steak and eggs. Tell them to never mind those things they call potatoes. They fry them in coal oil. And just plain bread. I don't want toast burned to a cinder. A jug of black coffee."

The woman began arranging her hair and pinning on a bonnet. Niles closed the door, waited until sure she had left.

Then his manner changed. He smiled and extended a hand. Zack, surprised, accepted it.

"Good morning, Keech," Niles said. "You look healthy and fit. You had a strenuous introduction to Sioux Wells yesterday, but seem to have survived."

"Yeah," Zack said, baffled.

"We'll keep our voices down," Niles said. "I know why you're here, of course. I know because I was there when we got our orders from J. K. Tolliver."

"So this J. K. Tolliver really is here—in Sioux Wells?"

"Yes. That's between the two of us. The three of us, counting Hickok. Here's our plan. We want you to join these outlaws who have been robbing us."

"Join them?"

"Right. J. K. Tolliver is prepared to give you six thousand dollars if you break up this gang. The only way seems to be to get inside the gang itself."

"Why hasn't that been tried before?" Zack asked.

Niles picked up a cigar which lay smoking on an ash tray, revived the red glow and blew smoke reflectively as he considered his answer. "It has," he finally said. "With bad results, evidently. Hickok brought in a friend of his to attempt to get information on this outfit. He pretended to be a down-and-outer who swamped at the saloons for enough to live on in the hope of picking up information. He has disappeared."

"Disappeared. You mean he's run out?"

Niles shrugged. "We hope so. He was known as Jimmy Broom around the barrooms. Nobody has seen him for days."

There was silence for a time. "Before that," Niles went on, "we hired two experienced detectives for the same purpose. One was found dead, a knife in his back. The other quit and left Sioux Wells."

Zack could hear the telegraph instrument rattling faintly in the distance. Other sounds came from the bookkeeping room which was separated from Niles' office by a painted wooden wall. A door back of Niles' chair evidently led to a small inner office. The door was slightly ajar and Zack fancied he heard another faint sound from that direction.

"What makes you think I could swing a thing like this, even if I wanted to try?" Zack asked.

"You've got more in the pot. And more on the ball.

They were hired detectives. They had only their fees to lose."

"And their lives."

"Six thousand dollars is a nice sum," Niles said. "And J. K. Tolliver might be induced to sweeten the pot if things worked out."

Again Zack heard movement beyond the partly open door. He guessed the answer. J. K. Tolliver was there, in person, listening. That meant that he was in reality dealing directly with the president of the railroad and that Frank Niles was only acting as a mouthpiece.

Zack was caught on the horns of a dilemma. While six thousand dollars, if lost, would not cripple the K-Bar-K, there was the matter of his own pride. He had come to Sioux Wells to collect on the loss of the cattle, and his mission was public knowledge. J. K. Tolliver had cleverly placed him in a rather untenable position. He could throw up his hands and leave Sioux Wells admitting his defeat. Or he could follow his pride.

He raised his voice a trifle to make sure that whoever was listening could hear clearly. "I might try this," he said, "on one condition. The money is to be paid to Brandy Ben Keech, win or lose."

"What do you mean, win or lose?" Niles demanded.

"You know what I mean. From what you just told me these outlaws play for keeps. They've wrecked trains, murdered men. They tried to kill Hickok last night. They missed. They won't always miss."

"But that's the beauty of our plan," Niles said. "You're going to try to be one of them. An enemy of the Rocky."

"Beauty is the wrong word," Zack said. "Skunk might come closer to it. But you heard my terms. The Rocky pays my father, win or lose. I'll try to give them their money's worth. Being a spy sort of leaves a bad taste in me, but everything's fair in dealing with cutthroats."

Niles coughed, clearing his throat. "Pardon me a moment," he said. "I seem to be picking up a cold. I've got some tablets around somewhere."

He arose and entered the inner room, closing the door behind him. He returned after a few minutes. "I've thought it over," he said. "All right. Your father will be paid, win or lose—provided, of course, that we are satisfied that you have given us an honest effort."

Zack was sure beyond all doubt that Niles' superior was in the inner office and had given the word to go ahead. There could be many reasons why J. K. Tolliver did not want to appear in public in Sioux Wells, but the main one, no doubt, was that the railroad president did not want to become a target of the highbinders as Hickok had been.

Niles extended a hand. "It's a deal, then?"

Zack accepted it. Niles' grip was strong, very strong. He was a bigger man than Zack had believed. He was as tall as Zack himself and handled himself with the poise of a man who kept in trim and took pride in his physique. In spite of himself Zack was thinking of the Miss Smith with the snapping dark eyes. Only a strong man, educated, poised, such as Frank Niles, would interest a girl who had proved that she was no weakling herself the day she had drawn the derringer to back up her grandmother in the matter of the wounded antelope.

"Just how will we go about this?" Zack asked. "Any ideas as to the best way to weasel into the confidence of these train wreckers?"

"You've already made a good start at proving you've got no use for this railroad," Niles said. "I'd say your best path is to continue along that line. Convince everyone that you have every reason to hold a grudge against the Rocky."

"Build up a feud?"

"Exactly. We might add fuel to the flames right now. Everybody in town knows by this time that you came to my office this morning for a showdown. It's my bet that half of the town is waiting to see what happens. Let's give them a run for their money. What if this talk ended up in anger and threats of vengeance?"

Niles, not waiting for an answer, took the initiative. "And I tell you, sir, that I will not sit here and be threatened!" he shouted. "I must ask you to leave at once."

Zack got to his feet, taking his cue. "You'll be the sorriest man in Sioux Wells before I'm through with you, Niles," he thundered. "And so will the Rocky."

"I'm not armed!" Niles howled. "You wouldn't shoot an unarmed man, would you? If its a gunfight you want, I'm willing to oblige. I left my weapon at my home. Give me a chance to arm myself."

Zack thought this was carrying it a little too far. He kicked his chair against a wall with an impact that undoubtedly could be heard in the waiting room below. "No you don't, Niles," he said. "I want only the money that's coming to me. Don't try to fix it so that you can get some of your railroad gunmen to shoot me."

He stamped out of the office, slamming the door back of him. Jenny, the plump secretary, was just returning with a cloth-covered tray containing the breakfast Niles had ordered. Zack lifted the tray from her hands and hurled it against a wall.

Dishes shattered amid the debris of eggs and steak. Coffee streaked the wall and floor. Zack headed for the stairs with Jenny uttering weak moans of dismay. Niles shouted furious threats that were not all faked, for he was staring angrily at his ruined breakfast.

Descending the stairs to the waiting room, Zack found himself facing a lake of startled faces. He barged roughly among them, shouldering men aside. Reaching the outer platform, he was confronted by a different type.

Railroad men were gathering. Brawny brakemen,

switchmen, oilers, firemen, section hands. More men were leaving the repair shops at a distance and were racing to join the gathering. The word had spread. It occurred to Zack that it had spread too rapidly. It was as though the railroad's employees had expected that his talk with Niles would end in a declaration of war, and they were more than ready for it. Here was the man who had knocked out their champion, and they believed it had been a lucky punch. They were out to humiliate Zack, not only because of the raw wound to their pride, but because they were railroad men and Zack was a cowboy—an alien.

Zack found his path blocked by muscular men, some in greasy jumpers, some in the rough garb of section hands. "If'n he's a cowboy," someone shouted. "Let's see how he can ride. Fetch a crosstie, boys."

Howls of agreement arose. Men went racing off the platform to where a stack of crossties was stored. They lifted one of the ties and came hurrying back.

Zack moved to a wall, stood with his back against it. He had a hunch that all this had been planned beforehand—by Niles, no doubt, in order to add fuel to the appearance of a feud. But it was carrying the scheme too far. The mob meant business. It was being egged on by half a dozen loud-voiced, hard-eyed men who were heavily armed. Zack doubted if they were railroad men, although they wore striped caps and checked shirts. However, instead of brogans they had on high-heeled saddle-boots.

He had not drawn his six-shooter. He knew that to do so might change the situation. At the moment the members of the group were only in a mood to humiliate him. Bloodshed might change their temper and they would become a lynch mob.

Then he spotted Stan Durkin. The big, redheaded man, evidently no worse for wear, was standing at the back of the circle that ringed Zack in. He was taking no part in the taunting and profanity, but neither was he making any attempt to intervene

Zack singled him out. He lifted his voice so that he could be heard above the jeering. "Durkin! You, there! Your pals seem to think I was lucky yesterday. Maybe they'd like for you to have a second chance. I'm willing to give you another try."

Durkin straightened, bristling. Then he seemed to have a second thought. "I wouldn't want to rob the boys of their fun, cowpoke," he said. "They still want to see if you can ride a rail."

A new voice broke in. A feminine voice. "Surely, Mr. Durkin, you're not afraid of this Texas lout are you? You ought to be able to put him in his place without trouble, being as you're a railroad man."

The speaker was the comely Miss Smith. Apparently she had just entered the station from the door that faced on Railroad Street. She wore a neat, short-sleeved white dress and had a handbag dangling from an arm.

She also had command of the situation. She looked at the group that surrounded Zack. "Never let it be said that it takes twenty railroad men to lick one cowboy. It would be a blot on the honor of Sioux Wells forever."

Stan Durkin was palpably flattered at being singled out as a champion by such an attractive creature. He began to swell with importance and with the realization that he had a chance to redeem himself and quench his thirst for vengeance on Zack.

"Afraid!" Durkin roared scornfully, and came pushing through the group to face Zack. "Me, afraid of the likes of this saddle bum? He was lucky yesterday. Such luck can't last a second time. Put up your dukes, Texas."

Frank Niles descended the stairs from his office and joined the dark-haired girl. A self-satisfied smile tugged at the corners of Niles' mouth. That clinched Zack's belief that Niles had arranged this beforehand, even to the threat of the rail-riding. No doubt it was part of the scheme to build him up as a bitter foe of the railroad, but there were features of the confrontation that were puzzling. The majority of the men who were jeering him were railroad men, beyond question, but he could not shake off the belief that the real ringleaders were from a different stratum.

However, if it had been staged, Stan Durkin evidently had not been aware of it. He stood with fists poised in a boxing attitude before Zack. "This time I'm going to beat you to a froth," he promised. "Stand back, boys. Give me room to operate."

The group hastily moved back, forming a circle. Stan Durkin moved in on Zack. He was wary this time. Very wary. It was evident he hadn't forgotten the impact of the one blow Zack had landed the previous day. He began retreating, feinting, dancing aside, ducking. He was trying to lure Zack into making a rush, intending to trap him off balance.

Zack moved. He faked a rush and Durkin fell for it. Durkin jabbed eagerly with a long left, his right fist poised for a smash to the jaw. Zack let him start that intended knockout swing, let it whiz past harmlessly.

Then he swung his right. The same blow he had struck the previous day, on the same jaw. And with the same result.

Whack! Stan Durkin collapsed at the knees and pitched forward into Zack's arms to be lowered gently to the floor.

Zack looked around at the bystanders. Once again complete, unbelieving silence reigned.

The girl with the snapfinger eyes was the first to speak. "Holy cow!" she gasped. "Not again!"

Zack blew on his knuckles. "I don't believe we've ever been introduced, miss," he said. "I go by the name of Zachary Keech. From Round Butte, Texas. That's down in the Brazos River country."

He lifted his hat. "And you?" he asked.

"My name is Smith," she said. "Anita Smith. Congratulations seem to be in order again. And here's something else by which to remember me."

She lifted a slipper and once more stamped it down on his foot. Luckily it was the left foot this time. Zack's right foot was still tender from the event of the previous day.

Zack reeled to a wall, nursing the injured foot. "Miss, you *are* a hard loser," he mumbled.

"Indeed I am," she said grimly.

"I'll be careful in the future not to get within stompin' distance," Zack said. "Just why are you so down on Texas folks? Did someone from down our way do you dirt at one time or another?"

She started to answer that, then thought better of it. She turned away and took the arm of Frank Niles.

"My advice to you, Keech," Niles said, "is to take the next train out of town. There's nothing in Sioux Wells for you. Good day, sir."

He walked away with Anita Smith clinging to his arm.

Chapter 5

Men were bringing water and dousing it on Stan Durkin. Zack lingered until certain Durkin had suffered no serious injury. Then he left the depot, walking through the scattering drift of spectators who were now returning to their various pursuits. The ringleaders of the gathering had faded into the background.

The day was turning blazing hot again and Zack walked into the first saloon, moved to the bar and ordered a mug of beer. The barkeeper, who had entered just ahead of him after having been among the onlookers at the brief encounter in the depot, moved with haste to fill the order, so much so that he overfilled the mug, loosening a foaming Niagara across the bar top.

Other men came crowding into the place in Zack's wake, giving it the biggest rush of patronage at this hour of the day in its history. Zack, embarrassed, and trying to ignore it, was the center of all eyes, and most of those eyes were envious. One man even had the temerity to hurriedly place a hand on Zack's biceps. "What muscle!" the man said admiringly.

Others might have attempted the same thing, but a sudden hush came, a taut stillness. A new arrival had entered the saloon. A path magically opened for him.

The arrival was Wild Bill Hickok. The badge was pinned to a suspender. He stood at a short distance from Zack, staring with his sad eyes for a space. "Sunup," he said. "Be long gone from Sioux Wells come daylight tomorrow, Keech, or I'll be lookin' for you. Two fist-

59

fights, two insults to a lady, a try to have me killed and bein' mixed up in a hotel-room brawl all in twenty-four hours has tried my patience. Sunup."

Zack couldn't believe it. Hickok had been friendly to the point of fatherliness only a short time earlier. Now he was pronouncing that sentence that men had learned not to ignore. Deadline!

Zack felt the cold chill of the presence of sudden death. He could not understand this sudden change in the attitude of the marshal. He knew that men around them were suddenly crowding away to safer distance. He stood facing Hickok, still frozen by that inner knowledge that a wrong move might be his last.

Then he believed he understood. Once more it was all stage setting, melodramatic fakery. Like his feigned quarrel with Frank Niles this was to build him up further as an enemy of law and order—and of the railroad.

He turned away, pushed men aside, walked out of the saloon and headed down the sidewalk to the Traveler's Rest. Mounting to his room he unlocked the door, entered and locked the door back of him. The heat of the day gripped the room. He hung his hat on a peg, pulled off his boots and stretched out on the bed, trying to think.

He was confused. He was unable to decide where the stage play started and stopped and where he had faced reality. The threat of rail-riding had been very real. And his second encounter with Stan Durkin had not been prearranged. His aching wrist and hand assured him of that. His hand had taken real punishment.

He watched a fly make its erratic way across the ceiling. He was trying to decide whether to go through with this. By this time the K-Bar-K herd should be fifty or sixty miles up the trail—barring further obstacles such as the one that had got him involved with the Rocky Mountain Express. He was asking himself if he had not made a mistake in trying to force his claim on a railroad that already had deep trouble.

A hand tapped softly on the door, obviously being careful not to attract attention elsewhere. He got off the bed and lifted his six-shooter from the holster on the wall peg. "Who is it?" he called.

"Open," a muffled voice said. It was a feminine voice, and that voice belonged to the one who called herself Anita Smith. Zack hesitated. Anita Smith, if that was her real name, had proved that she was far from enthusiastic about his presence in Sioux Wells.

"Who's with you?" he demanded.

"Nobody. Open this door, you fool." That was Anita Smith, beyond a doubt. Headstrong, sassy.

He opened the door, still cautious. She pushed it wide open, sending him staggering. She slipped inside the room and locked the door while he regained his balance.

"You *are* very awkward, aren't you?" she commented. "And suspicious. Did you think I was bringing a posse to ride you on a rail?"

"Now I don't want to get into any fuss with you," Zack raged.

She lifted a warning finger to her lips. "Please speak softly. You are not bellowing at a herd of cattle. I have very good hearing. Furthermore, you know what it might do to my reputation if it became known I was here."

"How about my rep?" Zack replied. "And no stomping on my feet. I haven't even got boots on to protect me right now." In spite of himself he was obeying her warning to lower his voice so that it could not be heard beyond the door.

"My, my!" she said. "You do handle the language nicely. I thought all Texans talked like they had sand burs under their tongues."

Zack glared at her, but she did not wilt. "What do you want?" he demanded.

"Want? How fantastic. I only came here to give you some advice."

"Now that's mighty considerate of you," Zack said. "Of course, if I needed any such, you would be the very last person I'd apply to."

"Don't make rash statements," she said. "I came to tell you that, if you are smart, you should get out of Sioux Wells as fast as you can."

Zack eyed her for a long space in a silence during which he could hear the ticking of his watch which he had laid on the bureau.

"It seems like a lot of folks don't want me around here," he said. "First Hickok, then that Niles fella. Now you. It doesn't happen that all of you are interested in getting rid of me and that six-thousand-dollar claim I've got against the railroad?"

"Perhaps," she said. "But there could be other reasons."

He was remembering that he had seen Hickok coming from the suite occupied by Granny Smith and this girl the previous afternoon.

"How long have you called yourself by that name, Anita Smith?" he asked abruptly.

She arched her brows. "Why, everyone in Sioux Wells knows my name. Are you insinuating that I'm traveling under false colors?"

"I'm saying it out loud."

"And too loud," she murmured. "I came here to ask you to stay out of all this. Money isn't worth it. Six thousand dollars isn't worth your life."

"So that *is* it!" Zack said harshly. "It's the railroad that sent you to try to spook me. It was your fine friend, Frank Niles, who put you up to this, wasn't it? He only wants to get rid of me and my claim against his railroad. What will you get out of this?"

She glared at him, anger pushing a pink tide into her cheeks. "I sized you up as being intelligent, but you're only being pigheaded," she said. "Well, you've been warned. That's all I can do."

She turned, opening the door to leave. "Wait!" Zack exclaimed. "I want to know more about—?"

"About my private life?" she said. "About Frank Niles? That's none of your concern."

She was gone, closing the door after her.

He heard her move down the hall, heard the door of the suite at the front open and close. Then silence. He locked his door again and stretched out on the bed once more. He tried to figure out this new puzzle. The big question was: Who is this Anita Smith and what is her purpose in warning him to pick up his marbles and quit the game? She was a puzzle indeed. And so was her grandmother. Zack believed Anita Smith had not come here voluntarily. She had been sent by someone, and that someone might have been the wispy, gray-haired sharp-tongued grandmother.

He tried to look at it from every angle, including this new phase. There were a multitude of angles, it seemed, each with a sharp corner that could wound. Or even kill!

That thought aroused him. He gazed around and found that anyone peering from the tops of buildings that stretched ragged down Railroad Street from the hotel might have a view of him here in broad daylight.

He moved hastily to correct this, remembering the Ogallala Kid and Matt Pecos. And there was Stan Durkin, of course, who had reason to hold a real grudge against him, but Durkin, at the moment at least, could hardly be expected to be in shape to notch a fine sight on a target at that distance.

As he moved, the bullet came. It shattered glass in

the window. Much glass. The window was of the sash type, with the lower half raised for ventilation. The bullet tore through both panes, littering with glistening shards both the floor and the bed where Zack had been reclining.

Zack crouched, snatching his six-shooter from the holster on the wall. He crawled to the window, peering. The bright sun of early afternoon was in his eyes. The sheet iron and tarpaper and shingled roofs of Sioux Wells baked peacefully in the sun. What powder smoke there might have been had been dissipated swiftly by the brisk plains wind. What windows were in sight looked back at him vacantly.

The shrill voice of a woman sounded. It was the large, frizzle-haired woman, Gussie Bluebell, who had castigated Ed Hake the time of the water tank shooting. She was leaning from the windows of the Good Time.

"More trouble at the hotel!" she was screeching. "A shootin' this time. Where's Hickok? Can't he keep law an' order to this town? I declare, its' nothin' but fightin' in the street, shootin' up water tanks an' brawls at the hotel."

Footsteps came pounding to his door. Zack, careful to stay out of line of fire through the window, turned the key and opened the door. It was about the same group of guests and loungers who had come up from the lobby as had gathered here the day before The same turkey-necked desk clerk, who was also the owner.

Anita Smith also appeared, wide-eyed. She looked at Zack and there was an I-told-you-so expression in her face. She seemed greatly upset, and also thankful to find him uninjured. With her was Julia Smith who looked as though she had been interrupted at her knitting. In fact, she still carried the knitting. There was one exception to this picture of peaceful demeanor. Zack was positive he saw Granny Smith conceal a weapon beneath the knitting in her hands. It was a business-looking six-shooter.

"You again?" the hotel owner raged, staring aghast at the shattered glass. "How did this happen?"

"If you've got any notion that I shot them out just for fun, then get another notion," Zack said. "How in blazes do you think it happened? It wasn't done by kids throwing stones, you can take my word for that."

He moved to a wall, drew out his pocket-knife and dug a spent bullet from the plaster. "A .45," he said. "Not much help there. Half the population carries that gun."

"I'm asking you to leave my establishment," the hotel man thundered. He added hastily, "The cost for the windows will be two dollars."

Zack turned bleak eyes on the man. "In the first place, you miser, I doubt if fixing them will cost much more than half that. In the second place, I'm staying here until I decide to leave."

"That won't be any too soon," the man said. "At least I'll be rid of you before too many hours. I hear that Wild Bill has deadlined you. Even Hickok is tired of you and the brawls and shootings you've been in. And I want you to know that, as an honest Sioux Wells business man, you are less than welcome here."

"He's a saddle bum!" It was Granny Smith who spoke from the background. "Just a ruffian. I hear he even had the gall to threaten the superintendent of the railroad here about some foolish claim he is trying to press about a few cows he says were lost down the country."

Here it was again. The case of Zack Keech against the beneficent Rocky Mountain Express upon whose payrolls the majority of the population of Sioux Wells depended. Granny Julia Smith had drilled into a very live nerve with her interference in the discussion. Zack once more felt alone, facing the hostility of a community.

Once again it was Hickok who arrived and calmed

the angry waters. He looked at Zack with his pale, un-readable eyes, looked at the broken panes. "Did you see where the shot came from?" he asked.

"No," Zack said. "Maybe Gussie Bluebell did. She was the first to begin yowling."

"I'll talk to her," Hickok said. "Looks like I ought to shorten your stay in Sioux Wells. For your own sake if nothin' else. If you pulled out of town pronto, everybody might feel better about it. I mean pronto."

"I don't pronto very fast under these circumstances," Zack said. "Somebody just took a shot at me. Maybe he'll try again. That might give me a chance to drive a nail in his coffin."

Hickok shrugged. "Have it your way." He looked at the hotel owner. "Did I hear you tryin' to make this cowboy pay for these busted windows, Jud?" he asked. "Why?"

"I figger he shot 'em out himself," the man said. "Just to bring attention to him. He seems to like such."

"Now you know that ain't right, Jud Gregg," Hickok said mildly. "That bullet came from outside an' you know it. Otherwise the glass would have been scattered in the other direction. It's a case of damage at the hands of persons unknown an' you could hardly hold Keech responsible. I say to drop the subject."

"Just as you say, Marshal," Jud Gregg agreed hastily. "Just as you say."

"Otherwise, I'll run you in for makin' a false claim for damages," Hickok continued in his soft voice. "An' give you a boot under the coat tail in addition, for tryin' to take advantage of a guest in your hotel."

"I advise you not to skyline yourself while you arrange to leave town," he added, addressing Zack. "You've rubbed the fur of a lot of people the wrong way. Stay away from windows. Mind me now."

Hickok left, descending to the lobby. No sound came

back. Zack noticed with the annoyance of a man proud of his own poise that the stairs, which squeaked unmercifully under the tread of himself and other persons, gave forth no sound beneath Hickok's boots.

Jud Gregg left also, grumbling. The others drifted away. Granny Smith and her deadly bundle of knitting vanished into her quarters down the hall along with her granddaughter, who gave Zack a glance back over her shoulder—a glance that he believed bore concern for him.

An Indian woman appeared with broom and dustpan and swept up the broken glass. After she had left, Zack moved the bed out of range of the window. He wedged a chair under the doorknob to reinforce security, and placed his pistol on the stand within reach.

He stretched out on the bed, trying to think. Suddenly, he sat up and leaped from the bed. He moved to the gouge in the plaster where the bullet had imbedded, and lined it up with the approximate spot where the slug had crashed through the panes of glass.

He stood rubbing his chin in perplexity. He had a new problem to add to the rosary of problems over which he kept mulling. The bullet had passed at least four feet from him and a foot higher than his head. The marksman could hardly have been that poor a shot, which meant that he had made sure of missing by a wide margin.

Zack resumed his recumbent position on the bed, trying to fit this new piece of the puzzle in with all the hectic events that had dogged him almost from the moment he had stepped off the train at Sioux Wells.

He did not know that he had fallen asleep until a cooling breeze was moving through the empty frames of the window. The sun had gone down and the first lamps were being lighted in the town.

He was chagrined. "Somebody might have got in here

and cut your throat and you'd never have found it out," he told his reflection in the small mirror.

Inasmuch as he likely wouldn't have another chance to take advantage of the ultra-modern bathing facilities down the hall, he made his way there with towel and soap that he ordered from the flunky, and his razor. He had shaved that morning before going to court, but his dark beard was already roughening his lean jaws. Ordinarily he wouldn't have endured the nuisance of running a razor over his face twice in a day, but he went through the routine again and was very critical of the effect in the mirror above the washbasin, vaguely lighted by an oil lamp.

He showered, dressed and redid his string tie three times before he was partly satisfied with the result. He combed his thick hair with great care. He wouldn't admit to himself the real reason for all this extra grooming even while he was walking down the hall to the door at the front—the door back of which he expected to find the beautiful Anita Smith.

He was successful, up to that point. It was she who opened the door after he had finally steeled himself to tap on the panel. That had taken a little time. He had poised his knuckles four or five times above the panel, only to panic and stand motionless and perspiring a little as though some force had paralyzed his arm.

She stood looking at him with an inquiring smile. A cool, knowing, feminine smile. It came to him with freezing embarrassment that she must have been aware that he had stood there at the closed door for seconds, fighting the urge to retreat in disorder. A wise smile it was, the smile of one who was sure of herself and her power over him.

"Well, this *is* a surprise," she said. "Zachary Taylor is the name, I believe."

"Keech," Zach croaked. "Zachary Keech. Zachary Taylor was President a long ways back."

"Of course," she purred. "How could I have got it so wrong after the way you've turned this town upside down? You have become famous."

Zack waved that aside. He didn't want to talk about the past. He had removed his hat. He dropped it accidentally on the floor. He lunged to pick it up and butted his head against the door jamb. He straightened, beet-red. The girl was smiling coolly as though all this was only to be expected on his part.

"Can I do something for you?" she asked. "A cold, damp cloth on the head, perhaps? You might be developing a lump there."

Zack grinned. Somehow he felt suddenly at ease. "No bump," he said. "Skull's too thick. So's the brain."

Her smile changed. It matched a sudden intuitive feeling that between himself and this dazzling creature was an understanding.

"Affairs have been rather quiet with you lately, I imagine," she said. "It's been several hours since you've been shot at or have knocked out Stan Durkin. It must be monotonous. Are you here to try to stir up excitement?"

"Something like that," Zack said. "I likely will be stomped on again for being forward, not knowing you very well, but down in Texas we learn that if you don't throw your loop mighty quick and sudden, you'll never rope a steer."

"Or a heifer," she said.

Zack eyed her with growing respect. "Now, who'd ever guess that you'd know the difference."

"You'd be surprised at how many facts of life I'm acquainted with," she said. "Now, just what, or who, did you come here to catch in your loop?"

"I don't know what Sioux Wells has to offer in the way of eating places that would appeal to folks like you and your grandma," Zack said, "but I noticed one named the Delmonico that had the earmarks of being respectable and clean. I'm hoping that you and Mrs. Smith would do me the honor of having supper with me."

He saw that she was starting to refuse. "I promise not to get into any more trouble while I'm with you ladies, and will keep away from windows," he added hastily. "I imagine this place could serve up a beefsteak, or at least buffalo or antelope that might—"

Granny Smith's voice spoke from somewhere in the room. "Beef! That's my pick. Sticks to your ribs. I've had enough of buffalo hump and goat meat in my time."

Anita Smith hesitated. Zack believed the regret in her face was genuine. "I'm sorry," she said, "but we have a previous engagement for the evening."

Zack stood, fiddling with his hat. "Well, I missed," he said.

"Try again, sonny," Granny said, without appearing in person. Then she added as an afterthought, "Oh, I forgot. You won't be around long. I hear Bill Hickok has deadlined you."

"I'll be around until I decide to hit the trail on my own decision," Zack said.

"Good luck," Granny said. "You'll need it. 'Specially if you keep on tryin' to buck both Bill Hickok an' the Rocky. So long, sonny. Better to have loved and lost than never to have loved at all."

"Grandma!" the girl exclaimed, her composure fractured for the first time. "That's no way to talk."

"Heck, it was just a figure of speech," the invisible Granny snorted. "I don't put no stock in this love at first sight hocus-pocus. After all, you two only laid eyes on each other just lately, an' have been at sword's point ever since."

"For *goodness* sake, *will* you be quiet," her granddaughter demanded.

Zack found himself suddenly master of the situation and in a position to square up for several things, such as being stamped on. "I only came here to ask for company to supper," he said. "I didn't figure I was proposing marriage."

Anita Smith glared at him, her lips tightening. "Well, I never!" she exploded. "You *are* a barbarian, aren't you?"

Zack backed out of reach. "I don't aim to have another toe mashed," he said. "I'll say good evening, ladies. I hope I have better luck next time."

He turned away and Anita Smith slammed the door shut. Faint words came from beyond the panel. He knew she and Granny were engaged in heated talk, but he did not linger to attempt to eavesdrop.

He made his way down the hall toward the stairs that led to the lobby. As he reached it he encountered a man who was ascending. The arrival was Frank Niles. He wore a natty dark cutaway coat and trousers that matched the derby that was perched on his head. A polka-dot cravat carried a pearl stickpin. He bore the fresh aroma of barber's bay rum and hair oil.

Zack could not explain why he took the next step. It was perhaps because he understood that Frank Niles was arriving to escort Anita Smith and probably Granny out to supper. This was the previous engagement she had mentioned, no doubt.

He grasped Niles' derby by its curled brim and jammed it down over its wearer's ears. For an instant both he and Niles were stunned by this unexpected turn of events.

Then Niles, with a snarl of fury, wrenched the ruined derby from his head. "Why you . . . !" he frothed.

He started swinging with both fists. This was not play-acting as part of the plan to build up the feigned feud between Zack and the railroad company. This was the real thing.

Zack weathered that first flurry, but was forced to

come to close quarters. Wedged on the narrow stairway between the rail and the wall they could do little but claw and maul at each other for a moment. Niles teetered back, losing his balance. He grasped Zack's arms as he fell and carried him along as he plunged backward down the stairs, the two of them rolling over and over.

The stairs stood up under the punishment and they reached the floor of the lobby with Zack underneath. Niles rammed a knee into his stomach, driving from him what little breath he had left. He retaliated by managing a left uppercut with his only free arm to Niles' throat. That caused Niles to weaken enough for him to twist free.

They got to their feet and went at each other with the primal ferocity of two evenly matched males who were not too sure what they were fighting over, except that they had known from the first moment they met that they had little use for each other and now was the time to prove their dislike.

Three or four of the customary idlers had occupied the two rocking chairs and the sofa in the lobby. They scattered like quail as the avalanche descended and the two antagonists came battling among them. One, too slow to escape, fell, and avoided being trampled underfoot only by rolling and crawling free, squeaking in terror.

Hotel manager Jud Gregg, horror-stricken, came timorously from the shelter of his counter. "Stop it!" he quavered. "Stop it this instant! You're wrecking—"

It ended in a groan as the two men, swinging wildly at close quarters, fell over one of the rocking chairs. The chair disintegrated.

Niles seized up a rocker to which clung one of the legs and attempted to bring it down on Zack's head. The unwieldy weapon missed, and Zack landed a short right to the body—the same right that had twice leveled Stan Durkin. But it lacked steam after these hectic moments of supreme activity. However, the blow still had enough authority to drive Niles staggering back against the counter which Jud Gregg had just deserted.

The counter toppled. The ledger, which contained the names of guests, fell amid the clatter of pens, inkstands and handbills. Jud Gregg uttered another moan of horror. "Stop it!" he wept.

Niles picked up the ink bottle, which was a hefty object made of glass, and hurled it at Zack. Zack ducked and the bottle shattered one of the large front window panes. Ink was splattered over the ceiling and walls. Jud Gregg covered his eyes.

"Someone get Hickok!" he implored.

A gunshot roared in the room. Dust gusted up from the floor near the feet of the struggling men. "You fools!" an authoritative voice snapped. "Stop it, before I put a slug where it'll hurt."

Zack and Niles quit a combat that had reached the point of futility, due to sheer exhaustion. Gunplay was not in the mind of either man. What they sought was physical victory. Zack was beginning to feel utterly foolish for having started this. He was entirely to blame. He admitted that. No self-respecting man would have reacted any other way than had Niles to the affront.

He backed away from Niles. He discovered that the gunshot had not come from Wild Bill Hickok. There was no sign of Hickok. The street windows were lined with pop-eyed citizens, peering into the lobby. The stairs were packed with spectators who had come from the guest rooms or by way of the rear outer stairs.

In the forefront of the group on the stairs stood Granny Julia Smith. She held in her hand a wicked-looking, snub-nosed pistol. The powder smoke from the shot was still coiling up the stairway.

"What in blue blazes started all this?" she demanded.

"This fellow insulted me," Frank Niles panted. "He's

been asking for trouble with me because I'm in charge of the railroad's business here."

Blood dripped from Niles' nose, staining his fine garb. One sleeve of his tailored coat was ripped. His hair was matted with perspiration and gore, some of which had come from Zack who had a gashed cheekbone and other bruises.

Niles said to Zack, "I'll kill you the next time."

There was ferocity in the man, a cold savagery that appalled Zack, and brought him up alert and ready for anything.

Hickok arrived, jostling spectators aside and forcing his way into the lobby. He looked at Niles. "My God, Frank!"

He turned to Zack. He lifted his eyes upward as though appealing to a higher power. "All right," he said in a strained voice. "This will cost you fifty dollars tomorrow, not to mention maybe thirty days working on the road gang. There'll be damages to this hotel in addition."

"Sorry, Marshal," Zack said. "As I recall it, you told me to dust out of here before sunup."

"I'll see to it that you stay a little longer," Hickok said. "Who started this?"

"I did," Zack said.

"Naturally," Hickok sighed. "How and why?"

"I didn't like the way his hat fitted him. He sort of resented it, and that's how it went."

"Is that all there was to it, Frank?" Hickok demanded.

"There's a little more to it than that," Niles said. "He made threats this morning when he came to my office and demanded that I fork over a lot of money for some cattle that he claims were killed because of the railroad. He admitted that not one cow was hit by our rolling stock and that they died in a stampede which he claims was caused by one of our trains. He ignored the fact that the cattle should not have been held so near our right-of-way. It's my guess they were held there deliberately, just so they could put in a false claim against us."

"They were there because we couldn't prod them into crossing your blasted track," Zack said.

Granny Julia Smith intervened. "Better go see a saw-bones and get that cut on your face taken care of, cow-poke," she said. "Looks like it needs some stitchin'. As for you, Mr. Niles, I think me an' my granddaughter can take care of that nose. It don't look like it's busted. Come with us. I've got medicine an' court plaster."

"I'll go along with you," Hickok said to Zack. "It looks like I better keep a closer eye on you. I never saw anybody what could get into more trouble in a hurry. Now you've about wrecked a hotel."

"Who's goin' to pay for this?" Jud Gregg howled. "Look at this lobby, Marshal! That window alone will cost ten dollars, if a cent. Two busted chairs. My counter wrecked, papers scattered and tromped on. Who's—?"

"You'll be paid, Jud," Hickok said. "Quit yowlin'."

Hickok led Zack out of the Traveler's Rest and headed down the sidewalk. Once they were out of hearing of others, the marshal snarled, "You sort of overdid it, cow-boy. You really didn't have to pick a brawl with Frank Niles to prove your point did you?"

"Point?"

Hickok glared at him. "Have you forgot you can get your cattle money by trying to get the goods on these highbinders? You've already made yourself unpopular enough with railroad people without pickin' a fight with Niles. You tried to make his face over. Niles is on our side. Your side."

Zack was holding a handkerchief to his dripping injury. "He's a lot tougher man than Stan Durkin," he commented. "Fact is I was mighty glad when that old lady interfered. I wonder who she is? I've seen trail bosses that were milk and water compared to her. Did you see that gun she fired? You'd be surprised at other things I happen to know about her."

"Nothin' would surprise me from now on," Hickok said. "Here's Doc Appleton's office. It's unlocked. Likely he's over at the Ox Yoke, playin' monte. I'll round him up."

"Why did you fake that shot at me in my room this afternoon?" Zack asked.

Hickok smiled. "So you knew it was me? I just wanted to find out somethin'."

"And did you?"

"Maybe. Most people, if they had any sense, would have cleared out of town after bein' shot at, or been jumped with clubs like you've been. I wanted to know if you'd stampede."

Hickok walked away then. Zack waited in the doctor's office until the marshal returned with the pudgy, bulbous-nosed medic who was testy at being called away from the monte table.

Zack, his injuries doctored and court plastered, paid the two-dollar fee and left with Hickok "I'll see you in court in the mornin'," the marshal said.

"I thought you might throw me in jail," Zack said.

"Jail's full. If I was you, I'd spend the evenin' at the Good Time."

"The Good Time? That'd be the last place I'd want—"

"For what you've got in mind, I figure that's a fine place to hang around tonight," Hickok said.

"I see," Zack answered. Reluctantly, he took the marshal's advice and headed for the bawdy music hall alone.

Chapter 6

The Good Time was attempting to live up to its name. A four-piece band consisting of a trumpeter, a clarinet, a drummer and an ump-ah tuba, came to life occasionally and beat out deafening sounds that went for music. Now and then a girl in tights offered song and dance numbers on a small stage set at an angle in a corner. A tiny dance floor was available for those who bought tickets for the privilege of struggling around the enclosure with one of the girls. Between times a mechanical piano kept the pace going.

The Good Time was busy. It was a large wooden structure with tinsel hanging from the beams, and posts bearing advertisement from breweries and distilleries.

Zack bought a mug of beer at the bar. The beer was pleasingly cold. "We git ice by the carload from Omaha, mister," a barkeeper informed him. "This here is the classiest emporium between Chicago an' Frisco, if you ask me, an' I've seen 'em all."

Zack carried his mug to a table that had just gone vacant, and at which there was no gambling and took one of the chairs. He expected company, which was the rule in places like this, and he did not have to wait long. Also, as he had expected, the company was feminine. His uninvited table companion was the buxom, peroxide blonde whose head he had seen at a window above the day of the water tank episode.

"Howdy, cowboy," she said in a graveled voice as she gave him a slap on the shoulder and seated herself in

77

the nearest chair which she hitched closer. "What name do you go by?"

"Captain Kidd," Zack said. "And you?"

She threw back her head and laughed loudly. "I happen to know different," she said. "You've made a rep for yourself here in Sioux Wells in the last couple of days. Keech is your name and everybody in town knows it. As for me, you can call me Gussie."

"Gussie Bluebell?"

"You know me, cowboy? Now, I can't recall—"

"I was around when a buffalo hunter baptized you with a bullet through a water tank," Zack said. "Something tells me that was your first baptism."

Gussie Bluebell again threw back her head and shook the room with great laughter. She slapped him once more on the back. "So we're old acquaintances," she roared. She beckoned another girl who had been hovering close. "Two, Mabel," she said. "Old Kentucky straight. The best is none too good for this man here."

The drinks were brought.

"Here's to sin and the devil," she said, holding aloft her glass. "And to the Rocky Mountain Express. I hear they've kicked you around some."

Zack hesitated. Gussie Bluebell's bluff, coarse manner did not ring exactly true. Beneath the powder, rouge and peroxide she seemed to be a woman of forty, marked by lines of care rather than dissipation. He felt that she was studying him beneath that hail-fellow manner as though asking herself an urgent question.

"I'll drink to that," he said. He noticed that she barely touched the glass with her lips. She again pounded him on the shoulder, spilling the contents of her glass into the sawdust, apparently accidentally. "You look like my kind of man, cowboy," she said.

Then a cool, authoritative voice said, "Hello, Texas man. Good evening, Gussie."

Gussie was replaced at the table so swiftly and expertly that Zack blinked. Evidently Gussie knew better than to protest, for she moved away to give her attention to other patrons.

The new arrival was neither coarse-voiced, blonde nor dressed in spangles. She was good-looking, very much so and was considerably younger than Gussie, but still mature. She had coppery-red hair, very straight lips and green-flecked eyes. She had character—the character of a diamond. Wise, sophisticated, hard.

"Hello, Mr. Keech," she said. "Oh, yes, I know your name. You've become famous in the Wells lately. My name is Lila. Do you want another drink?"

"Lila what?" Zack said. "Let me guess. Lila Lilac? Or Lila Hyacinth. Or maybe Lila—"

"Any will do," she said, smiling. "To you, I'm just Lila. That's good enough, at least for now."

"Meaning our long friendship might not last?"

"I hope not. How about that drink?"

"I have a feeling I better keep my wits about me tonight," Zack said. "Are you Gussie's daughter, by any chance?"

She laughed. "Better not let Gussie hear a remark like that. She's not that old. Besides, she works for me."

"Works for you?"

"It happens that I own the Good Time," she said. "This is how I make my living." She saw him admiring the dark evening dress that she wore. It was rich and expensive in contrast to the tinseled, knee-length costumes the percentage girls had on. "It isn't too bad a living," she added. "But I want to do better."

Zack understood that he had been dropped a cue. "We all do," he said.

It *had* been a cue, and he apparently had given the right answer. "It's so noisy here," she said. "We can talk in my office without having to shout."

She arose and led the way down the length of the room through a rear door. Zack was aware that many curious eyes followed them, and some were envious. To the left was a small stage and a girl in tights was standing there awaiting the rise of the curtain to begin her song-and-dance number.

A stairway led to the second floor, and there was a rear door that evidently opened into the outdoors. Lila unlocked a door to the right which had painted on it the word Private.

It turned out to be a business office—and just that. A closed roll-top desk, filing cabinets and a slanting bookkeeping table with its high stool occupied the major part of the wall space. There were swivel chairs with worn leather cushions, cuspidors, a table bearing ash trays and a large iron safe. The floor was covered with faded green carpet. The stubs of cigars lay in the ash trays and the room carried the reek of recent smoking. Zack noticed the band on one of the half-smoked cigars that proclaimed it as an expensive make.

Lila had a twinkle in her eye as she watched him take in the drab surroundings. She seated herself at the closed desk and motioned him to take one of the swivel chairs. "You seem to have expected something else," she said. "This is really my office. I don't live at the Good Time."

Zack grinned. "I'm doubly glad I didn't take that second drink. Something tells me this is not a social event."

She glanced toward the door, making sure it was tightly closed. "We can talk freely here," she said. "The walls are padded with straw and double to kill sound. Even so, it will be best to keep our voices down."

"Seems like I've heard that before somewhere," Zack said. "Doesn't anybody trust anybody in this town?"

"Where did you hear it?"

"A little bird told me. What's the subject for tonight's discussion?"

"I understand you've had no luck with trying to squeeze money out of the Rocky," she said.

"None so far," Zack replied.

"Maybe you're not using the right approach."

Zack delayed his answer, trying to choose the right words. There was humming excitement within him. He was sure now what this was all about and why Hickok had advised him to spend his evening at the Good Time. The honky-tonk was apparently an important link in the outlaw organization, and this cool, handsome young woman might even be its head.

Their eyes met. She nodded. "You want money from the Rocky," she said. "I want money too. So do some of my friends. We intend to get it."

Zack debated whether to feel his way, or to rush in. He took the plunge and rushed. "From what I hear, some folks have already been cashing in pretty good."

"The hard way," she said. "Freight car robbing is hardscrabble, penny-ante stuff compared to other ways. Ladies underwear and washing machines and truck like that eat up all the profits peddling them."

Zack was of a notion to mention that stealing forty thousand dollars' worth of gold dust hardly could be listed as penny-ante profit, but decided against it.

She suddenly arose, moved to his side and kissed him. "That's only to seal the deal," she said.

She moved to the door, opened it and called a name so softly Zack could not catch it. Footsteps approached, and she ushered in a man. He was burly, garbed in the dungarees, striped cap and blue shirt of a railroad worker —with exceptions. He wore cowboots and carried a brace of six-shooters in holsters. His eyes were smoky dark, wise, without warmth. Zack remembered him. He had been the ringleader in the rail-riding demand at the depot the previous day.

"This is Jim Axel," she said. "The Ax. You'll enjoy knowing him better."

Zack doubted that. There was nothing particularly friendly in the inspection The Ax was making of him. The man finally shrugged, and said, "Come on, Keech."

Zack debated it. Prudence told him that he was wading into waters whose depth was unknown. Black waters. But, within him was a stubbornness, a humming anger at the arrogance of these people who were taking it for granted that he would do their bidding.

He made his decision and moved to leave the room with the swarthy man. Lila spoke. "One thing," she said. "From this point on, tall man, there is no turning back. Let that be understood."

Zack looked at her. "For either of us," he said.

The Ax led the way out of the Good Time by way of a rear door that avoided parading through the main gambling room before the eyes of patrons. They emerged into starlight. A prairie wagon, its weathered canvas tilt sagging drunkenly over the bows, stood nearby. A four-horse team stood in harness, the animals drowsily slapping at mosquitos with tails and twitching manes A bearded driver lolled on the seat, the reins wrapped around the whipstock. In the darkness, all that Zack could make out about the man was that he was garbed as a freighter. Like The Ax, he was heavily armed.

"We're goin' for a ride," The Ax said. He parted the ragged curtain that hung over the rear bow, and motioned for Zack to mount.

At that moment a commotion arose in the distance. The sounds came from the direction of the depot, which was not far from their position. "Git Hickok!" someone was shouting. "Fetch the marshal an' the coroner! My God! You ought to see *this!*"

"Let's take a look," Zack said. The Ax started to protest, but Zack was already on his way, and the man had no alternative but to follow. Zack walked to the street along a passageway between the Good Time and a neighboring building. Men were pouring from the music hall, and other citizens were passing by on the run, heading for the depot. Zack followed them. Hickok passed him, moving in long strides, and reached the scene ahead of him. He shouldered through the increasing press of onlookers.

A single night lamp in the waiting room gave light through the dingy windows. That vagueness was a blessing, hiding some of the horror of what lay at the feet of the staring arrivals.

Zack went cold to the marrow. It was the body of a man. He had been tortured. His body was naked, and the scars of the ordeal he had endured were ghastly visible.

"Injuns!" someone croaked.

Hickok knelt by the body and removed a paper that had been hung by a thong around the victim's neck. On it was a message printed in big letters:

HICKOK HERE'S YOUR SPY

"Not Indians," Hickok said. "White men."

His eyes lifted. The one he singled out was Zack. Then, quickly, the marshal turned away. But Zack had got the warning. Beyond a doubt, this was the missing man, known as Jimmy Broom, whom Hickok had brought in to attempt to get evidence against the train thieves.

Hickok had said that Jimmy Broom was his personal friend. Jimmy Broom had not died easily. There was no expression in the marshal's lined face, but he had the capacity for curbing his emotions, veiling them from public gaze.

"Who is he?" someone in the crowd asked.

Hickok did not respond, but the information was supplied by other bystanders. "He's been hangin' around town lately," someone volunteered. "A month or so. Ain't he the one that showed up, busted, an' lived on what money he could pick up out of the sawdust by swampin' an' sweepin' out at the Good Time? They called him Jimmy Broom, fer he always had a broom in his hand."

Zack saw that The Ax was drifting out of the circle. The Ax looked in his direction, and that was an order to follow. Zack hesitated, then left the group, acting as though he had seen enough of this horror. The Ax was ahead of him, and both drifted off the sidewalk into the darkness between buildings and returned to the waiting prairie wagon. Zack was remembering Lila's words that once he went with The Ax there would be no turning back. That would be doubly true, he realized, if he entered the wagon for the ride The Ax had mentioned.

Without a word he climbed into the interior of the wagon. The Ax joined him, the driver kicked the brake loose, spoke to the horses and the vehicle lurched into motion.

There were packing boxes aboard that served as seats. Zack tried one, but preferred to sit on the floor, wedging himself into place as best he could as the springless wagon jolted over rough going.

The Ax managed to roll a cigarette and get it lighted. The flare of the match accented the sardonic look on his tough face. His hair jutted like crow's wings from beneath the brim of his hat.

The wagon lurched ahead. The rear curtains swayed open with the motion of the vehicle, giving fleeting glimpses of their route. The wagon was following a traveled road southward out of Sioux Wells. It paralleled the railroad yards for a time, then swung away from the tracks. The Ax, who had chosen to place himself near the rear bow, seemed particularly interested in some object outside. Zack peered. What The Ax was looking at was a single railroad car that stood alone on a remote sidetrack, well removed from the clutter of boxcars and gondolas that cluttered the yards they were leaving.

The Ax became aware that Zack was gazing also. "Damned rich bugs," he growled. "Ride on velvet an' eat off gold plate while the likes of me sit in a stinkin' hide wagon."

Zack saw that the car glistened with varnish, and its platforms and windows were trimmed in polished brass. It was dark and silent, but he could see fine curtains at the windows.

"Who?" he asked.

"J. K. Tolliver, that's who," The Ax said. "It's the Tolliver private car. It's been settin' there for a month, waitin' fer his majesty to find time to use it. They say it cost a pretty penny to build."

"But I understood that the Rocky is scratching bottom," Zack said. "If they can afford a car like that they can afford to pay what they owe me."

"They'll pay you an' everybody else before this is over," The Ax promised.

The glittering palace car and the lights of Sioux Wells faded back of them as the wagon creaked along the wheeltrack that wound through the sea of buffalo grass which clung tightly to the earth, still hot from the day's sun. A pair of coyotes, sounding like a pack, lamented their passing with weird, shrilling chorus. The driver, on one occasion, aroused and said, "Bufflers! Half a dozen of 'em. They're gittin' scarce in these parts. I'll come back tomorrow an' git me some horns an' hides."

Zack began to doze. One thing he could tell The Ax for sure. J. K. Tolliver was already in Sioux Wells, secretly and under another name to avoid persons like Zack who were pressing claims, or creditors clamoring for money from the railroad.

He had been maneuvered into this by the invisible J. K. Tolliver in the hope of saving the Rocky Mountain

Express from bankruptcy. He was also being led by a Delilah who called herself Lila into pretending that he was joining the Rocky's enemies. He was being used by both sides. He was sure that it had all been too easy—this being invited to join the outlaws. They were either giving him rope to hang himself and suffer the same fate as had Jimmy Broom, or were using him for some other purpose he could not imagine.

He only knew that The Ax distrusted him, and would kill him, no doubt, if he made a wrong move. Lila probably would do the same. She posed as an important person in the outlaw setup, perhaps its head. He wondered if that were true. As for J. K. Tolliver, that individual was risking only money. And then there was William Butler Hickok. Zack was not sure just where the marshal stood in this arrangement. He had come stampeding into Sioux Wells to do battle with the Rocky Mountain Express, and now he was riding to some sort of a rendezvous with the outlaws who were preying on the railroad. The maneuvering had been done mainly by Wild Bill. It was Hickok who had talked him into trying to pull the Rocky's chestnuts out of the fire. It was Hickok who had dangled the six-thousand-dollar bait in front of him.

Then there were two persons named Smith who fitted into this somewhere, he was sure. But where? Grandma Julia and her gorgeous granddaughter were sailing under false colors. He was also sure of that. Were they working with the highbinders also?

The wagon jolted on hour after hour through the night. Zack tried to sleep, but failed. He had too many perplexing problems that kept rearing up, nagging him. He believed The Ax dozed occasionally. At times the driver would arouse to remind loafing horses that he held a whip or to curse chuckholes and condemn all prairie dogs to perdition.

The thud of hoofs became audible. The Ax awakened completely, but after a moment or two settled back with a grunt of disinterest. At least three riders overtook the wagon and moved ahead, but they swerved off the trail, giving the vehicle a wide berth. There was no reaction at all from The Ax or the driver. It was as though this had been expected. Zack caught only a vague glimpse through the rear curtain of the riders in the starlight. He had the impression that one wore a slicker and was small. A woman, perhaps.

The wagon rolled onward. The trail carried them up-grade for miles out of the rich river basin and to the dryer, buffalo-grass plains. From far away came the lonely wailing of a train whistle. Such a sound could carry for miles in this stillness.

Dawn was at hand when they reached their destination. The fragrance of newly cut hay and running water was in the air. The horses quickened their pace, eager to be free of the harness.

Buildings loomed up and took form as the roofs and walls of a ranch spread. Someone outside said grumpily, "A hell of a time fer everybody to pull in. I'll help with the hoss's, Simmons."

There was an oath. "No names, you fool!" The Ax snarled, leaping from the wagon. "Next time, you'll re-gret it."

"We're here," he said to Zack. "We'll find some cawfee an' a bait of grub, then I'll locate a bunk fer you."

Zack alighted from the wagon. The layout straggled across a flat between swells in the plain. There was a rickety pole corral, a slab-sided wagon shed, a squatty house with weather-boarded sides that had never been painted. A huge haybarn dominated the spread. On the flats beyond he made out the shape of half a dozen siz-able haystacks. This was new country, but this ranch already seemed defeated, its buildings weathering into the darkness of the land. A windmill creaked, and Zack heard the throb of the valve stroke as water was being pumped into the hayfields.

"This way," The Ax said. Zack followed him toward the house where lamplight showed. Back of him he heard the rattle of chains on the swingles and the creak of harness as the driver and the grumbling man freed the horses and led them away.

They mounted patched steps to a crooked stoop. The door was opened by someone inside. Zack followed The Ax into what turned out to be the kitchen, and found himself facing the steely-handsome girl from the Good Time—Lila.

"Good evening, Keech," Lila said calmly. "Or good morning, rather. Did you enjoy the trip?" Before Zack could answer, she continued, "I was one of the riders who passed the wagon down the trail. I couldn't get away from the Good Time until after you and Axel were well on your way."

She was sitting at a table, a cup containing coffee in her hand. Two other men also were at the table, which was long and built of solid planks, flanked by wooden benches. The table would take care of more than a dozen at one seating. Zack began to realize that this house, which appeared so small and dilapidated from the outside, was surprisingly big and not at all shoddy in furnishings or comfort.

"Welcome to Box Springs Ranch," Lila said. "You'll find this a very interesting place. This gentleman with the coffee dripping from his mustache is Jerry. The other one is Kerry. As a matter of fact, we don't worry about names. We only use them for the sake of convenience We *do* put much stock in action."

Lila's companions were garbed similarly to The Ax, but they were no more railroad workers than was he. And just as hard-eyed and just as heavily armed

"When do we begin this action?" Zack asked.

Lila smiled and looked at her companions. "Now that's what we like, isn't it, boys? A man of action. Of course, he's already proved that. I didn't see it with my own eyes, but he knocked out Stan Durkin with a single punch. To prove it was no accident he did it again. And he fought a pretty rough brawl with Frank Niles."

"Niles?" one of the men said, and eyed Zack with increased interest. "The big augur of the Rocky? How did it come out?"

"He found Niles tougher and faster with his fists than Stan Durkin, so I understand," Lila said.

She smiled at Zack. "It's time you got some sleep. Axel will show you to a bunk. As for action, my friend, you'll soon find some. Get plenty of sleep. You're likely to need it. But, first, have some grub and coffee."

Chapter 7

The Ax led Zack out of the house and across the ranch yard to the huge haybarn. The structure looked as though it might collapse at any moment under the weight of the wild hay in the loft.

Once they were inside the building The Ax lighted a lantern and Zack discovered that, like the ranch house, the outer appearance of neglect was a deception. The barn was braced strongly inside with beams and supports.

The Ax opened a trap door and they descended a steep stairway into a sizable dugout beneath the structure. This was a hidden sleeping quarters and there were half a dozen bunks in the place, with four occupied by sleepers who began stirring and mumbling profane objections to being awakened at this hour.

"Here's yours," The Ax said, indicating an empty bunk. "Help yourself to whatever you need. There's plenty to pick from."

He swung the lantern around so that Zack could see that the dugout was piled high with an astounding assortment. There were mattresses, pillows, sheets, blankets.

"Take yore pick," The Ax said grinning. "Ever sleep on a silk sheet? Here's yore chance. Sleep like a king fer once. When you git tired of them jest throw 'em away an' git new ones."

This was loot from Rocky Mountain Express trains. A wealth of it. Zack hesitated, then selected bedding and made up the bunk while The Ax waited with the lantern.

"Good night," The Ax said. "Sleep good. There won't be anythin' doin' all day."

He mounted the steps and the trap door dropped in place back of him. Daylight had strengthened enough so that wan light filtered into the dugout through cracks in the floor. Zack settled down on the bunk. He had plenty of time to think, for sleep eluded him. The other occupants of the hideout finished their interrupted rest, dressed and left by way of the trap door before he became drowsy.

He could hear the muted sounds of activity. Dogs yammered and squabbled somewhere, evidently in kennels. Pans and dishes rattled and he caught the fragrance of bacon being cooked. Horses whickered somewhere.

Then he slept. It was past noon when he awakened. The other bunks were still empty. He suspected that someone had been left on watch over him, for The Ax returned and lighted a lamp that stood in a bracket attached to a post.

Zack dressed. He got a better look at the wealth of loot in the place. Along with the bedding there were crates of clothing, boots, shirts, underwear, trousers, hats.

"Help yourself," The Ax said. "If you ride with us, you dress in the best. It's all paid for by the Rocky. An' we can furnish the top in the way of saddles, guns an' such. Hair tonic, razors, bay rum. We got it. Just ask. An' firewater."

"Santa Claus?" Zack asked.

The Ax's broad, hard face cracked into a crooked smile. "You guessed it. You can wash up at the trough outside. You'll find razors, soap an' towels. We picked a thousand razors in one day off a razor tree."

"A tree named the Rocky Mountain Express," Zack said.

"The market wasn't ripe for sellin' razors at that time," The Ax said, "so we was stuck with 'em."

Zack gazed around at the wealth of offerings, particularly the clothing. "A man could make a dude out of himself in this place, so much so he'd spend most of his time admiring his shadow," he said. He looked down at his own garb and shrugged, making no offer to array himself in the more expensive displays.

The Ax was watching him without expression, but he suddenly knew he had made a mistake. He hadn't been able to bring himself to wear stolen property. His instincts were all against it. Brandy Ben Keech had always hewed strictly to the line of honesty, and it had become a part of Zack's code. He sensed that somewhere in the book The Ax was keeping on him a demerit had been placed.

He and The Ax mounted to the floor of the barn. A few pieces of wheeled equipment, rakes, harrows and a mowing machine that needed repair stood in the place. He wondered what additional loot was hidden under the hay in the loft.

Emerging into the ranch yard through the double wagon doors that sagged on rusty strap hinges, Zack saw before him a scene commonplace on the plains where ranchers and dirt farmers bet the government they could defeat time and the weather and the loneliness by acquiring land.

A man in bib overalls and ragged straw hat was working on the windmill while a mowing machine with a team of horses stood idle nearby. A slovenly woman in calico and sunbonnet was listlessly hanging out a washing on a line back of the house. A few cattle and horses dotted a pasture beyond the haystacks which were enclosed by high barbed wire.

A man appeared amid the haystacks and left the enclosure by way of a gate which he was careful to chain tightly shut. Zack could have sworn that the man had emerged from one of the stacks itself. He looked at The

Ax who scowled. "See nothin', say nothin', hear nothin'," The Ax warned.

The haystacks, no doubt, were false fronts, like the ramshackle appearance of the house and barn, serving as hideouts for members of the outlaw organization and likely also as storehouses for loot.

Zack was served food by the slovenly dressed woman who, on closer look, turned out to be much younger and more active than she had seemed at a distance. The slovenliness and the washing were part of the plan to represent Box Springs Ranch as not worth attention.

The woman, like Lila, was hardened by life. She also liked the attention of any males around, for she brightened when Zack appeared and moved around, skirt hem swinging as she fried steak and eggs and potatoes, and heated coffee in a pot. It was a solid, satisfying meal.

"We had fresh oysters from Chesapeake Bay, an' terrapin soup a couple weeks ago," she said. "But we run out of all that stuff. It was meant for some miner who had hit it rich in the diggin's, an' was tryin' to make a splash." She fluttered her eyelashes at Zack. "I'm Anna May," she added.

"And I'm the Queen of Sheba," Lila spoke, entering the kitchen. "Throw out that sludge you call coffee and make some fresh in the small pot. I need something to wake me up and not to shatter my nerves."

Anna May sullenly obeyed. Zack judged that she had started out as a percentage girl at the Good Time and had graduated or been demoted, according to the point of view, to a place at Box Springs Ranch. The Ax had entered the room and was glowering at her, promising her that her attitude toward a stranger like Zack would bring her trouble later on.

"Anna May's man-crazy," Lila said, indifferent to the fact that Anna May was listening. "Don't get any wrong ideas. She's already spoken for around here."

"Thanks for the information," Zack said. "And you?"

Lila stared at him, surprised in spite of herself. Then she laughed. "You *are* a cool one," she said. "That comes under the head of business to be taken up in the future. There are other matters to be discussed first."

Zack waited. He sensed that she was trying to decide whether to go ahead. He was sure she was waiting for some sign from The Ax. The Ax did not speak.

Lila was forced to go it alone. "All right. We know you are aware of what this place really is."

She paused. Zack heard the faint, but plain chatter of a telegraph sounder. Then that ended. It was as though a door had opened and closed somewhere.

Lila shot a glance at The Ax who turned and left the house, striding angrily. Zack guessed the answer. Evidently the railroad's telegraph line had been tapped, and a hidden wire ran to Box Springs Ranch. By that means the outlaws could keep track of train movements and other railroad information. It was a secret that The Ax apparently had not wanted revealed—at least to Zack.

Zack waited for Lila to do the talking. But she was waiting also, an annoyed frown creasing her brow. The wait went on and on. The new coffee eventually was ready. Zack sipped at the steaming contents of a cup. Still Lila did not break the silence. There was growing tension in her manner, however.

Once more Zack was sure he heard the sounder of a telegraph instrument. Only for a moment, as though a door had been opened and closed again.

The Ax returned. He gave Lila a look. Their eyes locked for an instant. Zack saw that in both of them was a burst of wild, fierce excitement. But along with that there was in both of them apprehension—fear. They had the attitudes of at last finding themselves face-to-face with a situation that fascinated them, but which they also dreaded now that the time had come.

"When?" she asked The Ax.

"Tonight," he said. "It'll be around midnight, but I want to pull out as soon as it comes full dark. I want plenty of time. And no mistakes."

"How many men?"

The Ax thought it over. "The fewer the better. Three ought to be enough. I want Ogallala and Matt Pecos."

"And our friend Keech," Lila said.

The Ax frowned. "I don't understand. I figure it'd be better if—"

Lila cut him off abruptly. "You know the ord—the plan, I mean. Follow it unless you want to find yourself in real trouble."

She looked at Zack. "You're going with The Ax and the boys tonight. It's going to be a surprise party on the Rocky. I'm sure you wouldn't want to miss it."

These people had wrecked trains, murdered and tortured. Zack believed they did not trust him—at least not yet. He decided that they might only be putting him to a test. He took it for granted that this was to be another looting expedition, but the limited number who would ride indicated that it was something far out of the ordinary. By going along with their plan he might learn something valuable about their methods. He was sure he had already come upon some information. Neither Lila nor The Ax were the leader of the highbinders. Lila had almost let slip the fact that they had precise orders as to the night's plan. Those orders must have come by telegraph over the tapped wire.

Both of them were waiting for him to speak. "If it means getting square with the Rocky," he said, "you can count me in."

The Ax had to accept that although Zack could see that he was dubious. "I could swing it with jest the Kid an' Pecos," he grumbled.

"Quit complaining," Lila snapped. "And remember, there's to be no shooting."

That lifted some of the burden off Zack's conscience. Looting a freight car might be condoned for the sake of his main purpose, but he knew that anything involving gunplay might force him to take sides and reveal that purpose. Evidently nothing as drastic as train wrecking was planned in view of the small force The Ax was taking with him. Still, his uneasiness deepened, for he could still see the wild emotions that ran in Lila and The Ax. This was something out of the ordinary for them, something the Box Springs outlaws had never before attempted.

Lila added a touch of cool water to the still-torrid cup that Anna May had petulantly placed in front of her. She kept waiting, trying not to look at Zack. But, being a woman she could not keep it up.

"Aren't you going to ask?" she burst out. "What are you made of—stone?"

The Ax spoke quickly. "Don't bother, fella. You'll find out tonight."

"That's good enough for me," Zack said. He pushed his coffee cup aside and arose, stretching. "Mind if I look around a little? I need to get the kinks out of my legs."

"We mind," The Ax snapped. "We don't wander around much in the open here at the Box. Not in daylight at least. Don't worry about the kinks. You'll get them out before long. You'll be most of the night in the saddle."

"I still don't savvy why the law men don't know about this place," Zack commented.

"What law men?"

"Well, there's Wild Bill Hickok for one."

"He's town marshal an' has his hands full in the Wells. Anyway, he's only one man. The sheriff's a long ways off, an' folks have learned not to be too nosy about the Box."

The Ax studied Zack for a space, then added, "A few have showed up around here. Some of 'em never seemed to find their way back to town to collect what money the Rocky was payin' for snoopin'. Them that did get back had sense enough to keep their mouths shut. 'Specially if they was family men. Sometimes things happened to their wives or kids. Accident-like. We've got good friends in the Wells. Lots of 'em. The Rocky ain't too popular there, except among them that work for the railroad. Even some of them railroaders sort of go along with us."

If there had been any exhilaration at the thought of the spice of danger in associating with these criminals, it faded entirely within Zack and was replaced by a sick and burning rage. He had already seen proof that they had committed murder and torture. Evidently there was nothing they would stop at to tighten the reign of terror they patently held over Sioux Wells and its citizens. The twinges of conscience that had been nagging him over infiltrating this organization also died.

He knew that Lila was studying him, trying to read his thoughts. Something of the revulsion he was feeling toward her and all these ruffians must have touched her, for her mouth tightened a little, angrily.

"There's one thing I want to make clear," The Ax said. "If shootin' is needed, I shoot. An' shoot to kill, no matter who it is I shoot at. I think of myself first, no matter what anybody says. I ain't too happy about this thing tonight."

"He's only trying to throw a scare into you, Keech," Lila said quickly. "He doesn't believe you take us seriously enough. This is not a thing that will call for gunplay."

She was only trying to smooth over the situation. There was a bitter, mirthless smile on The Ax's thick lips as he turned and stalked out of the door. "We ride tonight," he spoke before he closed the door.

The fading daylight showed the faces of the two men who were waiting in the barn when The Ax led Zack out of the hideout and into the meeting place among stalls unused by horses for a long time.

Zack peered closer. "Well, well!" he said. "We seem to have met before. The Ogallala Kid is the name, I believe. And this other one calls himself Matt Pecos."

The Ogallala Kid snarled something in a mumble that Zack could not interpret, but did not need to. He was well aware that the Kid had less than no affection for him. Nor did his companion. Matt Pecos said nothing, merely stared with flat eyes. He wore a strip of court plaster on his chin. Zack could not recall having landed a blow there, but evidently he was the person responsible, for the man fingered his injury, and his stare was that of one who was promising that he would never forget his grudge.

"You remember them, I see," The Ax said sardonically.

"Very much so," Zack said. "But we're not what you might call old friends."

"I won't ask you boys to shake hands," The Ax said, "but I want you to know that we're on the same side tonight, and I don't stand for anybody settling personal matters while we're on a job for the organization. Keep that in mind. We pull together or somebody finds hisself where he don't want to be—which might be in a bed six feet under."

Six saddled horses were waiting. They shaped up as sturdy animals, solid of leg and haunch—the sort of mounts men would want under them if called on to outdistance pursuers.

"You take the black gelding," The Ax said to Zack, indicating a powerfully built animal.

Zack adjusted the stirrups to his satisfaction and mounted. The saddle didn't particularly suit him, mainly because it was creakily new—more loot from a Rocky freight car, no doubt.

The other three mounted, and they rode away into the deepening darkness, leading the two spare animals whose stirrups had been tied across the saddles. The Ax set a leisurely pace as they headed away from the ranch, where, true to its pose as a rundown homestead, the only light was from a lamp in the kitchen.

However, Zack again heard the faint clatter of the telegraph sounder. The Ax called a halt and rode away into the darkness alone. He returned after a few minutes, breathing hard.

"It'll be a sweet long time before that fool brass pounder opens that door while that thing is tickin'," he snarled. "I cuffed him around some."

They rode on again in silence. This latest episode concerning the telegraph brought up questions in Zack's mind. On the face of it The Ax apparently had decided there was no point in keeping the presence of the tapped line a secret from him. That meant that he was being accepted at face value. Still, there was an uneasiness deep in his mind whose source he could not determine.

It was the Ogallala Kid who finally spoke. "I don't savvy this, Axel? There's only the four of us, countin' this cowboy. Just what are we supposed to be up to?"

"Shut up!" The Ax snapped.

"Cain't a fella even ask a question?" the Kid mumbled. "Seems like me an' Matt ought to know at least where we're goin'."

The Ax twisted in the saddle and glared at him in the starlight. He lapsed into surly silence.

Zack judged that they had traveled little more than two miles when they crossed what apparently was an abandoned stretch of railroad track. It was weed-grown, the rails appearing rusty in the faint light. Evidently it was a spur off the main line of the Rocky Mountain Express which was no longer used.

They paralleled this, still traveling at a slow pace. Finally, The Ax who had been rising in the saddle and peering ahead, gave a grunt of satisfaction. "Here we are," he said.

Zack made out the vague picket line of telegraph poles and saw the glint of steel rails. They had reached the main line of the railroad.

The Ax flared a match to look at his watch, then headed north, with the railroad track nearby. After less than a mile he seemed satisfied with the lay of the land and pulled up his horse. "All right," he said, dismounting. "We'll hang around here a while. It might be quite a few hours."

"Ain't no freight trains due along here 'til ten o'clock," the Ogallala Kid said uneasily. "An' with only four of us what could we do?"

"Shut up!" The Ax replied. "An' keep shut."

He led the way a short distance from the line of track and into the cover of a small gully. They tied up the horses to stunted brush and settled down to wait. As The Ax had predicted, the wait went on and on.

Eventually they heard the distant rumble of an approaching train. It was coming from the direction of Sioux Wells. The Kid and Matt Pecos, who had found places to recline while they puffed cigarettes, got to their feet expectantly.

But The Ax did not move "Keep yore fool heads down," he said. "We don't want to be seen."

The train rumbled past and the sound receded into the distance, then died. The wait went on.

The Ax finally moved to his horse, removed a bundle that was tied to the saddle. He dealt out rolls of grain sacks to Zack and the other two. "Don't put these on 'til the time comes, when I give the word," he said. "An' no shootin' unless I say so. 'Specially at the fellers on the engine. They're some of us."

Zack discovered that the grain sacks were masks, for they had eyeholes cut in them. He found a comfortable place to sit, apart from the others, and waited. The night was warm, fragrant with the perfume of grass and sage. The clean, gentle night breeze touched him. An old moon was rising in the sky. A man could be completely at peace with the world on a night like this, with no regrets for the past, no anxieties for the future. But there was no such tranquillity in him, nor in his three companions. They were all on edge, as taut as a stretched wire. And The Ax was the most nervous of all. He could not rest, but kept rolling cigarette after cigarette and peering at his watch in the matchlight.

Time dragged. Zack's watch told him that midnight was near when The Ax drew a long breath and stood listening. Zack made out the pulse beat of a locomotive far away. The sound also came from the direction of Sioux Wells to the north.

"Come on!" The Ax snapped. "Leave them horses here."

They left cover and moved nearer the right-of-way. Soon, Zack made out the beam of the engine's headlight fingering across the flats, appearing, disappearing. Finally, the light was sweeping the stretches of plains nearby, picking out larger clumps of brush, giving golden glow to outcrops of boulders. Then it was bearing down upon them, lighting up the rails and ties.

"Git them masks on," The Ax ordered. Zack pulled the grain sack over his head and adjusted it so that he could peer through the eyeholes. The other three were similarly arrayed.

The Ax had brought from a saddlebag a bull's-eye lantern. He lighted it and Zack saw that it was equipped

with a red lens. The locomotive was bearing down on
their position now.

"Hell, Axel!" Matt Pecos snarled. "It's only one car.
A passenger car, an' all dark an' looks empty. What'n
blazes!"

"All you need to do is follow orders," The Ax gritted.
"Anybody what makes any mistakes will pay fer it."

He began snapping the shutter of the bull's-eye, sending lances of crimson light down the track. The beat
from the stack of the locomotive slowed instantly. Zack
heard the grind of brakes on sanded tracks. The Ax
shifted to a white lens on the lantern, which gave better
light and in its beam Zack could see the face of the engineer, who was leaning from the window of the cab,
peering with the attitude of a man who had been expecting something like this. The fireman was standing in the
gangway, also taking this calmly enough.

The engine came to a stop. The Ax ran to the steps
of the single car back of the tender. Zack saw the gleam
of polished brass and gold paint. This was the ornate
private palace car that he had seen standing on a sidetrack in the Sioux Wells railroad yards, and which The
Ax had said belonged to J. K. Tolliver, owner of the
Rocky Mountain Express.

The Ax leaped up the steps to the platform of the
palace car, followed by the Ogallala Kid. The door was
locked, and he blew off the lock with two blasts from his
six-shooter.

A girl screamed in the car. The frightened voice of an
older woman also arose, demanding to know what in
condemnation was going on. Zack had heard those voices
before. They belonged to Granny Julia Smith and her
beautiful granddaughter.

He followed The Ax and the Ogallala Kid into the
car. The Ax bellowed an order for Matt Pecos to stand
guard outside. The beam of the bull's-eye showed that

they were in the narrow corridor that contained sleeping compartments, which occupied half of the car. Beyond was a lounge section with brocaded chairs and settees, and a small kitchen at the rear. Rich quarters.

"Git dressed an' come out, you two!" The Ax bellowed. "Right quick. Pronto! Quit yowlin' in there, young lady! An' you can stop cussin', old lady. You won't git hurt."

"Go to blazes!" the grandmother screeched. "What kind of scoundrels air you, tryin' to terrorize two poor, defenseless ladies in the middle of the night? What do you want? If it's money you're after, you're wastin' your time. We ain't got more'n a few dollars between us."

"Come out, afore I have to come in an' drag you out!" The Ax snarled. "You ain't goin' to be hurt. But you're goin' with us whether you want to or not."

"Goin' with you? Where?"

"You'll find out. We know who you are."

"Who are they?" Zack asked.

"The old biddy's real name is Julia K. Tolliver. I don't know what the K stands for. Cussedness, maybe. The young one's name is Anita Tolliver."

"Well, I'll be damned!" Zack said. "I should have known."

"Them two own this here Rocky Mountain Express, lock, stock an' barrel, between them," The Ax said. "They go under the name of Smith around Sioux Wells, for they don't want men to know they're workin' for a railroad owned by petticoats."

Chapter 8

The Ax pounded on the doors of two of the compartments with his guns. "Come out right now!" he roared.

"I'll come out when I'm dressed proper, an' not before, you blasted rascal!" the elder woman replied. "The first one that tries to come through that door before I say so gits a slug in his belly, an' that goes for my granddaughter's room too. I got a gun here that will do the talkin' for me."

"All right, all right!" The Ax said hastily. "But don't try any shenanigans. Before you come out, push that gun out ahead of you on the floor. Don't try anything foolish, like goin' out a window. We've got men on watch outside. You'd only git caught, an' maybe git hurt in the bargain."

Anita Tolliver was the first to emerge. She was still trying to twist her hair into a semblance of order, and was jabbing at hairpins with nervous fingers. She had hurriedly pulled on a skirt, blouse and shoes. She gave a startled little cry of fear when she saw the grotesque shapes of the three men in the masks, but recovered, refusing to show panic.

"What are you going to do with us?" she demanded.

"You'll jest be our guests fer a little while," The Ax said.

"Watch out fer that filly," the Ogallala Kid warned. "I happen to know she packs a derringer."

"Well, well!" Anita Tolliver said. "It's nice to know at least one of you. You're the coward who shoots game from railroad cars, then leaves them wounded to die."

"You fool!" The Ax snarled at the Kid. "Won't you ever learn to keep your yap shut?"

Julia Tolliver opened the door of her quarters and pushed a six-shooter ahead of her into the passageway with the toe of her slipper. The Ax snatched up the weapon.

"Now for thet derringer, you," he said, addressing Anita Tolliver. "Hand it over."

The girl hesitated, then shrugged and turned away. Evidently she was carrying the small weapon in her garter. When she turned again, she had the derringer in her hand. Reluctantly, she surrendered it to the outlaw.

"Don't you know that they string you up without a trial for mistreatin' women?" Julia Tolliver said scornfully. She was fully dressed, evidently even to stays beneath her neat, dark dress. She had donned a small bonnet and had a knitted shawl around her shoulders.

"Keep quiet!" The Ax snarled. "I'll do all the talkin'."

"Don't you ever again try to shut me up," Julia Tolliver rasped. "I'll see you do a jig at the end of a rope for this night's work."

"Hold your tongue, you old harridan!" The Ax raged. "I'd put a slug in you if it wasn't that—"

He decided not to finish it. "If it wasn't for what?" Anita Tolliver demanded. "Just what are you going to do with us?"

"Never mind that," he said. "Now git back in this sleepin' room, an' stay there. Don't close the door. You'll be watched every minute."

The Tollivers hesitated. Zack could see that they were mortally afraid, but trying desperately to show a brave front.

"Move!" The Ax said. There was a deadliness in him, a viciousness that belied his promises that they would not be hurt. Anita hurriedly seized her grandmother's arm and drew her inside one of the compartments. Zack watched them seat themselves close together on the berth and hold hands.

"You stay here," The Ax said, stabbing a finger at the Ogallala Kid. "Jest see thet the ladies stay there too. An' don't try to git gay with them."

"You," he said to Zack. "Come with me."

Zack followed him to the platform. Matt Pecos was standing on guard alongside the track. "You fetch the horses, Pecos," The Ax said. "See to it thet none git away. We're goin' to need 'em."

"Whar to?" Pecos asked.

"To that spot on the old Crown Point sidin' where we have worked before," The Ax said. "We're takin' this car up there an' spot it out of sight."

Then The Ax yelled ahead to the engineer. "All right, Hank. Git goin'!"

"You mean on up the line?" the engineer yelled back.

"Blast it!" The Ax screeched. "Can't anybody learn to do what they're told without askin' a lot of fool questions."

"But—!"

The Ax, cursing, scrambled up the short iron ladder to the water tank deck of the tender. He had his gun in hand, and was glaring down into the locomotive cab. "Git rollin'," he raged. "Afore I put a slug in you."

The engineer obeyed with such haste that the steam boxes gushed like geysers, the stack exploded into bellowing life and the drive wheels spun. Zack was staggered against the car's door, but managed to hang on until he recovered his balance.

The wheels found traction and the equipment got under way. The Ax had vanished, having scrambled down into the cab of the engine. Zack moved to the platform, swinging out by the handrails and looking ahead. He saw the fireman on the running board alongside the boiler.

Then the headlight died, and the engine was moving along unlighted rails.

Presently the pace eased as power slackened. Zack could see the head and shoulders of The Ax jutting from the gangway of the engine. The man was peering ahead, evidently seeking some landmark.

Then the brakes were applied and the train slowed, then stopped. The Ax leaped to the ground and ran ahead. Zack heard the squeaking of metal, and The Ax shouted, "All right! Come ahead!"

The train crept ahead again and swerved off the main line onto a spur track. No doubt it was the weedy, overgrown track they had crossed some distance west earlier in the evening, the Crown Point siding.

The engineer halted the equipment again, and metallic sounds told that The Ax had rethrown the switch. The man came running out of the darkness and mounted the steps to the lounge car platform where Zack waited.

"All right, Hank!" he shouted. "Pull ahead again. I'll tell you when to stop."

"Dang it, Axel!" the engineer shouted back. "This here spur gits more risky every time I run over it. We'll likely wind up ridin' on the ties."

"Take it slow," The Ax answered. "If it looks too risky, stop 'til we kin make sure. I don't want this outfit to be hung up out here in the open come daybreak."

The train got under way again, very slowly as the engineer felt his way along.

"What'n blazes is this all about?" the Ogallala Kid asked.

"What do you keer?"

"I got a right to ask," the Kid said sullenly.

"What right?"

"It's like the old lady said. They don't take kindly to roughin' up women in these parts. I've heerd of some terrible things that has happened to some what did things like that."

"You kin git off right now if you want. Either that or quit whinin'." The Ax had his six-shooter in his hand, and it was apparent he was ready to use it.

The Kid subsided. He had been very close to death and knew it. "Keep yore shirt on, Axel," he croaked. "I didn't mean nothin'. I just don't know what this is all about."

The Ax laughed with contempt. He shoved past Zack, walked down the corridor into the lounge section of the car. He moved to a window and kept peering out. After a time he hurried back to the platform and leaned from the steps. "We're about there, Hank. Stop in that cut ahead as soon as you're sure we're between banks high enough to hide this outfit."

The train crept along for a short distance. Zack could see brush-grown banks rising higher on either side of the track. Then the equipment jolted to a stop. The Ax leaped to the ground and surveyed the situation. "All right," he shouted. "This is good enough."

He returned to the car, walked to the open door of the compartment where the Tollivers waited. "Come out!" he commanded.

Anita Tolliver and her grandmother slowly emerged. "What do we do now?" she said.

"Wait a while. There'll be horses brought up directly. Kin the old lady ride?"

Julia Tolliver bristled. "I was ridin' high-steppin' horses afore you was born, you rascal. Where you takin' us?"

"Out to view the scenery," The Ax said.

Julia turned, peering through the window of the compartment. "I'd say we're on the old Crown Point spur that we built back into the hills to bring out gravel an' timber when we was constructin' the Rocky through this country."

"Could be," The Ax replied.

The wait did not last long. Zack heard the sound of hoofs and knew that Matt Pecos was bringing up the horses.

"All right, ladies," The Ax said. "We're all gittin' off here."

Zack was first to alight. He waited to help Anita Tolliver from the step of the car, but she knocked his hand aside, and turned to assist her grandmother to the ground. "Don't touch me, you scum!" she said.

The Ax, pistol in hand, followed, accompanied by the Kid. "Stay here, you two," The Ax called to the engineer and fireman. "I'll have horses brung over to take you to the ranch. You won't be needed fer a little while. Lila will tell you what to do."

"What the hell, Axel!" the engineer protested. "This special will be missed, an' it'll be found sooner or later. What's Joe an' me goin' to say about what happened to us?"

"That'll all be taken care of," The Ax said. "Now do what I say."

He turned and gave young Anita Tolliver a shove. "March!" he snarled.

"What about our luggage?" she demanded.

"Never mind that," The Ax said. "If'n it's clothes you need I kin skeer up enough to fix you two up and a hundred like you."

"Stolen from the railroad, of course," Julia Tolliver said wrathfully.

"March, I say!" The Ax rasped, and they all went stumbling over crooked ties and through weeds out of the cut to where Matt Pecos and the horses were waiting. The two women were lifted aboard the spare mounts and left to manage as best they could with their skirts.

"If you was halfway human, you'd have brung side-saddles so we could ride as ladies should," Julia Tolliver complained. "How did you know we was on that car?"

"We know everything."

"Where are you taking us?"

"Shut up!" The Ax snarled, resorting to his particular way of ending discussions.

"I told you not to say things like that to me ag'in!" Julia Tolliver snapped. She swung the ends of the long reins and caught The Ax across the cheek with whip-like force that brought a yelp of pain and fury from him. He yanked his horse close, a fist clenched, and would have smashed the elderly woman in the face.

Zack also kicked his horse within reach and managed to grasp The Ax's arm and halt the blow. This destroyed The Ax's balance and he nearly fell from his horse.

He recovered, dragging himself back into the saddle and whirled on Zack, his pistol in his hand. Again he was in a killing rage. It faded, for he was looking into the bore of Zack's gun inches from his face.

"I don't like any part of this," Zack said. "I didn't declare myself into this game to haze women around. And I don't stand for a man mauling a woman—and an old lady at that."

"She's got it comin'," The Ax gritted. But he now had control of himself and holstered the pistol. However, Zack doubted that he was responsible for quelling the storm. The Ax had thought of other and better reasons for not pursuing the matter. "But the next time you git out of hand—" he growled at Julia Tolliver. He let it ride there, but it was mere bluster now.

"You might as well take off that feed bag you've got over your ugly head," she said. "I know you. Your name is Jim Axel, and you was a straw boss on one of our track-layin' gangs when we was buildin' the Rocky. My son fired you for petty stealin', booted you out of camp. An' now you're still stealin' from us Tollivers."

The Ax yanked off his mask and hurled it away. His two outlaws followed that example, glad to be free of the confining burlap. Zack also rid himself of the disguise. The thought had struck him that the Tollivers might show some sign of gladness when they saw they had an ally at hand, but he felt that they had recognized his voice, also, by this time. They were equal to the occasion. They only glared scornfully at him in the yellow moonlight.

"Well, well," Anita Tolliver said. "This *is* a surprise. So you've joined the highbinders. I suppose that figures. I knew you had a grudge against the Rocky, but I really didn't think you would stoop so low as to kidnap women."

"Be quiet," Zack said. He was playing out his role, but in him was a chill realization. There could be only one answer to the removal of the masks. It was never intended that Julia Tolliver and her granddaughter would live to identify their captors.

The Tollivers must have understood this also, for Julia Tolliver had to try repeatedly before she could overcome the quaver in her voice and make herself heard. "Just what do you expect to get out of all this?"

"I've said all I'm goin' to say," The Ax growled. "No more talk, lest I have you gagged."

They were heading in the general direction of Box Springs Ranch, but Zack, after a time, discovered that their route was more westerly and would carry them a distance wide of that hideout. They rode in silence, the women boxed in by the outlaws to prevent any attempt at a break to escape.

Presently they entered broken country, with the horses laboring up rocky ascents, following the tumbling course of a fast stream. Jagged buttes and rims arose around them. Julia Tolliver was obviously having a trying time of it in the bulky saddle, and Anita was staying close at her side as much as possible, attempting to assist her.

"Dang it, 'Nita," Julia complained. "Quit cluckin' over me like I was stove up an' crippled. This cussed saddle is too big fer me, an' I rattle around in it like a dried pea in a pod, but I've rid worse, an' I ain't made of sugar an' salt. I won't melt."

Dawn was lighting the sky. Through breaks in the patchwork of ridges and low hills Zack sighted Box Springs Ranch only two miles or so away on the flats below the cover of the hills that they were following.

They were now following a faint horse trail, evidently seldom used, although there were the marks of a few fresh hoof prints. Riders had traveled this route both ways lately.

They emerged into a small flat where a spring was the source of a small stream that wound across the flat to join the bigger creek. Grass, aspen, spruce and pine grew here. There was a small corral, empty now and a log gear shed that also seemed to be seldom used. Dominating the layout was a well-built log cabin with a high gable, shake roof and a small veranda of rustic wood. The faded pelt of a grizzly was nailed to one wall along with wolf and cougar skins. The antlers of elk, deer and bighorns decorated the main house and gear shed.

A hunting lodge by the looks, Zack surmised. There was no sign of life about the house. The Ax led the way past without comment. They rounded an outthrust shoulder of a higher ledge and came upon a rude, sagging log shack which crouched, animal-like against the base of a cliff.

"All right," The Ax said. "We're here. Light down."

Zack slid from his horse and moved to help Julia Tolliver. Continuing the role they were playing, she slapped his hands away. "I don't want to be touched by the likes of you," she snapped, and accepted assistance from her granddaughter.

The Ax was standing a pace back. Before Zack realized what was happening his six-shooter had been snatched from its holster. He whirled and found himself facing his own gun, cocked and in the hands of The Ax.

"Put up yore arms, cowboy," The Ax said harshly. "It'd be a pleasure to put a bullet in you. We don't like spies. We don't like 'em none at all."

"What are you talking about?" Zack demanded.

"We know all about you, mister. You tried to worm your way into our bunch because Julia Tolliver promised to pay your claim for them stampeded cattle if you sent all of us to the gallows and the pen."

"But it was you people who invited me in," Zack protested.

"Sure, sure. You've heard of the spider and the fly, haven't you. Didn't it ever occur to you that we were making it easy for you to get this far? Too easy. You took us for fools. The fact is we sort of needed you. We took you along on this thing tonight because we figured these two gals would give us less trouble if they thought they had their hired spy along to maybe help them when the sign was right. And we had other reasons."

"What other reasons?"

"You better hope that you never find out," The Ax replied. "Matt, git the leg irons. You'll find 'em lyin' in the shack just inside the door. I put them there myself when I rode over here yesterday. I'll keep the key. No point in tyin' up his arms. He ain't goin anywhere when he's hobbled. Make sure he ain't got any hideouts, such as a knife or palm gun."

Zack and the two women were led at gunpoint to the shack and pushed through its crooked door. The clank of iron sounded and Matt Pecos brought up the leg irons.

"Courtesy of the Rocky Mountain Express," the man

said, grinning, as he clamped the irons around Zack's ankles. "These things was bein' shipped to the law dogs in the gold camps, but it happened that we inherited them an' figured we might have use for 'em from time to time. We was right."

The chain connecting the shackles was little more than a foot long, limiting Zack's activity to awkward hobbling. Remembering Jimmy Broom, he was wondering why they were permitting him to stay alive at all. The Ax guessed what was in his mind and answered the question. "You ain't worth near as much on the hoof as the hen an' chick," he said. "But you're worth enough to pay us for our trouble, if need be."

"How's that?" Zack asked.

"You're Brandy Ben Keech's son, ain't you? That's another reason we scooped you up in our net. He's on his way to the Indian agency up north to sell ninety thousand dollars' worth of beef, ain't he, barrin' a few hundred head that you say were lost in the stampede. Ninety thousand ain't in it with somethin' else we got in mind, but it ain't pocket change either. We got two barrels to our gun. If one don't bring down the big game, maybe the other will. An' maybe both barrels will score."

Zack looked at the Tollivers and saw the waxen set of their faces. More and more they were realizing that there was little hope they would live through this.

"Brandy Ben has a reputation for being a dangerous man to try to bluff," Zack said.

"It happens we ain't bluffin'."

"He won't pay. I know him."

"He'll change his mind after we start sendin' him little souvenirs. Such as an ear or two. If that don't convince him, we'll start on yore fingers an' toes. Or a nose. What kind of a father would turn his back on things like that, just to save a few dollars?"

"And then you'd have him hounding you the rest of

your lives," Zack said. "I know him. And there are a few more Keech's down in Texas who would join in the hunt."

The Ax tried to snort scornfully, but it was a failure. Evidently he had never given a thought to being marked for vengeance, and it worried him. He changed the subject and turned to the Tollivers.

"As for you two, I warn you not to try to git away. There'll be men on watch outside every minute. You couldn't git far even if you managed to sneak away. We've got dogs to bring up that'd run you down in no time."

He and his companions left the shack. They closed the door which was built of slabs, and Zack heard them bracing it securely with more slabs. Zack hopped to the door which was so poorly fitted there were slits that gave views of the surroundings. The Ax and Matt Pecos were heading on foot around the arm of the ledge, evidently in the direction of the hunting lodge. The Ogallala Kid was making himself comfortable on a log which he had dragged against a tree. He seated himself there, a rifle and his six-shooters handy, his position commanding their place of confinement.

Zack looked around the interior. "There's no place like home," he said.

The shack was about ten by twelve feet, with a dirt floor. The one window was fitted with a four-pane sash, but the outside was covered with crisscrossed barbed wire. There were two mattresses in the corners, along with sheets, blankets and pillows. One of the pallets had been used. The thought struck Zack that this was where Jimmy Broom might have been held until he was tortured for information and murdered.

He discovered a small opening at the rear. Hopping to it he discovered that the shack had been built as an addition to a dugout under the base of the cliff. The dugout

probably had been the quarters of the original resident, a
hunter and trapper, no doubt, and the shack had been
added later.

"A real two-room palace," he said. "I'll take the rear
bedroom. You ladies can sleep in the parlor."

"Sleep!" Julia Tolliver sniffed. "Who'll be able to
sleep with these cutthroats waitin' to murder us?"

"What's this all about?" Zack asked.

"I wish I knew," Julia Tolliver said dolefully. "I never
been kidnapped before. If it's money they want, they're
wastin' their time. Me'n 'Nita are as poor as church mice.
We've sold about everythin', tryin' to keep the Rocky
goin'. Fact is, we was headin' east to try to sweet-talk
bankers into loanin' us money, an' to sell the palace car."

"To sell it?"

"One of the bigwigs on the Union Pacific had offered
me five thousand dollars for it, an' we was takin' it east
to close the deal. Me an' 'Nita couldn't afford any longer
to ride in a private car. We ride the cushions like everybody else, as you saw the day you got mixed up with us
when that skunk shot the antelope. In addition we was
runnin' scared last night."

"Scared. Why were you two alone in that fancy car?"

"Bill Hickok come to us yesterday an' advised us to
git out of the Wells, an' git out fast. Somebody had tipped
him off that something big was in the wind an' that us
Tollivers was mixed up in it."

"Who tipped him off?"

"He didn't say, except that the person was a friend of
both him and us, and that there wasn't any question but
that the information was reliable. We hired Bill to come in
an' try to break up this gang that's robbin' us blind, but
it's been too tough a job even for him. He's bein' watched
every minute, an' that attempt to kill him the other night
wasn't the first, an' likely won't be the last. We got hit
by our biggest loss just recently. Forty thousand dollars

in gold dust that was brought by wagon from the mines to our end of steel at Summit, which is forty miles west of the Wells. The train was stuck up after if had gone through the Wells, bound east. We got to make that up to the shippers."

"How? You just said you were broke."

She made a helpless gesture. "How would I know? Another thing I don't know is how these rascals knew me an' 'Nita was aboard the car last night. We sneaked into it after dark as it set in the yards. Even the two on the engine wasn't told. They only thought they'd been called to take that empty palace car on a special run down to Buffalo Junction. Only Hickok an' Frank Niles knew we was aboard."

"Niles?"

It was Anita who spoke. "Frank was the only one with authority to call in the crew and order an engine out of the shop," she said slowly.

Nobody said anything for a space. It was Zack who broke the silence. "Did you know that the railroad telegraph line is tapped? There's a line running to their headquarters at a place called Box Springs Ranch, which isn't more than a couple of miles from here. That's how they've been keeping tab on which shipments are worth hitting. I think they've been using that old railroad spur at times for unloading freight cars. I think the word came through to Box Springs yesterday afternoon to The Ax that you two were to be on that special run last night."

"Word? From who?"

"Box Springs is a big setup," Zack said. "On the face of it you'd think it was a homestead on its last legs, but there are underground storehouses and haystacks that aren't haystacks but caches for what they steal. That young woman who calls herself Lila and runs the Good Time in Sioux Wells, is in on it. She seems to give the orders. Maybe she's the brains back of all this."

"I doubt if that hussie has got a real brain in her head," Anita spoke scornfully. "I suppose men like you are dazzled by good looks and a shape."

"She does have points there," Zack said.

Anita uttered only another disparaging sniff. Her grandmother spoke hastily. "Never mind discussin' things like that. I know the gal. Her real name is Martha Kelly, an' I ain't surprised to hear she's mixed up with the highbinders. Now why didn't some of them detectives we hired find out about this Box Springs hangout?"

"Some probably did," Zack said, "but didn't live to tell about it, like Jimmy Broom, or were too scared to talk. How long has all this highbinding been going on?"

"It started more'n two years ago," Julia sighed. "It was only petty theft at first, but it kept snowballin'. That's why I finally hollered for help from Bill Hickok. I met Bill years ago when my husband was layin' track for the Union Pacific an' I was helpin' with the books. Bill was scoutin' for the Army at the time."

"Your husband is dead, I take it?"

"Yes, God rest his soul. He was killed when a work train went through a temporary bridge not long after he had started buildin' the Rocky. Our son, who was 'Nita's father, took over an' finished the Rocky beyond Sioux Wells. We had put every cent we had in the world into the Rocky. When these highbinders hit us we had to stop construction short of the mountains. We'd really do business if we could git to the gold camps. Even so, it was a payin' proposition until the thieves got busy. Me an' 'Nita own it all. She lost her maw an' paw two years ago. Indians hit a stagecoach on which they were ridin' outside Denver City."

"Who besides Hickok and Frank Niles know that you two are J. K. Tolliver between you and not the Smiths?" Zack asked.

"Must be quite a few in Sioux Wells," Julia admitted.

"The Wells wasn't more'n a grease spot at first, but there's a few around who was with us when we built into it, an' set up a station an' a water tank. There's Jud Gregg at the hotel. He's known us for years. An' Sid Crain, the justice of peace. Ed Hake used to hunt buffalo fer us. There's quite a few others around who know who we really are, some of whom I don't care to name at this time. They're old friends. It might be what you call an open secret in the Wells. Our only reason is that railroad men are a proud lot. They don't like to be told that they're bein' bossed by womenfolk."

Zack eyed Anita. "Just why did you come down on me those times after I had trouble with that big hulk of an engineer who stampeded our herd."

"I'm railroad," she said. "I was given a railroad spike to play with in my crib. You're not railroad. To me you were just a big, overbearing cowboy not fit to humiliate people like us by knocking out our best man with one punch. I wanted you to lose. I wanted Stan Durkin to wallop you all over the street. But you disappointed me. Twice."

"I'll be careful to avoid you if I lock horns with Durkin again," he said. "But he's a sucker for a right cross. You did more damage to me than Durkin."

Chapter 9

Zack moved along the walls of the shack in the hope he might find something that would offer a chance of bursting free. He crawled into the dugout and inspected it almost inch by inch. It was all wasted effort.

The Tollivers helped as best they could, all maintaining silence so as to not arouse the Ogallala Kid's inspection. They all finally gave it up. The Tollivers sat together on one of the pallets. Zack used a wall of the shack for support and sat legs outstretched.

The morning advanced. They heard sounds, the sound of voices. But it was only the Ogallala Kid changing over the guard duty to Matt Pecos.

They continued to wait, a listless apathy claiming them. They aroused at every faint sound, but always they sank back, discovering that it was the scamper of a bird over their roof, or the changing of the guard. Even The Ax stood a three-hour vigil.

The torpid heat of afternoon began to invade their quarters. Still nothing. Zack became aware of nagging thirst. He began thinking of water, of cooling springs at which he had partaken in the past, of creeks and rivers in which he had swum. He tried to shake away such phantoms. They kept rising in his mind. He finally lifted his voice in sudden fury. "How about some food and water?"

He knew that The Ax was on guard. But there was no reply. He got to his feet, hopped to the door and pounded on the heavy slabs, shaking the barrier. "You heard me, Axel!" he shouted. "What are you trying to do —torture women? At least bring them water."

Still no answer. Julia Tolliver spoke wanly, "Looks like they don't care whether we suffer or not."

"What are they up to?" he asked.

"Maybe it'd be just as well if we never found out," she said grimly. "But I'm gettin' somethin' of an idea."

"What kind of an idea?"

"I could be wrong. No use borrowin' more trouble than we're already in. I reckon we'll find out sooner or later what this is all about if we wait long enough."

They waited. The afternoon stretched out interminably. Julia Tolliver stretched out on a pallet, attempting to sleep, but it was a failure. Anita moved about their crowded quarters, driven by growing tension. She paused often at Zack's side, but always found that she had nothing to say. He spent the time working at the shackles. It was futile effort, but at least it kept his mind out of other avenues—dark avenues.

Twilight came. And still no sign that their captors had any intention of heeding the demands Zack kept repeating that they be given water and food. It was apparent to Zack now that the real purpose was to weaken their spirit so that they would be more amenable to whatever plan was in store for them.

Full darkness had fallen when they heard the approach of a rider. Zack pulled himself to his feet, and he and the Tollivers crowded to slits in the door peering. But their limited view of the surroundings told them nothing. Apparently the arrival had dismounted at the hunting lodge. After that they heard momentary rumor of voices. Then a door closed, and silence came.

The wait finally ended. The Ax came striding to the shack. The bars were lifted and the door opened. They were blinded by the beam of the bull's-eye lantern in The

Ax's hand. Zack made out the dim shapes of the Kid and Matt Pecos at the shoulder of The Ax.

"Come out you two women!" The Ax said harshly. He came into the shack, seized Anita Tolliver by the arm, sending her staggering toward the door where the Kid grasped her and hustled her outside. The Ax pushed Julia ahead of him and out of the door.

Zack hopped toward the man, a fist clenched, but The Ax was carrying a wagon-spoke club, dangling by a strap from his wrist, and used it. The club landed a glancing blow on Zack's head and sent him reeling, stunned against a wall.

Then they were gone and the door was tightly barred shut again.

"You devils!" he heard Anita Tolliver scream. Then they were gone out of hearing.

Silence again settled over the camp. Time passed, time whose length he could not judge. He had recovered from the glancing blow. It had brought another streak of blood which had dried. He stood at the door, peering, listening. And still no sound that would tell him anything.

Presently they came again, The Ax with his club and bull's-eye lantern, the other two thugs with their guns. The door was opened.

"Tie his arms," The Ax ordered. "An' make blasted sure they *are* tied."

Zack was seized by the desperadoes and his arms were lashed to his sides.

"Start movin'!" The Ax said, and poked the muzzle of a six-shooter into his back.

He was pushed out of the shack and half-dragged along by the Kid and Matt Pecos. They rounded the rock ledge and The Ax called a halt when they reached the shake-roofed hunting lodge. "All right, you two," he said to his companions. "There's a jug over by the water trough. Help yourselves—but don't git drunk. We've all got some more work to do tonight. I'll call you when you're needed. An', above all, don't git curious. Stay away from the house."

The two evidently knew better than to ask questions, for they walked hurriedly away. The Ax opened a door and pushed Zack ahead of him into the house.

It was a big room. Game pelts and woven rugs adorned the walls and floor. A long table of handsawed design, with a polished cedar top dominated the room. Easy chairs and two davenports, made in the rustic style, stood along the walls. Antler racks held a liberal display of hunting rifles and fowling pieces.

A single oil lamp stood on the table, bearing a shade which restricted its glow. Julia and Anita Tolliver sat at the near end of the table, side by side, their backs turned to Zack and The Ax. Their hands, unbound, lay on the table. They seemed to be caught in some sort of a trance. He realized it was cold fear that gripped them.

Another figure sat at the far end of the table. It was a grotesque, formless shape. Zack realized that what he was looking at in the shaded light was a man wearing one of the shapeless grain-sack masks. Two cocked six-shooters lay on the table at his side. An inkstand stood nearby, and smoke from an expensive, lighted cigar coiled up from an ash tray where it had been placed.

The Ax pushed Zack closer to the table. The masked man spoke. "You know what to do, Axel, if he gets rough."

Then the man addressed the Tollivers. "I had hoped you would be reasonable and not force me to take drastic measures to convince you that I'm offering you the best way out. Anything that happens from now on will be on your conscience, Mrs. Tolliver."

Zack recognized that voice. So had the Tollivers. "You treacherous devil!" Anita Tolliver said huskily. "I had begun to suspect, several days ago, that something was wrong with you, but wouldn't let myself actually believe it. To think that we were fools to treat you as a friend, to trust you even up to a few days ago."

Julia Tolliver spoke bitterly. "You might as well take off that mask, Frank. You was the only one besides Hickok who knew we were aboard that car last night. Take it off. We all know who you are."

The masked man laughed. He was Frank Niles, division head of the Rocky. "I prefer to keep it on," he said. "I never doubted but that you people would recognize my voice. It really doesn't make any difference. However, except for Axel here, nobody else around here really knows that I am what I might modestly refer to as head of the highbinders. They think that The Ax, or perhaps Lila, might be the one. I prefer that the lesser members continue to remain in doubt."

"You—you thief!" Julia said grimly. "And to think that your brother is in on this too. How could we misjudge men so far?"

"I'm beginning to lose patience with you two," Niles said. "All I'm asking is that you sign this paper. It will only take a moment.

He was tapping a paper that lay on the table beneath his hands. He moved it closer so that even Zack could read the words written in legal penmanship. But they seemed meaningless in the brief glimpse he had.

"Never!" Julia gritted. "Never!"

"What is it?" Zack asked. "What is he asking you to sign?"

"It's an authorization to his brother to sell all our stock in the Rocky."

"Absolutely correct," Niles said. "It is duly witnessed and notarized, as you will note."

"It's hard to believe that both of you could turn out so vile," Anita said. "You two have wormed your way into our confidence while driving us almost into bankruptcy with your gang of thieves. And now you aim to steal the Rocky itself. You probably expect to pick up the stock at a penny on the dollar—and pay for it with the profits from what you stole from us."

"Go to the head of the class," Niles said. His voice was growing ugly. "Once we are in control we will soon get rid of the highbinders. We know who they are, you see, but they don't know who we are, excepting, of course, Jim here and Lila. They are partners with us. The Rocky can be turned again into a prosperous railroad. We expect to be worth a million or more in a year, and more millions when we build on into the camps."

"Like perdition you will," Julia Tolliver said, shaking with anger. "I'll see you in the flames, with the devil pokin' his pitchfork into you before I sign that paper."

"I'm sure you'll change your mind presently," Niles said. "You can't expect Willis and myself to resist such a bargain after we've planned and worked for so long, now could you?"

"Who's Willis?" Zack asked.

Anita answered. "Willis Niles is Frank's older brother. He has been company attorney ever since the Rocky was organized. He holds the title of executive manager, and is chairman of the board. After the death of my father it seemed better to appear that the Rocky was still run by men."

"Can they get away with this kind of fraud?"

It was Niles who answered. "You just heard Anita say that Willis is chairman of the board, company attorney and general manager. Who would question the sale of stock by such an executive in a company on the verge of bankruptcy?"

He dipped the pen into the ink well, arose and moved the document within Julia Tolliver's reach. "Being the senior stockholder it would be proper for you to sign first, my dear," he said.

Instead of accepting the pen, Julia Tolliver knocked it from his hand. Niles stood for an instant, his eyes cold with rage, and malevolent. Zack believed the man was about to use his fists on the frail, elderly woman, and started to move forward to once again attempt to intervene, but The Ax gripped his arm, holding him back.

Niles thought better of his intention. He forced a smile, bent and retrieved the pen from the floor. "That was foolish of you, Julia," he said. "Don't be difficult again. You're forcing me to take measures that I dislike. Sign."

"No!" Julia said huskily. "Never!"

"It happens I can't spare any more time in debate," Niles said. He spoke to The Ax. "Tear off Keech's shirt. The ladies seem to need an object lesson as to what will happen to them if they continue to be obstinate."

The Ax ripped Zack's shirt from his shoulders, letting the shreds fall from his bound arms. Niles lifted the cigar from the ash tray, blew off the long ash that had formed, blew on the tip until it burned hot and crimson. He moved toward Zack.

"No!" Anita Tolliver choked. "He had no part in this. Why him?"

She tried to arise from the chair. It was then that Zack discovered she and the older woman were tied to the chairs. Niles pushed her roughly back.

"This is one of the reasons we brought this cowboy into our outfit," he said. "We figured you might need a little persuasion."

He advanced on Zack. His features relentless, he slapped Zack with his left hand. A blow that staggered Zack. Then, with deliberation, he pushed the glowing end of the cigar against Zack's bare chest. In spite of himself, Zack uttered a gasp of agony. He felt The Ax's six-shooter hard against his side.

The ugly, acrid tang of burned flesh arose. The act

had been done so casually, so callously he could hardly believe that this was real.

Niles studied the horrified expressions on the faces of Anita Tolliver and her grandmother. They too seemed caught in a dream—a dream of horror. Julia Tolliver's lips were moving, but no sound came out. She was trying to scream, but failing.

Anita was looking at Zack, her dark eyes no longer snapfinger bright, but deep and sunken with pity and misery for him. "I'm so—so sorry," she said brokenly.

Niles drew back a fist with deliberation and smashed Zack in the face. Zack managed to turn his head so that he caught the blow on the cheekbone. He felt blood flow as flesh was gashed. Another blow brought more blood.

Julia Tolliver managed a despairing sound. "Dear God, strike him down!"

"Sign!" Niles gritted.

"Tell him to go to hell," Zack said between lips that were crushed and bleeding.

"Ever see a man's eyeballs burned out?" Niles asked. He held the cigar aloft and once more blew the burning end into a glow. He moved again upon Zack. His face still bore that implacable determination that was driving him. Frank Niles meant exactly what he said. He meant to destroy Zack's sight while the Tollivers watched.

"No! No!" Anita choked. "Don't! Please!"

"Then sign," Niles said icily.

"Don't do it," Zack said hoarsely. "Don't you understand what this means? This man can't afford to let any of us li—"

The glowing cigar came closer. Zack managed to duck, and the crimson end only blistered his cheek. But it had been meant for his eye.

"We'll sign," Julia Tolliver moaned. "We'll sign. Don't torture him any more. We'll sign."

Niles relaxed. "That's better," he said. Again he

casually drew back a fist and smashed it into Zack's face. "You're lucky, Keech," he said. "Or I might have a lot of fun with you. But I've got to get back to the Wells."

He moved back to the table, pushed the document in front of Julia and handed her the pen. She had to try several times before she could control the quivering of her hand enough to affix her name.

Anita Tolliver hesitated. She looked at Zack, her eyes glistening. "Don't sign it," he said.

"And watch this man burn out your eyes?" she sobbed. "You know I can't do that."

She took the pen that Niles handed her and added her name to the paper.

Niles studied the document. "Write in the date," he said to Anita. "This is August 15."

"That was three days ago," she said.

"Do as I say," he replied. "Or would you like to watch Keech really lose an eye?"

She sighed, picked up the pen again and wrote in the date. Niles picked up the document, studied it for a time, then drew on his cigar and blew smoke with an air of complete satisfaction.

He nodded to The Ax. "All right. Take them away."

Then he disappeared through a rear door into an unlighted room that evidently was a kitchen. Another door opened and closed. Zack heard the creak of saddle leather as Niles mounted. Then came the receding sound of hoofs.

The Ax, his pistol covering them, moved to the front door and called out. Matt Pecos and the Ogallala Kid responded, and entered the house. They stared at the blood and signs of torture on Zack and darted uneasy glances at each other, their Adam's apples bobbing.

"This feller," The Ax said, "fell ag'in the lamp an got burned an' bruised some. It was an accident. Right?"

The Kid and his partner swallowed hard. "O' course, o' course!" the Kid said hastily. He had the bravo to sniff the air. "Somebody's been here, smokin' a good cigar, Axel. You don't smoke cigars, now do you?"

"You just keep on askin' smart questions," The Ax said, "until you find yourself in a lot worse shape from fallin' into lamps than this feller here."

"Sure, sure," the Kid agreed quickly. "Where we goin' now?"

"Just fer a little ride," The Ax said. "Saddle up the horses for the three of us, an' fer the ladies an' the cowboy here. Move! Or are you deef? Git them horses up here in a hell of a hurry!"

The pair went stampeding out of the house to where the horses evidently had been corraled. Zack and the Tollivers waited in silence. Zack's injuries bled for a time, then clogged. The burns on his chest continued to plague him. "I wish I could do something for you," Anita spoke, her eyes still swimming.

Zack managed a twisted grin. "I've been in worse shape and survived," he said. "You ought to have seen me after I tried to ride a Longhorn bull on a bet down at the ranch."

The saddled horses were brought up, the same mounts on which they had been brought to this place. The Tollivers were freed from their chairs, and lifted onto mounts and tied there. The Ax produced a key, freed Zack from the leg irons, then prodded him into mounting the black gelding. His arms remained tied, and the Ogallala Kid and Matt Pecos helped lift him into the saddle. His ankles were lashed tight beneath the horse's belly. The cavalcade set off in the darkness.

"Where are you taking us?" Anita demanded.

"Back to whar you come from."

"Back to Sioux Wells?" she asked dubiously.

"O' course not. I mean we're takin' you back to that

fancy car you was holed up in. You ladies like that sort o' thing don't you? Fuss an' feathers. We aim to make you comfortable."

The Tollivers became silent, puzzled. Zack finally spoke to Julia. "How are you making out?"

"Instead o' frettin' about me you ought to be blamin' us for what happened to you," she said exhaustedly. "It was me that sent Hickok to talk you into joinin' these devils, usin' that cattle money as bait. Please forgive me. It was Frank Niles that really put me up to it. I never knew that he'd been waitin' a chance to kidnap me an' 'Nita an' force us to sign that order to his brother."

"I'm tellin' you people for the last time to keep quiet," The Ax snarled. He brought his horse alongside and whipped the muzzle of his pistol across Zack's face. The blow did little more than bruise and scrape the skin, but it brought a new streak of blood to add to the damage Zack had sustained.

He would have struck again, but Anita Tolliver managed to knee her horse near and lean far enough from the saddle to take the glancing blow on her shoulder. "Why be so cruel?" she implored. "What kind of a man are you?"

The Ax settled back in the saddle. He was a savage man in the habit of giving in to unbalanced emotions. "Next time I'll cut him to pieces," he frothed. "An' you too, if'n you git gay."

"At least do something for him," she sobbed. "Look at him! Burned, beaten. Why add to his suffering? You and your boss have got what you wanted haven't you?"

"He won't suffer much longer," The Ax said. "Neither will you."

That silenced her. If there had been any lingering hope in the minds of any of them that they might be allowed to live, it faded. The Ax was deadly, capable of more torture. Murder would be very easy on his conscience.

Julia Tolliver began to weep softly. "Be quiet!" The Ax snarled. "Next one that whimpers will be without a tongue."

He had a skinning knife in his hand. He meant what he said. Julia Tolliver still had the courage to look up into the sky and say, "Lord, have mercy on us. We're in the hands of demons."

They rode slowly. The Ax was apparently wasting time for some reason of his own. Although they had traveled this route in darkness the previous night Zack saw outcrops against the stars that, with a cattleman's mind for recording landmarks, he remembered. They were heading in the direction of the spot where the engine and palace car had been halted on the abandoned spur.

He glimpsed the single window light that marked the location of Box Springs Ranch again reminding him that the hunting lodge and shack where they had been held was within easy distance of the main outlaw stronghold.

Within less than an hour at the slogging pace The Ax demanded, they reached the abandoned track—the Crown Point spur, Julia had termed it. The smell of coal smoke was in the air. The Ax called a halt. Zack and the Tollivers were freed from the ropes that bound them to the horses and dragged to the ground. They were pushed roughly down a descent into the cut where the engine and palace car stood.

The engine was being manned by its crew. The boiler was being stoked and the steam boxes were alive. The engineer was at his seat in the cab, but he did not look out as The Ax moved past with the captives and the two gunmen.

The palace car was dark. Zack and the Tollivers, their arms bound, were pushed up the steps and marched into the lounge section. The Ax produced his bull's-eye lantern,

and also more thongs for bonds. The thongs were used
to lash the three captives securely to heavy swivel chairs
whose bases were fastened to the floor.

"All right, you two," The Ax said to the Kid and
Matt Pecos. "Go to the ranch. I'll be along later. Leave
my horse and talk to nobody about what you've seen
or where we've been."

The pair left the car and Zack presently heard them
riding away, leading the unneeded horses.

"You're going to kill us, aren't you?" Anita spoke.
Her voice was steady.

"Not me, miss," The Ax answered in pretended horror. "You're just goin' to start on your way up the line
again."

Although the car retained the stuffy heat of the day,
The Ax piled wood and scrap papers into a brass heating
stove that served the car in cold weather. He dashed on
some kerosene from a tin, struck a match and the stove
roared into life. He stood by pretending to briskly rub
his hands together against an imaginary chill. "Nothin'
like a warm fire to make a man happy," he remarked.

In the glow from the doors of the stove Zack saw
that three or four more five-gallon tins of kerosene had
been brought into the car and were standing dangerously
close to the roaring stove.

"Now wouldn't it be a shame if'n this here special got
to runnin' wild an' didn't make the curve at the bottom
of Rincon Hill?" The Ax said.

The man was looking at them with a death's-head grin.
He was torturing them, telling them their fate, enjoying
it. They were to be sent to their death in a wrecked train
which would burn and destroy all evidence that they
had been murdered.

"Bill Hickok will pay you off for this, Axel," Julia
Tolliver said hoarsely. "There won't be a hole deep

enough for you to hide in once he takes after you. You know him."

"Hickok won't be alive long enough to pay off anybody," The Ax grinned. "He'll be taken care of the minute he shows up tomorrow in Sioux Wells. We've got fellers in the bunch who'd enjoy puttin' a slug in his back. He's been kind of rough on some of 'em here an' there along the line."

The Ax closed the shutter on the lantern and they heard him leaving the car, heard his boots grind the gravel as he moved ahead toward the engine, which he boarded.

There was a faint refrain of conversation. Evidently Hank, the engineer, seemed to be debating a point. Zack heard The Ax cursing him and giving orders.

With a jolt, their car ground into motion. The engine and car were being backed down the spur, returning to the main line.

Zack strained wildly at his bonds. He failed. He could not escape. Anita and her grandmother burst into frenzy also, fighting to free themselves. That was also futile and the three of them were forced to fall back, exhausted.

"Where is this place The Ax mentioned?" Zack panted. "This Rincon Hill."

"Not far," Julia said dully. "Not far enough. 'Twon't take long to git there once we're on the main line. It's two miles of downgrade an' at the bottom there's a curve with a rock wall on one side called Castle Gate an' a gully on the other that's usually filled with dry brush an' driftwood at this time o' year. These devils figured it out good. If we go into the ditch that kerosene will go up like a volcano. We'll all burn, even these ropes they've tied us with. It'll look like an accident."

They again fought the bonds, but Zack only felt the knots grow tighter, threatening to entirely cut off circula-

tion in his arms and legs. They were finally forced to
give it up, lungs heaving.

The train slowed, jolted over switch frogs, then came
to a stop. "Main line," Julia said.

There was silence for a time, except for the throbbing
of the steam boxes. Then two pistol shots sounded. They
looked at each other questioningly, but had no answer
to what the gunplay meant.

Presently the drive wheels began to spin as though an
inexperienced hand had yanked open the throttle. Their
car rocked unevenly ahead. The locomotive wheels found
more traction and the car began to roll faster, more
smoothly. Zack heard the crunch of gravel and was sure
that it meant that The ·Ax had leaped from the moving
engine.

Their car rolled faster. Zack again made an agonized
effort to break free. He managed to rip the swivel chair
from its moorings and he toppled on his face on the thick
carpet, the chair still bound to him. He was in a more
helpless position than ever.

"It's no use," Julia said, and now her voice was
calm. "Make our peace with the Lord. We've only got a
few more minutes to live. We can only give our souls
over to the mercy of—"

She broke off. Zack realized they were not alone in
the car. A figure stood over him. "Stay quiet," a voice
husked. "I've got a knife. I'm tryin' to cut you free."

"Gertie!" Julia Tolliver gasped. "Dear God, where
did you come from?"

"No time for that," the husky voice said. Zack now
recognized the arrival in the glow from the stove. She
was the coarse-voiced, loud-talking dance-hall woman,
Gussie Bluebell.

She was using a carving knife she evidently had got
from the pantry. "Hurry!" she husked. "Stop that engine
before we all git killed!"

Zack found himself free. The car was gaining speed. He ran to the front platform and mounted at frantic speed the iron ladder that reached the tender. He stumbled past the hatch of the water tank, and plunged to the floor of the cab amid an avalanche of coal.

He had a working knowledge of the operation of railway engines, having spent time with engine crews during switching operations at cattle shipping points.

He leaped at the figure that sat in the engineer's seat on the right side of the cab. He expected battle and his hands grasped for the throat. What he seized was a dead man. The corpse slumped from the seat and he saw the bullet wound and the fresh blood. The engineer had been shot in the back of the head. The fireman was slumped on the opposite seat. He too had been murdered. Undoubtedly they had been members of the outlaw organization. They were the men who had manned the engine the previous night. And undoubtedly they had been killed by The Ax to silence them as witnesses to the murder of the Tollivers.

Zack grasped the lever to reverse the drive wheels. The heavy lever did not move. He discovered that the crowbar the fireman used to loosen coal in the tender had been wedged into the slot in which the lever moved.

He yanked desperately at the crowbar, but it had been jammed too tightly in place. He had no time to labor over it. There was only one other hope. He knew that he could have leaped from the cab at that time and, with luck, emerged with no more than bruises. But there were the three in the lounge car. Julia Tolliver, in particular, would likely never survive such an effort.

He scrambled back over the tender and leaped to the platform of the parlor car. Gussie Bluebell had freed the Tollivers and all three of them were on the platform. He landed among them. The car, like all passenger cars, had the wheel of the handbrake on the platform.

"We've got to uncouple!" he panted. "I can't stop the engine! Help me! Start turning that hand brake!"

He vaulted the railing, pulled the coupling pin by its chain and yanked the lever that parted the jaws of the couplings.

Anita and her grandmother, being railroad people, had already grasped the idea and were frantically turning the iron brake wheel. For a moment there was no result. Then, the locomotive, its stack thudding faster each second, drew clear.

Zack leaped to the brake wheel, replacing Julia, and put his greater strength to the task. For heart-freezing seconds he feared that it was too late and that the car had gained too much momentum to be checked in time.

The car slowed suddenly. The engine pulled ahead and the car continued to lose speed. Wheels groaned and chattered, but the brakes were taking effect. The locomotive faded into the starlight ahead and Zack saw open track lengthening between it and the car.

The sagebrush slid past sluggishly now. There came a screeching of tortured metal ahead, then a heavy, booming crash. The engine, now more than a quarter of a mile ahead, had reached the curve at the foot of the Rincon and had plunged into the ravine.

Their own vehicle had slowed to a respectable pace, but was still drifting ahead. Zack kicked in place the ratchet that held the brake. "We've got to jump!" he panted. He indicated Anita Tolliver. "You first."

Without hesitation she descended the steps, poised a moment, then leaped. The pace was still a trifle fast, and Zack saw her stumble and sprawl.

"You!" he said to Gussie Bluebell. "Land running and you'll be all right."

But Gussie, not as young nor as experienced with trains as Anita, fell when her feet touched the ground.

Zack turned and kicked free the brake ratchet. The wheel spun violently as the brakes were released.

Julia Tolliver was already on the steps, ready to leave the car. "I kin make it," she said.

But Zack pushed past her, dropped to the ground and caught her as she followed him. They both fell, but he managed to twist so that he took the brunt of it.

"Dang it, I could have made it better by myself," she complained, scrambling to her feet. "I was hoppin' trains afore you was born."

Zack had picked up a few more bruises and had lost some cuticle. Anita and Gussie Bluebell came scrambling to join them. They also were nursing skinned hands and knees and had torn clothing, but all of them had come out of it without broken bones.

The car, gaining speed again, vanished into the darkness. A heavy explosion sounded down the grade. The boiler of the ditched engine had exploded.

Then came a new grinding crash. The palace car had left the rails and plunged into the ravine. A burst of flame rose, turned into a fireball that floated majestically higher. The kerosene had ignited from the wrecked stove.

"There goes five thousand dollars' worth o' rollin' stock," Julia Tolliver moaned. "An' me an' 'Nita as poor as church mice. Why did you wreck it, cowboy?"

"I'm trying to make them believe we're all dead," Zack said. "If we had left that car sitting on the track they'd be after us as fast as you can wink. I'm not too sure they won't be suspicious anyway because there were two wrecks instead of one. In any event we're a long way from being out of the woods. The Ax and those two leppies who are his heel dogs will likely do some scouting to make sure things went their way."

"My husband had that purty car built 'special for me as a weddin' present years ago," Julia sighed.

"Keep your voices down," Zack cautioned. "I tell you—"

His warning had come none too soon. He heard the sounds of hoofs in the night. He pushed Julia and the two younger women down, and they flattened in the weeds alongside the track.

By this time the fire below the grade had grown to a giant torch that lighted up the flats and ridges around them. They flattened still more. Evidently the dead brush in the ravine was adding to the blaze. The riders came nearer.

Chapter 10

The padding of hoofs passed by, and Zack chanced a glance. Two riders, rifles jutting from saddle slings, were moving past. They were lax and hipshot in the hulls—the posture of men who believed they were wasting time. They were so close Zack recognized them. The Ogallala Kid and Matt Pecos. Zack crouched back again and waited until all sounds had died. The course of the two desperadoes indicated that they were heading for Box Springs Ranch.

He lifted to his knees, listening. The Ax was still to be accounted for. But, after a time, he decided that there was no immediate danger from that source.

He spoke to Gussie Bluebell. "Now, where in blazes did you drop from? Why and how?"

"Her real name ain't Gussie Bluebell," Julia said. "It's Gertrude Hanson. She's an old friend of mine. She was cookin' fer one of our gradin' crews when we was buildin' the Rocky west into Sioux Wells."

"She will always be Gussie Bluebell to me," Zack said. "But how—?"

"I work in a dance hall these days, fer there ain't been any cookin' jobs open since the Rocky had to stop buildin' west," Gussie said. "I don't claim to be an example of refinement, but I ain't as bad as some folk think. An' I don't forgit my friends. Mrs. Tolliver, here, has done me some big favors in the past. She always had treated me like a lady, an' she pulled me through some bad spots when I needed help. I never had any hand in

139

what these highbinders was doin', but I had eyes an' ears. I overheard Lila an' that scoundrel, Jim Axel, whisperin' together a few nights ago. I didn't git the drift of it, but somethin' big was in the wind, an' I heard the Tollivers mentioned. I knew it meant harm to Julia an' Anita, so I tipped off Bill Hickok to warn them that it might be better if they got out of Sioux Wells."

"Hickok wouldn't tell us where the warning came from," Anita said. "He probably was afraid the outlaws might find out and take it out on you."

"But how did you get into that car?" Zack asked.

"It was that buffalo hunter, Ed Hake," Gussie said. "He likes to rile me up with things like shootin' holes in the water tank, but we're old friends. He had heard rumors there was a big herd of buffalo out in the direction of the old Crown Point spur an' rode out there to take a look-see. He didn't find any sign o' buffalo. I was havin' a beer with him an' he mentioned that he'd sighted J. K. Tolliver's private car an' an engine spotted on the spur. He thought it was a little odd. So did I, for I knew the Tollivers had pulled out the night before on the fancy car. Hickok had told me so. They should have been in Junction City an' headin' east. It didn't smell right to me, so I hired a horse an' buggy at the livery this afternoon, sayin' I was just goin' for a ride. I headed for the Crown Point sidin', an' got there at dark. When I found they was gittin' up steam, I decided I'd wait it out. So I tied up the horse an' rig an' sneaked aboard, figurin' somethin' would turn up sooner or later. An' it did."

"Oh, Gertie, how can I tell you how grateful we air," Julia said, and kissed the dance-hall woman. "You know what will happen to you if they find out what you did."

"I know," Gussie said. "But they got to ketch me first. I knew somethin' bad had happened to you an' Anita when I saw how your clothes was strewn around your staterooms. I got a .32 an' I figure that I might be killed, but I might take some of them skunks with me."

Anita also kissed Gussie and hugged her. "We would all be down there, burned to death, if you hadn't risked your life for us," she said.

"I don't like to mention this," Zack said, "but I've got a sort of feeling up my backbone that by this time The Ax is beginning to really wonder why the car was ditched minutes after the engine. Come daybreak he might have a lot of people looking for sign of anyone who might be wandering around this country. They've probably got lookouts stationed on the hills around Box Springs to keep track of anything that moves, such as us. The Ax might not even wait for daybreak if he starts adding two and two."

"Daybreak ain't too fur away," Granny Tolliver said. "We better hole up. This country's full o' gullies an' brush."

"Hickok!" Zack said, and let it ride there.

They all peered at him, a new freezing chill on them. "You heard what The Ax said," Zack went on. "Hickok is marked to be killed, and they likely won't waste any time. They're out to wipe out all witnesses, even among their own outfit. Hickok has got to be warned—and fast."

He looked up at the stars. As Julia had said, the night was well along. "Where are we?" he asked. "How far are we from Sioux Wells?"

Julia answered that. "The Crown Point spur is fifteen miles out," she said. "We're a couple of miles or more beyond it now. I'd say eighteen miles." She added spunkily, "We ain't never goin' to git there by standin' around here talkin' about it. Let's git movin'. Eighteen miles ain't much fer healthy, spry people. I've walked a lot farther'n that in a day, an' drove a six-horse team an' a load o' crossties in the bargain."

They set out, Zack leading the way. They moved along

in silence for a space. Granny Julia finally broke that lull. "What I need is about a gallon of water all in one gulp," she said. "I'm so thirsty I could even enjoy alkali gyp water."

"And a nice big steak with fried spuds, apple pie and a slab of cheese," Zack said. "It just occurred to me it's been a long time between meals."

Anita moved in and pretended to stamp on his foot— but lightly. "Won't you ever learn not to provoke me?" she said.

They came presently to a small seep of water. It was fairly fresh, and they reveled in it for minutes, dousing their heads, satisfying their parched tongues. After that they moved along almost light-heartedly, carrying with them the belief that they had risen from the grave.

"When we git to town we'll put a crimp in Frank Niles an' his brother," Julia said as she trudged along over the rough going. "An' put them both in the pen."

"Would those papers you signed be legal?" Zack asked.

"Not when we kin prove duress," Julia said. "But they figgered it out mighty slick. The paper they forced us to sign was dated the day we got back to Sioux Wells. That was the same day you got mixed up in things. We're supposed to be dead. There will be plenty of witnesses, honest people, who will testify that we was friendly with Frank Niles that day, an' not actin' like we suspected him of anythin'. Fact is, we wasn't. Except for Niles an' Bill Hickok, there's nobody but them two on the engine crew who knew we left Sioux Wells on that special last night an' not tonight. As fur as folks know, we was killed in a train wreck. There'll be no evidence of us havin' been tied up, fer the fire will destroy all that sort of evidence. Them two that was on the engine won't tell the truth, bein' as they acted like they was highbinders too."

"They'll never tell," Zack said. "They're dead The

Ax killed them before he started the engine running wild. Their skeletons in the fire would only be taken as further evidence the wreck was accidental."

That brought gasps of horror. "They're even killin' their own kind to protect themselves," Julia moaned.

Anita spoke. "We can't think of trying to walk to Sioux Wells. We couldn't possibly make it until late in the morning. By that time it would be too late. That devil, The Ax, said Hickok would be killed as soon as he appears in town this morning."

Zack turned to Julia. "A train? Won't there be a train along that we can stop?"

She shook her head dolefully. "Ain't nothin' scheduled eastbound out of the Wells until ten in the mornin'. The last eastbound went by before The Ax had our car backed off the spur. He made sure of that. It was why he dallied around so long before puttin' us on the main line."

"Westbound?" Zack asked hopefully.

"There'll be a passenger due along about eight o'clock, but it won't be able to git past the Castle Gate wreck," Julia said.

"Won't they be sending out a work train from the Wells to clean up the wreck?" Zack said.

"Likely they don't know about it," Julia said. "The telegraph line probably is burned out at Castle Gate."

Zack whirled on Gussie, snapping his fingers. "How stupid can I get," he exclaimed. "Your livery rig! Where did you leave it?"

"I tied up the horse in a gully near the place where I found out the engine and the Tolliver car was standin'," she said.

"We've got to find it," Zack said. "You ladies, at least, can make it to the Wells, maybe in time to warn Hickok."

They surged ahead faster, buoyed by new hope. Zack stayed with Julia as they made their way at as fast a pace as possible through the brush and outcrops, their shoes sinking into the loose, shifting soil of the plains. They were not always successful in avoiding obstacles. They often stumbled, or went sprawling, tripped by roots and gopher holes that threatened them with sprained ankles. Once, disturbed rattlesnakes sounded their fearsome shrilling, freezing them in their tracks, causing them to slowly backtrack and circle far wide of the area.

Julia began to fail. Zack swung her to his shoulder and swung along in the wake of Gussie and Anita. "I kin make it," she wailed. "Put me down."

"You'll get your chance," Zack told her. "I'm not of a mind to pack you all the way into the Wells."

The weed-grown spur track appeared abruptly out of the darkness across their path. "Here we are!" Gussie said exultantly. "It must be west of us where I left the horse an' buggy. It can't be too far."

Enlivened they moved along at a fast gait. Even Julia's frail weight was telling on Zack when he suddenly called a halt. "Listen!" he breathed.

They could hear faint, far sounds in the windless stillness. They were rough voices, profane voices. Zack was certain he made out the rasping tones of The Ax, angry and fuming.

"We're too late," he whispered. "They've found Gussie's livery rig. Now they really can add two and two and figure out that we must have had help and are probably alive and on foot."

They retreated, freezing disappointment replacing their eagerness. They left the railroad spur and headed northward through the open brush. There was no sign of immediate pursuit. Hope began to grow in them again, but Zack was sure The Ax would guess that they would have attempted to reach the livery rig, and would eventually decide they had been warned away

However the country was big, vast. Hope grew that

they might escape under cover of darkness. They were following the pointers on the Big Dipper which marked the North Star, for in that direction lay Sioux Wells. But daybreak was now little more than an hour away.

"We'll never make it in time to save him," Gussie finally said in a flat voice.

"We'll make it," Anita said. "You think a lot of Bill Hickok, don't you?"

"There was a time some years ago when I was cookin' for the U.P. an' Bill was scoutin' for the Army that we talked about maybe gittin' ourselves a claim an' settlin' down," Gussie said. "I was younger then, an' wasn't bad lookin', even if I do say it myself. But it didn't turn out that way. I never forgot how we talked an' dreamed. An' I know he's never forgot. He told me just lately he wished things hadn't turned out the way they did for him. Whether we git there today in time won't make much difference in the long run for him. Some day he'll be shot —likely in the back. He knows it, I know it. It's the way men like him die. Death has always followed him."

"We can't give up," Anita said. "We've *got* to get there in time and warn him."

They were driven now by a determination that overcame weariness and weakness. Julia seemed to have been rejuvenated, and insisted on walking on her own feet the greater part of the time, submitting to being assisted by Gussie and Anita at times, or carried over some of the harder going on Zack's shoulder. At times she hopped agilely along over obstacles, setting a pace that was almost too much for the others.

"It was me that brung Bill Hickok into the Wells," she said once. "If'n he's murdered, it'll haunt me to my grave. He only took the job as a favor to me."

Anita tripped over some hidden snare and fell. Zack lifted her to her feet. She looked up at him, then reached up, and tenderly stroked his cheek with her fingertips.

He kissed her and she clung to him for a space, word-lessly.

Then they hurried on. The hope grew brighter in Zack with each passing minute. There was now the possibility they might build up distance that could not be overcome even if their trail was cut at daybreak.

Then they heard the dogs. The sound was far away, coming to them over dark distances, but it was unmistakable. Julia uttered a small despairing sigh. Anita moved closer to Zack and took his hand. She was trembling.

Zack was remembering the sounds of kenneled dogs that he had heard while he was at Box Springs Ranch. He feared that he now heard the occasional tolling bell voice of a bloodhound amid the screeching of the pack.

Gussie, weeping, began to run, but Zack caught her by the arm. "No! Easy! The dogs haven't cut our trail yet. They're only circling and yipping. They're mainly catch dogs, trained to trail horses, but there might be a hound among them. The hound doesn't act like he's on the scent either. When they pick up what they want they'll settle down to steady screeching. The hound will say nothing."

"There's one thing I want understood," Gussie said. "I ain't lettin' them take me alive. That man, Axel, ain't human. He likes to torture an' see folks suffer. My gun is only a .32 but it'll serve the purpose." She looked at Julia and Anita. "An' I advise you to decide the same."

She had produced a short-muzzled weapon from some-where. "Never mind thinking about anything like that," Zack said. "Maybe you better give me that gun."

"Only if an' when I figure you're goin' to need it worse than us ladies," Gussie said.

They pushed ahead as fast as the terrain permitted. The sounds of pursuit had died. But that proved to be only a trick of the wind. The clamor of the dogs came again, louder, nearer. They had picked up the trail, but they were still a long distance behind them—a mile or more, Zack judged.

They came upon a wide stream bed with a rushing creek in its midst. They fell gratefully into the cold water, slaking their thirst. The yammer of the dogs was undeniably closer now. They followed the stream, wading often to their waists, fighting against the rush of water. They kept this up for exhausting minute after minute, hoping to at least throw the pursuit off for a time.

They found themselves confronted by a cascade where the creek plunged down a twenty-foot drop. Zack carried Julia up that water-greased ascent over rocks on which he somehow found foothold. Gussie and Anita followed him and it was sheer will and desperation that brought them to the top where the creek leveled and flowed gently through mounded sandbars.

Zack staggered upstream for a time, with Julia clinging to him, then fell, utterly spent, on a sandbar. Julia, weeping and crooning over him, brushed the hair back from his forehead. "An' to think that it was me that brought not only Hickok into all this, but you too, cowboy," she sobbed.

Anita and Gussie had sunk down also, too spent to go on for the moment at least. They lay there, listening. They could hear the dogs far in the distance. The sounds became confused, fading, rising, fading, rising again. Finally silence.

"They've lost us," Zack finally decided. "It's my guess they're covering both sides of the creek downstream, figuring we would head in that direction rather than go against the current. But they'll swing this way before long."

They finally took to the stream again, taking advantage of the easier going through the flats. An old sickle moon was in the sky now, giving faint light.

"Wasn't it me that was so thirsty I said I could drink a river dry a little while ago?" Julia croaked. "The Lord sometimes provides too much." In spite of the milder current she was able to progress only by constant help from Zack or the girls.

Zack saw that Anita and Gussie were also nearing their limit. In the faint moonlight he saw a ledge near at hand that rose twenty feet or more from the water's edge. It appeared to be part of an outcrop that extended some distance north of the stream.

"All right," he said hoarsely. "We'll try it here."

Standing in a pool to his waist, he lifted Granny Julia to a foothold. The ledge was broken and fissured so that Julia was equal to the occasion. She found a new reservoir of strength and climbed upward. Zack mounted just below her, ready to catch her if she fell. The two girls followed close below him.

They all scrambled safely to a broad ledge and sank down to regain their strength. Now that they were away from the babble of the stream, they again could hear the distant yelping of the dogs. Zack said nothing. The dogs were still circling, but they were casting the area along the stream, heading in their direction once again.

They huddled together, listening, waiting. The sounds of the chase bore relentlessly down upon them. Zack placed an arm round Julia Tolliver, drawing her against him. She was quivering, but still brave. She sighed and murmured, "It's been a mighty long time since I let a man cuddle me."

Another head leaned against Zack's shoulder. Anita. She remained there for comfort and courage. Gussie Bluebell sat like a statue, her small pistol in her hand—alone as she had fought her way through life.

The yapping of the dogs became more distinct. Zack found one note of hope. The deep voice of the bloodhound sounded only intermittently. The dog was keeping its whereabouts known, but Zack was certain it was grow-

ing tired and disinterested. Their battle upstream had
left no scent for the animal to pick up.

Presently, they made out the approach of riders, and
finally heard an occasional voice as men called to each
other.

The dogs, the horses, the voices, moved past. The
sounds faded into the mellow, faint moonlight. Zack began to breathe more deeply. He felt the Tollivers quivering
more violently. Gussie bowed her head and uttered a
prayer of deliverance.

Chapter 11

"We're safe now, aren't we?" Anita said. She was forcing conviction into her voice, more for her grandmother's sake and the rest of them than for herself.

"Of course," Zack said. But he knew better, and he was aware that so did she. But, at least they had gained time—many minutes at least, and perhaps much longer before the searchers swung back to again circle the area.

"We can't stay here," he said. He looked at Julia. "Where are we in relation to the railroad? How far?"

"I'd say two miles," she said. "East of us." Then she uttered a little cry of self-condemnation. "If'n I ain't a fool! The Sand Crick sidin'. It ought to be somewhere about directly east of us if'n I'm thinkin' halfway straight."

"The Sand Creek siding? What good will—?"

"It's a sidetrack for layin' over work trains an' such," Julia explained. "There's a tool shack there an' there might be a handcar to be had. It would be a lot better and faster than walkin' all the way to the Wells—even if the highbinders wasn't around to scoop us up."

Enlivened by hope once again, they stumbled their way out of the outcrop and reached more level ground. They found themselves in a devil's garden of sharp-fanged boulders that jutted like the fins of sharks through the surface, which was soft and was certain to leave footprints.

Heavy clouds blotted out the moon and stars. A chill wind assailed them—their garments still wet from the stream. The wind opposed them, as had the stream. They bent against it, moving into its teeth. It moaned and whistled along the brush, and some of those sounds came not from the wind but from the throats of coyotes who were seizing this chance to pounce on prairie dogs and jack rabbits under cover of the drive of the storm.

Julia said brokenly, "God, why have You forsaken us?"

The faint moon began playing tag with scattering clouds, and in that elusive light Zack kept peering ahead, but all that loomed were more hummocks of grass, more patches of brush, more needlerocks—more distance.

"I never figured I'd be so anxious to see a train track again after all the grief one caused me," he mumbled as they were all forced to pause and rest.

They wandered into a prairie dog village and worked their way among mounds and treacherous burrows without meeting new disaster.

Anita spoke in a strangled voice. "Look!"

Telegraph poles loomed close at hand, linked by the gossamer threads of wires. They saw the rise of the embankment, studded with the ends of crossties. They had reached the main line of the Rocky Mountain Express.

"Forgive me, Oh Lord, for doubting You," Julia said.

Zack halted, motioning for silence. He stood, listening, combing the night for sound. The wind brought nothing but the sighing and complaining of the brush.

"This Sand Creek sidetrack?" he asked Julia. "Which direction would it be?"

"I just don't know," she said exhaustedly. "I cain't pick out any landmarks to tell me where we air. It might be south of us, it might be north. One thing I'm sure, it ain't fur away."

"Sioux Wells is north of us," Zack said. "We might as well take a chance and try in that direction. At least we won't be losing any distance if we have to make it all the way on foot."

They stumbled along the ties. They were moving mechanically now, with Zack again carrying Julia the major part of the time.

Dawn was pink in the sky when Zack saw a shape looming up ahead. Anita saw it also and uttered a little sighing sound. "The siding," she mumbled. "Sand Creek. And there's the tool shack."

"And, glory be, there's the handcar standin' alongside the shack if my eyes ain't deceivin' me," Julia exclaimed. "We'll now have wheels under us. Railroad wheels. It ain't hard goin' from here into the Wells, mainly level with only a couple of rises to pump over, an' then some downgrade the last couple o' miles into town."

It was then they again heard the dogs. The sound was brought from a distance by the wind. It faded, but rose again. Pursuit was coming up—and fast.

They raced to the shack. The handcar, which was propelled by manually-operated bars that turned cogs and wheels, stood on the travel ramp alongside the shack, where it had been left overnight by the section hands.

With the sounds of pursuit growing in their ears, they desperately seized the vehicle, intending to set it on the rails. It was made of good railroad iron and strong lumber and very heavy. Even so, their desperate efforts began to move it.

But only a foot or two. Then they stopped. They discovered that it was secured to a ringbolt in the tool shed by a stout length of chain, and padlocked.

They halted, panting. "There'll be tools in the shanty to bust the padlock," Julia gasped. "Sledges, crowbars."

But the shanty was also padlocked. Gussie pushed her pistol into Zack's hands. "Blow it off," she said.

Zack knew the sound would carry to the oncoming pursuers. Then he blew off the padlock with two shots. Hurling the door open he scrabbled around in the interior and found a sledge hammer. Emerging, he smashed the padlock that linked the chain, freeing the handcar.

They once more strained at the vehicle. They could now hear the hammering hoofs of the horses as the chase came up. The gunshots had been heard, and the pursuers knew that their quarry was near.

With Zack using a crowbar that he had taken from the tool shack, they inched the heavy car astride the rails. He was prying the flanged wheels into place when Julia uttered a despairing cry. "We're too late! They're upon us!"

Zack made out the shape of oncoming riders. Screeching dogs came out of the darkness to surround them, snarling and darting at them in pretended attack.

He got the wheels in place on the rails, felt the vehicle move freely. He lifted Julia onto the car. "All aboard!" he panted. "Get pumping!"

Julia already was straining at the bars with her frail strength. Anita and Gussie joined her. Zack remained on the ground, digging his heels against the crossties, putting his shoulder against the car, veins bulging in his forehead as he strained to force the ponderous weight into motion.

The wheels began to turn—slowly, agonizingly. They creaked and grated on the rails. The cogs protested with metallic groaning. With dogs snarling at his heels, their teeth clashing, Zack strained harder.

A voice shouted, "They're tryin' to git away on a handcar!"

That voice belonged to The Ax. Zack found the strength for supreme effort. The bars were beginning to rise and fall faster as inertia was overcome. Zack leaped aboard and put his strength to the bars.

A gun opened up, then another. The flashes were lurid in the dawn. Zack heard the sullen buzz of a spent bullet, for the range was long for a pistol. Another spent slug struck metal on the handcar and dropped at Zack's feet.

He fired one shot from Gussie's pistol in reply, but only

for effect, for he knew it was wasted as far as finding any human target was concerned. The handcar was moving faster now with each rise and fall of the bars. The landscape began to slide past at an unexpected pace. Zack realized they were on a downgrade and the handcar was beginning to run out of control. The bars were whipping up and down so violently they were being nearly torn from the grasp of the four passengers.

"How do you slow this thing down?" he shouted.

"Step on the brake!" Julia panted. "It's that pedal on your side. Don't you cowpokes know anythin'? Hurry, before we go flyin' into the ditch! But careful, too, or you'll derail us! Easy does it!"

Zack found the brake and tried to get their careening vehicle under control. "Hang on!" he gritted. For a freezing space he thought he had failed and that the handcar was going to leave the rails under the grip of the brake. Then it held to the track and began to slow. And just in time, for the flanges screeched wildly as the car rounded a curve. But the wheels clung to the rails. Then they were on more level track.

All sounds of pursuit had been left far behind. Zack manned the bars again. Anita sat down weakly in the limited deck space, keeping her head clear of the bars. "I think I'm going to throw up," she stuttered faintly.

"Me too," Gussie groaned.

"Do it downwind, both of you," Julia commanded. "I'm surprised you kin find anythin' to throw. It's been so long since I had a bite to eat my stomach's wearin' itself out ag'in my backbone. You young ones ain't got a bit o' spunk."

Then she leaned over the side of the car and was sick herself. That seemed to be the tonic the younger pair needed, for they crept over to help her, then arose and manned the bars of the handcar with new strength, for their vehicle had found a slight upgrade and needed motive power now.

Zack felt a little limp himself, but it was Granny who drove that out of him. She recovered swiftly. "I guess it must have been somethin' I et a couple of days ago," she said, forcing herself to restore her brassy bravado.

Zack looked at the lightening sky. "As I judge it, we're still a dozen miles or so out of the Wells," he said. "It's going to take us up to two hours to make it, for this thing isn't what might be called a ball of fire. The sun will be up long before that."

"You mean you're afraid The Ax might catch up with us?" Anita asked apprehensively.

"There's not much chance of that," he said. "Not unless they've got fresh horses somewhere, which isn't likely. After all, those animals they had been riding were pretty well used up after a night's work. But you forget that there's a person in Sioux Wells named Frank Niles who will be even more anxious than The Ax to be the first to greet us. And he's got help. That's for sure."

They all knew what he meant. Not only Bill Hickok's life was at stake in the town now, but their own if they dared appear openly in broad daylight with Niles' gunmen waiting.

"Maybe Frank ain't in the Wells," Julia quavered. "Maybe he's hid out somewhere to make sure things will blow over."

"He's there," Zack said. "And waiting for us."

"How come?" Julia protested. "Maybe he don't even know we're alive. He might not—"

"He knows. And he knows by this time we're on our way on this handcar. You forget that telegraph line to the ranch I told you about. The Ax is sure to have sent someone to the ranch to warn Niles. They'll be waiting for us—and for Hickok. Niles has got everything to lose now, including his neck, if any of us are alive when the day is over, and he knows it."

"They'll be sendin' out a work train to clean up the wreck," Gussie burst out. "We kin stop an' wait. They won't be highbinders on the work train. They'll help us."

"I'd say that there won't be any wreck train called until Niles gives the word," Zack said. "After all, nobody is supposed to know about that wreck, and you can bet he's got one of his crooked telegraph operators on duty at the Wells."

They labored woodenly at the bars, drugged by exhaustion, weighed down by the fear that they were continuing a race they had no chance to win. Julia's small, delicate face was gray, drawn. Zack took her hands gently from the bars and said, "Lie down and rest. Don't you know when to quit?"

She sank down, too spent to spark a protest. Zack and the two girls put their own fading strength to the bars. They were opposed now by another of the slight upgrades and Zack knew their vehicle was slowing little by little in spite of their efforts.

"Just a little piece more," Anita mumbled. "We're near the top of the rise. "Then we can almost coast into the Wells."

The sun was peering over the horizon, flooding the hills around them with golden tints. Those hills remained silent, devoid of life except for birds of prey which were rising to soar the sky in search of morning meals.

The handcar slowed still more. The clanking of the cogs was weary. Zack slid off and began pushing. The two girls followed his example, feeling that they could better utilize their strength in that manner.

The handcar's stolid weight fought them now. It became a malevolent foe instead of a friendly ally that had carried them out of the grip of their pursuers.

Then Zack felt the weight lighten. The vehicle lost its

opposition, became alive again. Zack pushed Anita and Gussie aboard. They had reached the crest. Ahead, the track stretched straight as a ruler along a gentle downgrade toward a sprawling settlement some two miles ahead. Sioux Wells.

They clung to the handlebars, letting the vehicle coast, as they watched the town take shape. In the early sun Zack could make out the structures along Railroad Street, the water tanks on the roofs of the Good Time and Travler's Rest, the red-painted railroad station with its peaked second-floor roof. There were the railroad yards with boxcars, flats and slat cars idle on the sidings. Smoke lifted from the repair shops that flanked the sidetracks. A switch engine, miniature at that distance, moved among the yards. Workmen in dungarees and carrying lunchpails were walking to work.

"Looks normal," Zack said.

"Not exactly," Anita spoke. "They *are* making up a wreck train. The yard engine is pulling out the crane car. That means that Niles knows everything. The telegraph line is in operation."

The handcar was entering a cut whose rims hid the view of the town. "We better get off here," Zack said. "We'll be in plain sight if we roll on out into the open. Once Niles sights us they'll be watching. I will try to go in first to scout around and warn Hickok."

"Not a chance," Anita said. "I've got a better idea. First, we must ditch this jig car. If they've already sighted us, they'll likely be sitting tight, waiting for us to come rolling right into their arms. But I doubt if they've spotted us. We've got the sun right at our backs, and we're still a long way out. Follow me and do as I say."

They managed to move the unwieldy vehicle off the rails and let it roll down the embankment into the weeds.

"We need a friend now," Anita said, "and we Tollivers

still have some around here. They aren't all highbinders, not by a long shot."

Now that she had taken charge and was coming to grips with her foes she was all strength and determination. They followed at her heels as she led the way through brush and small ridges that still cut them off from possible observation of watchers in town.

They descended an embankment to the course of a small stream. Beyond the watercourse stood a small farm on a flat. The house was a patchwork, hip-roofed structure, its walls built of railroad ties and scrap lumber, its roof of sheet iron and tarpaper. It was flanked by a small, flourishing cornfield and a well-kept truck garden where beans and peas were luxuriant on poles. There were patches of cabbage, carrots and a potato field. The stream had been dammed with logs and an irrigation system devised.

Julia suddenly came to life after having followed her granddaughter dubiously. "Of course!" she exclaimed. "Of course! The Washburns! Why didn't I think of them?"

They waded knee-deep across the stream and ran toward the house. A small, black child, no more than four, who was playing with a wooden doll, fled in fear around the corner of the house, screaming for her mother.

Beyond the house a black man in linsey and cotton jeans was loading a rickety wagon with a canvas top with baskets of vegetables, fresh-picked. A mule was in harness. The black man seized up a shotgun that had been thrust inside the wagon and came running, the weapon ready. He raised the gun, then slowly lowered it, staring in growing amazement at these apparitions that had appeared on his farm.

"Glory, glory be!" he exclaimed. "That ain't you, is it Misses Tolliver? An' you, Missy 'Nita? You ain't ghosts ris' from the daid, are you?"

Zack could understand. He looked at the three female members of his party. Their hair hung long and stringy. Gussie's peroxide had faded. Julia was witchlike in her ragged, tattered, worn aspect. Only Anita seemed a vestige of her real self. She was still beautiful, pale, eyes sunken, but beautiful. As for himself, he could imagine the black man's consternation. Fragments of his shirt still hung from his belt. The blood had matted on the hair of his chest. One eye was nearly closed, and his face was puffed and colored with more dried blood.

"We're all alive, but we thought we were goners several times lately, Noah," Julia said. "Hide us. We're in deep trouble. The binders are after us to kill us. Frank Niles is their leader. We just found it out. Hide us until we can collect our wits."

A handsome, barefoot black woman in calico and sunbonnet appeared. "Mattie!" Julia sobbed. She turned to Zack and Gussie. "These are the Washburns," she explained. "Old friends. Noah and Mattie Washburn. Gussie, you know them, of course. They also worked for us when we were building the Rocky. They settled here at the Wells and took up farming."

Mattie Washburn embraced Julia and Anita, and shook hands with Gussie. She led the way into the house. The small girl they had seen peeked cautiously at them from around a doorway. A baby of less than a year gurgled in a homemade crib, smiling happily up at Anita who moved to hover over the crib, saying things women say to babies. Zack saw filled washtubs at the rear of the house and clotheslines from which many garments dangled.

"Noah farms and peddles vegetables in town," Anita explained. "Mattie takes in washing. You can trust them."

Noah Washburn and his wife listened, wide-eyed as Anita hurriedly told their story. "I always knew thet slick-talkin' Frank Niles was crooked somewhere," Noah said.

"But I never knew he was all bad. Now, you all, jest keep hid here. I'll go into town an' sorta size up the situation."

Zack looked out at the vegetable wagon. The mule stood hipshot, idly switching at flies. "Have you got a gun?" he asked Noah. "A real hammerhead, I mean. One that knocks holes in things. This shooter I'm carrying is a lady's gun, and there's only a live shell or two in it. I haven't had time to check. I need something that packs more authority."

"All I got is this here scatter-gun," Noah said. "An' it's only loaded fer birds to keep eagles an' such off'n my hen roost."

"The .32 will have to do," Zack said. "I'm going into town with you. I've got to warn Bill Hickok that he's ticketed for over the hill. Let's go. I'll hide in your wagon. The ladies will stay here."

"Not this gal," Julia Tolliver said emphatically. "After goin' this far, I ain't of a mind to hide under a bed while you an' Bill Hickok take on Frank Niles an' his thugs."

Gussie Bluebell spoke. "I'll be needed too. I know what goes on in the Wells. Hickok will be gettin' up an' settin' out for the Good Time about this time for his mornin' pick-me-up, an' will then go over to the Delmonico for breakfast. I figure we might have an even chance of sneakin' into the Good Time by the backdoor. From my room you get a good view up an' down Railroad Street, an' maybe we kin git there in time. All the other girls will still be asleep at this hour. We can hide in Noah's wagon. But, hurry. We might be too late already."

Zack seized Gussie's arm and they ran out of the house. He lifted her into the rickety wagon and she squeezed among the fragrant baskets of vegetables. He started to climb in to join her, but was pushed aside.

It was Anita. "Do you think I'm going to let you go into that place alone?" she said. She scrambled past him into the wagon, and gave him a twisted smile. "Besides, Grandma and I can't stay here. If things went wrong and they found us here they'd take it out on Noah and Mattie."

Zack found himself again being pushed aside, this time by Julia who crowded herself into the wagon between the younger pair. "Git goin'!" Julia said.

Zack started to debate it, then realized that it would only be a waste of very precious time. He slid into the wagon, folding his long legs in the cramped quarters.

Noah arranged the ragged top to better cover them and brought a worn tarp to throw over them and the vegetables. "May de Good Lawd look after us," he said as he climbed into the seat. "Now, you gals keep as quiet as though you was daid. I got a feelin' there's goin' to be big trouble in Sioux Wells before this mawnin' is over, an' thet somebody is goin' to be really daid! Let's hope it ain't none of us."

He mounted the seat and released the brake. He slapped the reins on the mule's back. The mule leaned into the collar, then, surprised by the unexpected weight, looked around reproachfully at Noah. Noah lifted the whip from the socket and brandished it threateningly. "Git along, you lazy scamp," he said. "For once, you are goin' to earn your keep."

The mule heaved a sigh and buckled down to the task. The wagon lurched along on crooked wheels over the chuckhole path out of the Washburn farm and onto the main wagon road that led toward the outlying shacks and farms around the town.

Zack found an eyehole in the weathered top and followed their progress. The wagon jolted across a spur track, creaked deeper into the town and turned up a weedy alleyway at the rear of the business structures which fronted on Railroad Street.

The sun was now high enough to beat down on the

canvas within inches of his head and he became aware
again of the need for food and water—food above all.

"See anything out of the ordinary, Noah?" he whispered.

"Sure do," the driver murmured. "Dar's a man on de
roof of de hotel, hidin' under de watah tank. He got a
rifle. I see him clearer now. He is one o' de highbinders.
Name of Buck Anders. A bad one. He's killed two men
here in de Wells in saloon brawls. He takes apples an'
peaches off'n my wagon, an' laughs at me when I ask
him to pay. An' dar's another one up in de loft o' de barn
at Tim Sullivan's livery yard. I jest got a peek at him as
he leaned out to signal to de one on de hotel. He's got a
rifle. I'd say de marshal, glory be to de Lawd, ain't
showed up yet, an' dey're still waitin' fer him."

The vehicle was approaching the rear of the Good
Time. "Anybody else in sight?" Zack whispered.

"Cain't see a soul," Noah breathed. "I'll stop as close
to the door o' the Good Time as possible, an' give the
word if the coast is still clear so you folks kin slip inside."

The wagon halted. Noah uttered a word of caution,
and they remained rigidly silent while the steps of a
passer-by approached and continued on down the alley.

"Now!" Noah whispered. Zack alighted, lifting Julia
and the younger pair down. Gussie opened the door, made
sure the coast was clear and they crowded in.

"This way," Gussie breathed and led the way up a
stairway that was enclosed, shutting off the view of the
bar and gambling room. They reached a hallway on the
second floor, with the doors of several rooms to their left.
They tiptoed in Gussie's wake toward the front.

One of the doors opened, and the disheveled, sleepy
face of a girl appeared there. Her eyes widened in surprise, then in consternation. Gussie placed a hand against
the girl's eyes and pushed her back into the room. "See

nothin', hear nothin', dearie, an' you'll live to a ripe old age," she said.

She led the way to a door at the far end of the hall, tried the knob, and to her relief, it was unlocked. She ushered them into a room that was evidently larger than most, with a bed, two easy chairs and other furniture.

"My room," she whispered. The two windows had drawn blinds and curtains. Zack moved to one of the windows, parted the curtains and knelt, raising the blind enough for vision. The room overlooked the greater part of Railroad Street. Alongside the Good Time was an open lot, studded with hitch racks for the use of patrons on busy nights.

Except for a dozen or so pedestrians and a few pieces of wheeled equipment, Railroad Street seemed normally inactive and drab at this breakfast hour. But Zack saw the shadow of the man Noah had spotted lurking beneath the water tank on the roof of Traveler's Rest which stood on the opposite side of the hitch lot. He could see only the front of the livery barn beyond the hotel, and had only a slanting view of the big window in the loft which faced on Railroad Street.

He flipped open the cylinder on Gussie's small gun. There was only one live shell left in the weapon. Gussie saw his grimace. "I'll fix that," she said and hurriedly left the room.

Zack kept watch on the street. The marshal's office and quarters were in sight beyond the livery yard, for the street meandered eastward in stride with the railroad track. The marshal had his living quarters at the rear of the office, for Zack had glimpsed into those rooms the morning he had been assessed a fine by the judge.

Gussie returned, closing the door behind her as silently as possible. She carried a holstered pistol—a .44 that looked well-kept and efficient.

"I know where Mel Lang, the night trouble-shooter, hides his artillery when he's off duty," she said.

Zack buckled on the belt, made sure the gun was loaded. Anita, who had taken his place at the lookout, spoke. "Riders coming in."

Zack crouched beside her. Three horsemen were entering town. One was The Ax. With him were the Ogallala Kid and Matt Pecos.

The Ax was warily scanning the street as he rode closer. He particularly appraised the marshal's office and apparently decided that Hickok had not yet appeared.

The Ax located the gunman on the hotel roof, and peered toward the livery barn, evidently having received a signal. He did not look again, but his attitude was of approval and satisfaction. The trap had been set. Set by Frank Niles, beyond a doubt.

The three men turned into the hitch lot almost below the window from which Zack and Anita were peering, dismounted from their jaded horses and walked tiredly into the honky-tonk. Their footsteps came up from below, indicating that they had gone to the bar and were ordering drinks.

Zack returned to his lookout point, with Anita crouching at his side. It was her quick eyes that saw the movement first.

"Hickok!" she breathed.

The gun marshal had stepped from the door of his office.

Chapter 12

Wild Bill Hickok was immaculately garbed, as always. He wore his spotless Panama hat, a white shirt and dark, thin tie, with black sleeve supporters and tailored dark trousers tucked into expensive, hand-tooled boots. He wore his brace of six-shooters. They had polished cedar handles with silver mountings.

Zack saw the shadow beneath the water tank on the hotel roof come to life. Zack lifted the blind higher and pushed up the lower sash of the window. The gunman, whose name was Buck Anders, according to Noah, was now creeping toward the front parapet of the flat-roofed hotel building. He had two six-shooters in his hands. He crouched there, waiting for his prey to come within certain range, lifting his head occasionally for quick glimpses.

Zack saw a head appear from the loft window of the livery. That assassin was closer to Hickok and was almost sure to fire at any moment.

The man on the roof arose also, lifting one of his six-shooters and taking aim.

Zack shouted, "It's a trap, Hickok! Duck!"

He fired at the man on the roof as he spoke. His bullet struck home. The impact sent the man twisting and reeling backward, his fingers convulsively tripped the hammer of his weapon but the bullet only blew a cloud of dust in the street yards from the marshal. Then he toppled backward from the roof and landed on the wooden awning that shaded the office and lobby. He lay there twisting in the agony of violent death. His pistol lay beside him.

Hickok had crouched and leaped aside. He stared up, locating Zack by the powder smoke that spun into the bright sunlight. His six-shooters were in his hands, the hammers tilted back.

"The hayloft!" Zack yelled. "Look out! There may be others! Take cover!"

A gun opened up from the livery hayloft, but the assassin evidently had been rattled by the shooting, and he was firing fast and wildly. Hickok was not hit. The marshal's two guns answered in split-second reply to that attack. Evidently he had his target in sight, for the weapon in the loft went silent.

Hickok remained crouching for a space, his guns swinging from side to side like the heads of serpents as he conned the street for more opponents.

"Take cover, I tell you!" Zack shouted. "There are three more of them, at least, in the bar. The Ax is one of them."

Hickok did not take cover. Instead, he arose and began running directly toward the Good Time, his guns gripped for battle. He was following the hard code he had learned that attack was always the best defense.

Zack heard the stampede of running feet and the slam of the rear door being thrown open. More running feet in the rear of the building. The Ax and his companions had chosen to escape rather than face Hickok in a gun duel.

Girls were screaming in the rooms. Anita screamed also, but, for her, it was the set expression on Zack's face at which she stared in fear. He turned to leave the room, but she darted in front of him, trying to stop him.

"No!" she sobbed. "No. Please! There are too many of them."

He kissed her. "This has got to be settled now and once for all," he said. "We both know that we could never live in peace with ourselves again if we let Niles get away now that we have him on the run."

She sagged a little, but stood aside. "I'll wait," she choked.

Zack raced to the stairs, descended and pushed open the door to the main room. "It's me, Zack Keech!" he shouted. "Hold your fire, Marshal. They've pulled out. They're likely joining up with Niles at the railroad station."

Wild Bill had entered by way of the swing doors at the front and was standing aside, against a wall, his guns ready to kill. The few patrons were cowering under cover of upended poker tables. The bartender was not visible back of his customary barrier.

"The Tollivers are upstairs," Zack said quickly. "With Gussie Bluebell. She saved all our lives. Frank Niles is ramrod of the highbinders. He kidnapped the Tollivers, forced them to sign an order to sell the Rocky at bankruptcy prices, then tried to murder them and me and all other witnesses who could tell the truth—including you."

Hickok was staring at him. "My God, Keech!" he exclaimed. "What have they done to you?"

He was seeing Zack's injuries—the matted, dried blood, the bruises, the ugly blotches of cigar burns.

"Never mind that," Zack said. "We've got to find Niles and finish this before he can organize for a stand."

Hickok studied him. "How many?"

"I can't say," Zack said. "The Ax, the Ogallala Kid, Matt Pecos, at least. Maybe others, but my bet is that the bulk of them don't really know what this is all about and will fade out. We know for sure there are two less than there were a few minutes ago."

"You better get yourself another gun, at least," Hickok said. "And full loads in that one you have. That will still make only the two of us against stiff odds."

"Make it three of us," the deep voice of Noah Washburn spoke. He stepped into the room by way of the back door. He had his shotgun in his hands. "I got myself some buckshot shells at the store," he added. "Traded in a bushel o' turnips. I've been tormented an' robbed by them whelps, an' it's time everybody in this town stood up to be counted an' help make this country fit for honest people to live in."

Another voice spoke. "I don't aim to miss this party either. I've been pushed around by these thugs. They wrecked my train once. Killed my fireman. I'm in this too."

The speaker was a big man who had emerged from back of an upended table. "I thought it was a private fight, but it seems anybody can pitch in," he added. He was the rawboned, redheaded engineer, Stan Durkin, who had been the victim of Zack's knockout punches on two occasions.

Durkin looked at Zack. "I ain't sayin' I was right in stampedin' your cattle that day," he said. "I ain't sayin' I was wrong. Nor I ain't sayin' you're a better man than me, even if you did level me twice. But I don't run with outlaws or thieves. I got scores of my own to settle with some folks."

Another man moved in. "Count me in," he said. "There'll likely be others as soon as the word spreads. We ain't lettin' you two go ag'in odds like that. We've been pushed around by these scum long enough."

The speaker was the grizzled buffalo hunter, Ed Hake, who had punctured the water tank on the roof of the Good Time with a bullet the day Zack had arrived in Sioux Wells. He was carrying his heavy buffalo rifle and had a six-shooter in his belt.

Hickok looked at the army that had suddenly sprung up. "Noah," he said gently. "You've got a family to support. Stay out of this."

"Nope," Noah said. "There's a time when a man's got to stand up for hisself. Mattie kin git along if anythin' happens to me."

"Of course, of course," Hickok said. He eyed Stan Durkin. "I don't see any gun on you. What are you goin' to use, rocks?"

Durkin clenched his fists, poised them and laughed. "I ain't exactly unarmed. I'll get more satisfaction usin' these."

The barkeeper had emerged from hiding. Zack spoke to him. "You've got artillery back there, hidden. Pass it over, along with any shells you can rake up."

The bartender hurriedly produced from various hiding points, two six-shooters and a sawed shotgun. Zack thrust one of the pistols in his belt after making sure it and the gun he already had were loaded. He offered the shotgun to Stan Durkin, but Durkin refused it. However, reluctantly, he did accept the other six-shooter.

"Come on!" Zack said, and led the way out of the Good Time.

"I could round up a few more of the boys," Durkin said. "A lot of us railroaders have scores to settle with these thugs."

"No time," Hickok said. "Time's one thing we can't afford. We've got to hit them now, and fast. Likely they'll run."

"The Ax won't run," Zack said. "I've had experience with him."

"That's his choice," Hickok said.

He and Zack walked side-by-side down the sidewalk, with Noah and Stan Durkin and the buffalo hunter following. They kept to the shade of the balconies and wooden awnings, then right-wheeled and crossed the unpaved street toward the railroad station.

The station was silent, standing stark and ugly in its red paint, flanked by its plank sidewalk and the steel rails and the greasy ties, all beginning to simmer in the hot sun. The baggage truck stood untended, no clatter came from the telegraph sounders. There was no sign of life in the ticket booth.

A head appeared at a window in the offices above. It was that of Frank Niles. He was hatless, unshaven, and even in that glimpse Zack saw the man's desperation, his bitterness. Niles had six-shooters in his hands.

"You! You!" he shouted, as though he could think of no greater expression of hatred. He fired at Zack, not Hickok, as though that was the epitome of his plight.

But Zack was moving, ducking aside and the shots missed. He fired one pistol in return, but his shot was only an echo to the roar of Hickok's guns, so swiftly had the marshal replied to Niles' murder try.

But Niles had vanished from the window in time and Hickok's bullets only shattered glass. The other guns opened up from hiding places. One outlaw was in the baggage room, firing through its wide open door from its interior gloom. Gunflame spurted from the slit in a partly opened door of a boxcar sitting on a nearby sidetrack.

All the guns were now roaring. Zack and his contingent were scattering. He heard the boom of Noah's shotgun, saw splinters fly from the door of the boxcar. Hickok was running—straight ahead, carrying the fight to his opponent. Zack ran with him stride for stride, but Hickok's objective was the gunman in the baggage room. The marshal fired one gun and Zack glimpsed a figure reeling and crumbling in the baggage room. Matt Pecos.

Zack ran into the waiting room of the station and headed for the stairs and Frank Niles. And The Ax if he was up there.

He heard the deafening roar of guns back of him, saw glass and splinters fly from the ticket booth as it was shot full of holes by Ed Hake. An outlaw had been crouching out of sight below the counter, and the buffalo hunter had sent slugs smashing through wood to find him.

Gunfire had resumed from the boxcar. Noah Washburn

was busy reloading, but Stan Durkin raced across the track, fired twice through the slitted door into the car, then slammed the door and bolted it.

Zack mounted the stairs three steps at a time. As his head and shoulders cleared the upper floor The Ax appeared in the door of one of the offices, firing two guns. But he was dying as he pulled the triggers, for Zack had sent slugs through his stomach the instant he had appeared. The Ax toppled back into the office.

Zack ran to that door. Frank Niles was there, cornered. He began firing as Zack appeared. Zack felt the harsh drive of a slug along his side. Then he sent two bullets into Niles' body. He stepped over The Ax's writhing body, to deliver the death blow to Niles, but found that he could not pull the triggers again. It was not in him to put more bullets in a dying man.

Hickok arrived and ran down the corridor, kicking doors open. He fired into one room and a man gasped, "Don't shoot again, Hickok. I'm hit bad."

Zack, guns ready to back up the marshal, moved to that door. The Ogallala Kid lay there clutching at his stomach. "I'm done for," the Kid gasped. And he was right.

Two more outlaws, hands raised, came from hiding. "My God, Hickok!" one of them chattered, looking at the crumpled bodies. "You've got a charmed life."

Zack sat down, used the remnants of his shirt which still clung to his belt to stem the flow of blood from the wound in his side. He decided it was only an ugly flesh wound. The slug had glanced along a rib.

Frank Niles was still alive, but going fast. Zack stood over him. "That paper you forced the Tollivers to sign," he said harshly. "It won't do you any good now. Where is it?"

Niles managed a ghastly smile. "Go to hell," he said.

"None of this would have happened if you hadn't come to Sioux Wells."

Niles never spoke again. But the papers were still there. Zack found them in Niles' desk, ready to be taken east to Niles' brother. That was late in the day after the dead had been placed in a temporary morgue in Tim Sullivan's livery barn and the prisoners locked in the town jail.

That was after Gussie Bluebell had made a spectacle of herself by kissing and weeping over Hickok and Ed Hake and Noah Washburn and Stan Durkin, none of whom had suffered more than bullet burns.

That was after Julia Tolliver and her granddaughter had also made spectacles of themselves by kissing these same persons and by wailing over Zack as though he was dying, even though he kept trying to reassure them that it wasn't more than a scratch. And there was Anita babbling about how much she loved him, and how she didn't want to live if he died. It was all loud and unruly.

That was after half the citizens of Sioux Wells, sworn in as possemen, had headed out to Box Springs Ranch to clean out the last of the highbinders with plans for stringing up some they considered were likely candidates.

They started straggling back long after nightfall, somewhat disappointed, for they found Box Springs Ranch mainly deserted. The word had reached the hangout in time and the only person they brought back with them was Lila. She had been tied to a post and left to be caught by desperadoes whom she had browbeaten and scorned.

They brought back the first installment of the rich store of loot they found in the caches, but the biggest haul was the gold dust that had been taken from a Rocky express car not long in the past.

"Looks like we'll soon be able to start buildin' on west to the mines," Julia crowed exultantly.

It was a month later when Brandy Ben Keech and his K-Bar-K crew, who were on their way back to Texas, rode within sight of Sioux Wells. Zack led a welcoming party on horseback out to escort them. Fall was crisp in the air. The last of the leaves from the cottonwoods were blowing in the wind. Sioux Wells was beginning to button up for winter.

Zack dismounted and gripped hands with his father, and the crew. "Welcome to Sioux Wells," he said.

Brandy Ben was staring at Zack's companions. He was answering his son's questions numbly, still staring. "Yeah," he mumbled. "We sold the herd. Beat the deadline. Got your telegram at North Platte that you was hangin' out at this place, so we headed this way. Say, that's a mighty purty gal there with you. Never saw purtier dark eyes. An' ain't that feller with the long mustache Wild Bill Hickok?"

"Sure is," Zack said. "And you're right about the young lady being rather pretty. But watch out for her. She stomps on you when she's riled. Packs a derringer at times too. Fact is, she sort of used stomping and a derringer to rope me into marrying her."

"Marryin'?"

"We've been holding off on the ceremony until you and the boys show up. It's to be held tonight in the Good Time, an establishment which is now owned by a fine lady they call Gussie Bluebell. She's furnishing all the refreshment. Wait until you meet my future ma-in-law. She's something. She and Anita here own the Rocky Mountain Express railroad."

"Railroad?" Brandy Bill stuttered. "Say, as I recall it, you went stampedin' off to this town to collect—"

"We'll discuss that later," Zack said. "There's much to be said on both sides."

"He's our division superindendent," Anita explained. "I'm sure you'll get a square deal from him, but the Rocky isn't in shape right now to throw money around recklessly. Isn't that so, Zachary?"

"Well I'll be double-da—danged!" Brandy Ben gasped. He started to hurl his hat on the ground, then thought better of it, for he had paid thirty dollars for it at Miles City.

He looked at Hickok. "You the law here?" he asked.

"Not any longer," Hickok said. "Feller named Stan Durkin is marshal now. I might ride along south with you boys as far as Dodge an' might winter there. Next year I'm of a mind to take a peek at the Dakota country. I hear there's a lot of action at a gold camp named Deadwood up that way."

Ø

More Westerns from SIGNET

Buy them at your local

bookstore or use coupons

on following pages for ordering.

⊘   ⊘

Buy them at your local

bookstore or use coupon

on next page for ordering.

Big Bestsellers from SIGNET

- [ ] **THE SHINING** by Stephen King. (#E9216—$2.75)
- [ ] **THE STAND** by Stephen King. (#E9013—$2.95)
- [ ] **NIGHT SHIFT** by Stephen King. (#E8510—$2.50)*
- [ ] **CARRIE** by Stephen King. (#E9223—$2.25)
- [ ] **'SALEM'S LOT** by Stephen King. (#E9231—$2.50)
- [ ] **THE BLOOD OF OCTOBER** by David Lippincott. (#J7785—$1.95)
- [ ] **VOICE OF ARMAGEDDON** by David Lippincott. (#E6949—$1.75)
- [ ] **SAVAGE RANSOM** by David Lippincott. (#E8749—$2.25)*
- [ ] **TWINS** by Bari Wood and Jack Geasland. (#E9094—$2.75)
- [ ] **THE KILLING GIFT** by Bari Wood. (#J7350—$1.95)
- [ ] **COMA** by Robin Cook. (#E8202—$2.50)
- [ ] **THE LONG WALK** by Richard Bachman. (#J8754—$1.95)*
- [ ] **THE MESSENGER** by Mona Williams. (#J8012—$1.95)
- [ ] **THE MANHOOD CEREMONY** by Ross Berliner. (#E8509—$2.25)*
- [ ] **PHONE CALL** by Jon Messmann. (#J8656—$1.95)*

*Price slightly higher in Canada

Buy them at your local bookstore or use this convenient coupon for ordering.

THE NEW AMERICAN LIBRARY, INC.
P.O. Box 999, Bergenfield, New Jersey 07621

Please send me the SIGNET and SIGNET CLASSIC BOOKS I have checked above. I am enclosing $_____ (please add 50¢ to this order to cover postage and handling). Send check or money order — no cash or C.O.D.'s. Prices and numbers are subject to change without notice.

Name _____

Address _____

City _____ State _____ Zip Code _____

Allow 4-6 weeks for delivery.
This offer is subject to withdrawal without notice.

Superthrillers from SIGNET

☐ **EYE OF THE NEEDLE by Ken Follett.** "An absolutely terrific thriller, so pulse-pounding, so ingenious in its plotting, and so frighteningly realistic that you simply cannot stop reading. This World War II espionage tale is right up there with the best of them . . . masterful on several levels . . . a blazing and unexpected climax!"—*Publishers Weekly*
(#E8746—$2.95)

☐ **OPERATION URANIUM SHIP by Dennis Eisenberg, Eli Landau and Menahem Portugali.** Now the first full account of the most dazzling espionage strike Israel ever made. The true inside story of near-incredible planning and execution as an entire ship is stolen, disguised, and stealthily sailed to Israel with the ultimate cargo of salvation.
(#E8001—$1.75)

☐ **PHOENIX by Amos Aricha and Eli Landau.** The best espionage thriller since THE DAY OF THE JACKAL! The contract is three million dollars to kill Moshe Dayan; the conspirators are shadowy figures in the highest circles of Mideastern power; the assassin is Phoenix, code name for the best professional killer on earth and the newest name for terror!
(#E8692—$2.50)*

☐ **BLOCKBUSTER by Stephen Barlay.** A high-intensity superthriller—a city held hostage by a terror beyond imagining. . . . "Exciting . . . nervewracking!"—*Springfield News and Leader*
(#E8111—$2.25)

☐ **SHADOW OF A BROKEN MAN by George C. Chesbro.** Meet Mongo, a private detective who specializes in solving cases that Sam Spade would have found too kinky to cope with. "One of the best detective novels of the year . . . it has everything!"—*The New York Times Book Review*
(#J8114—$1.95)

* Price slightly higher in Canada

Buy them at your local

bookstore or use coupon

on next page for ordering.